DEC 2017

My Absolute Darling

My Absolute Darling

GABRIEL TALLENT

RANDOM HOUSE
LARGE PRINT

Copyright © 2017 by Gabriel Tallent

Published in the United States of America by Random House Large Print in association with Riverhead Books, an imprint of Penguin Random House LLC, New York.

Cover by Jaya Miceli
Cover Image: Amen Moawad / EyeEm / Getty Images

The Library of Congress has established a Cataloging-in-Publication record for this title.

ISBN: 978-0-5254-9884-1

www.randomhouse.com/largeprint

FIRST LARGE PRINT EDITION

Printed in the United States of America

10 9 8 7 6 5 4 3 2

This Large Print edition published in accord with the standards of the N.A.V.H.

for Gloria and Elizabeth

My Absolute Darling

One

THE OLD HOUSE HUNKERS ON ITS HILL, all peeling white paint, bay windows, and spindled wooden railings overgrown with climbing roses and poison oak. Rose runners have prized off clapboards that now hang snarled in the canes. The gravel drive is littered with spent casings caked in verdigris. Martin Alveston gets out of the truck and does not look back at Turtle sitting in the cab but walks up the porch, his jungle boots sounding hollowly on the boards, a big man in flannel and Levi's opening the sliding glass doors. Turtle waits, listening to the engine's ticking, and then she follows him.

In the living room, one window is boarded over, sheet metal and half-inch plywood bolted to the frame and covered in rifle targets. The bullet clustering is so tight it looks like someone put a ten-gauge right up to them and blew the centers out; the slugs glint in their ragged pits like water at the bottom of wells.

Her daddy opens a can of Bush's beans on the old stove and strikes a match on his thumb to light the burner, which gutters and comes slowly to life, burning orange against the dark redwood walls, the unvarnished cabinets, the grease-stained rat traps.

The back door off the kitchen has no lock, only holes for the knob and deadlock, and Martin kicks it open and steps out onto the unfinished back deck, the unboarded joists alive with fence lizards and twined with blackberries through which rise horsetails and pig mint, soft with its strange peach fuzz and sour reek. Standing wide-legged on the joists, Martin takes the skillet from where he hung it on the sprung clapboards for the raccoons to lick clean. He cranks the spigot open with a rusted crescent wrench and blasts the cast iron with water, ripping up handfuls of horsetail to scrub at problem places. Then he comes in and sets it on the burner and the water hisses and spits. He opens the lightless olive-green refrigerator and takes out two steaks wrapped in brown butcher paper and draws his Daniel Winkler belt knife and wipes it across the thigh of his Levi's and sticks each steak with the point and flips them one by one onto the skillet.

Turtle hops onto the kitchen counter—grainy redwood boards, nails encircled by old hammer prints. She picks up a Sig Sauer from among the discarded cans and slivers back the slide to see the brass seated in the chamber. She levels the gun and turns around to see how he takes this, and he stands leaning one big hand against the cabinets and smiles in a tired way without looking up.

When she was six, he had her put on a life jacket for cushion, told her not to touch the hot ejected casings, and started her on a bolt-action Ruger .22, sitting at the kitchen table and bracing the gun on a rolled-up towel. Grandpa must've heard the shots on his way back from the liquor store because he came in wearing jeans and a terry-cloth bathrobe and leather slippers with little leather tassels, and he stood in the doorway and said, "Goddamn it, Marty." Daddy was sitting in a chair beside Turtle reading Hume's **An Enquiry Concerning the Principles of Morals**, and he turned the book upside down on his thigh to keep his place and said, "Go to your room, kibble," and Turtle walked creakingly up the stairs, unrailed and without risers, plank treads cut from a redwood burl, old-growth stringers cracked and torqued with their poor curing, their twisting drawing the nails from the treads, exposed and strained almost to shearing, the men silent below her, Grandpa watching her, Martin touching the gilt lettering on the spine of his book with the pad of his forefinger.

But even upstairs, lying on her plywood bed with the army surplus bag pulled over herself, she could hear them, Grandpa saying, "Goddamn it, Martin, this is no way to raise a little girl," and Daddy not saying anything for a long time and then saying, "This is my house, remember that, Daniel."

They eat the steaks in near silence, the tall glasses of water silting layers of sand to their bottoms. A deck of cards sits on the table between them and the box shows a jester. One side of his face is twisted into a manic grin, the other sags away in a frown. When she is done, she pushes her plate forward and her father watches her.

She is tall for fourteen, coltishly built, with long legs and arms, wide but slender hips and shoulders, her neck long and corded. Her eyes are her most striking feature, blue, almond-shaped in a face that is too lean, with wide, sharp cheekbones, and her crooked, toothy mouth—an ugly face, she knows, and an unusual one. Her hair is thick and blond, bleached in streaks by the sun. Her skin is constellated with copper-brown freckles. Her palms, the undersides of her forearms, the insides of her thighs show tangles of blue veins.

Martin says, "Go get your vocabulary list, kibble."

She retrieves her blue notebook from her backpack and opens the page to this week's vocabulary exercises, carefully copied from the blackboard. He places his hand on the notebook, draws it across the table toward himself. He begins to read through the list. "'Conspicuous,'" he says, and looks at her. "'Castigate.'" In this way he goes down the list. Then he says, "Here it is. Number one. 'The **blank** enjoyed working with children.'" He turns the book around and slides it across the table toward her. She reads:

1. The _____ enjoyed working with children.

She reads through the list, cracking the knuckles of her toes against the floorboards. Daddy looks at her, but she doesn't know the answer. She says, "'Suspect,' maybe it's 'suspect.'" Daddy raises his eyebrows and she pencils in

1. The <u>suspect</u> enjoyed working with children.

He drags the book across the table and looks at it. "Well, now," he says, "look here at number two." He slides the book back to her. She looks at number two.

2. I _____ we will arrive late to the party.

She listens to him breathing through his broken nose, his every breath unbearable to her because she **loves** him. She attends to his face, its every detail, thinking, you bitch, you can do this, you bitch.

"Look," he says, "look," and he takes her pencil and with two deft strokes strikes out **suspect** and writes in **pediatrician.** Then he slides the book over to her and he says, "Kibble, what's number two? We just went over this. It's right there."

She looks at the page, which is the thing of absolute least importance in that room, her mind filled with his impatience. He breaks the pencil in two, sets both pieces in front of the notebook. She stoops over the page, thinking, stupid, stupid, stupid, and shitty at everything. He rakes his fingernails across his stubble. "Okay." Stooped in exhaustion and drawing a finger through the scum of blood on his plate. "Okay, all right," he says, and throws the notebook backhanded across the living room. "Okay, all right, that's enough for tonight, that's enough—what's wrong with you?" Then, shaking his head: "No, that's all right, no, that's enough." Turtle sits silently, her hair straggled around her face, and he cocks his jaw open and off to the left like he's testing the joint.

He reaches out and places the Sig Sauer in front of her. Then he draws the deck of cards across the table, drops it into his other hand. He walks to the blocked window, stands in front of the bullet-riddled targets, shucks off the deck's case, draws the jack of spades, and holds it beside his eye, showing her the front, the back, the card in profile. Turtle sits with her hands flat on the table looking at the gun. He says, "Don't be a little bitch, kibble." He stands perfectly still. "You're being a little bitch. Are you trying to be a little bitch, kibble?"

Turtle rises, squares her stance, levels the front sight with her right eye. She knows the sight is level when the edge appears as thin as a razor—if the gun tips up, she gets a telltale sheen off the sight's top surface. She revises that edge into a thin, bare line, thinking, careful, careful, girl. In profile, the card makes a target as thick as a thumb-nail. She eases the play out of the 4.4-pound trig-ger, inhales, exhales to the natural slackening of her breath, and rolls on those 4.4 pounds. She fires. The top half of the card flutters down in a maple-seed spiral. Turtle stands unmoving except for quivers that chase themselves down her arms. He shakes his head, smiling a little and trying to hide it, touching his lips dryly with his thumb. Then he draws another card and holds it up for her.

"Don't be a little bitch, kibble," he says, and waits. When she doesn't move, he says, "God-damn it, kibble."

She checks the hammer with her thumb. There is a way it feels to hold the gun right and Turtle dredges through that feeling for any wrongness, the edge of her notch sight covering his face, the sight's glowing green tritium bead of a size with his eye. For a suspended moment, her aim follow-ing her attention, his blue eye crests the thin, flat horizon of the front sight. Her guts lurch and drop like a hooked fish going to weeds and she does not move, all the slack out of the trigger, thinking, shit, shit, thinking, do not look at him, do not look at him. If he sees her across those sights, he makes no expression. Deliberately, she matches the sights to the quaking, unfocused card. She exhales to the natural slackening of her breath and fires. The card doesn't move. She's missed. She can see the mark on the target board, a handsbreath from him. She decocks the hammer and lowers the gun. Sweat is lacy and bright in her eyelashes.

"Try aiming," he says.

She stands perfectly still.

"Are you going to try again or what is this?"

Turtle locks back the hammer and brings the gun from hip to dominant eye, the sights level, coequal slots of light between the front sight and the notch, the tip so steady you could balance a coin upright on the front post. The card in contrast moves ever so slightly up and down. A bare tremor answers to his heartbeat. She thinks, do not look at him, do not look at his face. Look at your front sight, look at the top edge of your front sight. In the silence after the gunshot, Turtle relaxes the trigger until it clicks. Martin turns the unharmed card over in his hand and makes a show of inspecting it. He says, "That's just exactly what I thought," and tosses the card to the floorboards, walks back to the table, sits down opposite her, picks up a book he'd set open and facedown on the table, and leans over it. On the boarded-up window behind him, the bullet holes make a cluster you could cover with a quarter.

She stands watching him for three heartbeats. She pops the magazine, ejects the round from the chamber, and catches it in her hand, locks the slide back, and sets the gun, magazine, and shell on the table beside her dirty plate. The shell rolls a broad arc with a marbly sound. He wets a finger and turns the page. She stands waiting for him to look up at her, but he does not look up, and she thinks, is this all? She goes upstairs to her room, dark with unvarnished wood paneling, the creepers of poison oak reaching through the sashes and the frame of the western window.

That night Turtle waits on her plywood platform, under the green military sleeping bag and wool blankets, listening to the rats gnawing on the dirty dishes in the kitchen. Sometimes she can hear the **clack clack clack** of a rat squatting on a stack of plates and scratching its neck. She can hear Martin pace from room to room. On wall pegs, her Lewis Machine & Tool AR-10, her Noveske AR-15, and her Remington 870 twelve-gauge pump-action shotgun. Each answers a different philosophy of use. Her clothes are folded carefully on her shelves, her socks stowed in a steamer trunk at the foot of the bed. Once, she left a blanket unfolded and he burned it in the yard, saying, "Only animals ruin their homes, kibble, only **animals** ruin their fucking homes."

IN THE MORNING, Martin comes out of his room belting on his Levi's, and Turtle opens the fridge and takes out a carton of eggs and a beer. She throws him the beer. He seats the cap on the counter's edge, bangs it off, stands drinking. His flannel hangs open around his chest. His abdominal muscles move with his drinking. Turtle knocks the eggs against the countertop, and holding them aloft in her fist, purses open the crack and drops the contents into her mouth, discarding shells into the five-gallon compost bucket.

"You don't have to walk me," she says, cuffing at her mouth.

"I know it," he says.

"You don't have to," she says.

"I know I don't have to," he says.

He walks her down to the bus, father and daughter following ruts beside the rattlesnake-grass median. On either side, the thorny, un-blooming rosettes of bull thistles. Martin holds the beer to his chest, buttoning his flannel with his other hand. They wait together at the gravel pullout lined with devil's pokers and the dormant bulbs of naked lady lilies. California poppies nest in the gravel. Turtle can smell the rotting seaweed on the beach below them and the fertile stink of the estuary twenty yards away. In Buckhorn Bay, the water is pale green with white scrims around the sea stacks. The ocean shades to pale blue farther out, and the color matches the sky exactly, no horizon line and no clouds.

"Look at that, kibble," Martin says.

"You don't have to wait," she says.

"Looking at something like that, good for your soul. You look and you think, goddamn. To study it is to approach truth. You're living at the edge of the world and you think that teaches you something about life, to look out at it. And years go by, with you thinking that. You know what I mean?"

"Yes, Daddy."

"Years go by, with you thinking that it's a kind of important existential work you're doing, to hold back the darkness in the act of beholding. Then one day, you realize that you don't know what the hell you're looking at. It's irreducibly strange and it is unlike anything except itself and all that brooding was nothing but vanity, every thought you ever had missed the inexplicableness of the thing, its vastness and its uncaring. You've been looking at the ocean for years and you thought it meant something, but it meant **nothing**."

"You don't have to come down here, Daddy."

"God, I love that dyke," Martin says. "She likes me, too. You can see it in her eyes. Watch. Real affection."

The bus gasps as it rounds the foot of Buckhorn

Hill. Martin smiles roguishly and raises his beer in salute to the bus driver, enormous in her Carhartt overalls and logger boots. She stares back at him unamused. Turtle climbs onto the bus and turns down the aisle. The bus driver looks at Martin and he stands beaming in the driveway, a beer held over his heart, shaking his head, and he says, "You're a hell of a woman, Margery. Hell of a woman." Margery closes the rubber-skirted doors and the bus lurches to a start. Looking through the window, Turtle can see Martin raise his hand in farewell. She drops into an open seat. Elise turns around and puts her chin on the seat back and says, "Your dad is, like—so **cool**." Turtle looks out the window.

In second period, Anna paces back and forth in front of the class with her black hair gathered into a wet ponytail. A wetsuit hangs behind her desk, dripping into a plastic bin. They are correcting spelling tests and Turtle hunches over her paper, clicking her pen open and closed with her index finger, practicing a trigger pull with no rightward or leftward pressure at all. The girls have thin, weak voices, and when she can, Turtle turns around in her chair to lip-read them.

"Julia," Anna says to Turtle, "can you please spell and define 'synecdoche' for the class? Then please read us your sentence?"

Even though they are correcting the tests, and even though she has another girl's test right in front of her, a girl Turtle admires in a sideways-looking and finger-chewing way, even though the word **synecdoche** is spelled out in the other girl's neat script and glittery gel-ink pen, Turtle can't do it. She begins, "S-I-N . . ." and then pauses, unable to find her way through this maze. She repeats, "S-I-N . . ."

Anna says gently, "Well, Julia—that's a hard one, it's **synecdoche**, S-Y-N-E-C-D-O-C-H-E, **synecdoche**. Would anyone like to tell us what it means?"

Rilke, this other, far prettier girl, raises her hand, forming an excited O with her pink lips. "Synecdoche: a figure of speech in which the part is made to represent the whole; 'the crown is displeased.'" She and Turtle have traded tests, so Rilke recites this from memory, without looking at Turtle's page, because Turtle's page is blank except for the first line: 1. Suspect. **Believe. I suspect we will arrive late to the party.** Turtle does not know what it means, when the part is made to represent the whole. That doesn't make any sense to her, nor does she know what it means, **the crown is displeased.**

"Very good," Anna says. "Another one of our Greek roots, the same as—"

"Oh!" And Rilke's hand shoots up. "'Sympathetic.'"

Turtle sits on the blue plastic chair, chewing on her knuckles, stinking of the silt from Slaughterhouse Creek, wearing a ragged T-shirt and Levi's rolled up to show her calves, pale and swatched with dry skin. Under one fingernail, a rusty grime of synthetic motor oil. Her fingers have its prehistoric smell. She likes to massage the lubricant into the steel with her bare hands. Rilke is applying her lip gloss, having already gone down Turtle's test with a neat little **x** beside each empty line, and Turtle thinks, look at this slut. Just look at this slut. Outside, the windswept field is spotted with puddles, the flooded ditch cut from the ash-colored clay, and beyond that, the forest's edge. Turtle could walk into those woods and never be found. She has promised Martin that she will never, not again.

"Julia," Anna says. "Julia?"

Turtle turns slowly around to look at her and waits, listening.

Anna, very gently, says, "Julia, if you could pay attention, please."

Turtle nods.

"Thank you," Anna says.

When the bell rings for lunch, all of the students stand up at once and Anna walks down the aisle and puts two fingers on Turtle's desk and, smiling, holds up one finger to indicate that she needs a moment. Turtle watches the other students leave.

"So," Anna says. She sits down on a desk and Turtle, quiet and watchful, attentive to faces, can read almost everything in her; Anna is looking Turtle up and down and thinking, I like this girl, and weighing how to make this work. It is unreasoningly strange to Turtle, who hates Anna, has never given Anna any reason to like her, does not like herself. Turtle thinks, you whore.

"So," Anna says again, "how did you feel about that one?" Her face becomes gently questioning—biting her lip, allowing her eyebrows to climb up, wet strands of hair escaping her pony tail. She says, "Julia?" To Turtle's north-coast ears, Anna has an accent, cool and affected. Turtle has never been south of the Navarro River, and never north of the Mattole.

"Yeah?" Turtle says. She has allowed the silence to go on too long.

"How did you feel about that one?"

"Not that good," Turtle says.

Anna says, "Well, did you get any of the definitions?"

Turtle does not know what Anna wants from her. No, she hadn't, and Anna must know that she hadn't. There is only one answer to any of Anna's questions, which is that Turtle is useless.

"No," Turtle says, "I didn't get any of the definitions. Or, I got the first. 'I suspect we will arrive late to the party.'"

"Why do you think that is?" Anna says.

Turtle shakes her head—it's beyond saying and she won't be bullied into saying something else.

"What if," Anna says, "you stayed in, some lunchtime, and we made flash cards together?"

"I **do** study," Turtle says. "I don't know if that would help."

"Is there something you think would help?" Anna does this, asking questions, pretending to make a safe space, but there is no safe space.

"I'm not sure," Turtle says. "I go over all the words with my daddy—" And here, Turtle sees Anna hesitate and she knows that she has made a mistake, because other Mendocino girls don't use the word **daddy**. Mostly, they call their parents by their first name, or else Dad. Turtle goes on. "We go over them, and I think what I need is just to go over them myself a little more."

"So just, put a little more time into it, is what you're saying?"

"Yes," Turtle says.

"So how do you study with your dad?" Anna says.

Turtle hesitates. She cannot sidestep the question, but she thinks, careful, careful.

"Well, we go over the words together," Turtle says.

"For how long?" Anna says.

Turtle works at one finger with her hand, cracks the knuckle, looks up, frowning, and says, "I don't know—an hour?"

Turtle is lying. It's there in Anna's face, the recognition.

"Is that true?" Anna says. "You're studying an hour every night?"

"Well," Turtle says.

Anna watches her.

"Most nights," Turtle says. She has to protect the way she cleans the guns in front of the fire while Martin waits reading by the fireplace with the firelight escaping onto their faces and escaping out into the room and then being dragged hard back across the floor to the coals.

Anna says, "We're going to need to talk it over with Martin."

Turtle says, "Wait. I can spell 'synecdoche.'"

"Julia, we need to talk to your dad," Anna says.

Turtle says, "S-I-N," and then stops, knowing that it's wrong, that she is wrong, and she cannot for the life of her remember what comes after that. Anna is looking at her very coolly, interrogatively, and Turtle looks back, thinking, you bitch. She knows that if she protests more, if she says anything more, she will give something away.

"Okay," Turtle says, "okay."

After school, Turtle goes to the office and sits on a bench. The bench faces the front desk, and beyond the front desk, the administrative assistant's desk and a short hallway to the green-painted door of the principal's office. Behind that door, Anna is saying, "God love her, Dave, but that girl needs help, real and substantive help, more help than I can give her. I have thirty students in that class, for crying out loud." Turtle sits cracking her knuckles, the receptionist giving her quick, uncomfortable glances over her computer. Turtle is hard of hearing, but Anna is talking in a flustered, raised voice, saying, "You think I want to talk to that man? Listen, listen—misogyny, isolation, watchfulness. Those are three **big** red flags. I'd like her to see a counselor, Dave. She's a pariah, and if she goes on to high school without us addressing that, she will fall **further behind**. We can chase down that gap now—yes, I know we've been trying—but we've got to **keep** trying. And if there **is** something wrong—" Turtle's guts clench. Christ, she thinks.

The receptionist racks a stack of papers sharply on the desk and walks down the hall to the door, Principal Green saying something and Anna flustered, "No one wants that? Why does no one want that? There are **options** is all I'm saying— Well. No. Nothing. All I'm—" And the receptionist stands at the door and knocks and slips her head into the room, saying, "Julia is here. Waiting for her dad."

There is a hush. The receptionist walks back to her desk. Martin pushes the door open, looks once at Turtle, and walks to the counter. The receptionist gives him a hard look. "You can just . . ." she says, motioning with the papers that he can go right in. Turtle rises and goes after him, past the desk and down the hall, and he knocks once and pushes the door open.

"Come in, come in," Principal Green says. He

is an enormous man, pink-faced, with large, soft pink hands. His fat hangs down and fills up his pleated khaki trousers. Martin closes the door and stands in front of it, as tall as the door itself, almost as broad. His loose flannel shirt is partly unbuttoned and shows his clavicles. His thick, long brown hair is in a ponytail. His keys have begun to cut their way out of his pocket, leaving patches of white threads. If Turtle hadn't known, she could have told that Martin had the gun just from the way he wore his flannel, just from the way he took his seat, but neither Principal Green nor Anna thinks of it; they do not even know such things are possible, and Turtle wonders if there are things that she is blind to that other people can see, and what those things might be.

Principal Green picks up a bowl of Hershey's Kisses and holds it first to Martin, who shows his palm to decline, and then to Turtle, who doesn't move. "So, how has your day been so far?" he asks, setting the bowl back on his desk.

"Oh," Martin says, "I've been better." Turtle thinks, that is wrong, that is the wrong way, but how could you know better, you're just a bitch.

"And, Julia, how have you been?"

"I'm good," Turtle says.

"Ah yes, well, I bet this is a little stressful," Principal Green says.

"So?" Martin says, gesturing him on.

"Let's talk about it, shall we?" Principal Green

says. The new teachers go by their first names, but Principal Green is a generation older, maybe two. "Since we last spoke, Julia has continued to struggle in her classes and we're concerned about her. Part of the problem is her grades. Her reading comprehension is not where it could be. She struggles on tests. But for us, the problem—more than any question of her aptitude—is her sense of, well, perhaps her sense that the school may not be welcoming, and we do believe that she needs a certain level of comfort, a certain level of **belonging** before she can begin to thrive in school. This is the problem as we see it."

Anna says, "I have been working with Julia quite a bit, and I think that—"

Martin interrupts her, leans forward in his seat, clasps his hands. He says, "She will make the work up."

Turtle stifles her surprise, looking over at Martin, thinking, what are you doing? What she wants is for Martin to look right at Anna, and she knows he can do it—look right at her, and make her feel good about this whole thing.

Anna says, "Julia seems to have particular trouble with girls. We were thinking—perhaps she might be willing to see Maya, our counselor. A lot of our students find talking to someone very grounding. We believe Julia might gain from having a friendly face here at the school, somebody she can confide in—"

Martin says, "You can't make Julia's graduation contingent on her seeing a counselor. So what can we do to make sure she graduates?" He looks at Principal Green. A kind of rising horror is on Turtle, and she quells it, because perhaps she doesn't understand, and perhaps Martin does. She thinks, what are you doing, Daddy?

Anna says, "Martin, I think there's been a misunderstanding. Julia will not be held back. Since we no longer have the budget for summer school, and since any continuation school is very limited, all students are promoted into high school. But if she leaves middle school without robust friendships and with her current study skills and level of reading, poor grades will affect her high school curriculum and subsequently her college opportunities. Which is why it is important to continue addressing these questions **now**, in April, while there is still time left in the school year. It is strictly an issue of Julia's welfare, and we think that a weekly meeting with somebody she can talk to should be a part of any solution."

Martin leans forward and his chair creaks. He makes eye contact with Principal Green, presents his hands as if asking, if there are no consequences, what the hell are we doing here?

Principal Green looks at Anna. Martin looks at her as if wondering why she is being looked at. Then he looks quickly away, engaging Principal Green's attention. Martin thinks Principal Green is in charge and that Principal Green is the nut he can crack. To Martin, Anna seems both too bothersome and too powerless. Turtle doesn't know why he thinks this. In all of these conversations, she's never known Principal Green to be anything but unimpressed with Martin. She can see it, how solid he is. He has, Turtle knows, a squinty-eyed son with Down syndrome and he has been principal here for well over twenty years, and Martin is not talking his language. Nothing Martin can say will convince Principal Green of anything. This meeting is all about being polite and showing that Turtle is engaged, showing that Martin is also engaged with Turtle's teachers, and Martin isn't doing it right, isn't saying the right things, is trying to bully Principal Green like he's tried to bully Principal Green before.

"Martin," Anna says, "I am very committed to working with Julia and doing **whatever** is necessary to prepare her for high school, but there are limits to what I can do when Julia is disengaged here at school, unfocused."

"Mr. Green," Martin says, as if going argument and counterargument with Anna. Principal Green frowns deeply, swinging a little side to side in his chair, hands clasped over his enormous belly. "Julia's success is not contingent upon special attention or upon therapeutic intervention. It's not so complicated. Her schoolwork is boring. We live in exciting and terrible times. The world is at war in the Middle East. Atmospheric carbon approaches four hundred ppm. We are in the middle of the sixth great extinction. In the next decade, we will be over Hubbert's Peak. We may be over it even now, or we may continue with the present course of fracking, which represents a different but no less serious risk to the water table. And for all your efforts, our children might as well believe their tap water arrives by magic. They do not know that there is an aquifer beneath their town, or that it is dangerously depleted, or that we have no plan for how to supply the town with water **after** its depletion. Most of them do not know that five of the last six years have been the hottest on record. I imagine that your students might be interested in that. I imagine they might be interested in their future. Instead, my child is taking spelling tests. In **eighth** grade. Are you puzzled that her mind is elsewhere?"

Turtle is looking at him and trying to see him as Principal Green and Anna see him, and she hates what she sees.

Principal Green looks as if he has heard this objection before, put more forcefully, from others. He says, "Well, Marty. That's not quite true. Our students have their last spelling test in fifth grade. Eighth graders learn vocabulary words with Greek and Latin etymology, all of which are useful in preparing students to understand and articulate the phenomena you describe."

Martin stares at Principal Green.

Principal Green says, "Though, it is true that they are required to spell the words correctly."

Martin leans forward and the Colt 1911 prints against his flannel at the small of his back, and despite how cool his face is, the movement expresses his physical power and menace. It is clear, watching Principal Green and Martin across from each other, that they may even be of a weight, but where Principal Green is spilling hugely off his chair, Martin is solid as a wall. Turtle knows that this meeting is about showing a willingness to address their concerns. Martin doesn't seem to know it. "I think," Martin says, "that we should allow Julia to navigate her own relationships with her peers, and her own relationship to her schoolwork, in whatever way is best for her. You cannot dictate that a girl be an extrovert. You cannot dictate that she see a therapist, and you cannot pathologize her boredom and disenfranchisement with a tedious curriculum. In her place, you or I would be bored and disenfranchised. So I will not tell her—nor will I permit anyone to tell her—that she needs special attention. I hear your concerns about the rigors of high school, but I cannot help but think that such rigors can only be a profitable contrast from this mind-numbing gauntlet of spelling tests and plotless children's books. She will rise to whatever challenges the coming year brings. However, I am cognizant of your concerns and I can commit right now to finding more time to help Julia study and to teaching her the study skills you believe she may lack. I can find more time for that, every night and on weekends."

Principal Green turns to Turtle and says, "Julia, what do you think of all this? Would you like to meet with Maya?"

Turtle sits frozen, one hand grasped by the other, right on the cusp of cracking a knuckle, mouth open, and she looks from her daddy to Anna. She wants to put Anna at her ease, but can't contradict Martin. Everybody watches her. She says, "Anna is really helpful, and I don't think I do a good job of letting her help." Everyone in the room seems surprised. "I think," Turtle says, "that I need to work a little harder, and let Anna help a little more, listen to her more, maybe. But I don't want to see anybody."

When they are done, her daddy rises and opens the door for Turtle and they walk to the truck together and get in and sit in silence on the bench seat. Martin puts his hand on the ignition and seems to think about something, looking to the side window. Then he says, "Is this the sum of your ambition? To be an illiterate little slit?"

He starts the truck and they pull away, out of the parking lot, Turtle repeating the words **illiterate little slit.** His meaning comes to her all at once like something lodged up in a can glopping free. She leaves parts of herself unnamed and unexamined, and then he will name them, and she will see herself clearly in his words and hate herself. He shifts gears with quiet, forceful anger. She hates herself, hates that unfinished and unchinked gap. They go up the gravel drive and he parks in front of the porch and shuts the truck off. They climb the porch steps together and Daddy walks to the kitchen and takes a beer from the fridge and knocks it open on the counter's edge. He sits down at the table and chisels at a stain with his thumbnail. Turtle gets down on her knees and puts her hands on the faded indigo of his Levi's and says, "I'm sorry, Daddy." She slips two fingers through the white distressed threads, laying the side of her face against the inside of his thigh. He sits looking away from her, holding his beer encircled by thumb and forefinger, and she thinks desperately about what she can do, a slitted little girl, slitted and illiterate.

He says, "I don't even know what to say. I don't know what to tell you. Humanity is killing itself—slowly, ruinously, collectively **shitting in its bathwater**, shitting on the world just because they cannot conceive that the world exists. That fat man and that bitch, they don't understand. They make up hoops for you to jump through and they want you to think that **that's** the world; that the world is made up of hoops. But the world isn't, and you must never, ever think it is. The world is Buckhorn Bay and Slaughterhouse Gulch. That

is the world, and that school is just—shadows, dis-
tractions. Never forget that. But you have to pay
attention. If you stumble, they will take you away
from me. So what do I tell you . . . ? That school
is nothing, and still, you have to play along?"
He looks at her, gauging her intelligence. Then he
reaches out, takes hold of her by the jaw, and says,
"What goes on in that little head of yours?" He
turns her head this way and that, looking into
her intently. Finally, he says, "Do you know this,
kibble? Do you know what you mean to me? You
save my life every morning that you get up and
out of bed. I hear your little footsteps padding
down your stairwell and I think, that's my girl,
that's what I'm living for." He is silent for a moment. She shakes her head, her heart creaking with
anger.

That night, she waits silently, listening, touching
the cold blade of her pocketknife to her face. She
opens and closes it silently, tripping the liner lock
with her thumb and lowering the lock into place
to keep it from clicking. She can hear him pace
from room to room. Turtle pares crescents from
her fingernails. When he stops, she stops. He is
silent down in the living room. Slowly, quietly, she
folds the knife closed. She cracks the knuckles of
her toes with the heel of her other foot. He comes
up the stairs and lifts her up and she drapes her
hands around his neck and he carries her down
the stairs and through the darkened living room

to his bedroom, where the moon-cast shadows of the alder leaves come in and out of focus on the drywall, the leaves themselves the darkest waxen green against the window glass, the rust-black floorboards with cracks like hatchet wounds, the unfinished commissure of the redwood and the drywall a black seam opening into the unplumbed foundation where the great old-growth beams exhale their scent like black tea, like creek stones and tobacco. He lays her down, fingertips dimpling her thighs, her ribs opening and closing, each swale shadowed, each ridge immaculate white. She thinks, do it, I want you to do it. She lies expecting it at any moment, looking out the window at the small, green, new-forming alder cones and thinking, this is me, her thoughts gelled and bloody marrow within the piping of her hollow thighbones and the coupled, gently curving bones of her forearms. He crouches over her and in husky tones of awe, he says, "Goddamn, kibble, goddamn." He puts his hands on the shallow horns of her hip bones, on her stomach, on her face. She stares unblinking. He says, "Goddamn," and runs his scarred fingertips through the tangle of her hair, and then he turns her over and she lies facedown and waits for him, and in the waiting she by turns wants and does not want. His touch brings her skin to life, and she holds it all within the private theater of her mind, where anything is permitted, their two shadows cast across the sheet and knit together. He runs his hand up her leg and cups her butt in his hand and he says, "Goddamn, goddamn," and he walks his lips up the knobs of her spine, kissing each, waiting on each, his breathing choked with emotion, saying, "Goddamn," her legs parted to show a gap admitting to the black of her guts and he takes this for her truth, she knows. He lifts her hair in handfuls and lays it over the pillow to expose the nape of her neck and he says, "Goddamn," his voice a rasp, teasing the small stray hairs with his fingers. Her throat lies against the pillow, filled with papery wet leaves, like she is a cold seep in autumn, the wintry water sieving through them, peppery and pine-tasting, oak leaves and the green taste of field grass. He believes her body to be something that he understands, and, treacherously, it is.

When he is asleep, she rises and walks through the house alone, holding her engorged pussy to catch the unspooling warmth. She crouches in the bathtub, looking at the copper fixtures, ladling the cold water onto herself, the coarse spiderweb texture of his spunk among her fingers clinging even under the running water and seeming only to thicken. She stands at the porcelain sink, washing her hands, and they are her father's eyes in the mirror. She finishes washing, cranks the copper finial, looks into that chinked, white-threaded blue, the black pupil dilating and contracting of its own.

Two

WHEN THE FOG LIFTS FROM GRASS STILL smoking with dew, Turtle takes the Remington 870 down from its wall pegs, trips the release, and slivers back the slide to show the green buckshot hull. She jacks the shotgun closed and tilts it over her shoulder and goes down the stairs and out the back door. It is beginning to rain. The drops patter down from the pines and stand trembling on the nettle leaves and sword fronds. She scrambles along the joists of the back deck and clambers down the hillside alive with rotting logs and roughskinned newts and California slender salamanders, her heels breaking through the gooey crust of myrtle leaves and churning up the black earth.

She comes cautious and switchbacking down to the wellspring of Slaughterhouse Creek, where the maidenhair ferns are black-stemmed with leaves like green teardrops, the nasturtiums hanging in tangles with their crisp, wet, nasturtium scent, the rocks scrolled with liverwort.

The spring here pours from a mossy nook in the hillside, and where it falls, it has carved a basin out of the living stone, a well of cold, clear, iron-tasting water, big as a room, thatched with logs worn feathery by age. Turtle sits on the logs, taking off all of her clothes and laying the shotgun among them and slipping feetfirst into the stone pool—because here she seeks her own peculiar solace, and here she feels it to be the solace of cold places, of a thing that is clear and cold and alive. She holds her breath and sinks to the bottom and, drawing her knees to her shoulders with her hair rising around her like weeds, she opens her eyes to the water and looks up and sees writ huge across the rain-dappled surface the basking shapes of newts with their fingers splayed and their golden-red bellies exposed to her, their tails churning lazily. They are bent and distorted, hazed the way things are under water, and the cold is good for her, it brings her back to herself. She breaks the surface and heaves out onto the logs and feels the warmth return and watches the forest around her.

She rises and climbs carefully back up the hill-side and walks heel to toe across the joists of the back deck in the gathering rain and then into the kitchen, where the black-tailed weasel startles and looks up, one paw raised above a plate covered in old steak bones.

She sets the shotgun on the counter and goes to the fridge and opens it and stands wet, her hair slicked to her back and straggled around her face, racking the eggs on the counter's edge and breaking them into her mouth and discarding them into the compost bucket. She hears Martin walk out of his bedroom and down the hallway. He comes into the kitchen and looks past her through the open kitchen door to the rain. She says nothing. She lowers her hands to the counter and lets them rest there. Water is beaded on the shotgun. It clings to the corrugated green hulls in the shotgun's sidesaddle. "Well, kibble," he says, looking past her. "Well, kibble."

She puts the carton of eggs away. She takes out a beer and tosses it to him and he catches it.

"Time to take you down to the bus?"

"You don't have to come."

"I know."

"You don't have to, Daddy."

"I know that, kibble."

She doesn't say anything. She stands at the counter.

They walk down the road together in the gathering rain. The drive runs with water, laddering the ruts with pine needles. They stand at the bottom of their driveway. Along the tarmac's crumbling edge, sweet vernal grass and wild oats nod in the downpour, bindweed twining up the stalks. They can hear Slaughterhouse Creek echoing in the culvert beneath the Shoreline Highway. On the nickel-gray ocean, whitecaps ship cream against the black sea stacks.

"Look at that motherfucker," Martin says, and she looks, not knowing what he means—the cove, the ocean, the sea stacks, it isn't clear. She hears the old bus shifting as it comes around the bend. "Take care of yourself, kibble," Martin says darkly. The bus creaks to a stop, and with an exhausted gasp and the thwacking of rubber skirts, throws open its doors. Martin salutes the bus driver, holding the beer over his heart, somber in the face of her derision. Turtle climbs the stairs and walks down the corrugated rubber runner lit by panel lights in the floor, the corrugations now filled with rainwater, the other faces dim white smudges disordered in their dark green vinyl pews. The bus heaves, and with it, Turtle jars sideways and drops into her empty seat.

Each time the bus slows, the water drains forward beneath the seats and through the rubber corrugations of the walkway and the students pull their feet up, disgusted. Turtle sits watching the water pass beneath her, carrying with it a hull of pink nail polish, which has come off all of a piece and lies upturned on the tide. Rilke is across the aisle from her, knees pressed against the seat back, bent over her book, running a hank of hair between thumb and forefinger until she has only the fan of ends, her red London Fog coat still beading with water. Turtle wonders if Rilke wore it to school thinking, okay, but I have to take good care of this coat. The rain is unseasonable, but she's heard no one say so. Turtle doesn't think anyone else but her daddy worries about that. She wonders what Rilke would think if she could see Turtle up at night, sitting under the naked bulb in her redwood-paneled room with its bay window looking out on Buckhorn Hill, stooped over the disassembled gun, handling each piece with care, and she wonders, if Rilke could see that, would Rilke understand? She thinks, no, of course not. Of course she wouldn't. No one understands anyone else.

Turtle is wearing old Levi's over black Icebreaker wool tights, her T-shirt clinging to her stomach with damp, a flannel, an olive drab army coat much too big for her, and a mesh-back cap. She thinks, I would give anything in the world to be you. I would give anything. But it is not true, and Turtle knows that it is not true.

Rilke says, "I really like your coat."

Turtle looks away.

Rilke says quickly, "No, like—I **really** do. I have nothing like that, you know? Like—cool and old?"

"Thanks," Turtle says, pulling the coat up around

her shoulders, drawing her hands back into its sleeves.

"It's this whole, like, army surplus, Kurt Cobain chic you have."

Turtle says, "Thanks."

Rilke says, "So, Anna is, like—**killing** you on those vocab tests."

"Fucking Anna, fucking whore," Turtle says. The coat sits huge about her shoulders. Her hands, white-knuckled, wet with rain, are clenched between her thighs. Rilke barks out a startled laugh, looking forward down the aisle and then in the other direction, to the back of the bus, her neck very long, her hair falling about her in straight, black, glossy strands. Turtle does not know how it is so glossy, so straight, how it has that sheen, and then Rilke looks back to Turtle, eyes alight, putting a hand over her mouth.

"Oh my god," Rilke says, "oh my god."

Turtle watches her.

"Oh my god," Rilke says again, leaning in conspiratorially. "Don't say that!"

"Why?" Turtle says.

"Anna's really very nice, you know," Rilke says, still leaning in.

"She's a cunt," Turtle says.

Rilke says, "So you want to hang out sometime?"

"No," Turtle says.

"Well," Rilke says, after a pause, "good talk," and returns to her book.

Turtle looks away from Rilke, at the seat ahead of her, and then out at the window, sheeted with water. A pair of girls tamp a bowl into a blown-glass pipe. The bus shudders and jars. I would just as soon, Turtle thinks, slit you from your asshole to your little slut throat as be your friend. She has a Kershaw Zero Tolerance knife with the pocket clip removed that she carries deep in her pocket. She thinks, you bitch, sitting there with your nail polish, running your hands through your hair. She does not even know why Rilke does this; why does she examine the ends of her hair; what is there to see? I hate everything about you, Turtle thinks. I hate the way you talk. I hate your little bitch voice. I can barely hear you, that high-pitched squeak. I hate you, and I hate that slick little clam lodged up between your legs. Turtle, watching Rilke, thinks, goddamn, but she is really looking at her hair as if there is something for her to see about the ends.

When the bell rings for lunch, Turtle walks down the hill to the field, her boots squelching. She wades out toward the soccer goal, hands in her pockets, and the rain sweeps across the flooded field in drifts. The field is enclosed by a forest black with rain, the trees withered and gnarled with their poor soil, thin as poles. A garter snake skates across the water, gloriously side to side, head up and forward, black with long green and copper runners, a thin yellow jaw, a black face, bright black eyes. It crosses the flooded ditch and is gone. She wants to go, to bolt. She wants to cover ground. To leave, to take to the woods, is to throw open the cylinder of her life and spin it and close it. She has promised Martin, promised, and promised, and promised. He cannot risk losing her, but, Turtle thinks, he will not. She doesn't know everything about these woods, but she knows enough. She stands enclosed in the open field, looking out into the forest, and she thinks, the hell, the hell.

The bell rings. Turtle turns and looks back to the school above her on the hill. Low buildings, covered walkways, throng of raincoated middle schoolers, clogged downspouts sheeting water.

Three

IT IS MID-APRIL, ALMOST TWO WEEKS since the meeting with Anna. Blackberries have clambered into the old apple trees and are knitted into a wildly blooming canopy. Quail mince in nervous coteries, topknots bobbing, while sparrows and finches go wheeling and banking among the trunks. She comes out of the orchard and through the staked raspberry field to Grandpa's trailer. Streaks of mold have run down the panels. The aluminum coping around the windows is caulked with moss. Pockets of leaf litter grow cypress shoots. She hears Rosy, Grandpa's old dachshund/beagle mutt, heave herself up and come to the door, shaking herself and setting her collar to tinkling. Then the door is thrown open, and Grandpa stands in the doorway and says, "Hey there, sweetpea."

She climbs up the steps and leans the AR-10 against the doorjamb. It is her gun, a Lewis Machine & Tool rifle with a U.S. Optics 5-25x44 scope. She loves it, but it's too damn heavy. Rosy hops up and down, flopping her ears.

"Who's a good dog?" Turtle asks Rosy.

Rosy shakes herself excitedly, wagging her tail.

Grandpa settles at the foldout table, pours himself two fingers of Jack. Turtle sits down opposite him, takes her Sig Sauer from a concealment holster in her jeans, drops the magazine, and leaves the gun on the table, locked open, because Grandpa says that when a man plays cribbage with his granddaughter, the two of them should be unarmed.

He says, "Have you come to play some cribbage with your grandpa?"

"Yeah," she says.

"You know why you like cribbage, sweetpea?"

"Why, Grandpa?"

"Because cribbage, sweetpea, is a game of low animal cunning."

She looks up at him, smiling a little, because she does not at all know what he means.

"Ah, sweetpea," he says, "I'm joking with you."

"Oh," she says, and allows her smile to overtake her whole face, turning a little away from him, touching her thumb to her teeth shyly. It feels so good to have Grandpa teasing with her, even if she doesn't understand.

He is looking at her Sig Sauer. He reaches across the table, sets a hand on it, lifts it up. The slide is locked back, the barrel is exposed, and he inspects it for fouling and touches it with a finger pad for grease, turning it this way and that way in the light. "Your daddy takes care of this gun for you?" he says.

She shakes her head.

"You take care of this gun for yourself?" he says.

"Yeah."

He swings the takedown lever and drops the slide catch. Carefully he removes the slide from the frame, sits inspecting the rails.

"But you never fire this thing," he says.

Turtle picks up a deck of cards, shucks it out of the case, splits the deck, shuffles and bridges them. The cards slither with satin-finish friction. She racks the deck sharply against the tabletop.

"You do fire it," he says.

"Why is it a game of low animal cunning?" she says, breaking the deck and examining the halves in either hand.

"Oh, I don't know," he says. "That's just what they say."

Every night she disassembles the gun and cleans it with a brass-bristled brush and with cotton patches. Grandpa sits looking into the clean, well-worn rails, and then he returns the slide to the frame. His fingers shake, holding the slide in place against the recoil spring. He seems to have forgotten how to engage the takedown lever, sits looking at the catches and levers as if hesitating, as if for a moment he has lost his bearings on the gun. Turtle does not know what to do. She sits with the halves of the deck still in her hands. Then he finds the takedown lever and tries it twice before he manages to get the tight-fit steel tab to rotate, and then he pushes it into place, his hands shaking, and lets the slide relax forward. He sets the gun aside and looks at her. Turtle shuffles, bridges, slaps the deck down in front of him.

"Well," he says. "You're not your old man, that's for sure."

"What?" Turtle says, curious.

"Oh," Grandpa says, "never mind, never mind."

He extends a shaking hand and cuts the deck. Turtle picks it back up and deals them each six cards. Grandpa fans the cards before him, and sighs, making slight adjustments with thumb and forefinger. Turtle discards her crib. Grandpa sighs again and encircles his whiskey in one big hand and sits, turning it slowly in the ring of its condensation, the soapstones sounding softly against the glass.

He tosses back the drink, sucks air through his teeth, pours himself another. Turtle waits, silent. He tosses this back, and pours himself a third. He sits rotating it slowly. Finally, he picks two cards and tosses them into the crib. Then he cuts the deck and Turtle draws off the start card, the queen of hearts, and lays it faceup. He seems about to remark on how the start card has determined the fate of his hand, as if—on the verge of this observation— he is struck mute by the complexity of it.

"The rails on that gun," he says after a minute, "look pretty good."

"Yeah," Turtle says.

"Well, they look pretty good," Grandpa says again, doubtfully.

"I keep them oiled," she says.

Grandpa looks around the trailer, suddenly, wonderingly. His eyes run across the ceiling, across the ersatz wood paneling peeling away in places, over the dingy little kitchen. There is laundry on the floor in the hallway and Grandpa frowns severely, looking at it all.

"It's your play," Turtle says.

Grandpa teases one card from the others, throws it down. "Ten," he says.

Turtle throws down a five, pegs two for fifteen.

"Grandpa?" she says.

"Twenty," he says, pegging two for the pair.

"Thirty," Turtle says, throwing down a jack.

"Go."

Turtle pegs one for the go, throws a queen. Grandpa lays down a seven in seeming exhaustion. Turtle throws a three, for twenty. Grandpa throws a six, says, "Here, sweetpea," and unbuckles his belt and draws off it the old bowie knife. The belt leather is worn shiny black from the sheath, and he holds it out to her in his open hand, hefting it. "I don't use it anymore," he says.

Turtle says, "Put that down, Grandpa. We still need to score the hand."

"Sweetpea," Grandpa says, holding out the knife.

"Let's see what's in your hand," Turtle says.

Grandpa puts the knife down on the table in front of her. The leather handle is old and black with grease, the steel pummel dark gray. Turtle reaches across the table, collects Grandpa's hand, and pulls it forward to her. She gathers the four cards together and looks at them: the five ofspades, the six of spades, seven of spades, ten of spades, and the start card, the queen of diamonds. "Well," Turtle says, "well." Grandpa doesn't look at his cards, he just looks at her. Turtle's mouth moves with her counting. "Fifteen for two, fifteen for four, the run for seven, and the flush for eleven points. Did I miss anything?" She pegs him eleven points.

Grandpa says, "Pick that up, sweetpea."

She says, "I don't understand, Grandpa."

He says, "You're entitled to a thing or two of mine."

She cracks one knuckle, then another.

He says, "You'll take good care of it. It's a good one. You ever stick a son of a bitch with this, he'll sit up and take notice. This knife comes from me to you."

She draws it from the sheath. The steel is smoky black with age. Oxidized in the way of very old carbon steel. She turns the blade to face her and it shows a single unbroken, unglinting line without nicks or flaws, a shining, polished edge. She passes the blade gently up her arm and golden hairs accumulate in a tide line.

He says, "Go get the whetstones, too, sweetpea."

She goes to the kitchen and opens a drawer and pulls out the old leather bundle with the three whetstones and carries it back to the table.

He says, "You take good care of that."

She sits looking at the blade, mute. She loves taking care of things.

Rosy, sitting on the floor between them, perks up, her collar tinkling. She looks toward the door, and then there is a loud knocking. Turtle flinches.

"That'll be your father," Grandpa says.

Martin swings the door open and steps inside. The floor complains beneath him. He stands spanning the hallway.

"Oh Christ, Dad," Martin says, "I wish you wouldn't drink in front of her."

"She doesn't mind me taking a drink," Grandpa says. "Do you, sweetpea?"

"Christ, Daniel," Martin says. "Of course she doesn't mind. She's fourteen. It's not her job to mind, it's mine; it's my job to mind, and I do. It should be your job, too, but you don't make it your job, I guess."

"Well, I don't see the harm."

"I don't mind it," Martin says, "if you have a beer. I don't mind that. I don't mind it if you're gonna pour yourself a finger or two of Jack. But I don't like it when you've had more than a few. That's not all right."

"I'm fine," Grandpa says with a wave of his hand.

"All right," Martin says thinly, "all right. Come on back home, kibble."

Turtle picks up the pistol, drops the slide, slaps in the magazine, holsters it. Then she rises, holding the knife and the bundle of whetstones, and walks toward the door, where Martin puts an arm around her shoulder. She slings the AR-10 and turns to look back at Grandpa. Martin hesitates there in the doorway, holding Turtle.

He says, "You all right, Dad?"

Grandpa says, "I'm fine."

Martin says, "I don't guess you'd want to come over for dinner?"

"Oh," he says, "I have a pizza in the freezer."

"You're welcome to dinner. We'd like to have you over, Dad. Wouldn't we, kibble?"

Turtle is silent, she does not want to be in this, does not want Grandpa to come over.

Martin says, "Well, have it your way. If you change your mind, you just call, and I'll drive the truck up here and pick you up."

"Oh, I'm all right," Grandpa says.

"And, Dad," Martin says, "take it easy. This girl deserves a grandfather. All right?"

"All right," Grandpa says, frowning.

Martin continues to hesitate in the doorway. Grandpa watches him, his head trembling a little bit, and Martin stands as if expecting Grandpa to say something, but Grandpa doesn't and Martin tightens his grip on Turtle's shoulder and they walk down together, following the old gravel road through the orchard. He is a big, silent presence beside her. They go through the evening woods, past where Grandpa parks his truck. Blackberry runners have knit over the median. Wild chamomile sprawls in the gravel. "Don't take this the wrong way, kibble," Martin says, "but your grandpa is a real son of a bitch."

Father and daughter climb the porch steps together and go in through the living room. Turtle vaults onto the counter and sets the knife down beside her. Martin strikes a match on his Levi's to light the burner, takes down a frying pan, and begins to prepare dinner. Turtle sits at the counter's edge. She unholsters the gun, racks the slide, and sinks four shots into a single mark. Martin looks up from cutting a squash and watches her empty the magazine. The slide locks back, smoking, and he returns his attention to the butcher block, smiling tiredly and lopsidedly, smiling so that she can see it.

"Is that your grandfather's knife?" He dusts off his hands, holds one out.

Turtle hesitates.

"What?" he says, and she picks up the knife and hands it to him. He draws it from the sheath and walks around the counter to stand beside her, turning it to the light. He says, "When I was a kid, I can remember your grandfather sitting in his chair—he'd get in a mood and he'd drink bourbon and throw this knife at the door. Then he'd stand up and get it and sit down again, and he'd look at the door and then he'd throw the knife. It'd stick in the door and he'd walk over and get it. For hours, he'd do that."

Turtle looks at Martin.

"Watch this," he says.

"No," she says, "wait."

"It's fine," he says.

He walks to the hallway door beside the fireplace and closes it. He walks back and squares against the door. He says, "Watch this."

She says, "It's not a throwing knife."

"The hell it isn't," he says.

She grabs on to his shirt. "Wait," she says.

"Watch this," he says, seeming to gauge the distance. He tosses the knife in the air and catches it by the spine. Turtle watches silently, putting her fingers in her mouth. Martin winds up and throws the knife and it ricochets off the door and strikes the hearthstones. Turtle lurches after it, but Martin is faster, shoving her aside and picking it off the river stone hearth and bending over it, putting his back between Turtle and the knife, saying, "Nah, it's fine."

"Give it back," Turtle says.

Martin turns away from her, bent over the knife, saying, "It's fine, kibble, it's fine."

"Give it back," Turtle says.

"Just a moment," he says. Turtle, hearing some dangerous note in his voice, steps back. "Just hold on just one goddamn moment," he says, holding the knife to the light while Turtle waits, her jaw flexing in annoyance. "Well, fuck," he says at last.

"What?"

"It's this fucking carbon steel, kibble, it's like glass."

"Give it back to me," she says, and he hands it back. The blade is chipped.

"It doesn't matter," Martin says.

"Fuck!" Turtle says.

"That high-carbon steel is worthless," Martin says. "Like I told you, it's like glass. That's why they make knives out of stainless steel. That carbon steel, you just can't trust it. Holds an edge like a motherfucker, but it shatters and it rusts. I don't know how the man kept it like that, all through the war. Grease, I guess."

"Fuck," Turtle says, flushed with anger.

"Well, here, I'll make it good."

"Forget it," Turtle says, "it doesn't matter."

"It does matter. You're mad about it, my love. I'll make it good."

"No, I don't care," she says.

"Kibble," he says, "give me the knife, I'm not going to have you pissed at me because that knife is as fragile as a fucking toy. I made a mistake, and I can set that knife up just like you want it, good as new."

Turtle says, "It's something you have to care for."

"Well, that's fucked, because," Martin says, laughing at her anger, "I thought a knife was supposed to take care of you. I thought that was the point."

Turtle stands, looking down at the floorboards, feeling that she has flushed red to the roots of her hair.

"Give me the knife, kibble. A pass on the sharpener and that mark won't even be there."

"No," she says. "It doesn't matter."

"I can see on your face that it does matter, so give it to me, and let me make it right."

Turtle gives him the knife and Martin opens the door and goes down the hall, past the bathroom, the foyer, and into the pantry, where there is a long wooden workbench along one wall, with clamps and vises and above that a wall of pegboard covered with mounted tools. The opposite walls are lined with gun safes, stainless-steel cabinets of reloading materials, stacked thousand-round boxes of 5.56 and .308. A spiral stairwell leads into a cellar, which is a room of damp, moldy earth filled with five-gallon buckets of dehydrated food. They have enough food stored down there to keep three people alive for three years.

Martin goes to a grinder bolted to the workbench and turns it on.

"No, wait," Turtle says over the roar of the grinder.

Martin stands gauging the angle of the bevel by eye. "Fine," he says, "it will be **fine**." He passes the blade across the grindstone. It screams. He plunges it, hissing, into a coffee can of mineral oil, returns it to the wheel, holds it steady, his whole face intent, runs it across the grindstone, throwing a brilliant rooster tail of orange and white sparks, the edge feathering white, heat markings spreading across the steel. He lifts the blade away, plunges it again into oil, turns it over in his hand, and returns it to the grinder. He inspects it again, and stands testing it against his thumb, nodding and smiling to himself. He turns off the grinder and the grindstone begins to coast, some hitch in the mechanism so that the sound of the slowing grindstone has a faint irregularity, a **whump-whump, whump-whump**. He passes her the knife. The mirror polish of the razor edge is gone, the cutting edge scored and uneven. Turtle turns the knife to the light and the blade throws a thousand glinting sparks from chips and spurs in the edge.

"You've ruined it," she says.

"Ruined it?" he says, hurt. "No, that's just because— No, kibble, this is a hell of a lot better than whatever edge Grandpa put on there. That grindstone, it'll put a perfect edge on that blade, a hundred microscopic serrations, that's what really gives the blade a cutting edge. The razor edge you had on that before, that's just the vanity of patient men—that's no good for the real activity of cutting, kibble, which is to **saw** through things. A mirror polish like that—that's only good for a push cut, you know what that is, kibble?"

Turtle knows what a push cut is, but Martin can't resist.

He says, "A push cut, kibble, is the simplest kind of cut, when you lay the knife down on a steak and **press** without **drawing** the blade across it. But, kibble, you don't just **push** the knife into a steak, you **draw** the knife across it. That, what you had before, was a glorified straight razor. In life, you **drag** a blade across something. That's the business of cutting, kibble, a **rough** edge. That mirror polish is meant to distract from the knife's purpose with its beauty. Do you see— Do you see—? That razor edge, it is a beautiful thing, but a knife is not meant to be a beautiful thing. This knife is for slitting throats, and for that you want the microscopic serrations you get from a rough grindstone. You'll see. With that cutting edge on there, that thing will open flesh like it was butter. Are you sad that I took your illusion away? That edge was a shadow on the wall, kibble. You have to stop being distracted by the shadows."

Turtle tests the edge against her thumb, looking at her father.

"That's a goddamn lesson in life, right there," he says.

She turns the knife in her hands, uncertain.

He says, "You just don't trust me, do you?"

"I trust you," she says, and she thinks, you are hard on me, but you are good for me, too, and I need that hardness in you. I need you to be hard on me, because I am no good for myself, and you make me do what I want to do but cannot do for myself; but still, but still—you are sometimes not careful; there is something in you, something less than careful, something almost— I don't know, I am not sure, but I know it's there.

"Here," he says, taking the knife from her and shoving her down the hallway, leading her to the living room. They go back through the door and he points to a chair. "Step up on that," he says. Turtle looks at him, steps onto the chair. Martin points to the table, and she steps up onto it, stands among the beer bottles and old plates and steak bones.

"That rafter," he says.

She looks up at the rafter.

"I want to show you something," he says.

"What?" she says.

"Jump up to the rafter, kibble."

"What are you going to show me?"

"Goddamn it," he says.

"I don't understand," she says.

"Goddamn it," he says.

"I know the knife is sharp," she says.

"You don't seem to know that."

"No," she says, "I trust you, I do. The knife is sharp."

"God fucking damn it, kibble."

"No, Daddy, it's just that it was Grandpa's knife, and he'll be disappointed."

"It isn't his anymore, is it? Now grab on to that rafter."

"I wanted to try taking care of that mirror polish," she says, "just try and take care of it, that's all."

"It doesn't matter. That steel, it's gonna rust away into pits by the end of the year."

"No," she says, "no it won't."

"You haven't had to take care of a thing like that yet, you'll see. Now jump up on the rafter."

"Why?"

"God fucking damn it, kibble. God fucking damn it."

She jumps and captures the rafter.

Martin overturns the table from beneath her, spilling the deck of cards, the plates, candles, beer bottles. He puts his shoulder against it and shoves it out from beneath her, carrying all of its detritus along like a bulldozer, leaving Turtle hanging from the rafter above the floor.

She racks and reracks her fingers so they lie

comfortably against the grain. Martin watches her from below with a grimace gathering almost to anger. He walks to her and stands between her feet, turning the knife this way and that.

"Can I come down?" she says.

He stands looking up at her, his face growing stiffer, his mouth setting. Turtle, looking down at him, can almost believe that looking at her like this makes him angry.

"Don't say it like that," he says. Then he raises the knife and lays the blade up between her legs, stands scowling up at her. He says, "Just hang in there."

Turtle is silent and unamused, looking down at him. He presses up with the knife and says, "Upsy-daisy."

Turtle does a pull-up, places her chin on the splintery beam and hangs while Martin stands below her, his face stripped of all warmth and kindness, seeming fixed in some reverie of hatred. The knife bites into the blue denim of her jeans and Turtle feels the cold steel through her panties.

She looks across to the next rafter, and the one after that, all the way to the far wall, each rafter felted with dust and showing wandering rat tracks. Her legs quiver. She begins to lower herself, but Martin says, "Uh—" abruptly and warningly, the knife resting against her crotch. She trembles, not able to fully raise herself back to the rafter and so puts her face against its splintery side, holding her cheek there. She strains, thinking, please, please, please.

Then he lowers the blade and she comes down with it, unable to do otherwise, trembling and shaking with the effort of lowering herself as slowly as he lowers the knife. She hangs at the full extension of her arms and says, "Daddy?"

He says, "See, this is what I'm **goddamn** talking about."

Then he begins to raise the blade again, clucking his tongue warningly. She goes up into a full pull-up and hooks her chin on the rafter and hangs there, quivering. She starts to lower herself and Martin says, "Uh—" to stop her, grimacing as if it's sad the way things are, and he would even change it if he could, but can't.

Turtle thinks to herself, you bastard, you fucking bastard.

"That's two," he says. He lowers the blade and she lowers herself with it, and then he raises it, saying, "With a little incentive, you can really rack up those pull-ups, huh?"

He makes her lower herself with agonizing slowness. She does first twelve, and then thirteen. She hangs trembling from her exhausted arms, and Martin, raising the blade with a slow and menacing pressure, says, "You all done? Tapped out? Dig deep, kibble. You better find something. Let's go for **fifteen**." Her fingers ache, the grain cuts into her flesh. Her forearms feel numb. She doesn't know if she can do another.

"Come **on**," he says. "Two more."

"I can't," she says, almost crying with fear.

"You think the knife's sharp now, don't you?" he says. "You believe it now, don't you?" He saws the blade forward and she hears the denim whisper apart. She digs deep for any last ounce of strength, trying desperately to hold on, and Martin says, "You might want to hold on, kibble. You might not want to let go, little girl," and then her fingertips peel off the rafter and she comes down onto the blade.

Martin jerks the knife out from under her at the last possible moment and it saws through her thigh and buttock. She lands on her heels and stands there splay-legged and astonished, looking down at her crotch, where there is no sign except a cut in the denim. Martin holds the bowie knife bloodless and unmarked, his eyebrows going up in astonishment, his mouth opening into a grin.

Turtle sits on her butt and Martin begins to laugh. She stoops forward to look through the parted cloth and says, "You cut me, you cut me," though she cannot feel or see any cut.

"You should've," Martin says and stops and bends double with laughter. He waves the bowie knife through the air to try and get her to stop so he can get his breath.

"You should've—" he gasps.

She lies back and unbuttons her jeans. Martin sets the bowie knife on the counter and grabs the bottoms and upends her out of them. She spills across the floor, recovers herself, and then stoops over her thighs, trying to see the cut.

"You should've—" he says. "You should've—" And his eyes clench with laughter.

Turtle finds the cut and a whisker of blood.

Martin says, "You should have seen—**your face.**" He screws his own face up in a mimicry of adolescent betrayal, opening his eyes wide in astonishment, and then, waving one hand through the air as if to brush all teasing aside, he says, "You'll be okay, kiddo, you'll be fine. Just, next time—**don't let go!**" At this, he begins to laugh again, shaking his head, his eyes slitting closed and leaking tears, and he inquires of the room, "Jesus! Am I right? Am I right? Jesus! Don't let go! Isn't that right? Fuck!"

He kneels down and takes her naked thigh in his hands and, seeming to see her distress for the first time, he says, "I don't know why you're so afraid, baby, you're hardly even nicked. See, I wasn't going to cut you. I took it out from under you, didn't I? And if you're so afraid, goddamn, next time, don't let go."

"It's not that easy," she says from behind her hands.

"It is, you just—**don't let go,**" he says.

Turtle lies flat on the floor. She wants to smash to pieces.

He rises and walks down the hall and into the bathroom. He returns with a first aid kit and kneels between her legs. He tears open a green disposable wound sponge and begins to dab at the cut. He says, "This? You're worried about this? There, I'll take care of it, there." He unscrews the cap on the Neosporin and begins to dab it into the wound. His every touch sends ripples of sensation through her body. He opens a Band-Aid and lays it flush against her skin and smooths it to ensure the contact is good. "All better, kibble, look at that, it's all right."

She raises her head and ropes of muscle stand out from her mons pubis to her sternum like a bread loaf. She watches him and then she lays her head back down and she closes her eyes and she feels her soul to be a stalk of pig mint growing in the dark foundation, slithering toward a keyhole of light between the floorboards, greedy and sun-starved.

Four

IT IS FRIDAY AND THEY HAVE A FRIDAY ritual. Turtle walks up from the bus stop to the two fifty-gallon drums where they burn their trash, flooded with rainwater the way any bucket, any barrel or pot left in their yard fills with water, and will keep filling until June, though the weather has been unpredictable. She takes the fire poker laid crosswise over the barrel mouth and plunges it deep into the ashen water and draws out an ammo can on a looped steel runner. She pops it open and takes out a 9mm Sig Sauer and a spare magazine. She is supposed to take the precaution of clearing the house slowly and carefully, from the front door and into every room, discovering every target. But Turtle has grown bored of the process, and so she goes up the porch steps and throws open the sliding glass door, gun up, and there are three training targets by the kitchen table, plywood and sheet-metal stands with printed silhouettes stapled to them, and Turtle takes them one at a time, sidestepping out of the doorway with tight double taps, one after another, six shots in a little less than a second, and in all three targets the shots are between and slightly below the eyes, so close together that the holes touch.

She walks casually to the hallway door, stands off to the side of it, on the hearthstones, and soft-tosses it open and moves in a swift arc across the doorway, three steps back and then sidestepping so that the hallway comes into view by degrees, and she takes each of three plywood and sheet-metal targets as they appear around the jamb, tight double taps into the nasal cavity, then she steps through the door and quickly out of the fatal funnel. Gunman's shuffle down the side of the hallway, into the bathroom, clear—into the foyer, one bad guy, two shots, clear—into the pantry, clear. She ejects the magazine and replaces it with her spare and moves to Martin's bedroom door at the end of the hall. There is not enough room to pan across the threshold, so she tosses open the door and takes three swift, retreating steps back down the hallway, firing as she goes—six shots, two seconds, and when her field of fire is clear, she advances on the door again and finds three more targets, taking each in turn. Then there is silence except for the hot brass rolling around the bedroom and the hallway. She walks back to the kitchen and sets the Sig Sauer on the counter.

She can hear Martin coming up the drive. He parks outside and throws open the sliding glass doors and walks right through the living room and sits down heavily on the overstuffed couch. Turtle opens the fridge and takes out a Red Seal Ale and pitches it underhand to him and he catches it and fits the bottle cap between his molars and pops the bottle open. He begins to drink, taking long satisfied gasps, and then he looks back to her and says, "So, kibble, how was school?" and she walks around the counter, sits down on the arm of the couch, both of them looking at the ashy fireplace as if there were a fire there to absorb their attention, and she says, "School was school, Daddy."

He rakes a thumbnail across his stubble.

"Tired, Daddy?"

"Nah."

They sit and eat dinner together. Martin keeps looking at the table, furrowing his brow. They continue to eat in silence.

"How did you do, clearing the house?"

"Well."

"But not perfect?" he says.

She shrugs.

He sets his fork down and considers her, his forearms resting on the table. His left eye squints. His right eye is bright and open. The two compose an affect of complete and nuanced absorption, but when she looks at them carefully it is upsetting and strange to her, and the more genuine her attention to his expression, the more alien it seems, as if his face were not a single face at all, and as if it were trying to stake out two contrary expressions on the world.

He says, "Did you check the upstairs?"

"Yes," she says.

"Kibble, did you check the upstairs?"

"No, Daddy."

"It's a game to you."

"No, it's not."

"You don't take it seriously. You come in here and you saunter around, placing your shots right into the ocular cavity. But you know, in a real firefight, you can't always count on hitting the cavity exactly, you might have to fire for the hip—break a man's hip, Turtle, and he goes down and he does not get up—but you don't like that shot and you don't practice it because you do not see the necessity. You think you're invincible. You think you won't ever miss—you go in there just cool and relaxed, because you're overconfident. We need to put the fear on you. You need to learn how to shoot when you're shitting yourself in fear. You need to surrender yourself to death before you ever begin, and accept your life as a state of grace, and then and only then will you be good enough. That is what the drill is for."

"I do all right when I'm afraid. You know how I do."

"You go to shit, girl."

"Even if my spread goes to shit, Daddy, it's still two inches at twenty yards."

"It's not your spread, and it's not how strong you are, and it's not how fast you are, because you have all those things, and you think that means something. That means **nothing**. It's something else, kibble, it's your heart. When you are afraid, you clutch at your life like a scared little girl, and you can't do that, you will die, and you will die afraid with the shit running down your legs. You need to be so much more than that. Because the time will come, kibble, when just being fast and accurate won't be enough. The time will come when your soul must be absolute with your conviction, and whatever your spread, and howsoever fast you are, you will only succeed if you fight like a fucking angel, fallen to fucking earth, with a heart absolute and full of conviction, without hesitation, doubt, or fear, no part of yourself divided against the other; in the end, that's what life will ask of you. Not technical mastery, but ruthlessness, courage, and singularity of purpose. You watch. So it's fine that you saunter around, but that's not what the exercise is for, kibble. It's not for your spread. It's not for your aim. It's for your soul.

"You are supposed to come to the door and **believe** that hell awaits just on the other side, **believe** that this house is full of nightmares; every personal demon you have, every worst fear. That's what you stalk through this house. That's what waits for you down the hallway. Your worst fucking nightmare. Not a cardboard cutout. Practice conviction, kibble, strip yourself of hesitation and doubt, train yourself to an absolute singularity of purpose, and if you ever have to step through a door into your own personal hell, you will have a **shot**, a **shot** at survival."

Turtle has stopped eating. She watches him.

"Do you like your cassoulet?" he says.

"It's fine," she says.

"You want something else?"

"I said, it's fine."

"Christ," he says.

She goes back to eating.

"Look at you," he says, "my daughter. My little girl."

He pushes aside his plate and sits there looking at her. After a while, he nods to her backpack. She walks to it, opens it, brings out her notebook. She sits down opposite him, notebook open. She says, "Number one. 'Erinys.'" She stops, looks up at him. He puts one large, scarred hand across the open book, draws it across the table. Looks down at it.

"Well, now," he says. "Look at that. 'Erinys.'"

"What is that?" she says. "What does that mean, 'Erinys'?"

He looks up from the book, his attention is fixed on her, and it is enormous with his affection and with something private. "Your grandfather," he says, careful, wetting his lips with his tongue, "your grandfather was a hard man, kibble, he still is: a hard man. And do you know that your grand-father— Well, fuck, there is a lot your grandfather never said or did. There is something broken in that man, profoundly broken, and his brokenness is in everything he's done, his whole life. He never could see past it. And I want to say, well, kibble, how much you mean to me. I love you. I do things wrong, I know I do, and I have failed you, and I will again, and the world I am raising you into— it is not the world I would want. It is not the world I would choose for my daughter. I do not know what the future holds, not for you and me. But I am afraid, I will say that much. Whatever you lacked, whatever I haven't been able to give you, you have always been loved, deeply, kibble, ab-solutely. And I wanted to say, you will do more than I have. You will be better and more than I am. Never forget that. Now, here it is. Number one. 'Erinys.'"

Turtle wakes in the predawn dark thinking about that. Thinking about what he'd said. She cannot get back to sleep. She sits at the bay window and looks out at the ocean, the rose thorns itching at the panes. What had he meant, **there is something broken in that man**? Outside, it is clear. She thinks, you will be better and more than I am, reproducing his expression in her mind, trying to get at what he meant. She can see the stars out above the ocean, though when she looks north, she can see the lights of Mendocino reflected in the clouds. She turns, feet on the floor, elbows on her knees, and looks at her room. The beam-and-cinder-block shelves, her clothes neatly stowed. Her plywood platform bolted to the wall, with its sleeping bag and folded wool blankets. The door, the brass doorknob, the copper lock plate, the old-fashioned keyhole. She pulls on her jeans and she belts on Grandpa's knife and adds a concealment holster, telling herself, just in case, just in case, walking to her bed and reaching under it and pulling her Sig Sauer from the brackets there. She shrugs into a thick wool sweater, and over that a flannel, and walks barefoot through the hall, holstering the pistol.

She climbs down the stairs, but stands on the lowest step, hesitating, soaking up the loneliness of the house in some way, as if it had something it could tell her, the generations of Alvestons who have lived here, and all of them, she thinks, unhappy, all of them bringing their children up hard, but all of them having something to them.

Just down the hall, Martin is in his huge redwood bed, the moon casting the shadows of the alder leaves onto the drywall, and she imagines him there, solid, one hand resting on that enormous chest. She walks into the kitchen and eases open the back door. The night is clear. The moonlight is bright enough to see by. She walks along the joists and stands looking down into the black ferns. She can smell the creek. She can smell the pines. She can smell their curling, dusty needles.

She switchbacks through myrtles and rusty fronds. She comes into the rocky creek and wades up it, her feet numb with cold. The trees rise blackly into the star-glittered vault. She thinks, I will go back now. Back to my room. I have promised and promised and promised and he cannot bear to lose me. To the east, the stream shines glassy from out the riotous dark. She stands breathing, taking in the silence for a very long time. Then she goes.

Five

TURTLE CLIMBS OUT OF SLAUGHTERHOUSE
Gulch and comes into a forest of bishop pine and
huckleberries, deciphering them in the darkness
by the wax of the leaves and the brittle mess of
their sprawl, the dawn still hours away. At times
she breaks from the woods into moonlit open
places filled with rhododendron, their flowers pink
and ghostly in the dark, their leaves leathery and
prehistoric. There is a part of Turtle that she keeps
shut up and private, that she attends to with only
a diffuse and uncritical attention, and when Martin advances on this part of herself, she plays him a
game of tit for tat, retreating wordlessly and almost
without regard to consequences; her mind cannot

be taken by force, she is a person like him, but she is not him, nor is she just a part of him—and there are silent, lonely moments when this part of her seems to open like some night-blooming flower, drinking in the cold of the air, and she loves this moment, and loving it, she is ashamed, because she loves him, too, and she should not thrill this way, should not thrill to his absence, should not need to be alone, but she takes this time by herself anyway, hating herself and needing it, and it feels so good to follow these trackless ways through the huckleberries and the rhododendrons.

She walks for miles, barefoot, eating watercress from ditches. Bishop pine and Douglas fir give way to stunted cypresses, to sedges, pygmy manzanita, to Bolander's pines stooped and ancient, hundreds of years old and only shoulder-height on her. The ground is hard-packed and ash-colored, puzzled over with tufted, gray-green lichens, the land studded with barren clay ponds.

In the dawn, the sun still banked among the hills, she climbs a fence and walks across the tarmac of a small airport, all shut up and quiet, the runway all her own. She's been walking for just over three hours, groveling through the underbrush. She should've taken shoes, but it doesn't much matter. She is so far accustomed to going barefoot that she could strop a razor on the soles of her feet. She climbs over the fence on the other side and walks out onto some other, larger road.

She stands in the middle of it, on the double yellow line.

A rabbit breaks from the underbrush, dim gray movement against the black. Turtle draws the pistol, racks it in one smooth movement, and fires. The rabbit pitches over in the salal. She crosses the road, stands with the kicking, delicate creature at her feet, and it is smaller than she thought. She picks it up by the back legs, a bare skim of soft fur over the coupled bones, articulated and sinewy, sawing back and forth in her hand.

Turtle comes to an old roadbed lined with Oregon grape, cluttered with fallen leaves. She stands looking down into the Albion River basin. The sun has risen a handsbreadth above the horizon, crowning the eastern hills, sheaves of light slanting through the stunted trees. The road winds out below her, following a ridge with thickly wooded gulches on either side. She eases along, stopping to watch the silk-lined burrows of spiders in the cut bank, raking through grass for the grass-colored mantises, turning over roadside stones. She has an image of Martin in the kitchen, cooking up pancakes for a Saturday morning breakfast, humming to himself, and expecting her to come down any minute. Her heart breaks at this thought. He will be riddling over what to do as her pancakes get cold, and he will stand at the bottom of the stairs and call up, "Kibble? You up?" She thinks that he will go upstairs and open her door, look at her empty room, scraping his stubble with the edge of his thumb, and then he will go back downstairs and look at all the plates and pancakes and warm raspberry jam he'd set out.

The morning turns to early afternoon, blue, cottony, flat-bottomed clouds towing shadows across the forested slopes. At a barren clay promontory, the road makes a turn and descends into the easternmost of two gulches, and here a clay pullout overlooks the valley. Long dried ruts. An old VW bus with its tires rotting into the ground, ceanothus growing up against the driver's-side quarter panel.

Turtle lays the rabbit across the dirt and opens the van's rusted door and finds it stuffed with Oriental rugs. She drags out a rug, unrolls it, and finds nothing but sow bugs and wolf spiders. She walks to the front of the van. She opens the passenger-side door and sits inside, looks carefully around the front of the van. There is a strange, intermittent squeaking. It sounds like a loose spring in the upholstery, but it isn't that. She opens the glove box and finds decaying maps and something long rotten. She leans down and walks her fingers along the footwell where the moldy upholstery has wrinkled up from the frame. She draws her grandpa's bowie knife, cuts through the carpet, and pulls it aside. There are three pink newborn mice, the size of her fingertips, laid up along a mounded fold in the carpet, eyes closed, paws folded in small fists, squeaking furiously. Turtle lays the carpet back over the mice.

She climbs out of the bus and walks to where the rabbit lays on the dirt. She collars its feet, slits it from anus to throat, pulls its fur off like a bloody sock, and pitches the pelt into the brush. She scoops out the guts and pitches those after the pelt. Then she makes a fire of dry grass and dead wood, skewers the rabbit, and roasts it over the fire, looking by turns at the fire and out at the valley.

A mouse comes out from the undercarriage of the VW and she watches it wander about. It clambers awkwardly up a shoot of grass to get at the seeds in their papery chaff, bowing the sprig over. It extends its muzzle, sniffing and finally opening its mouth to show the chisel of its teeth. Its ears are small and round and the sun shows pink through them with just a single, snaky pink vein at the center of each ear, catching the light.

Turtle takes the rabbit down from the skewer and the mouse bolts, feinting right and then changing directions in a desperate bid for a nearby rock. But whatever hiding place it expects isn't there, and it performs a panicked circuit of the rock. In a last-ditch effort, the mouse squashes itself up against the rock and waits, panting. Turtle prizes ribs off the rabbit's spine and chews the flesh from them, letting the juice run down her scabby fingers. In time, the mouse comes back and wanders the clay promontory, lifting one tiny hand to lean on this or that stalk of grass, flouncing its whiskers when it sniffs. Turtle finishes the carcass and pitches it over the ledge into the trees below. Her fire smolders. She sits, hands folded, watching.

She needs to get up and go home. She knows it, but she just doesn't go. She wants to wait out here, on this clay promontory above the river valley, and wants to watch the day go by. She needs time to sit and go through her thoughts like going through a colander of snow peas. It's not like Martin does, when he paces **thinking** and **thinking** and sometimes gesturing to himself as he tries to think out something difficult. The day warms, turns to late afternoon, and still Turtle does not go, does not move.

Then she sees a spider. It is the silvery color of sun-bleached driftwood. It sits sullen at the edge of its hole, eyes hidden behind a mess of hairy legs. The legs unfold and reach carefully out of the cave like ghastly, creeping fingers. She can see no eyes and no face, only the clutch of fingers. It has a speculative creep. The mouse crouches several feet away, hunched over another seedpod, its potbelly pooched up between its legs. When it is done with its seed, it looks down and gives the short hairs on its pink belly a hard look, then riffles through them with its fingers in a sudden, urgent little search, and dives its muzzle into its belly and chews intently for a moment.

The spider moves carefully. Stricken, Turtle watches it circle the tuft of grass, drawing closer. She hears then a noise from down the road— someone walking along the roadbed, and she thinks wildly of Martin. It is more than possible that he has managed to follow her. He has done it before. It is even likely. She rises slowly, silently, drawing the pistol from its holster and slivering back the slide to see the bright brass in the chamber, her every movement swift and quiet, but then she stops to watch. The spider emerges behind the mouse and crosses the last six inches and then rears and sinks two black hooks down into the mouse's shoulder. The mouse jerks spasmodically, one hind leg pedaling through the air. She hears more footsteps, but Turtle is captivated, watching the spider drag the mouse backward to the burrow, where it lodges crosswise against the silky-webbed sides. Knuckles in her mouth, Turtle watches the spider come half out again, fangs buried in the mouse's back. It turns the mouse with deft legs and then pulls the mouse down into the dark, the pink tail twitching.

She chews her fingers in anguish. The footsteps draw closer, and Turtle ducks into the woods, lies down behind a log. A slender, black-haired boy comes down the road, her age or a little older, fifteen or sixteen, not watching his feet, wearing a backpack and board shorts, an old T-shirt with a single candle and a twist of barbwire around it,

some word she doesn't know. He stands, survey-
ing the clay promontory, chewing on the water
reservoir's bite valve. He isn't much experienced.
The board shorts are a bad idea. His trail-running
shoes are unscuffed, the backpack new. He doesn't
know what he's looking at or what he's looking for.
His gaze just wanders. He seems delighted.

Another boy comes down the road behind him,
this one with an old leather-and-Cordura backpack molding apart, a huge blue tarp rolled up
and bungee-corded to the side. This new boy says,
"Dude! **Dude!** Check it out! A van!" He's holding a spray can of Easy Cheese and piling it onto
a Butterfinger. She places her front sight on the
can. "Dude, Jacob!" he says to the black-haired
boy. "Dude, Jacob! You want to sleep in that sick,
righteous-looking van?" He stuffs the Butterfinger
into his mouth and chews. His grin is so big that
his jaw stands out and shows his chocolate-stained
teeth. He's having trouble eating the bar all at once
and it slips partially out of his mouth, so he pushes
it back in with a forefinger. Turtle could shoot the
can right out of his hand.

Jacob smiles and squats down at the coals of
Turtle's fire, raking through it with a stick. She's
seen both boys before, last year when they were
eighth graders and she was a seventh grader. The
candy-eating boy is Brett. They must be high
school freshmen now, and she doesn't know how
they've gotten here, but they must be a long ways

lost. She wonders what the black-haired one is thinking. He is hurtful to look at, his face beautiful and unguarded. They must be on some kind of weekend adventure. Their parents dropped them off, they were going to spend one night out here and walk out the next day, something like that. Jacob sets his backpack down and eases a map from the mesh access pocket. He smooths it flat and says, "Well."

"This cheese," Brett says, holding up the cheese can, Turtle placing the front sight perfectly on it, "is **sick**. I mean, fucking **dank**, is all." He props his backpack against one of the VW's wheels and lies down, pillowing his head against it, jetting Easy Cheese into his open mouth from the can. "I know you don't believe, but truth, I mean **truth**."

Jacob, looking by turns at the map and at the valley, says, "Man, we suck at this."

Brett says, "Just because it's in a can doesn't mean it's not 'real' cheese, you know?"

"We are extremely, I mean **extremely**—I don't want to say 'lost,' but I am not entirely sure of where we might actually be."

"You're cheese-prejudiced, is what you are."

Jacob lies back on the rug that Turtle unrolled hours ago. He says, "Our powers of navigation **astound**." He opens his backpack and pulls out a wedge of Jarlsberg and a loaf of focaccia still in its Tote Fête bakery bag. He and Brett pass these items back and forth, lying propped up on their packs, stretched at length on the Oriental rug with small powdery gray moths struggling up from the nap. They take bites directly from the wedge of cheese.

"Let's camp here."

"There's no water."

"I wish there was a girl here," Brett says wonderingly, looking up at the sky. "We could woo her with our powers of navigation."

"If she were blind and had no sense of direction."

"That's sick," Brett says, "sick, deceiving a blind girl like that."

"I'd date a blind girl," Jacob says. "Though, not just because she was blind. What I mean is— I don't think it'd matter."

"I'd date her just for being blind," Brett says.

"Really?"

"How's it any different from objectifying her for her intelligence?"

"Her intelligence cannot be abstracted from her personality, whereas her blindness is incidental to who she is, and **can** be abstracted," Jacob says. "I.e., she's not a **blind chick.** She is a chick who is, incidentally, **blind.**"

"But," Brett says, "but, dude! She is not, like, **responsible** for her intelligence in any meaningful way. That's **shallow**, dude."

"She isn't **responsible** for her blindness, either," Jacob says, disgusted.

"Unless she plucked out her eyes in a fit of rage."

"You'd date a girl who **plucked out her eyes in a fit of rage**?"

"You **know** she's feisty. You just **know** it."

"That feels like an understatement**.**"

"Dude, bring it. I'm all about it."

"I bet she has a wicked temper."

"Girls have to start spunky, Jacob, or ninth grade grinds it out of them."

Turtle lies in the brush, the sight laid first on Brett's forehead then on Jacob's, and she thinks, what the fuck? What the fuck? They recline on their rug, ripping off strips of focaccia. Brett gestures to the view. "Gods," he says, "but I wish we had some more Easy Cheese."

When they are done, the boys help each other up and trudge bantering along the jeep track into the redwoods. Turtle rises and stands there for a moment and then slips into the trees after them. The road is hardly better than a streambed. Gangly brown roots stick out from the cut bank. They walk for hours and climb finally into a clearing with a cottage built from scrap lumber. It is unlit and the door stands open. Turtle squats behind a burned-out stump, coal-black, eaten by fire into a helix laddered by mushrooms with flat brown tops and bottoms like frogs' throats. It is shading into early evening. Everything is painted in deep green and sumptuous purple. She watches the boys walk out into the clearing. The clouds look like candles that have burned down to tiered pools of blue wax.

Brett says, "Dude, **dude**, what if you go in there—and there's just, like, one deformed blind albino child on a rocking chair with a **banjo**?"

Jacob says, "And he takes us prisoner and makes us read **Finnegans Wake** to his peyote plants?"

Brett says, "You can't tell anyone that my mom made us do that. You can't."

Jacob says, "Why **Finnegans Wake**, do you think? Why not **Ulysses**? Actually, why not just read **The Odyssey**? Or—or **The Brothers Karamazov**?"

"Because, **dude**—you read fucked-up Russian bullshit to your peyote plants, you're gonna have a bad time."

"Okay, so: **To the Lighthouse**. Or—you know what?—people die in subordinate clauses in that book. Maybe D. H. Lawrence? For a passionate, make-love-to-the-gamekeeper kind of high."

"Dude, with your voice you are like, 'Look at all these books I've read,' but with your eyes you are like, 'Help me.'"

"You know what would be good, actually? Harry Potter."

"Well, I guess we'll never know what's beyond that door," Brett says.

"We already know, Brett."

"We do?"

"Adventure," Jacob says. "Behind every door lies **adventure**."

"Only if by 'every' you mean 'some' and by 'adventure' you mean 'sodomical hillbillies.'"

"Nah."

"Dude. It could be dangerous. **Actually** and **in reality** dangerous."

"It's fine," Jacob says, and goes up the steps and in through the door.

"Physically perilous, Jacob," Brett calls after him, "in an entirely real, entirely not-hilarious way."

"Come on!"

Turtle follows the edge of the forest around the back of the cottage, slipping through the brush. She thinks, stay calm, stay easy. She steps up onto the creaking back deck and stands looking out into the woods. There are big black coils of irrigation hoses and heaped fifty-pound bags of organic fertilizer at the foot of the deck. There are clipped hoses and coupling links lying beside an overturned bucket with a coffee-can ashtray. The deck has an outdoor bathroom with a toilet and shower, the drain cut crudely into the redwood boards with a PVC pipe running to a sump hole. There's a PBR can beside the toilet and when Turtle picks it up she can hear the ticking of its carbonation. She sets down the beer and opens the door and steps into a bare kitchen. Now she is in the back of the house and the boys are in the front, separated from her by a dividing wall and a closed door. She can hear them.

"Dude," Brett says, "I don't like this."

"You think someone lives here?"

"Dude—**obviously** someone lives here."

"They're reading **The Wheel of Time**."

"Probably to their peyote plants."

"That's so epic. Just read them, like, all thirteen books, drop a bunch of peyote buttons, and then, like, **hold on to your hat**."

She walks through a kind of living room. There is a worktable with hand loppers and garden shears and a copy of the collected essays of Thomas Jefferson. Unopened boxes of Hefty garbage bags are stacked beside a six-foot-tall wooden Quan Yin, ornately carved. The ceiling is crisscrossed with white cotton clotheslines. She goes into a bedroom with a large four-poster bed and a dresser with a mason jar of bud, a stack of Robert Jordan novels, and a copy of **Overcome Your Childhood Trauma**.

She returns to the back door and slams it behind her to startle them, and it works. She hears Brett whisper, "Shit! **Shit!**" and she can hear Jacob laughing. They scramble out of the house. She looks into the forest with the gun in her hand.

The road does not continue beyond the cabin and the nervous boys take off south, going cross-country down into the river valley. She listens to the silence of the clearing for a long time. Then she follows them. They walk along a high hedge of thimbleberry in a clearing of velvet grass and sweet vernal grass. Turtle goes quietly among the stumps of old trees. She stops at a large concrete circle in the grass, and beside it, the form of a pump, covered in a tarp.

She can hear the boys, but she isn't listening to them. She thinks, stop and look. She goes in a half crouch, moving swiftly through the high grass, thinking, oh god, for christsakes, you two, stop and look. She sees them ahead, beside a stream at the border of the forest, the stream half overgrown with bracken.

She opens her mouth to call to them, but then she sees a man on the far side of the stream, wearing camo pants and a Grateful Dead shirt, a woven-hemp necklace with silver wire twining a large amethyst, a lever-action twenty-gauge shotgun slung on his back. He's a small man, with a big rotund belly and a bright red face turned to leather with years of sunburn. The tip of his nose is waxy and bulbed, with little red veins standing out of it. He's got a lemon-echinacea juice bottle in one hand. Turtle swings the Sig Sauer up and at him, placing the front sight over his temple, thinking, only if I need to, only if I need to.

"Hello, boys," he calls out. "How you do'en today?"

Brett straightens and looks around to locate the man. Jacob spots him and calls back, "We're good, a little lost, how about you?"

Turtle goes through the weeds, thumbing back the hammer. She thinks, easy does it, easy and slow, you bitch, and don't fuck this up, just do this, every part of this, exactly fucking right, every moment of this; do exactly and only what is necessary, but you do it well and you do it right, you slut.

"Where you boys from?" the man asks.

"Well, I'm from Ten Mile and he's from Comptche," Jacob says. He walks up to the man, holds out his hand. "I'm Jacob. This is Brett." They shake, and Jacob says, "A pleasure to meet you, friend."

Turtle kneels behind a stump, places the sights on the man's temple.

"All right, all right," the man says nodding. He takes out a can of Grizzly chew, thumps it once with the ball of his thumb, pinches up a huge dip, and folds it into his lip.

"You chew?" he says.

"No," Brett says.

"Only on special occasions," Jacob says.

"Ah," the man says, "well, don't start. Myself, I'm trying to quit. They put fiberglass in this stuff. Can you believe that? So, boys, you take it from me, if you're going to take it up, and it has its perks, I'll give you that, you pay the extra dollar and go organic. All right?"

"Right," Jacob says, "that's solid advice."

"Organic, that's the way," the man says, "not

these chemicals. I believe in organic myself. Better yet, just stick with the marijuana. If it weren't for nylon, that's all we'd ever be smoking."

"Speaking of that," Jacob says, unshouldering his backpack and setting it down. "Is there any chance we can buy some from you?"

"Well," says the man, turning the can of chew over in his hands. He frowns.

"It's no worries," Jacob says, "we were just looking for something to add to our adventure."

"I can appreciate that," the man says, nodding. "Sometimes you're just looking for a little something to take the edge off all the walking, and it helps bring out the details, doesn't it? You notice things you otherwise just plain wouldn't."

"That," Jacob says, "is exactly what I mean. I can tell, sir, that you are both a poet and a scholar."

"Well, I'd hate to leave a friend in need," the stranger admits.

"My man," Jacob says.

"I can help you out," he says, after a hesitation.

What the hell? Turtle thinks. She stands in the grass, gun leveled at the man. Jacob passes the man a twenty-dollar bill, and the man opens a canvas pouch on his belt and takes out a tea canister. He pulls the cap and dispenses several buds into his hand, passes them to Jacob. Then he takes out a pipe made from a deer's leg bone, with a wooden mouthpiece whittled to the bone flute, a bowl augured out of the jointed end. He begins breaking apart another bud in his fingers and packing it into the end, going on: "This stuff. This stuff, now. Not like tobacco, which is as addictive as anything— as addictive as heroin, and will kill you. Why I ever started smoking tobacco is beyond me. Trying to quit. Hence the chew, you understand. Only problem with the marijuana is that when you grow it out here, the fertilizer isn't good for the salmon, even the organic fertilizer, and that gets to me. Looking at ways around it. Also, another thing is that we have rodents and things come out of the forest to chew on the stalks of the plants and you have to poison them or put up with them. I put up with them, and that's why you should buy local. Those Mexican growers, those guys don't care, this isn't their home, right? They just lay down rat poison and it's awful, just awful, kills the ringtails, the raccoons, the weasels, all those critters. That's why you gotta buy your weed from guys like me. Locals. Supports the economy and it's better for the environment. Where you headed, by the way?"

"We're just trying to find a place to camp," Jacob says.

The man nods, working his fat lip of tobacco. "You're all right, boys, you're all right, well, I'll get you pointed in the right direction." He squints off west.

"Why fiberglass?" Brett asks suddenly.

"Huh?" the man says. "What's that?"

"You said they put fiberglass in the tobacco, but why would they do that?"

"Oh, well," the man says, "the fiberglass now, it cuts your lips so that the tobacco gets absorbed faster, makes it more addictive. It's the same thing with all of this packaged food they're selling, don't ever trust a corporation, boys, and especially don't trust a corporation to make the food you eat. This is why I don't have a car, you understand. Can't conscionably have a car. Not when I've been down to South America myself, lived among jungle tribes in the Amazon and seen the damage the petroleum industry is doing down there. We should all eat a lot more local food, smoke a lot more pot, and drive a lot less, as far as I'm concerned. And love one another. I believe that. Community, boys, that's the way." He lights the bone pipe and takes a long draw. He puffs, and then hands the pipe to Jacob. They stand nodding and passing the pipe around.

"Well," Brett says, "I admire that, but I have to ride the bus to school. No other way to get there."

"Me too," Jacob says, "though sometimes I drive. But you've given me something to think about."

Turtle doesn't know what to do. She watches, relaxing her finger on the trigger, but she doesn't lower the gun. After a silence broken only by the stranger's sumptuous chewing and by the boys firing the lighter, Brett says, "Do you know where we go next? We're a little turned around."

Jacob says, "Our path to glory has been swift and clear, but our destination eludes us."

The stranger nods down the gulch. "That way, keeping to the stream," he says, and then turns and nods back the way they came, "or that way back."

"The stream will take us to a road?"

The man nods, either agreeing or seconding the question, it isn't clear to Turtle. He says, "There's roads down there."

"All right," Jacob says, "thanks for the advice, man."

"Yeah, dude, we appreciate it," Brett says.

"Well, off you go," the man says.

Brett and Jacob begin down the slope, following the stream. The man taps out the pipe, puts it away, turns and forges back through the bracken. Turtle tracks him with the Sig until he is gone. Then she looks south, into the gulch. The plan is a bad one. I should go back, she tells herself. Then she thinks, what will Martin do? It will go badly for me, but the hell. I am a girl things go badly for. A light rain begins to fall, and Turtle holds out her hands and looks up at the sky, huge, misshapen towers of clouds, and then the rain begins in earnest, wetting her hair, wetting her shirt, and she thinks, well, we're in for it now.

Six

TURTLE STANDS ON A FALLEN LOG IN the pouring rain. Fifteen, twenty feet below her the flickering yellow beam of Brett's flashlight plays across the seamed and shaggy bark of redwoods, sword ferns, thimbleberry, the scaly, fluted trunks of western hemlocks, across the stream swollen high above its banks. She picks her way down to them. Water runnels, tea-colored with tannins, wind down between the knotty fern rhizomes, cutting dollhouse waterfalls, the soil spangled with something golden but not gold, tiny wafery minerals that circle the tiny catch pools, reflecting what light there is. The flooding washes millipedes out from beneath the logs, some trick of the current sorting dozens of them onto muddy washes so they lay stacked together, nearly all curled up, blue and yellow and glossy black.

She thinks, these useless boys, useless. She needs to leave, she needs to go, but they are lost and won't make their way down this hillside without her. Still, finding her way back home is easier said than done. Walking cross-country under a bright moon and a clear predawn sky is something entirely different than finding your way through this cloud-throttled black. It would be hard going.

Beside her, Brett says, "I don't know, dude."

Jacob says, "Yeah. I don't know either, man."

Turtle boosts herself up onto the log and backpedals quietly into the ferns, going on hands and feet just before Brett sees the log and moves to it, leans against it to take some of the weight off his pack.

"Keep going?"

Jacob shakes his head, but they can't stop here, that much is apparent. The ground is a mess. Turtle thinks, say something, say something to them, point the way for them, but she cannot seem to say anything. The only glimmer is the treacherous light of glowworms, nearly the same phosphorescent green as the tritium sights on her Sig Sauer, and she puts her hand on it now, thinking, I am not afraid of these boys, and if I have to make my way in this dark, I will. But she is afraid of them. She knows just from wrapping her hand around the Sig Sauer's comforting grip, that grip that says, **no one will ever hurt you**, just from her own willingness to brave this flooded dark alone, she knows that she is afraid of the boys.

Jacob hitches his backpack up on his shoulders and they continue down the hillside, following the stream, which has overrun its narrow trough and flooded the nearby banks so that the boys splish-splash through ankle-deep water. She thinks, I will wait and see if we come to a road. And if we do—I don't need to do anything; they will go one way, and I the other. But if there is no road, then they're going to need me.

They descend into a basin where the stream forms a pond before pouring over the edge, the marshy banks thicketed with cattails. The pond is full of chorus frogs, and when Brett pans the pale yellow beam across the water, Turtle can see their hundreds of eyes, the distinct ridged shapes of their heads breaking the surface.

"Let's strike out that way," Jacob says, and motions west across the side of the drainage, not down it. "If we follow this stream, it is gonna be too steep."

"Dude," Brett says, "this stream takes us to the road. That's what the guy said. We aren't good at, like, improvising this navigation thing."

"What possible reason have I ever given you to doubt **my** navigation?" They both laugh, Jacob looking down into the gulch, nodding. "All right, bud, all right, you wanna go right down this stream?"

"Yeah," Brett says, "that's the way he told us."

"All right, lead—"

"Shh!" Brett says, and turns and swings the flashlight almost onto Turtle. She sits embowered in ferns, grinning. You fuck, she thinks, delighted. You fuck! She thinks, what gave me away? She can feel it in her own face; her pleasure; her eyes slitted with happiness; she thinks, you fuck, did you hear me, did you see me, some movement? She is delighted with herself, and with him, for almost having seen her, thinking, ahh, ahh, Easy Cheese Boy isn't blind after all.

Jacob looks at Brett.

Brett says, "Sorry, man, I just had this, like, feeling—I don't know. I just had this feeling."

"What feeling?"

"There's nothing out there," Brett says, panning the flashlight across dripping ferns, across the tangle of cattails, almost over her.

You bastard, she thinks, delighted with him, you motherfucking bastard. She is full of joy.

They go through the pond with their backpacks held above their heads, crushing their way through cattails. They climb to the muddy edge, with the waterfall pouring down beside them, and the two boys look down into the gulch. Turtle cannot see what they see, but Jacob leans out, says, "It looks pretty steep down there, bud."

Brett nods.

Jacob says, "All right." He sheds his backpack and goes down over the lip. Brett passes him the backpacks one at a time, Jacob carefully banking them into the hillside. Then Brett climbs down. They help each other with the bags, and then drop out of her sight. When they have gone, Turtle crawls through the water after them. The muck of the pond bottom is knotted with water lily tubers. They are as thick as her arm, their flesh ridged and scaled, textured almost like pinecones not yet sprung. The drifts of algae feel like thick, sodden spiderwebs. She comes to the pond's edge and climbs out, shedding water in curtains. Below, the gulch is dark except for the blue glow of Jacob's headlamp and the lance of Brett's flashlight. Over the sound of the rain and the torrent of the water-fall, she can hear them calling out to each other. Their heads cut above the ferns like rats through water.

Brett pauses and looks back in Turtle's direction, and Turtle lowers herself into the weeds. Jacob plays his headlamp through the dark. Brett says, "I swear, I just—I had this bad feeling."

She lies perfectly still and looks right back at them.

"Like what?"

"Something," Brett says.

Jacob wades out toward her, moves the headlamp in meticulous search. "There's nothing here," he says.

"Just a bad feeling, a spooky feeling."

Jacob stands, turns a slow circle, peering into the dark. He looks back at Brett helplessly.

Brett says, "If there's nothing there, then there's nothing there."

"I don't see anything."

"I just hope it's not that guy."

"It's not that guy."

"I just hope he's not, like, following us through the dark."

The gulch narrows and grows steeper, spanned by fallen redwoods, the banks scarred by mudslides. Twenty feet below, it is finally blocked by an impenetrable wall of poison oak. Brett's flashlight grows pale, dim, and then dies. He slaps the light into the palm of his hand and it glows to life, a sullen filament lit for a moment before it dies again. Turtle waits above, nervous, thinking, just do it, Turtle. She thinks, nothing for it now, but still she cannot. She is going to have to get down on hands and knees and beg Daddy's forgiveness, beg, and maybe then he will let her off.

She hears Brett work the cap and dispense D-cell batteries into his hands. He cups them in his palms and blows on them.

Jacob says, "If there's a road, we've got to be right on it."

"Shit," Brett says, "oh shit."

"There's no alternative."

"That's a lot of poison oak we'd have to go through."

"The road's gotta be right past it."

Brett hunches over the flashlight, whispering to the batteries. "Come on, come on, come **on**."

In the moment of silence, all they can hear is the rain, soft, padding on leaves, and the crackling of the wet soil, the sound of the river.

"He **said**," Brett says, sounding betrayed, "that we just go this way, and we'd hit the road."

"We must be right on it," Jacob says, "we've got to be right **goddamn** there." He starts precariously down, clutching at ferns and shoots of poison oak, each step sinking into the mud. Turtle can see that he will never make it down the hillside, and before she can stop herself, before she can hesitate, she rises out of the weeds and steps up onto a log above them and says, "Wait."

They both turn and search the dark for her, and then suddenly she is bathed in Jacob's bright LED light, standing among cow parsnips and nettles, conscious of her ugliness, her lean bitch face and tangles of silt- and copper-smelling hair, half turning away to hide the pale oval of her face. For a moment, no one says anything.

Then she says, "Are you lost?"

Jacob says, "Not so much lost as unmoored from any knowledge of our location."

Brett says, "We're lost."

Turtle says, "I don't think that's the way."

Jacob looks down the gulch. The light pans over the riot of poison oak, the mud, the water sheeting the ground. He says, "I don't know what would make you think that."

Brett says, "Are we above a road?"

"I don't know," she says.

Brett says, "Who are you?"

"I'm Turtle." She comes down and stands in front of Jacob, and he reaches out and they shake hands.

"Jacob Learner," he says.

"Brett," Brett says, and they shake.

Jacob says, "What are you doing here?"

"I live near here," she says.

"So we're near a road?"

"No," she says, "I don't think so."

Brett looks wonderingly up at the hillside. "People live near here?"

"Sure."

Jacob looks back at her, and she is blinded with the blue light again. "Sorry," he says, angling the light away. "Can you lead us down to the river?"

Turtle looks away into the dark.

Brett says, "What happened? Is she still there?"

"She's thinking," Jacob says.

"Did we make her mad?"

"She's speculative."

"She's still not talking."

"Okay: She's **really** speculative."

"This way," Turtle says, leading them in a muddy traverse along the hillside, looking for a clear place farther out.

"Holy shit," Brett says, "holy shit. Look at her go."

"Hey!" Jacob says. "Wait up."

Turtle leads them across fallen redwoods and then descends to the river among grand firs on a low, sloping ridge, Jacob's light casting her shadow out ahead of her, the boys crashing behind.

The river has flooded its banks and Turtle comes down into a great tangle of alders hip-deep in water, long whips of stinging nettle bent in the current and swinging like seaweed, submerged skunk cabbages nosing out of the torrent, rafts of dead leaves scummed up against every nook and cranny, eddies circling blackly with huge dollops of foam.

"Holy shit on a shitty, shitty shingle," Brett says, and whistles.

"There's no road," Jacob says.

"We're fine without it," Turtle says.

"Maybe **you** are," Brett says.

Jacob stands there, sheathed to the waist in mud, and laughs and says, "Man," drawing it out into a long syllable, his voice giving it somehow a richness of humor and a depth of optimism that she is unused to, running his tongue along muddied lips with pleasure and saying again, "Oh man,"

like he can't believe the incredible good fortune
of being so entirely lost beside a river so flooded,
and Turtle has never seen anyone confront misfor-
tune this way.

Brett says, "Oh man," and he says it differently,
and then he says, "We are **fucked**."

Turtle looks from one to the other.

"We are **fucked**," Brett says. "We will never, ever
get home. We are fucked."

"Yes," Jacob says in hushed awe, weighting his
words with relish. "**Yes**."

Brett says, "It's ironic, because we were fine
before, we had the perfect campsite before, but
nooooo, we needed water."

"And look," Jacob says. "Hashtag success!
Hashtag winning!"

"We need somewhere to hole up," Brett says,
then, to Turtle, "Do you know where we are? Is
there somewhere we could sleep? It's all mud, isn't
it? There's nowhere not covered in mud."

It is still raining hard, and everyone, including
Turtle, is cold, and there is nowhere level here, not
with the river flooded, and to find a campsite, they
would need to climb the ridge again, and though
Turtle could, she doesn't know about the boys.

"I'm so cold," Brett says, "dude, so incredibly
goddamn cold."

"It's chilly," Jacob agrees with deep humor, trying
to wipe the mud out of his eye sockets. He stands
stiffly, in the way of people whose clothes are cold

and for whom every movement brings new flesh into contact with gritty wet fabric. He looks at Turtle, and something occurs to him. "How did you find us?"

"Just ran into you," she says.

The boys look at each other, shrug, as if to indicate they've heard stranger things.

"Can you help us?" Brett asks. He hunches shivering under his backpack. Rain sleets around him. Jacob finds a poison oak leaf stuck to his cheek, flings it disgustedly away into the dark. Turtle chews her fingers in consideration.

"Jesus," Brett says, "you don't feel any urgent need to fill the gaps in conversation, do you?"

"What does that mean?" Turtle says.

"Nothing," Brett says.

"You seem very patient," Jacob says.

"You move at your own pace," Brett says.

"Speculative," Jacob says.

"Speculative, that's right, **thoughtful**," Brett agrees.

"Like, where did you study Zen Buddhism?"

"And was your Zen master the ancient, slow-moving reptile on whose shell rests the entire universe, known and unknown, fathomed and unfathomed?"

"Is that what your name means?"

"Is this a koan? Can you help us? To which the reply is, and can only ever be: silence."

"Dark, dude."

Turtle is surprised that they would go on like this in a cold downpour and then she thinks, they're waiting on you, Turtle. They're waiting on you and the talking helps them. "This way," she says, and leads them back into the forest.

In the dark, she circles the largest trees, Jacob shining his light on them. She leaves the boys huddled together and ventures out in every direction, cutting back to them when she doesn't find what she's looking for. She is hoping for a burned-out redwood with a hollow chamber, but the best she finds is a stump, crosscut long ago, with axe-cut notches in the sides where the scaffold was pegged to the trunk.

She looks up at the stump's hidden crown and Jacob watches her, shading his eyes from the rain, and then follows her gaze. Lightning strikes on Albion Ridge across the river, and Turtle counts it, two miles before the thunder comes, rolling with the distance.

She climbs up the bark, hooks the top with a long reach, and drops into a deep, circular pit where the heartwood has rotted out. The hollow crown is ten feet across and tall enough to sit in without being able to see over the sides. A single huckleberry grows up through the middle in a rough circle of punky wood that drains the water. She wraps her fist around its base and rips it out and pitches it into the dark. She helps Brett and Jacob up, and they begin digging out leaf litter. She opens Brett's backpack, finds a hundred feet of parachute cord still in its tight store-bought bundle, teases the bundle apart, quarters the line, and passes her knife through the loops to make four twenty-five-foot lengths.

They unfold the blue tarp and Turtle bowlines the parachute cord to the corner grommets. Then she drops off the stump, and Jacob after her, while Brett holds the tarp. She pitches Brett a center pole, and he holds it in place. She wraps the first line around a stob, passes the bitter end back to the standing line, and ties a tautline hitch, a slide-and-grip knot that can be cinched up the wet line, though she wonders, even as she is tying it, if a tarbuck knot would be better. She guys out each line in turn. When she comes to the last, she finds that Jacob has already guyed it out and tied the tautline hitch. Water runs down the line, gathers just above the knot, and streams off in a single ribbon. The blue light from the headlamp follows the water on the parachute cord. She runs the knot between thumb and forefinger, finds it tight and well dressed. Jacob stands beside her.

She says, "You knew this knot already?"

"No," he says, "just saw you make it."

She plucks the line, and it thrums. She looks at him but doesn't know what to say, because he'd made the knot well, in the dark, not knowing how to make it, and she thinks he should be told how good that is, how rare, but she doesn't know how to say such a thing. She undoes Jacob's knot, then makes the next knot with conspicuous slowness. She ties a slipknot high on the standing line. She takes the bitter end, which passes around a branch, and brings it through the slipknot and bends it back down, making a pulley. She hauls on the line until the cord cuts paling corrugations across her palms. The pulley tightens the whole system; the tarp creaks with strain. She looks at him again.

Rain runs down his face, and he wipes his eyes, nodding.

She ties the tension off with half hitches, making them with exaggerated slowness. She glances back at him again, and plucks the cord.

"Ahh," he says.

"The rain," she says, "loosens the lines."

He nods again.

Here is the difference between me and Martin, she thinks, here is the difference—it is that I know the rain loosens the lines and I care, and Martin knows that the rain loosens the lines and he does not care, and I do not know why, I do not understand how you could not care, because it is important to do things right, and if that isn't true, I don't know what is.

She circles the stump, testing each guyline, cinching them down and doubling them up with half hitches, thinking, goddamn Martin, and how I will pay for this, how I will get down on my knees and beg not to pay and how I will pay anyway.

"It's like she can see in the dark," Brett says.

"She can," Jacob says. "You can tell she can."

"No, like she can really **see in the dark**. And not just a little."

"Yeah," Jacob says. "That's what I mean."

"Where do you think she is right now?"

"In her head," Jacob says.

"I can hear you," Turtle says. She climbs up the side of the stump and helps Jacob after her.

"She's so quiet."

"Not all of us," Jacob says, "go through life in a caffeine-fueled rage, Brett."

"Hey," Brett says, "it's good for your stomach. The coffee burns the ulcers right off your stomach lining."

"What are you talking about?" Turtle says.

"Coffee," Jacob says, "and how it mineralizes your bones."

"Is that true?"

"No," Jacob says.

Inside, they have made a kind of dark, wet grotto, ten feet across, maybe four feet deep. Brett has laid down a heavy-duty plastic ground cloth, and now he hunches at the far end of the grotto, huddled up in his sleeping bag, his arms wrapped around himself, shivering. Jacob is unpacking his bag. He takes out a siliconized nylon stuff sack and offers it to her.

"What?" she says.

"Take my sleeping bag."

"No way."

"You're shivering."

"So are you," she says.

"I'm going to spoon Brett," he says.

Brett says, "What?"

"Take the bag," Jacob says.

"No," she says.

"First of all, we owe you," Jacob says. "We never would've found somewhere dry if not for you. Second of all, Marcus Aurelius says—"

Brett groans. "If only," he says, "the emperor's journal had been burned, as he asked. Should we really follow the instructions of a man whose final instruction was that his former instructions be destroyed?"

"Marcus Aurelius says," Jacob continues, "that 'joy for humans lies in human actions: kindness to others, contempt of the senses, the interrogation of appearances, observation of nature and of events in nature.' This—loaning you my bag—satisfies all of those conditions. Please take it."

Turtle is looking at him, incredulous.

"What's happening?" Brett says.

"I don't know," Jacob says. "Maybe she's making an expression?"

"What?" Turtle says.

"Please, let me give you the bag."

"No."

Brett says, "Turtle, take the bag. Seriously. His grasp of reality is tenuous at best, so arguing with him is dangerous. Nobody knows what will shake off that last handhold and send him spiraling into madness. Also, I have a sleeping bag that we can sort of spread out like a blanket."

Turtle looks from one to the other of the boys, and tentatively accepts the sleeping bag and begins pulling it out of its sack. The nylon is of such a high grade that it is soft as silk. It is homemade and has no zipper. She slips into it. The rain drums on the plastic ceiling, filling the chamber with noise. She can feel her breath in moist plumes, and she runs her cold hands together, the fingertips turned to raisins. She can hear the boys in the dark, their ragged exhalations, their movements as they huddle close under the one sleeping bag.

Brett says, "Jacob?"

"Yeah?"

"Jacob, do you think she's a ninja?"

She says, "I'm not a ninja."

Brett says, "She's a ninja, isn't she, Jacob?"

"I'm not a ninja," she says.

"Hmmm . . ." Brett hems and haws. "Hmmmm . . . sort of, yes, actually, sort of a ninja."

"No."

"Where is your ninja school?" Brett asks.

"I didn't go to ninja school," she says.

"She's bound by covenants of secrecy," Jacob observes.

"Or perhaps," Brett says, "perhaps, the animals of the forest taught her."

"I'm not a ninja!" she yells.

The boys sit in chastened silence for a long moment. Then, as if her denial has given final proof to a theory once tenuous, Brett says, "She's a ninja."

Jacob says, "But does she possess preternatural powers?"

The boys talk in a way that is alarming and exciting to her—fantastical, gently celebratory, silly. To Turtle, slow of speech, with her inward and circular mind, their facility for language is dizzying. She feels brilliantly included within that province of things she wants, lit up from within by possibility. Giddy and nervous, she watches them, chewing on her fingertips. A new world is opening up for her. She thinks, these boys will be there when I go to high school. She thinks, and what would that be like—to have friends there, to have friends like this? She thinks, every day, get up and get on the bus, and it would be, what, another adventure? And all I would have to do is open my mouth and say, 'help me with this class,' and they would help.

Slowly, the boys drop off to sleep, and Turtle lies opposite them. She thinks, I love him, I love him so goddamn much, but, but let me stay out. Let him come after me. We will see what he does, won't we? Here is a game we play, and I think he knows we play it; I hate him for something, something he does, he goes too far, and I hate him, but I am unsure in my hatred; guilty and self-doubting and hating myself almost too much to hold it against him; that is me, a goddamn slut; and so I trespass again to see if he will again do something so bad; it is a way to see if I am right to hate him; I want to know. So you take off and you ask yourself: should I hate him? And I guess you will have your answer when you come back, because he will respond to your absence in a way you can love or he will respond beyond all reason, and that will be the proof, but always, Turtle—and you know this—he is ahead of you in this game. He will look at you and know exactly how far he can go and he will take you right to the brink, and then he will see he has come to the brink and he will step back; but perhaps not, perhaps he will go too far, or perhaps there is no such calculation in him.

An itch is developing on her lower back. She runs her hand along the waistline of her jeans and finds the tick just above the elastic of her panties. She can feel its pearl-smooth body.

"Brett?" she breathes, unbelting her pants and removing the holster, sliding it deeper into the bag to hide it. "Jacob?"

"Yeah?" Jacob breathes back.

"Do you have tweezers?"

"Brett does," Jacob says, "in his bag." She hears

Jacob sit up in the dark. He rustles around in the bag for seemingly a very long time before he finds them.

"Got them," he says. "Tick?"

"Yeah, tick," she says.

"Where is it?"

"Low down on my back."

"All right," he says.

"I can't get it myself," she says.

"All right."

She rolls over onto her belly, hitches her jeans down and her shirt up to bare her lower back. Jacob crawls quietly over to her, trying not to disturb the sleeping Brett. She lies with her cheek resting on the cold black plastic of the ground cloth. Jacob kneels beside her. He turns the headlamp on, and they are bathed in its blue glow.

"I've never done this before," he says.

"Get the head," she says.

"Do you twist it clockwise?" he asks. "I've heard they screw themselves in. Their mouthparts are an auger."

"No. It'll vomit out its stomach contents when you start on it. Just pull it straight out in one go if you can," she says.

"Okay," he says. He puts one hand on the small of her back, framing the tick between thumb and forefinger. His hand is warm and confident, her skin ringing electric. Her vision is narrowly of the black ground cloth, dirty, lapped up in wrinkles, but her focus is entirely on him, unseen, bending over her.

"Just do it," she says.

He is silent. She feels the tweezers fasten down on the tick. They bite into her flesh, and then there is a plucking sensation.

"You get it all?" she says.

"I got it," he says.

"You get it all?"

"I got it all, Turtle."

"Good," she says. She hitches her T-shirt down and rolls back over. She can hear Jacob crushing the tick to death with the tweezer points. The rain drums on the tarp stretched taut above them. Jacob switches off the light, and she listens to them, there in the dark with her.

Seven

TURTLE AWAKES WITH A START, HEART pounding, and waits, listening, eyes gummy from her dehydration, her mouth leathery. Someone has kicked the center pole away and the tarp hangs down cupped and half full of water, sunken leaves forming a black circle of detritus at the bottom. She waits, breathing, wondering what woke her, if Martin is standing outside, beside this stump, with his auto shotgun. Slowly, silently she draws the Sig Sauer and touches it to her cheek, the steel almost warm from the captured heat of the sleeping quilt. She can hear her own labored breath. She thinks, calm down, but she cannot calm down and she begins to breathe harder, and she thinks, this is bad, this is very bad.

Something strikes the water and Turtle jerks, watches a fist-sized object comet through the water toward her, touch the tarp, and float away. She waits, the gun held against her face in two shaking hands. It is a pinecone, probably a bishop pine-cone. This is what woke her: the cones splashing into the pool and striking the tarp. She takes a deep breath, and then startles as a second cone strikes the water and plunges down, slowing as it comes toward her. It touches the tarp, and then floats up and away. Ripples expand across the surface. Their shadows lave across the boys, the sleeping bags, the backpacks, the mess of this little hovel. She thinks, I love everything of theirs because it is theirs, and I like how crowded we are here with things, the riot and disorder, everything damp and warm, and she thinks, I love it. She pushes her feet down against the wet nylon of Jacob's sleeping bag. She lies, her muscles loosening, and when she can, she holsters the gun and waits with her hands on her throat, looking up at the pool. She wants to draw the gun and cannot bear to lie there without it, and she puts her hand on the grip and touches the uncocked hammer and she thinks, leave it, leave it, and she takes her hand away and lies listening to the water above and to the forest beyond.

She thinks, for a moment, I was sure it was him and the only thing I didn't know was how far he would go, and how angry he would be. She thinks, he has always been able to surprise me. When she is calm again she climbs out, slithering awkwardly through a gap between the tarp and the stump. She sits on the stump's crown, barefoot, jeans sodden and cleaving to her thighs, drinking from the tarp water.

She drops off the stump and sits on a log covered in translucent mushrooms shaped like deformed ears. She draws her knife and begins cleaning thorns and slivers from her callused feet. Around her, wild ginger grows among the redwood roots, its leaves dark green and heart-shaped, its purple flowers, with their open throats and liver-colored tusks, deeply buried in the foliage. She puts her fist against her forehead. If something happens to them, she thinks, what are you doing, Turtle? You are forgetting who you are and you are thinking that you can be someone else, and you will get yourself hurt and you will get Martin hurt, and god help you, you will get these boys hurt and that is the worst of it, but somehow you cannot care so much for the risk they are taking, being with you. It seems worth the risk and that shows that you aren't thinking clearly, because it isn't worth the risk, not for them, not if you put the question to them, and not if you could explain how far your daddy might go. She thinks, I know that he came after me and the only question is if he could find me out here, and I bet he could, but I don't know. She thinks, I can't seem to get that answer straight, because sometimes I think of him, and it seems to me he could do anything. He could, she thinks, hurt these boys. She knows that and she thinks, don't think of it.

She thinks, it is light enough now. I could make it back and it wouldn't even be hard, except—what are you giving up on, if you do that? She thinks, you know exactly what you're giving up on, and the question is, what are you willing to risk? When it comes down to it, she thinks, I am willing to risk a great deal. I am willing to risk these boys and it's just for myself and it's nothing to them, they don't even know, and I won't even tell them. She thinks, if they find out, they find out, and I will take that risk because I am a bitch.

Before long, Jacob crawls out and climbs with difficulty down the stump's side. He sits beside her and looks at her feet, which are small, with painfully high arches. They look lathed almost, or worked, articulated tendons and bones without any softness. Her callus is contoured like a stream-bed and grained like a fingerprint. Jacob watches for a moment. She is glad to see him, and she is particularly glad to see him because of the risks she is taking to make it possible. He doesn't know what he is involved in and it makes the moment of sitting on the log, beside him, important to her.

He says, "Well, that's strangely attractive." He nods to where she is digging into the callus with the knifepoint. His voice is guileless but full of humor, and she smiles despite herself. She does not know if he is making fun of her or if he is making fun of himself, and then, immediately after her smile, she understands.

She stiffens, stooped over her feet with knife in hand, tightening her jaw, acutely aware of her bitch face and ugly skin. Her whiteness is ugly and uneven, she knows, a freckled semitransparent whiteness so that her boobs, pathetically small and milkily untanned, are almost blue. She feels girded with imperfection and wants to play along with Jacob's teasing, as if her repulsiveness is a prank she's played on herself. She smiles her lopsided half smile, and smiling, wants to smash to pieces, because she has told herself not to play along when someone is cruel to her, but this boy has so unraveled her that she cannot stick to her intentions.

He has a way of watching her that makes her feel as if she is the most important thing in the world. She stoops there, thinking, slit, slit, slit, that unlovely slot lodged between her legs, unfinished by inattention or design, opening into her own peculiarity, its aperture and its sign, and she understands it now; the slit is illiterate—that word undresses her of all that she has knotted and buckled up about herself; she feels collapsed—every bitter, sluttish part of her collapsed and made identical to that horrible clam.

He says, "Where to next, Mowgli?"

"You want my help?" Still looking at him, willing to let it go, but unwilling to go without dignity. She is asking for something, and he gives her all of it in his expression alone, which is open and generous and sorry.

"Yes. Very much."

"No poison oak rashes yet," she observes.

"It's gonna be bad," he says.

"Yeah," she says, "I can help."

He says, "So, it's none of my business—"

"Yes?"

"But I couldn't help notice, just now, that you have a gun."

"Yeah."

"Why?" he says.

She leans and spits into the duff. "Because I can."

"Well, that's true," he says, "but are you—do you think that you might need to shoot someone?"

"It's a precaution," she says.

"Is it, though?" he says. "Owning a gun, you are nine times more likely to be shot by a family member than by an intruder."

She cracks a knuckle, unimpressed.

"I'm sorry," he says, softening. "I'm not challenging you, or criticizing—not at all—I just want to hear your perspective. That's all. I don't really think that you're gonna be shot by a family member."

Before she can answer, Brett groans and stirs, then peeks his head out from under the tarp.

They break camp. Jacob unknots each line and holds the raveling ends over a lighter, turning the nylon between thumb and forefinger to form a bulb of black. They shake the tarp out, and then she and Brett fold it together until they have a long rectangle. Jacob rolls the bundles on his thighs. Turtle parcels them with half hitches and lashes them to the backpack. Then she stands in the stump and throws down their things to them, and they load all this into the backpacks.

They follow the north bank of the river, eating focaccia and hunks of cheese, following broad avenues among the trees where the trickling runoff sorts the rust-colored needles into ripples.

Soon they come to a winding paved road, the asphalt seamed with tar where the cracks have been patched. She thinks, the hell, I'm just delaying the moment, but the moment will come, and then we will see, and he will be fair with me, or he will be unfair, and if he is fair, then it will be hard. They reach a large engraved redwood burl that reads RIVENDELL SPRINGS AHEAD. They have seen no cars and no other people. The world is theirs alone.

Brett says, "I think my mom does massage therapy here."

"You mean, she's there right now?" Jacob says.

"Probably. Most days. If she got called in."

"Would she give us a ride?"

"Sure."

They follow the turnoff to a parking lot with sprays of fairy wands in large blue and gold clay pots and a high redwood gate. A dozen run-down cars. Brett opens a Ford Explorer with a key from the gas cap and they stash their bags. A dream catcher hangs from the rearview mirror, the center console is filled with oils, sunscreens, hand salves, beeswax lip balms. Unopened bills clutter the dash. Jacob pulls off his muddy T-shirt and balls it up and throws it into the passenger footwell before pulling on a clean Humboldt T-shirt.

Turtle says, "I'm gonna leave you here." She looks back over the forest and she knows it's time.

"But you can't go," Brett says.

"Why?"

"What if we open that gate," Jacob says, "and they're all zombies?"

"What?"

"If we're forced to wander the postapocalyptic wastes of Northern California, we want you to be the reticent, shotgun-toting queen of our fellowship."

"I think she'd have to have a chain saw for melee," Brett says.

"For zombies," Turtle says, "I'd like a .308, but if we really had to hoof it, you could talk me down to 5.56."

"But seriously, what about a **chain saw**?" Brett says.

"You'd throw your chain," Turtle says.

"A samurai sword."

"If you're saying zombies," Turtle says, "I'd take

a tomahawk, sure. Use all the weight you'd spend on pistol ammo for more 5.56."

"A shotgun," Jacob says.

"Can't carry enough ammo. For every shotshell you can carry, you could carry three or four rifle shells. Plus, shotguns reload slowly."

Jacob says, "Couldn't you get an auto shotgun with a magazine, like they have for rifles?"

"Sure," Turtle says, "but rifle shells are metal-jacketed and do well in magazines. Shotshells deform under pressure and jam if stored in mags. Plus, auto shotguns are finicky. When you've got to shoot a lot, carry a lot, and scavenge for ammo, 5.56 is king."

"See, we'll never make it without you. Come on with us," Jacob says. "Please?"

"Please?"

She's grinning. "You'd make it."

"Not without you we wouldn't."

"She's coming," Brett says, "look at her."

"I'll come."

At the gate, they pull the bell cord and the three of them stand together, arguing about how to arm themselves for the coming apocalypse, Turtle barefoot, jeans rolled up to her knees and laden with drying mud. A shirtless man in hemp trousers opens the door, his chest tattooed with a Buddha over crashing waves, his hair in cigar-thick dreadlocks down to his waist.

"Hey, brother," he says to Brett. "Looks like the weather caught you by surprise."

"Hey, Bodhi—yeah, the weather surprised us some."

"Looking for your mom?"

"Hoping for a ride."

"Who's this?"

"My buddy Jacob, and this is Turtle, the future shotgun-toting, chain-saw-wielding queen of postapocalyptic America."

"Is she really?" Bodhi says with some interest. "Well, Jacob, Turtle. Come on in." He leads them through a meadow and among large glass pyramids into a redwood forest with moss-hung cabins and redwood barrel-style tubs of steaming water. There is a mineral scent in the air from a hot spring somewhere. They pass a group of naked women, Jacob acutely embarrassed, looking up at the shingle roofs, into the trees, anywhere. They pass another barrel-style tub where three old men bask naked, smoking a blown-glass bong.

They follow Bodhi to a cottage, the eaves hung with witch's hair, moss growing between the shingles, and they go into a warm interior with a woodstove in one corner. A naked woman sits cross-legged on a wooden pedestal, eating cherry tomatoes from a lacquered wooden bowl. Jacob's eyes goggle in surprise. The woman is olive-skinned, with wiry black hair bundled in hemp cords, her face pretty and open, her nipples big, the areolas soft brown and goose-bumpy, her belly somewhere between soft and firm, the skin healthy looking but worn. Her pussy has two little interior pieces of flesh hanging out. Turtle's own pussy is as trim and compact as an anemone bunkered down to wait out the tide.

Brett says, "Guys, this is my mom, Caroline. Mom, could you—" and the woman says, "Julia Alveston?"

Both Brett and Jacob turn toward Turtle in surprise.

Turtle says, "What?"

Brett says, "Mom—could you—could you put on some pants?"

Caroline says, "Oh, girlie. I haven't seen you since you were this high." She holds out a hand three feet above the ground. "Your mom, Helena, was my best friend, and boy—I tell you—she was a—well."

Turtle feels an immediate revulsion. She thinks, don't you talk about my mother, you cunt, you stranger.

Brett's mom now turns to look at the boys. "Tell me what's happened," she says.

Brett says, "Mom, could you—"

"Of course," she says, rising and pulling on hemp drawstring pants while the boys take turns explaining.

Jacob says, "She just sort of showed up."

"She was just out in the dark, no flashlight, no

backpack, no shoes, nothing, getting along just fine, like she could see in the dark."

"In the pouring rain, pitch-black."

"You should see her feet. Calluses—it's **insane**."

"She just walks everywhere barefoot."

"She doesn't feel cold."

"Or pain."

"Only justice."

"We think she might be a ninja."

"She denies this."

"But of course, she'd have to deny it."

"If she said yes, she was a ninja, we'd know she wasn't."

"I wouldn't describe the ninja theory as definitive, but it's a live possibility."

"Anyway, she led us out of the valley of the shadow."

"She can see in the dark."

"She can walk across water."

"She has her own pace. She just stops and she looks and she stands there looking and you're all, like, 'What are you looking at?' but she just keeps looking and you're like, 'Um, aren't you bored yet?' But that's because she's a Zen master."

"She's very patient."

"Her conversational pace isn't what you'd call **usual**."

"I'm right here," Turtle says.

"She's **thoughtful**, but there's something more and stranger than that."

"It's less thoughtful than watchful."

"Yeah—**yeah!** Watchful. You ask her a question and she just, like, **watches** you and you're like . . . 'Ummmm?' and if you wait long enough she comes out with an answer."

"She can tie knots, she can find her way in the forest."

"The animals speak to her and tell her their secrets."

When they are done, Caroline says, "Well, boys. That's very evocative." Then she turns to Turtle. "How is your father these days?"

"He's good," Turtle says.

"Is he working hard?"

"Not too hard," Turtle says.

"Is he dating?" Caroline asks. "I bet he is."

"No," Turtle says.

"No?" Caroline says. "He was always the kind of guy, had to have a woman in his life." She smiles. "A real charmer, your father."

"No, there're no women in his life," Turtle says, a little menacingly.

"Well, I'm sorry to hear that; must get lonely up on that hill."

"I don't know," Turtle says. "There's Grandpa, and there's the orchard, and the creek; and then, he has his poker buddies."

"Well," Caroline says, "people change. But your father was one of the handsomest men I ever knew. Still is, I bet."

"Mom," Brett says in exasperation, "that's gross."

"He was quite a looker," Caroline says, "and an intelligent man. I always thought he would do something."

"He hasn't done anything," Turtle says.

"He's raised you, and what a strong-looking girl you've come up to be," Caroline says. "Though, I have to say, you look about half wild."

Turtle says nothing to that.

Caroline says, "So, Julia, they met up with you a couple miles from here?"

Turtle nods.

"It sounds like it was pretty much in the middle of nowhere."

"I was on a walk," Turtle says.

"Starting where?"

"What?" Turtle cups her hand around her ear and leans forward.

"Where'd you start out?"

"At my house."

"You walked here from Buckhorn?" Caroline says.

"Yes, that's right," Turtle says, "came up out of Slaughterhouse Gulch, through the airport, and then above the banks of the Albion, sort of past people's backyards."

"Well, sweetheart, you look roughed-up enough for it, that's for sure. That must be miles and miles. With no water? No food?"

Turtle chews, opening her jaw and closing it. She looks at the floor.

Caroline says, "Sweetheart, I'm just worried about you. What were you doing out there in the middle of the night? How far is that from your home, do you think?"

"I don't know," Turtle says.

"Brett," Caroline says, "why don't you take Jacob out and show him the glass pyramids."

The boys exchange looks, and Brett jerks his head in a **come on** gesture and they both leave. Turtle stands in the middle of the floor, wringing her hands together and looking at the base of Caroline's pedestal.

"Did you know," Caroline says, "I was almost your godmother?"

Turtle cracks a knuckle, looks up at Caroline, and can almost remember her from a dim past. She senses a need to go carefully here and to protect her own small life on Buckhorn Hill.

"Your mother and I used to tear up the town together, and I tell you, we did our fair share of tramping around in these woods, when we were a little older than you, and it was all kissing boys and dropping acid. After school we used to go down to the headlands, and there was this cypress on the bluffs between Big River and Portuguese Beach. We'd hang our feet over the bluffs and look down at the little hidden coves and out at the islands and we'd **talk** and **talk** and **talk**."

Turtle is silent. She thinks, this bitch. This bitch.

"You have any good girlfriends in school?"

"No."

"Nobody?"

"No."

"How are you liking it?"

"Fine."

"But there are women in your life, I hope?"

Turtle says nothing.

"And Martin? I bet he's a wonder, helping you."

"Yeah. He is."

"He could explain anything, if he wanted."

"Yeah."

"He has a way with words, doesn't he?"

"Yes, he does."

"He was the most imaginative person I ever met. Goddess, he could read! And talk! Can't he?"

"Yes." Turtle smiles.

"He's a good guy," Caroline says, "but when he's angry, he sure can hit hard, can't he?"

Turtle runs her tongue along her teeth. She says, "What?" She thinks, you bitch, you whore. It is the kind of trick people play with kids, they try and get you to answer a lot of questions and then they ask you a question about your family. Turtle's seen it before. Women are always cunts in the end. No matter how they start up. Always some axe to grind.

Caroline sits cross-legged on her stool and watches Turtle with serene attentiveness, and Turtle thinks, you bitch. You fucking whore. I knew it would come and it came.

"Well," Caroline says, seeing her error, back-pedaling, "he used to have a temper on him."

Turtle stands there.

"I remember, when we were just kids—just—well, goddess, he had a temper. That's all I'm saying, just that sometimes he had a temper on him. So, how is he these days?" Caroline asks.

"I've got to go." Turtle turns.

"Wait," Caroline says.

Turtle strips all emotion out of her face but not quite out of her posture, and she thinks, look at me. She thinks, look at me. You know that I take this seriously. Look at me. If you ever try and take him away, you will see.

"Did I say something wrong?"

"I don't know what you're talking about."

"Julia, sweetheart, I'm just wondering how things are at home. I can't tell you how often I've thought of you over these years. How many times I thought I saw you at Corners of the Mouth, or waiting in front of the post office, or walking through Heider Field. And could never be sure, because, of course, I didn't know you. And now that you're here—well, of course it's you. You look just like your mom."

Turtle says, "My daddy would never."

"I know, sweetheart, I'm just curious," Caroline says. "You know, I was so close to your mother, I'm allowed to worry a little bit. You and I, we'd know each other if she was still alive, and you and

Brett would've grown up like brother and sister, but instead, I don't know you at all. I can't help thinking that it's a weird turn of fate, you know, that she left us and you grew up not even knowing me. And good goddess, girl, you need some women in your life!"

Turtle stares at Caroline, thinking, I have never known a woman I liked, and I will grow up to be nothing like you or like Anna; I will grow up to be forthright and hard and dangerous, not a subtle, smiling, trick-playing cunt like you.

"Oh," Caroline says, "sweetheart. Let me drive you home. I'd like to talk to Marty. It's been ages."

"I don't know," Turtle says.

"Oh, honey, I can't let you walk all those miles back home. I just can't. If you'd rather, I'll call your father and he can come pick you up, but it's an hour out of his way, and I'd much rather just take you home myself."

Turtle thinks, I will be in the car with this woman, and her thinking her things about Martin. But she wants to see how Caroline talks to him. She wants to be there, she half wants to know what Caroline thinks, and half she doesn't.

Eight

IT IS NEAR SUNDOWN WHEN THEY REACH the turnoff for Turtle's house. Caroline drives hard up the washboard gravel, just about six hundred yards, the Explorer lurching in and out of ruts. She keeps saying, "Look at this, Julia, goddess, if you knew how this place used to look." The boys have their hands and faces pressed to the glass and look out at the fields with fascination. The driveway runs up the northern edge of the hill, and on their left it's all shore pines standing above Slaughter-house Gulch, which cuts west below them. Above them, they can just see the house at the crest of the hill, all of the windows dark. On their right the fields run until they meet the orchard, be-

yond which, and hidden from them, are the raspberry fields and Grandpa's trailer. A stream cuts
its way through the grass, visible only as a seam of
thimbleberry and hazelnut. Turtle thinks, we will
see how this goes, but he will not be hard on me
until they are gone.

Caroline slows down, looking at pampas grass
beside the road, and says, "Daniel used to be more
proud of that meadow than anything, I think. I
don't know how many hours he spent tending
this meadow, and you know, it used to be just all
timothy—as far as you could see, just timothy.
But he's let it get away from him, hasn't he?"

Deer lying on the warm gravel lurch to their feet
and bolt into the grass. She looks at Turtle and
says, "It's a jungle you're growing up in, isn't it?"

"Look!" Brett says. "Look!" They can see a flat
shoulder of the hillside, not far from the orchard,
thickly overgrown in wild oats, where seven doors
stand in a circle, without any walls or framing.
Ravens stand on the lintels, cocking their heads to
watch the Explorer come up the drive.

Caroline looks over at Turtle, and then up to
the house, where the white roses have climbed
up among the windows and up onto the second
story, braided with poison oak, which throws long,
crinkly green-and-red shoots high into the air.
"Look at that," Caroline says, "look at that. Look
at all those roses. When I was last here, what—
over ten years ago—this was all different, Julia. All

of those roses were pruned and tied up on lattices, and the house was newly painted, that field had not a weed in it, and that driveway was beautiful new gravel. I can't believe how it's all changed. Those roses, no one even knows the cultivar. There was some kind of rose specialist out here to examine them once and take cuttings. Your great-great-grandma was a rose enthusiast and had all kinds of rose varieties, including some that were found only here in Mendocino that are now thought to be gone except, maybe, here they are. And there were pots on the porch, big glazed pots, just full of lettuce and kale and onions and garlic, squash and artichokes, and there were"—she points out by the deck off the master bedroom—"there were beehives."

"Oh," Turtle says, "Grandpa still has the hives. They are out in the orchard."

"And the orchard, it wasn't overgrown at all like that. Do those trees still fruit?"

"Not really," Turtle says. She looks at the orchard, the trees gone to shoots spring after spring without pruning, wickerwork hulks in a sea of blackberries.

"That orchard was in a lawn, I mean a lawn, that your grandfather used to mow. And look at it now. Just look at that. Those trees look awful. I mean, they look miserable. Oh, honey."

Turtle puts her fingers in her mouth. She doesn't like how Caroline is talking, like it's her daddy's fault that the trees stopped bearing fruit, her daddy's fault that the field is going to weeds, and what she's not saying is how Grandpa used up all the money, and her mother died, and how Martin is raising Turtle on his own, picking up jobs where he can, and isn't in the same position that maybe Grandpa was when Grandma was alive and he was retired and had money.

Martin is sitting in an Adirondack chair holding a Red Seal Ale in one hand, watching them. He's got his Colt 1911 .45 sitting on the arm of the chair, and laid up against the back of the chair, a Saiga shotgun. Evening light slants across the hill from the lambent blue ocean.

"Stay in the car, boys," Caroline says to Jacob and Brett, who peer through the tinted windows at the big man on the porch. He raises himself slowly, puts the Colt in the waist of his jeans, and walks carefully down the steps. Caroline winds down her window, and Martin comes abreast of the SUV, and then leans through the window, more than span-ning it with his shoulders, propping his elbows on the door so that the car sinks to the side. Turtle's vision flexes with anxiety, and her hair prickles up across her arms and legs, on her scalp, on the back of her neck, and a feeling of cold follows after, run-ning down her body. He looks into the interior, right at Caroline, and she doesn't talk for a mo-ment, and he seems to chew on what he's seeing before he breaks into a crooked grin.

"Well, Caroline," he says. "God, but it's terrific to see you."

"Martin, I've found your daughter."

"If only you'd found her mother," he says. At this, Caroline opens and closes her mouth, at a loss, but Martin goes on, almost kindly, almost as if to put her at ease, nodding to indicate Julia and saying, "That girl," sharing a roguish look with Caroline, a look so conspiring and full of good humor that she smiles despite herself.

"Marty," she says, trying to sound stern, "she was way out in Little River, almost in Comptche."

"Well," Martin says, "that's just a hop, a skip, and a jump for her. Between you and me, there's no holding that girl back, Caroline. I've known her to go thirty miles across country in a single day. The girl's part Helena Macfarlane, part wild-cat, you can't wear her out. Between you and me, Caroline, it is a thing out of myth, almost. You could hamstring her and drive her way out into the bush and leave her there, and you would come back to find she had taken up with wolves and founded a kingdom. When she was just a little thing, she'd walk all the way to the Little River Market. I am talking about a child in diapers, bare-foot, and the girls at the register would give her a stick of butter to eat and give me a call. Once, a little older, she walked all the way to the Ten Mile River before I found her. But if you're too hard on her about it, you just drive her away, isn't that right, kiddo?" Turtle, named this way, smiles and then looks quickly away. Martin is taking pleasure in talking. He goes on. "God, Caroline"—raking his fingers through his hair—"you look just like you did a decade ago, you know that?"

"Oh stop," Caroline says, smiling despite herself.

"Just the exact same way," Martin says.

"Little more gray in my hair," Caroline says.

"But it suits you," Martin says, turning his attention to her mop of wiry salt-and-pepper hair. "It's the only thing that keeps you from looking like a twenty-something. It's this sea air and that olive complexion of yours."

"How are things?"

"Are you sure there isn't a picture of you somewhere," Martin inquires, "getting more aged and wicked with every passing day?"

"No such thing," Caroline says.

"Just good living, then. As for me," Martin says, looking away from the car and out at the setting sun above the ocean, "things have never been better."

"Well," Caroline says.

"Well," Martin says, catching some meaning she conveys, "I have my daughter. And **god**, but that's more than enough for anybody. As you can see, she keeps my hands full. If you can't find happiness there, in a girl like that, Christ, I don't think it'd be worth living. She's everything to me, Caroline. Look at her, and a great beauty, too, isn't she?"

"Yes she is," Caroline says, sounding a little doubtful on the subject of Turtle's beauty.

"You know, you can't be too hard on the girl, she's just like you were, except so far, no boys and no psilocybin."

"I told her the same thing," she says, laughing. "That's exactly what I said!"

"Because it's true, look at her, I hope you weren't too hard on her," Martin says, and both adults look appraisingly at Turtle.

"I could use your advice, though," Martin says.

"You'll have it," Caroline says.

Martin looks out at the ocean and, narrowing his eyes as if describing something in the far-off distance, he says, "Kibble," and then pauses for a long moment to compose his description, "she struggles in school. Not with everything, but with English. With her vocabulary lists."

There is silence from the backseat, a creak of springs as Jacob leans forward to catch this. Turtle chews her fingers, angry that he would bring this up in front of her friends.

"Oh well," Caroline says with a sympathetic glance at Turtle, "don't we all struggle with that."

Martin nods in acknowledgment, slowly and humorlessly.

"There's nothing, I've found, but just to help them through it, though goddess knows that's not easy. Martin, this is my boy, Brett."

Brett leans forward, and they shake hands, Martin reaching in through the window and smiling at Brett with his jaw standing out and his flannel hanging open.

"Well, now," Martin says, "what a big handsome boy." He looks back at Caroline. She seems to be searching his face for something that isn't there. She is turned away from Turtle and Turtle cannot tell what she is thinking, but Turtle knows that Caroline must be putting on an act, that she must be worried and trying to suss something out. Turtle looks at Martin and wonders if he knows that, and looking at him, she thinks he does. Caroline says, "You should have me over more often, Martin. I'd like to be a part of the girl's life."

"Of course," Martin says.

"It's the same phone number," Caroline says.

"Truly?" Martin says. "The same number? Well, I have it then."

"The same house, even."

"Out on Flynn Creek Road? I remember that house **very** well. Still infested with brown recluses?"

"You have to knock every stick of kindling against a post before you can bring it inside."

"Well," Martin says in wonder. "Anyway, I have your number, and I will give you a call."

"I'd like that," Caroline says.

"Come on, kibble," Martin says, and Turtle opens the door and hooks something in the footwell with her toe and pitches it out into the grass unnoticed and then climbs out. She looks once at the boys and closes the door, and steps back from the car. Caroline waves a final good-bye to Martin, pulls the SUV around, and goes down the driveway, leaving Turtle and Martin standing side by side, watching them go.

Martin, silent, walks back to the Adirondack chair and sits down in it. He picks his cigar up from the arm and tosses open the Zippo's lid and lights it, puffing and squinting into the smoke. He draws on the cigar and then fits it between two fingers and she climbs up the porch steps and sits down on his knee and he pulls her back into the depths of the chair and puts one big, tobacco-smelling arm around her, cupping her hair to her neck, and they are silent for a long time. He puts his face into the nape of her neck and inhales. With the hand slung over her shoulder, he gestures down to the hill, to the fields.

"When you were just a little thing," he says, "you couldn't've weighed more than fifty pounds. Your mother, she'd let you out to play. You were way out in the field, at the edge of the orchard, and the grass was high that year, as high as you were. And I come out onto the porch to have a smoke and I'm looking, and I can just barely make you out. Down there, with this little toy monster you had, a toy Godzilla. You were making it walk through the grass and I could just barely see you. And not thirty feet from you, half hidden in the grass, was the biggest mountain lion I've ever seen. Sitting there, watching you. The biggest son of a bitch I've ever seen, kibble."

He has his arm around her, and his embrace is exceptionally gentle, but Turtle can feel the strength of it. He draws air sharply through his teeth, shaking his head, like he does when something hurts him. He says, "So I went into the house and I got the gun and I walked out onto the porch and I couldn't see the damn cat." She sits smelling him, enclosed within his embrace, looking over the fields and thinking about that. Where the field is still healthy, the timothy is all of a height, green and riffled by the wind. The wild oats stand with panicles arched, spikelets stirring. Soon, she knows, the meadow will be overgrown with weeds. She looks down at the decking and notices his boot prints, which are orange and gray clay. She sits looking at that, and then turns her attention to the ash-colored clay on the treads of his boots. There isn't any clay like that on their property, not that she knows.

He turns her in his lap so he can look at her. He says, "Goddamn it, kibble. I came to the porch and I looked out with the gun and I couldn't see the cat. It was summer, and all the grass was that yellow color it gets, and the cat was almost that same color. I knew it was out there, but I couldn't see it in the high grass. I just stood there, kibble, and I knew that the fucking cat was out there, and maybe if I called you that'd set him off, make him chase you. I could see you. You were just crawling around in the grass, and I stood there and I just—I just didn't know what to do."

She hangs her arms around his neck and presses her ear against the flannel breast of his shirt. She can feel the stubble of his chin, smell the smoke of the Swisher Sweets, the malty smell of the beer. There is clay on the edge of the stair where he wiped the mud free of the treads of his boots, clay and the small, brittle leaves of huckleberries.

Martin says, "I'm not sure that you understand what I'm trying to tell you, kibble. Because I thought I might lose you. And I didn't know what to do. I thought—I thought . . . You know what I thought, kibble? I thought that I could never lose you, never let you go. You are mine. But I might not always be there. I might not always be fast enough, or smart enough, kibble. And the world is a bad place. It's a really fucking bad place."

"What happened?"

"You stood up," he says. "You just stood up and you looked out into the grass, holding that goddamn toy in one hand, and I knew that you were looking at the cat, **Christ**, you must have been looking right at him. I was standing at the edge of the porch, I just couldn't find him in the grass. It was like he was invisible." He sucks air through his teeth. Veins stand out on his burnished forearms and snake over the backs of his hands. His knuckles are leathern burls, his fingers are crosshatched with scars. She looks down at the knees of his Levi's, stained with grease and rust, and she reaches down and picks at a scablike crust of epoxy. There are mud and leaves on the ankles of his Levi's. Lapped in a fold of denim, the tiny, tight-lipped pink urn and lipstick pedicel of a pygmy manzanita flower.

He says, "Those bastards, they can get so close to the ground and just wait. This motherfucker. I knelt at the edge of the porch and I found you in the scope and I put the reticule right on you. At first, I thought that I could catch him right before he was on you. And then I thought I'd kill you myself rather than let that cat have you. Rather than let you get dragged into the grass and disemboweled. That is what they do. Grasp you with their mouth and their forepaws, and then kick out with their hind paws to disembowel you. And the hell if I was going to let that happen. Put that reticule right on your temple, and it would be over—pffff, and a red mist. Rather than let that cat open you up."

"Did you see the cat, Daddy?"

"No. You just turned around and walked right up the hill and onto the porch and I knew that the son of a bitch was out there, ready to take you away from me. You came and held on to my pant leg, and I just stood there until you went inside. It got dark and you came out and said you were hungry."

"Would you really have shot me?"

"You're my little girl, kibble. You're everything to your old man, and I will never, ever let you go, but I don't know. I guess it's hard to say what's right."

"You and me," Turtle says, "against the world."

"That's right," he says.

"I'm sorry I went off, Daddy."

"Where'd you go?"

"East," she says, "east, above the Albion. There are redwoods out there, Daddy."

He nods and looks east. "There's growers out there, and I don't think any of them would ever hurt a child, I don't think, but they've got dogs that would. And, kibble, they're people, and in the way of people, they're not all of them good. You be careful. I think it's better if you don't ever go away like that again. But we'll let it go this once."

"Daddy," she says, "on a ridge, way over above the Albion, there was a tarantula."

He holds her for a while. Then he says, "No, kibble, there aren't any tarantulas over there."

"No, Daddy, I saw one. It was as big as my hand."

"You didn't see no spider like that, kibble."

"But, Daddy—"

"Kibble," he says.

"Yes, Daddy."

They sit there on the Adirondack chair, Turtle in his lap, he holding her, and they watch the clouds come toward them in rows. The setting sun lights a corona of aquamarine and purple ocean. The sea stacks stand in near-black outline. On their white-washed shoulders, the cormorants wait with their wings outstretched to the setting sun. His biceps are more in span than her hands, thumb to pinkie. The veins that cross them have more breadth than her fingerprints.

She hops off his knees and he rises and looks down at her and a spasm crosses his face. He drops to one knee and takes her into his arms. "Christ," he says. "Christ. Jesus Christ, kibble. Be careful. Christ, kibble. **Christ**." He holds her and she stands there, her waist encircled in his embrace. "How big you're getting," he says, "how strong. My absolute darling. My absolute darling."

"Yes," she says.

"Just mine?"

"Just yours," she says, and he crushes the side of his face against her hips, presses it urgently to her, looks up at her, his arms encircle the small of her back.

"You promise?" he says.

"I promise," she says.

"No one else's?"

"No one else's," she says.

He breathes her scent in deeply, closes his eyes. She allows herself to be held by him. Because he hadn't found her, she'd thought he hadn't come looking. She had figured he had just waited for her to return to him. But now she stands encircled by his arms, looking at his muddy boot prints and thinking, you followed me, and you didn't find me. It has always seemed to her that he could find her anywhere, that he could anticipate her every move better than she herself could. She thinks, it would've been better if you'd told me, Daddy, and we'd laughed about it. You could've made it a joke. You could've said, "how tall and strong you are, how trackless your ways." She thinks, you should've said something, rather than let me look at that mud and guess, let me guess that you came after me and that you didn't catch me, and so you had to come back here and just wait. She thinks, I would never have thought less of you, if you had just shared that with me.

Sometime in the night, she awakes, and lies silent, chewing on the wadded-up cotton of her sleeping bag. Then she rises and opens the window and steps up into the window frame, the moon shining on her naked limbs. She goes out the window and climbs down the rose canes, thick as knobby wrists, down into the muddy yard, and in the dark she goes out into the weeds. The motion-activated lights come on with a click and she lies there, breathing the wet scent of crushed radish and vanilla grass.

The door to the master bedroom's mudroom opens, and Martin comes out and stands on the small master bedroom deck, on the south side of the house, looking out over the field. He has a gun laid back over his shoulder, she can't tell which. With the spotlights shining down at her, he's nearly impossible to pick out on the deck, like a figure standing just to the right of the sun. He waits there, spread-legged and patient, and she can imagine his careful breathing as he looks out into the field. She buries her face, keeping the whites of her eyes in the grass, and she breathes, waiting for him, knowing that he will never see her. She thinks, there was something wrong with that story about that cat. He doesn't see things like they are, not clearly.

Martin walks back inside. She hears the door slam closed. She exhales, raggedly, and slithers through the wild oats, searching with her fingertips until she finds what she's looking for, what she'd pitched discreetly out into the grass when she'd gotten out of the passenger-side door.

She finds it, and puts it to her face, and breathes into it. Then she returns, the motion-activated lights clicking back on. She crosses the intervening space quickly, lays the shirt over her shoulders to free her hands, and mounts up onto the wall. She climbs around a window and steps into the inside corner formed between the walls of the foyer and the second story, scrambles up the foyer's roof, and then climbs across the side of the building toward her window. She hears Martin's door slam open, hears Martin come out onto the south deck. He is hidden from her by the foyer. Above her, the bay window projects out away from the wall by three feet. She clings to the rose canes beside and below it, looking up at it and hearing Martin's footsteps, and then she vaults up and out. She grasps the windowsill and hangs one-handed, her feet in open air. She matches her other hand onto the windowsill and slips through it and muddily onto the floor. She holds the cotton scrap. Below her, Martin walks out into the yard. She peeks over her window, breathing hard. He stands beside the trash barrel, looking into the grass, and turns to look at the house. When he is gone, she relaxes against the wall.

It's Jacob Learner's T-shirt. It shows a candle in the center, and around the candle, a twist of barbwire. Above that, an arc of stars. The shirt reads AMNESTY INTERNATIONAL. She sits chewing on her fingers, naked legs akimbo on the cold wood floor, scattered muddy prints of her heels. She plants her hands on the shirt.

Nine

ARRIVING FROM THE RASPBERRIES, TURTLE
hears Rosy heave herself up and come to the door,
shaking herself off and setting her collar to tinkling, then Grandpa opens the door and looks
down at her. "Sweetpea," he says, "would you give
me a hand with this pizza?"

She leans the rifle against the jamb, pulls the
pizza deftly out of the oven, and drops it onto
a cutting board. She accepts a chef's knife from
Grandpa, tests it with a thumb, and divides the
pizza into slices.

"Oh good," he says, watching the knife sticky
with cheese, "oh good."

"Grandpa," she says, "you have to eat some other things, sometimes, not just these pizzas."

"Oh, it's fine," he says, "it's fine. I'm long past worrying about my health, sweetpea."

They move to the table. "It's a rare thing, have you here for dinner," Grandpa says. He means it as a question.

"Yup," Turtle says.

He sits with one hand on a bourbon glass filled with chilled soapstones. His jowls hang down and he looks like he is frowning. She unholsters the Sig Sauer, drops the magazine, locks back the slide, and sets it on the table. It reeks of gunpowder. The exposed barrel is laddered with powder residue, the frame is smoked with it, her fingertips black with it, her trigger finger brassy. She shucks aside the card case, raps the deck smartly, shuffles.

"Well," he says. "Tell me you didn't take that to school."

"I didn't take it to school," she says, then cuts, shuffles, deals.

He collects his cards. They shake in his hand with a papery rattle. He says, "The pines on the north side of the gulch have started to die, and on towards Albion, along the highway there at the bend, more of them are dying. It may be that pine beetle that everybody is talking about, I don't know what, sweetpea."

Turtle discards into the crib. Those pines have been dead for a long time.

Grandpa touches and sorts his cards with a trembling hand.

"It's getting on towards the end of the year," he says.

She looks up at him. She doesn't know what he can mean. He sorts his cards.

"What was I—?" he says after a moment.

"I don't know."

His eyes are yellow. He runs his tongue over his lips.

"Well, what was I saying?"

"The pines, the end of the year, but it's not the end of the year, Grandpa."

"Well, I know that," he says. The game has stalled as he considers it. At last, he says, "The bees are dying. Six hives, sweetpea, and five of them dead."

She says nothing.

"I don't know why." He scowls. "Some mite, something. Maybe it's my fault."

"It's not your fault," she says.

"Maybe I—" He gestures. "Forgot something."

"You didn't forget anything."

"Six hives," he says, "and five of them dead, the larva capped in their cells. The workers just don't come back, I don't know why. Must be something I did."

She waits for him to discard into the crib.

"Can't think of what it might have been. Ah. Ah. The end of the year. Isn't there a thing you do?"

"Grandpa, it's May."

"A thing you do at the end of the year," he says.

"I've no idea what you're on about?" Turtle says.

"Prom," Grandpa says.

"Not prom," she says, because prom is high school. The dance is on May 16, in less than two weeks. The last day of school is June 10.

"Well, now," Grandpa says, and discards into the crib. Turtle cuts the deck, Grandpa draws the starter, a jack, and Turtle pegs two for his nibs. They are back on it now. "Well," he says, "well, now." He picks up his cards, throws an eight.

Turtle throws a seven, pegs two.

Grandpa throws a nine, pegs three for the run of 7-8-9.

"So will you go to the dance?"

She laughs. He nods to the Sig Sauer, and the gesture is very like Martin.

"I can't believe he lets you run around with this," he says.

"Yeah?" Turtle says.

"I can't believe how that man is raising you."

"He loves me," Turtle says.

Grandpa shakes his head.

"He loves me very much," Turtle says.

"Don't you do that, sweetpea."

"What?" Turtle says.

"Don't be twisting things up like that. You can't be saying one for the other like that, sweetpea, so don't you start."

She cracks her knuckles, thinking, sorry, I'm sorry.

"This is our town. This is **your** town. The people here are **your people**. And you're toting that thing around." He fastens on his whiskey glass, his eyes becoming harder and harder, his aspect changing very little or not at all, but suggesting somehow a slow solidifying of his bitterness. He picks up a bottle of Tabasco and begins dashing it onto the pizza. Then he lifts a slice and holds it in trembling hands and sets it down. He picks his cards up and the game moves on in silence. She can see it in his face, how he can't get it straight and how he sits there wishing he could.

After a while he says, "Well, isn't there a boy?"

"There's no boy."

Grandpa looks up at her now and looks at her very searchingly.

"How do you mean that?"

"There's no boy. That's all I mean."

"Are things hard for you at school? Are you bullied?"

"No," she says.

"That's good." He pours himself more whiskey. They turn over the crib, peg out the scores, throw down cards and count them. Grandpa collects the cards with difficulty. He shuffles them. They play a hand. He pours more whiskey, looks at it. They lay down their cards, peg points for the crib. He says, "If you went, what would you wear?"

"I'm not going," she says.

"I don't like to think that you wouldn't go."

"Well, Grandpa, then I'll have to go to the dance."

"Ah," he says, "is there a boy?"

"Sure," she says. "Sure there's a boy."

Grandpa's eyes are crinkled with his pleasure. He can't quit smiling. He sits raking his hand over his face, trying to quit because he knows that he looks like an idiot, and she can see he doesn't want to spoil it for her by looking like that, but he can't quit smiling and so sits pretending not to smile and looks down into his whiskey with his eyes squinting with pleasure.

"The little shit," Grandpa says.

"You don't know him. He's very nice."

"He's a little shit," Grandpa says. He can't quit smiling into his whiskey. He rakes his hand down his face again. He quits the smile for a moment and then it comes back with the left side of his face and he turns the glass in its ring of condensation.

"Well, you need a dress then, sweetpea."

"No dress," she says, holding the split deck, half in either hand. It feels like anything could happen. It feels as if the world could open up. Then

Grandpa says, "Martin's never, he's never really laid into you, has he?"

"No," Turtle says.

"Of course not. Of course not." He raises the glass, looks at the lights slanting through the whiskey, drinks it down. He sets it on the table. He seems to have forgotten about the card game.

"You ask him to go dress shopping."

"A dress," she says, and laughs.

"A dress. Here's what you say, here's how you do this," Grandpa says, and nods. "He'll like that. You tell him, 'I want to go to the dance.' He says whatever he says. Then you say, 'Daddy, take me dress shopping.' Then you shut up about it, that's the end of it, and you never mention it again and you let on like you've abandoned the idea, until he takes you dress shopping, and then you don't say anything about the dance, and you don't say anything about any boy. All it is, is the dress, and it's you, and it's him. Then, when the dance comes, you just go. You don't ask to go. You just go. And you come back, and you don't say nothing, and it's like the dance was between you and him and there might never have been a boy at all."

Turtle shuffles the cards, deals, sits looking at the two hands. Neither Grandpa nor Turtle turns them over. She thinks, the hell, that might even work, but there isn't a boy and there won't be a dress, and then she thinks, you're forgetting what your life is, Turtle, and you can't forget that and

you have to stay close to what is real, because
if you ever get out of this it will be because you
paid attention and moved carefully and did everything well. Then she thinks, get out of this, shit,
your mind is rotten and you cannot trust yourself
and you do not even know what to believe except
that you love him, and everything goes from there.

They pick up their hands. Turtle's cards are
no good. She'll wait and see what the start card
gives her, but her cards themselves are no good.
She might make something of them if she plays
well, but when her cards are no good it's always a
game about regret, because what she's put away in
the crib she may need and there's no way to know
in advance how that will go, but there's no way
around it. She sits sorting through them to see if
she can make anything of them and wondering
what the start card might give her. Grandpa sits,
turning his whiskey slowly, the soapstones sounding against the glass. Turtle waits for him to play,
and he does not play.

That night when she walks out of the orchard
into sight of the house, there is another truck
parked in the driveway, and Wallace McPherson's
orange VW Bug. She squats in the grass and yokes
the gun. She can see the shadows of the men
around the table and she thinks, he will be in a
mood, he will be in one for sure. She tears up red
sorrel and sits chewing on the tart leaves. Then
she rises and goes up the deck and in through the

sliding glass door. Martin sits at the table with Wallace McPherson and Jim Macklemore, beer bottles spread across the table, joints and cigars crushed into ashtrays, Martin dealing out poker hands. They look at her, and Martin brings his hand down on the table with a sound like a gunshot. "Well, there you are," he says.

"I was out with Grandpa," Turtle says.

"Out with Grandpa," Martin tells Wallace McPherson. "We were worried about her because she never came home, but as it turns out she is only out with her grandpa. Her beloved, beloved grandpa. I shouldn't have worried. What harm can it possibly do, to spend all your spare time with a remorseless psychopath? A man with no imagination huddled in a bleak, reeking trailer? A trailer filled with the stink of Jack Daniel's and of his poisonous dreams, the wretched exhalations of a bitter, hateful little mind? Only spending time with dear old Grandpa while he drinks himself to death."

Wallace McPherson looks at Turtle apologetically. His chair is tipped back on two legs. His black beard is groomed immaculately with waxed mustachios.

"Her dear old grandpa," Martin tells Wallace, "the gentlest of men, really. The kind of man anyone would want their daughter around." He slaps the table again and looks at Turtle.

"What are you up to now?"

"Bed."

"Bed? Well."

Jim Macklemore says, "That's an awful big gun for a little girl, isn't it?"

Turtle looks at him levelly.

"With a big—what kind of a scope is that you've got there?"

Turtle doesn't see the point in telling him.

"Can you even fire that thing?"

She doesn't answer.

"Can you hit anything?"

She stands jawing the sorrel.

"Well," and he shakes his head slowly. "Maybe you can, maybe you can't."

Martin says nothing.

Turtle walks quietly up to her room. She takes down her chest of tools and lays out a towel and sits cross-legged. She draws the Sig Sauer and drops the slide off the gun and sets it down in two pieces. She levers out the recoil guide rod. She takes a screwdriver from her tool chest and removes the polymer grips to expose the hammer strut and mainspring. Downstairs, she can hear Wallace get up and say, "Well, I guess I'm heading home." Then muttered and inaudible joking, laughter, the sound of Wallace putting on his coat, the swish and double kiss of the sliding glass door, and Wallace's footsteps down the stairs and into the grass, the ignition of the Bug, and Wallace backing around in the driveway. Turtle stoops over her towel, levering at the gun pieces with powder-black fingers. She ties her hair into a high, tight ponytail and goes on in a slow excavation of every cam and spring. She knows them all and she lays them carefully out on the towel. Downstairs, she can hear Jim and her daddy talking. Their voices are muted and broken by long silences. She can't make out the words, but she can make out the tone well enough. She rises and walks down the hallway. She lies down on her belly and slithers out onto the landing, which doesn't have a railing, just a frame of cracked redwood boards, black with age and with oil. She crawls right up to this beam, lies with her cheek against it, and she listens.

"That girl of yours."

"Christ," Martin says.

"Ain't she a wild thing."

"Christ," Martin says again.

"Looks just like her mother," Jim says.

"And nothing like me," Martin says.

Jim says, "It's in the eyes." There is a long pause as they both consider this. Then Jim says, "Cold blue eyes, full of murder and vitriol." He laughs at his own joke. Martin slaps the table, laughs. Both men fall silent. Turtle rolls onto her back, lies listening, looking at the ceiling.

"Her mother said that it was a mountain lion did it to her."

"What?"

Another long silence. Turtle hears the chapped

noise as Martin opens and closes his lips, prefatory to speech, fails each time to speak. Then, with a laugh like a murmur, he says, "She used to say that she was asleep in the bedroom and I was out cutting boards to repanel the bedroom upstairs. In the master bedroom, there's a mudroom and a porch beyond that. She says I'd left that door open."

"No shit?"

Silence. Martin is perhaps nodding. Soft noises of his lips, a kind of click he makes with his tongue when he's thinking or lost in memories.

"So she said that when she woke up, the mountain lion was in the bed with her, eight feet long, head to haunch."

"Never seen a cat that big," Jim says, "not that I live out here, like you guys."

"That's a big cat."

"She liked to rile you."

More silence, and then, "She said that the goddamn cat climbed on top of her and took her neck in his jaws and took her right there in the bed, from behind her, said it had like a hook, like a spine on its cock."

Jim laughs, slapping the table. "Oh fuck. She had some sass. Didn't she?"

"Hilarious," Martin says dryly.

There is another long silence. Then Jim says, "She's your daughter, all right, to her fucking bones. That girl is what, a hundred and ten pounds, all of it piss and vinegar and fucking murder. She's your daughter, all right."

Another long silence, and Martin says, "Christ."

"You know," Jim says, "most often, I worry about girls growing up in this world, right? Right? It's not the same as with boys, what can happen. But with your daughter . . ." He collects the deck of cards with a papery rasping, knocks it against the edge of the table. "The thing about Julia. The thing about that girl. Some asshole, right? You just . . . you pity that fuck and what he's about to find out." Jim coughs out a laugh.

"I don't think that's funny at all," Martin says.

"I know, I know," Jim says quickly.

"It's fucks like you," Martin says very quietly. "Fat fucks who've never seen a bad thing happen that think that just being good is enough. But the truth is, Jim, it can go any way, and sometimes it just doesn't matter how good you are."

"I know that, of course that's true," Jim says.

"So it's not funny. I've done all I can for her, but she's just a fourteen-year-old girl, Jim."

"I know, I'm sorry," Jim says.

"You never know how a thing's going to go," Martin says. "The outcome is just never certain."

"Of course, I'm sorry, Marty."

"And, Christ, the worry keeps you up late at night. You just worry about what kind of world she's growing up into, and what will become of her. Christ, it's an awful thing. And I wish it were like you say. But the truth is, it doesn't matter how tough you are."

She lies on the floor, listening to her daddy, his voice full of pain, looking up at the ceiling boards. They fit one to the other and go on, board after board, across the ceiling almost shrouded in darkness, and they are all of them miraculous in their strangeness and their particularity, and Turtle thinks, life is a strange thing, if you look around, if you look, you can almost lose yourself in it, and she thinks, stop, you are thinking like Martin. There is another long silence from below.

"That was a fucking awful thing," Jim says after a moment.

"Christ," Martin says.

"Hell, Marty, don't get on about her."

"Christ," Martin says again. "I could almost forget sometimes."

"Don't get on about her. It's done."

A noise as Martin shifts his chair. The table creaks as he puts his forearms against it, perhaps leaning in. He says, "And you just have to think, what do you tell a girl, what do you tell her about the world, what do you tell her about life. What do you say?"

"Oh fuck, Marty. I don't know."

"The temperature may rise six degrees in the coming decades, and that's not just 'rising temperatures,' that's a cataclysm. You think we can stop that? People don't believe in obesity, and **that** they can see in the fucking mirror. They can't take care of their own goddamn bodies. How many people die because their hearts are grimy with plaque, do you think? A lot. What is it—seventy percent of all Americans are overweight? Half of those are obese? And do you think—can this person, this average American, take care of anything? No. **Fuck** no. So the natural world, which they cannot see for all their roads and gas stations and schools and jails, the fucking natural world, which is more important and more beautiful than anything this average American has ever seen or understood in his whole fucking life, the natural world is going to die, and we're going to let it die, and there's no way we can save it. Fuck."

"Optimism?"

"Optimism, hell," Martin says. "You ask some-time, you ask somebody what they would do if the end came. You go ahead and ask them and there will be among those you ask a population who'll tell you that they would just die, and among those who didn't say it, more would mean it. People are content to live if the living should come easy. If it should stop being easy—well." A silence. They sit for some time, and then Martin grating, his voice harsh and low, raking his fingernails across the wood grain: "Well, I tell you, what that question is asking is—what will you do when things get hard? And life **will** get hard. Life will get hard, and to say that you will not fight for it—well. What intercourse can you have with such people? There can be none. Their life is a sham of circumstance only, their pretended agency is perfidy, a social lie, and to regard them as people is fetishism. So what optimism can there be? They will not fight for themselves—you think they will fight for a world outside themselves? A world troublesome to imagine, troublesome to understand? They have no language to understand it, even. They see no beauty in it. And you know what the proof is? The end is coming. And here we all are—waiting, with our dicks out in our hands."

"Well, fuck, Marty."

"You know what I think? She couldn't be fucking bothered. It got too fucking hard and the headaches were too bad and she gave up."

"Don't get on about her," Jim says.

"Why not?"

"You said yourself, anything can happen. It could've been some random thing. It wasn't a thing she meant to happen. You know that."

"Hell, I don't know shit."

"Don't let's talk about her."

"It's not a thing anyone can know, I guess," Martin says, "but you've got to fucking wonder."

"It was an accident, and if it wasn't, I don't see that it matters."

"It matters."

"No, Marty, I don't think so."

"You're a good guy, for a cocksucker. You know that, Jim?"

"I'm not a cocksucker."

"Being a self-hating Republican faggot doesn't make you any less of a faggot, Jim. It just makes you a faggot and also a blind and self-deceiving motherfucker."

"It's a wonder you don't have more friends."

Turtle waits for more, but there is no more, and she crawls back down away from the landing, and gets up and walks quietly into her bedroom, chewing on her fingers. She lies and looks at the square of moonlight cast by the window onto the floor. She thinks, you don't know what you heard, you don't know, so don't, and you don't know what they meant, so don't, Turtle, just don't.

Ten

IT IS JUST BARELY DAWN. LONG WET STALKS of red fescue are bent over her. Turtle lies looking through the scope. Close into the gun, she can smell its grease and the powder residue. Around her, the meadow is dew heavy, the mist purling down the hillside. As the day warms, long stalks weighted down with dew come suddenly untangled and spring up, their seed heads bouncing. There are yet no clouds in the sky except a single, distant lenticular toyed into strands by the breeze. Turtle dials in her distance and lies, cheek welded to the stock. The rifle target on its stand looks very far away. She thinks, no way would I ever take this shot. No reason to do it. At five hundred meters, you get up and walk away. I bet a lot of people think they can shoot out to five hundred meters and I bet there are very few that can. So just get up and walk away and take your chances. But, she thinks, I guess you can't always. She dials the illumination down, the crosshairs going from laser-red lines to black. She pulls the trigger. The gun kicks the hot shell into the grass. The target **pangs** and swings wildly on its hanger, Turtle grinning on the luck of that, of having doped out the shot on the first try. She fires again and the target **pangs** and swings and she waits for it to drop and she fires again and the target swings back up, Turtle smiling, the .308 shells nested, smoking in the wet grass. From behind her, chuckling laughter. She twists around. Martin is coming up through the field, his jeans wetted to his shins, holding a beer to his chest. He comes and lies down beside her. "Fuck," he says with slow pleasure, shaking his head, touching his dry lips speculatively and looking at the thing from every angle and ready to talk about it but not talking about it, a moment when the things he has wanted have come to pass, and here, in company with them, all the doubts, all the work to get here, all the expense, and she can see the darkening of the moment. "Fuck," he says, looking away down the sweep of the hill, past the line of the sun to where the shining waves buckle and succeed onto the unseen shingle.

"How did she die?" Turtle asks.

He turns to her, his face bereft. "How did she

die?" He shakes his head, inquiring mutely and wonderingly of her, of the moment, of the target down range, touching the pad of his thumb to his lips. "You don't know? How can you not know? I feel like I've told you this a hundred times. A **thousand** times."

"No," she says.

"Fuck." He stops, thinking about that. "Really?"

"I've never heard."

"Fuck, there you go," he says, gesturing to indicate the futility of the thing. He bends down a green stalk, begins tearing out the spikelets, the hulls cleaving wetly to his fingertips. Finally he says, "Well, she went abalone diving and she never came back."

"Really?" Turtle says.

"Right out there. Buckhorn Cove." He nods down to the bus stop, the ocean, the sea stacks black, verged with breakwater. "She went out alone, early that morning. It was a beautiful day. The surf wasn't rough. Around noon, I went down to the beach and found her boat. I swam out to it. She was gone."

"What happened to her?"

Martin probes his jaw.

"She just went down and never came back up?"

"That's right."

"Could it have been a shark?"

"Could have been anything." He drinks from his beer, tipping it up with difficulty from where he lies. "I'm sorry, kibble. If it had to be one of us, it should've been me. I wish it had been me. She was everything I had. Well. Not everything."

He rises and walks away. She puts her face in the grass. Then she struggles up and puts the spare magazine in her back pocket and follows him to the house. They climb up the porch steps together and he pitches his beer bottle out into the field. She goes to the fridge and takes out a Red Seal and tosses it underhand across the counter and he catches it and bangs it open on the counter's edge. She stands with the fridge door open, cracking eggs into her mouth, finishes the carton, discards it. They wait in silence. He offers her the beer. She drinks from it, cuffs her mouth.

"Time to go down?"

"You don't have to walk me."

"I know, kibble. I know that."

She nods. They walk down together. They wait at the gravel turnout.

"You don't have to wait here, Daddy."

"Look at that big goddamn bitch of an ocean, kibble." The cormorants stand on white-painted rocks with their wings spread, facing the sun. Spume lofts through the blowhole on Buckhorn Island. "It is all meaningless," he says, and she does not know why it would mean anything, or why you would look for meaning in it, and she does not understand why you would want it to be anything other than what it is, or why you would want it to be about you. It is just there, and that has always been enough for her. The bus comes gasping around the corner and pulls into the gravel drive and throws open its rubber-skirted doors and Martin salutes the bus driver with his beer and Margery looks straight ahead at the road. Turtle walks down the green vinyl seats and no one looks at her and she does not look at anyone.

She doesn't wait for the bus to go on to the middle school. Instead, Turtle stands up with the high schoolers and files out when the bus makes its first stop in town. She heads down the hill and out onto the headlands. She does not know where she is going, only that she can't go to school and nothing in her life is all right and that she needs to get away and get her head straight. What she wants, more than anything, is to be lost again on the muddy slopes above the Albion. A jogger coming the other way stops in front of Turtle and props one hand on her knees and takes her sunglasses off with the other, and then wipes sweat off her forehead with the back of her wrist. It's Anna, trying to get her breath, dressed in pink running shorts and a blue tank top, black hair gathered into a ponytail.

She says, "Julia? What are you doing here?"

Turtle says, "Oh shit."

"Julia?" Anna says again, in surprise.

"Oh fuck me," Turtle says.

"Are you all right?"

"What are you doing here?" Turtle says.

"I'm jogging," Anna says.

"But shouldn't you be at school?"

"Shouldn't **you**?" Anna says. "I don't have class until twelve thirty. But you should be in Joan Carlson's math class right now. Am I right?"

"Yeah," Turtle says.

"What's wrong?" Anna says.

"Nothing—I'm fine," Turtle says.

"Are you all right?" Anna says, coming closer, looking at her carefully.

"One fucking time, things could go well," Turtle says.

"What?"

"Why would I go to school?" Turtle says. "Why would I even go?"

"What?" Anna says.

"Why would I go? Have I passed a single one of your little fucked-up, stupid, motherfucking tests? You take me aside and you go after me like, 'Oh, Julia, why didn't you pass your test?' but isn't it fucking **obvious** why I didn't pass the test? What do you expect me to say? You're asking me to lie to you. I don't like to lie. I think there are good reasons **not** to lie, and I don't like that it asks that, your class. I need to get away, and **of course**, here you are—'Oh, why aren't you at school, Julia?' Fuck you, you sideways bitch. I suck at school be-cause I am useless, Anna. That's why. There's your answer." She raises her hands in helplessness and lets them drop. "I have tried and tried and tried and I **fail** and that's all I will ever do."

Anna stands, still winded, her hands on her hips. Turtle can smell the other woman, a healthy, sweaty runner's scent, her tank top plastered to her wet stomach. She wipes at her face again, panting and seeming to think that over. She says, "Julia, why do you think that?"

"Of course," Turtle says, "of course. **Of course** that's what you'd say. I hate these questions. Why do I think that? Because it's **true**. It is so obviously true, so clearly true, that I don't understand why you would ask. You only ask because you have nothing to contribute except open-ended questions, which isn't teaching, which doesn't help. Why do I think that? I think that because it's true. You **know** it's true."

"Do you really think that's true?"

"Oh, my fucking, motherfucking, shit-shitting **god**," Turtle says. "What is wrong with you?"

Anna blushes deep red. Even her ears go pink. She looks aside, off to the ocean, jaw open like someone struck. Stray hairs have escaped her tight, high ponytail and points of water cling to their tips. She says, "Julia, that's fair. I messed that one up; you told me what you didn't like and I went and did it." The road runs from town, where they can see low white buildings with peaked wood-shingle roofs and gingerbread weatherboard, water towers burned brownish-black with age. Opposite the town, an expanse of coastal prairie running out to coyote brush hedges, cypresses stooped and ragged, the ocean, sea stacks barren and carpeted with vast congregations of birds. Anna breathes deeply, doesn't seem to know what to say. Turtle watches her, feeling like she cannot exhale, her chest high and tight. She is ready for Anna to fuck this up, and Anna seems to be gathering herself and telling herself, don't fuck this up, Anna. Turtle thinks, I am screwed. I have said too much and I am so fucked it's not even funny and I've ruined everything and she's going to call CPS for sure.

Anna says, "Julia, do you know what I think?"

Turtle looks away, embarrassed, and Anna continues, blushing. "That was rhetorical, it wasn't a real question, what I mean, Julia, is that whatever you believe I think is mistaken. There has been a miscommunication here. I watch you every day and I know that you're smart. I know that you keep your thoughts to yourself and you don't apply yourself to your work, and that's why you're struggling—but that doesn't mean you're stupid. It means that, in class at least, you're nervous and shy."

"You don't know that," Turtle says. "I suck at this. I suck at all of this. I **can't do it**. That's like saying I'm good at math but just can't do math. I'm not smart, Anna."

"If you could just show some spine in that classroom—"

"I have spine," Turtle says.

"That's not what I meant," Anna says quickly, "that was the wrong thing to say, spine's not what I meant." She looks around, rolling her eyes a little at herself, and Turtle looks at this in wonder, and she thinks, is she rolling her eyes because I am so frustrating and stupid, or is she doing that because she wants this to go well and she is embarrassed that she has made a mistake? Turtle doesn't know.

Anna continues. "Julia, listen to me, you come to school, and you sit there and stare out the classroom window. You don't pay attention. You don't study. You don't have friends and you don't feel safe and you come to the first question on that test and you have this feeling of not knowing and you don't push through it, you just stop there, and you think, 'I don't know it,' and you sit there, hating yourself, that's what it looks like. That's my theory. But I think that half the time or more **you do know it**, and you would know it even better if you studied, and you'd be able to fill out those tests if you pushed through that moment of fear. You tell me you've done your hardest and that you've tried, but that isn't true . . ." She stops, knowing that she's said the wrong thing.

Turtle stands there, uncertain what to say.

"I'm sorry I said that, what I meant was that—"

"I know what you meant," Turtle says.

"Well, I didn't mean to say that," Anna says, "that came out wrong—I just mean, if you try, you

can do this. You just need to throw some gump-
tion at it."

"Is that what you think?"

"You'll be good at it. Just try."

"I **do** try."

"No you don't," Anna says, and then immediately bites her lip. "Shoot," she says, "I mean
that—"

"No, it's fine," Turtle says.

"It's not fine, I'm sorry, Julia— Jeez, this is not
my day! What I meant is, you need to commit to
it, and not be frustrated or alienated from it. Because I think you come to school and you think
you're bad at school and so you **are** bad at school.
But you're not bad at school." Anna reaches out
impulsively and grabs Turtle's hands. Holding
them, she says, "Just **try.** Just **try.**"

"Okay," Turtle says.

Anna lets go instinctively. "Sorry," she says.

"It's okay."

"Sorry," Anna says again. "I'm just not supposed
to touch students."

"You're a bitch. Do you know that?"

Anna looks more hurt than Turtle could think
possible. Her face closes and Turtle is miserably
sorry.

"Yeah," Anna says. "Well, I like you a lot, Julia."

Turtle says, "Can I ask you something?"

Anna walks over to one of the pressure-treated
beams that line the road. She sits down. She puts

her elbows on her knees. She looks out at the prairie. She says, "What's that?"

"Do you know if I can take a high schooler to the dance?"

"What?"

"Can I take a high schooler to the dance?"

"Sure," Anna says. "They have to be under seventeen and you have to have parental permission."

"There's a boy I'd like to take to the dance," Turtle says. She reaches down, picks up a stalk of sour grass, sticks it in her mouth. It is tart and crisp and crunches audibly.

"Who's that?"

"Is it just a paper my dad has to sign?"

"Yes," Anna says. She watches Turtle very carefully.

"You think my dad hits me," Turtle says.

"I worry about you. You show a lot of classic signs. Watchfulness. Isolation from peers. Misogyny."

"What is misogyny?"

"Hatred of women."

"He doesn't hit me," Turtle says. She watches Anna to see if Anna believes her, and herself, she believes it and cannot bear that there should be people out there in the world who could believe otherwise.

"Do you know that my mom died?"

"Yes."

"She died and I guess he never really got over it."

Anna is staring at her. Turtle thinks, I cannot think

of a time he ever hurt me, and she cannot. She thinks, and what was that with the knife? And she thinks, that was nothing, and the knife was nothing, it is just a knife, and it means nothing about care or about who you will grow up to be.

"I know how he is," Turtle says. "He's still hurt. He hurts pretty badly. But he's never laid into me."

"Okay," Anna says.

"I know that you think he's hurt me," Turtle says, "and it's hard to talk to you because I know you're thinking that." Turtle is thinking, I don't know if my mother's death hurt me at all. She thinks, if it did, I cannot feel it, and I cannot feel the loss. I do not miss her and I do not want her back and I cannot feel anything about it, anything at all, and if I am hurt it is because Martin hurt me, but I could almost believe that it's the tragedy and not his cruelty. Then she thinks, you are corrupting who you are and once you start lying you'll keep on lying and you'll start seeing things out of convenience and once you're there it's hard to go back. That's what Grandpa always says. Maybe you get started twisting things around, you may never get them untwisted. Maybe it's like your hearing, it doesn't come back and each day there is less of you.

Anna is looking at Turtle very closely now, and Turtle can tell that it's almost as if she is telling the truth and that Anna does not quite know what to say. Anna is good at looking at a girl and gauging, but Turtle has it all almost out of her mind and it's like it's true and the truth of it is surprising to Anna. The truth and the way she's put it.

"Oh, Julia. I'm so sorry to hear that. That must be terribly hard."

"I thought you should know."

"Julia, you're amazing."

Turtle says nothing.

Anna says, "You're very unusual, do you know that? You have an unusual mind. Okay, okay, Julia, that is fair; that is fair, and that would be upsetting to have someone be suspicious. You are so incredibly smart. I can see that you love your father, and it would be upsetting for anyone to have those suspicions, and I want you to be able to talk to me, and I want to be able to be your teacher. So I hear you, that your father is grief-stricken, and that things are hard at home, but that there's no wrongdoing. I hear you and I respect that. But let me say this—"

"No."

"Let me say this," Anna says.

"Don't."

"If it ever goes badly, I will be there for you. You call me, or you show up, any time of the day or night. You give me a call from anywhere, I will come and pick you up, no questions asked. All right? And you can stay with me for as long as you need to and I won't even ask until you start talking, okay?"

"You're not listening," Turtle says. "That will never happen."

"I hope not," Anna says, "but I will be there. You hear me, don't you?"

"I hear you," Turtle says. "Do you hear me?"

"I hear you, and I believe you're telling the truth. But if for some reason you were lying to me, if you felt like you had to lie to me, you wouldn't need to be embarrassed. You could still call me and I'd never think less of you." Turtle thinks, you suspicious bitch. That's true, what I told you, that's all true, even I believe that it's true, and thinking this, she smiles at Anna, can feel herself smiling affectionately, as she always feels affection for people who are difficult for her, smiling and cracking her knuckles, and Anna says again, "I hear you." She leaves it at that for a moment, and then she looks askance at Turtle again, and she says, "Day or night, and I will make it happen for you, Julia."

Turtle sits there hating the other woman, thinking, you bitch, but smiling, self-conscious of this ugly expression on her own lean bitch face.

Anna says, "You want a ride to school?"

Turtle looks around, embarrassed. "Yes," she says.

They walk back down the road in near silence. It is windy, and the grass and coyote brush lie this way and that in the blusters. Anna's car is a blue Saturn with a kayak rack and kayak on top, the passenger side-view mirror duct-taped in place. There is a great blue heron standing on the hood of the car, better than four feet tall, blue-gray, with a shaggy chest and clean, slat-feathered wings. When it sees them, it takes to the air, rising up and flying along the headlands.

Anna gets in first, does something to unlock Turtle's door, and Turtle has to lift up a colander of purple grapes from the passenger seat while Anna moves piles of books and papers, and then Turtle gets in and pulls her door closed, but it will not latch. Anna picks up a bungee cord bolted to the floor and strings it across Turtle's legs to an eye-bolt drilled into the door. Stone fetishes bound in grass and rawhide thongs hang from the rearview mirror and jostle one another. The front seats are covered in beach towels. The backseat has been laid down and covered in plastic sheeting and there's a half-dried wetsuit laid in drifts of black sand. Anna tries the ignition several times before it catches. Then she puts the car in reverse, really bearing onto the stick shift, and they wait.

"What's happening?" Turtle says.

Then Turtle hears the gears engage and the car startles and lurches back. Anna puts the car into gear and they go trundling away over the potholed parking lot, the car popping and lurching with un-expected engine noises. Anna drives up Little Lake and parks in the teachers' lot. They sit together in the car for a moment, Turtle with the colander on her lap. She is looking around at the car. She thinks, it is a little like the house, miscared for, and then she thinks, but that isn't true, because the car feels like home, and I am not sure if that's how the house feels, exactly, and this car feels lived in, and I am not sure if that's how the house feels, either. She thinks, it's a strange thing, isn't it? I like things that are well and carefully cared for, but this is something else. She thinks, what is this holding on to the car long after it has fallen apart? She thinks, I like that, too. Finally Anna says, "Well, I'm not glad you ditched class, but I am glad we got to have this talk."

Turtle purses her lips, looks up at Anna. Anna wraps her hands around the steering wheel, unwraps them, rewraps them.

"What?" Turtle says.

The bell rings for recess, and the doors are swung wide and kids come pouring out. Turtle cannot see the greens from here, but she envisions students slinging backpacks off shoulders, sitting down to eat bag lunches and talk. Others are heading to the library or out to the field or the basketball courts.

"Go on," Anna says, "it's your recess."

"What?" Turtle says again.

Anna sighs. She looks over at Turtle. She says, "It's dumb. But you know Rilke is being bullied?"

Turtle nods.

"She's new to the district, and she's kind of a know-it-all and kind of a kiss-up." Anna sighs again, and Turtle watches her. It's a little shocking to think that what the students see, the teachers might see, too. Anna says, "Sometimes all it would take would be for someone to be like, 'Hey, that's not cool.'"

Turtle looks Anna up and down, incredulous. Anna looks away, and then looks back at Turtle and says, "It just makes me wistful, because if you could—you know, if you could find it in you to be there, sometimes, and just be like, 'Hey, stop that.' Those girls, they're cowards. I don't know that you've ever talked to your peers. I don't think you care about them, but they respect you, Julia. There is something about you. I know you don't have **friends**, not really, but they're aware of you. It's your attitude. You have this certain, this kind of— you're not a girl anyone would try bullying. You have presence, I guess. I think you could stop it with a word. And you need help with your spelling and Rilke could help you with that. It just seems like an opportunity." She looks at Turtle again.

Turtle has nothing to say.

That night, Turtle sits cross-legged with the AR-10 broken open before her and the bolt carrier gutted from the receiver, shining red in the fire-light, stripped of bolt and cam and firing pin. She's poured the carbon solvent into a lowball glass. It's indistinguishable from whiskey. Turtle dips her rag in it, thinking, what if Anna is right and I am afraid to fail? She thinks, is it strange that Anna would tell me what Martin has told me—that I am afraid to fail and for that reason, too afraid to try?

Is it strange that they would see the same thing in me, my hesitation, my paralyzing self-doubt? She thinks, you are bound to make mistakes, and if you are unwilling to make mistakes, you will forever be held hostage at the beginning of a thing, you have to stop being afraid, Turtle. You have to get in the practice of being swift and deliberate, or one day, hesitation will fuck you.

THE NEXT MORNING, she comes down the stairs and stands in the kitchen cracking eggs into her open mouth, and when Martin comes down the hall buttoning his flannel, she slings him a beer across the counter. He catches it, hooks it on the counter's edge, bangs the cap off.

"You don't have to walk me," she says.

He drinks, exhales, holds the bottle over his heart.

"Everything all right at school?"

She purses an egg open, drops the contents into her mouth, pitches the shell into the bucket.

During study hall, in Mr. Krebs's classroom, she touches the letters of her vocabulary words with a firing pin, turning the pin between thumb and forefinger. Behind her, Rilke is wearing her red London Fog coat, even though it's too warm for it. Elise is ahead of her, leaning in to talk to Sadie, all blond hair and cherry lip gloss, all sly looks and embroidered jeans and matching tank tops, Elise's red, Sadie's blue, Elise saying, "She is such a **bitch**. I mean, **for serious**, such a be-**yotch**. And, like—if you needed reasons—(a) of all, her dad is a **cop**, and (b) of all, her name should be pronounced Rilk**ey**, and (c) of all, she, like—does her hair with, like—**honey**, and, like, **jojoba oil**. I can't even—" Turtle waits to hear what Elise can't even—but this is the end of the idea. Elise can't even. Turtle feels lost. More than anything, lost, and uncaring, it's like looking at a vocab sentence that doesn't make sense: "Rilke does her hair with jojoba oil and Elise can't **even**." Turtle thinks, what is a jojoba? Some kind of whale? Elise is writing Rilke's name on a note she's composed, saying, "She stuffs them. You just **know** she stuffs them. Like, her mom bought her that push-up bra so that the **boys** would like her, because her mom doesn't realize that **no one** likes her and that everybody can see how fake and ugly her fake, stuffed boobs are"—folding the note, creasing it with her thumb, applying her lipstick and kissing it, tauntingly, delightedly—"walking around everywhere with her stuffed bra stuck out in front of her like she's a **princess**. But I've seen them. They're **nothing**. They're **sad**. They're itty-bitty baby titties, **shrunken** and **gross** with black hairs all around the nipples." Sadie is laughing helplessly behind her hands. "You just know she stays up at night **crying** because they're so mean to her **at school**, and combing jojoba oil into her nipple hairs, probably, so they'll be silky smooth for **Anna** to suck on." Turtle has the Sig Sauer in the small of her back and she wears her flannel for this reason. The note is held out between two fingers like a cigarette and it goes hand over hand to the back of the class, where Rilke unfolds it and stoops over it and reads. She bends farther and farther forward and she makes no sound. She wears that coat, Turtle thinks, because she's embarrassed.

That afternoon Turtle stands on the last step of the porch with the chamber of the shotgun open and smoking, cardboard placards pegged into place at intervals in the yard, each with their cluster of buckshot, Martin sitting in the Adirondack chair. Turtle says, "I'd like to go to the dance."

Martin rubs his thumb along his jaw, still looking at her.

"I'd like to go dress shopping with you," she says. She looks back at him, and she thinks, I hope you understand what you and I have together, the two of us here on this hill, and I hope that is enough for you, I hope it is enough for you, because it is everything to me.

He says nothing and she lays the gun on the balustrade and walks out to the yard. She collects the cardboard placards and carries them back to the porch. She leans over them and measures the spread with a tape measure, noting the round in a notebook, the spread, and the distance in five-yard increments. Martin watches her with a book open in his lap. When she has written the numbers down, she collects the notebook and the shotgun and goes inside and up to her room. She closes the door and leans against it. She takes out Jacob's T-shirt and lays it over the floorboards. There is nothing, she thinks, except the thing itself. The shirt is stiffened in places with dry mud and it smells of leafy green thimbleberries and, too, it smells of Jacob, and she thinks, I am undivided in my intention and in my purpose, but she does not know half of what she does, or why she does it, and she does not know her own mind.

Turtle dreams of falling. Falling, and of the shotgun going off in her hands, and it is that feeling, that lurch, that shocks her awake, sitting upright in bed, silent, breathing hard, listening to a distant ringing, the sound of her auditory cells dying. The house smells of damp wood and eucalyptus. The sleeping bag is rucked and sweaty, black in places from grease. She waits, lowering herself slowly and silently back to the platform. He opens the door and she is careful not to move. The moonlight casts the window's rectangle on the floor.

He moves to pick her up, his hands callused and dry, and she twists in his grip, making a small mewing sound, and he takes ahold of her and hauls her out of the sleeping bag, spilling her onto the floor, and there she lies. He does not say anything for a moment, does not touch her or reach out to her, but kneels beside her in the dark.

She can feel him overestimating and misinterpreting her resistance, in the way he has, reading too much, but she is mute for hateful and reckless reasons, thinking, let him read too much in it then, let him think it goes deeper than it does. She lies looking at how the floor goes on, moonlight cast from the window and faint firelight cast from the door. He rises and walks across the room and stands before the window, looking out at the dark hillside.

She does not herself know what is wrong with her, but she feels it, and she will not admit that she does not know where the feeling comes from, or if it is right, so she continues to lie mute and unmoving, holding on to a grievance she cannot articulate, cannot even hold in her mind. She wishes she could tell Anna that he didn't make her this way. That he didn't make her fearful, isolated, girl-hating.

"What is it?" he asks, turning around, going down on one knee, tucking her hair back behind her ear. "What is it?"

She grits her teeth.

"Come on," he says, his voice dangerously impatient, and this hardens her resolve. "Talk to me," he says, still kneeling. She lies unmoving. "Kibble," he says, "don't play this game with me."

When she doesn't respond, he gets up, walks over to her bed. Her guns on wall pegs. Her wool blankets neatly folded. The sleeping bag unzipped. He lifts the sleeping bag up, lifts each blanket, weighing them in his hands. He walks around the bed, sits down at its foot. He opens the steamer trunk. Turtle sits up in alarm. "Ahh," he says, pursing his lips into a thin line. He leans over, stirs through the contents of the trunk, and then he lifts out the T-shirt. Holding it as if he doesn't know what it is, he brings it to his face and smells it. Turtle watches him from her position on the floor. He rises and walks out the door, holding the shirt draped over one arm, and for a moment she does nothing. Then she vaults up and runs after him, shrieking, "No, Daddy, no!"

She follows him out into the muddy yard. The motion-activated lights switch on, showing the flooded wash of driveway and the blackness beyond, the mud squelching up between her toes and the grass icy on her feet. Her father walks to the fifty-gallon drums where they burn trash and he reaches beneath the flooded brim and draws out the fire poker, his arm sheathed in ashen water, and he holds the dripping poker at the full extension of his arm with the shirt tangled on the spur. He has a bottle of butane in the other hand and hoses the shirt up and down, saying nothing at all, and she runs to him and throws herself on him, battering his chest with her fists. He squares his feet and endures this while the T-shirt wicks up the butane. Then he tosses open the Zippo and touches the flame to the dirty white scrap. The shirt goes up with a gasp and Turtle stops and watches the cloth blacken and scraps of char rise up through the air around them, cupping small bright embers. They gyre briefly and then fall, littering the grass and the mud, winking out. The shirt has burned incompletely and he flicks it contemptuously off the spur and into the water. It sits for a moment on the surface, then sinks.

"You are **mine**," he says, and swings the fire poker around and strikes her on the arm and she pitches onto her stomach in the mud, her left arm numb, her shoulder broken-feeling, and she tries to rise, gets one hand under herself and heaves up and he plants his boot on the small of her back and drives her to the ground. He raises the poker into the air, and she thinks, get away, get away, Turtle, for your life **get away**, but she is pinned in place by his boot and she thinks, you have to—you have to, but she cannot move, and he brings the fire poker down onto the back of her thighs, and she bucks, spasms.

"**Mine**," he says, his voice breaking. She rakes up handfuls of mud, tries to haul herself out from beneath his boot and cannot. She cannot let him bring the poker down on her again, she cannot. Her body is filled with pain. It is the only thing she can think of, and in her mind, she repeats it over and over—no, no, no, no—and her helplessness is the only thing, locking up her entire brain with mindless panic, and he does not even seem to care, leaning over her, bearing down with his heel. "You are mine," he says, "you little bitch, you are **mine**."

"Please, Daddy," she says, wrapping her hands together as if in prayer, laying her face into the mud, "don't, please don't, please, Daddy, **don't**." She cannot get a good look at him out of the corner of her eye, his figure stooped, hesitating, and she waits and thinks that he is done, and then she sees him raise his arm and the terror is like biting into a live wire, unendurable, and he brings the poker down hard onto her thighs and her body locks and bucks.

"Please," she says.

"Listen, Julia Alveston. Listen," he says, and he thrusts the poker forward so that the spur catches below her jawline, and he uses the hook to lift her face from the mud. "If you think I have not seen how you are **different**. If you think I have not seen you pulling away. If you think I have not had my suspicions."

"No," she says.

"You are mine," he says, and tosses the poker into the ashen water and steps away from her. "Get up," he says. Turtle struggles. She gets a hand under herself, goes onto a knee. "Get the fuck up," he says very quietly. She does not think she is going to be able to stand, and then she thinks, get your feet under you, Turtle. Get them under you. She rises, gripping the side of the trash barrel, white-knuckled.

"That's right, you fucking **stand**," he says to her. She straightens. "Go back to your room," he says, "and if we ever have this conversation again, if I ever see so much as an ounce of hesitation in you, of doubt, believe you me, I will **fuck** you with that poker." She starts limping away. With difficulty, she makes it up the porch steps. Martin says, "And, kibble?"

She stops. She isn't able to turn. It is all she can do to stay standing. He says, "Don't ever let yourself go down like that again. You understand? I don't care if you get hit by a fucking **truck**. You land on your feet. You hear me, kibble?"

She nods tiredly. She walks back in through the open sliding glass door, and she starts up the stairs, leaning against the wall with her good shoulder, making soft noises of pain. She limps to her room, shuts the door, and very slowly lowers herself onto her bed. She closes her eyes, and the dark blooms red and golden behind her eyelids. She thinks, this is me. This is me. This is who I am, and this is where I live. She thinks, my daddy hates me. Then she thinks, no, that's not fair. She goes to sleep thinking of it.

When dawn touches her window with gray light, Turtle struggles off the bed. She braces against the steamer trunk, bent over, breathing painfully through clenched teeth, but she stays on her feet. She thinks, I will not fall down. She takes measured and difficult steps to the doorway. She makes it down the stairs only with great difficulty, one step at a time, grimacing. Martin is standing in the open kitchen door, looking out on the back deck, as she comes into the kitchen. She opens the fridge and takes out her carton of eggs and a beer. She turns and pitches him the beer underhand. He catches it and opens it on his teeth, grimacing as he bites down on the cap. He stands drinking and holds it against his chest. Turtle lifts an egg, cracks it into her mouth, discards the shell into the compost. Martin comes over and proffers her the beer. She drinks and cuffs at her mouth. He accepts it back and drinks and exhales with the pleasure of it. She crosses painfully to her back-pack, kneels down, and with great difficulty pulls on her old combat boots. She struggles with the sliding glass door, using only her right hand, and walks down the driveway to the bus. He follows her out and down onto the bottom of the drive. They stand by the road together.

"You don't have to come," she says.

"Yeah," he says.

In the near-silence of the morning, she leans against the mailbox, snuffling and grimacing. When the bus does arrive, her limping gait draws looks from both sides of the aisle. She moves carefully, putting her hands on the backs of the seats. She passes Rilke, and Rilke turns around and looks and says, "Julie? Are you all right?"

Turtle stops, hate climbing up through her,

hate that Rilke—who is beautiful, who has lovely straight hair softened and glossy with honey and jojoba oil, whose parents love her and who has all the bobby pins and lip gloss and things she could ever need, Rilke for whom everything comes so easily, Rilke who is going to go on to high school, no question, and who will intrigue Jacob and Brett and everyone else with her shining little intellect and her bright little pens and her careful, studious way of doing things, this Rilke, whose life is **enchanted**, who is blessed above Turtle by the inscrutable order of things, Turtle hates that this Rilke should see her weak and tired, should see that her daddy hates her, should see that Turtle will never have a boyfriend, will never have anything, and so Turtle turns slowly and looks at Rilke, her face a rictus of disgust and scorn, and she says, "What do you know about it, sugar tits?"

A ripple of laughter runs down the bus, among people who were listening, and Turtle sees the succession of confusion to anger and then to hurt, and Rilke wraps her hands around herself, pulling her red coat up onto her shoulders, and she bends over her book, opening her mouth as if to say something, and not coming up with anything to say.

Turtle turns and walks away, and she thinks, that's not me, that's not who I am, that is Martin, that is something Martin does—his knack for finding the thing you hate about yourself and giving it a name. She thinks, Christ, that was so much more like Martin, derisive, condescending, than it was like me. She limps down the aisle, sits, and crushes her face into the vinyl seat ahead of her. She thinks, this is the part of him I hate most, the part that I revile, and I reached for it and it came easy. Christ, she thinks, Christ. Then she thinks, so what, so what if I am a misogynist. I never liked women anyway.

Anna stands at the front of the class and says, "Number one. 'Exacerbate.' Spell, define, and use in a sentence, please." Turtle puts pen to paper. She thinks, you are no good at this, and then she thinks, what if you never got knocked down and you always did your best to stand up and instead of being a little bitch you fought for it, and she thinks, you have Grandpa's knife and he never would've given it to you if he didn't think you were a fighter and not a coward, even if you have been a coward and will be again, maybe that is not all you will ever be, and what if you never let anyone knock you down, and she thinks, it would take a great deal of courage to be more than Martin believes I can be. Maybe I don't have to be what he thinks I am and maybe he would hate me anyway. Maybe he will hate me and love me whatever I do and it doesn't much matter. What are you thinking for, the difference is that today you have studied and you are ready for it and you never studied before, and heroism never got anyone anywhere unless they'd already done the work. She thinks, poor

Turtle, your life is so hard. Why don't you cry about it? She thinks, why don't you go away and cry and never do anything to make it better and never see Jacob again and then you can just cry and cry like the little bitch you are. She puts her pen to paper and writes:

> 1. Exacerbate. Make a problem worse. Being a cowardly little bitch only ever exacerbates the situation.

She smiles at her paper and looks up at Anna, still smiling. Turtle thinks, you see, all you have to do is stop failing. She thinks, oh, you'll like this sentence, Anna. Oh, you'll like it.

In front of the classroom, Anna says, "'Recalcitrant.' Please spell and define and use in a sentence. **Recalcitrant**." Turtle writes:

> 2. Recalcitrant. Stubbornly resistant to authority. I am a recalcitrant student and it's done me very little good, but elsewhere it has been good for me and that's made it hard to quit.

For the rest of the test, Turtle writes with focus and pleasure. When they are finished, they trade tests, Turtle handing her paper to Taz, and at the first question, Taz raises his hand. He says, "Anna?

I am not sure if this example sentence is appropriate." He looks at Turtle. "I'm not sure if it works."

Anna stands at the front, eyebrows raised, waiting to hear it.

"I'm not sure if I should read it," Taz says.

Anna walks over, stoops over Taz's shoulder. She laughs. She looks at Turtle. She says, "Yes, Taz. I see what you mean. She's used the word correctly, so let's give her full credit, and, Julia, I will need you to stay after class."

Turtle knows already that she won't. If she stays, Anna will notice how injured she is.

"What did she write?" Elise asks.

"Yeah," Rilke says, "what's the sentence?"

Anna looks up and around at her students, and she says, "Never mind. Next word. 'Recalcitrant.' Anyone?" Turtle keeps looking back at Taz to see how she has done, watching as Taz, lips pursed, makes a **C** for **Correct** next to each word and, at the top, writes, 15/15. Turtle looks back at Anna, a quick triumphant look, and she thinks, you see, you bitch, you whore, but she stops there because Anna has believed in her the whole way and it was only Turtle who did not believe in herself, and even if Turtle doesn't like Anna, she will not tell lies about her. Well, she thinks. You were right, I guess, but it doesn't mean I like you. When the bell rings, Anna collects the tests and walks back to her desk, bent over the stack reading and grinning. With all of the students standing up and dragging backpacks from beneath desks, Turtle stands up and limps into the crush of them and walks out before Anna can stop her.

That night, she lies on the Persian rug in front of the fire, propped on one elbow, reading the next week's vocabulary words. The fire is the heart of the room, the edges dark to Turtle's light-dazzled eyes, a two-inch gap between the hearthstones and the floor because the house, on its redwood piers, has drifted away from the fireplace over time. Above her, Martin is staring into the flames. His attention is fixed, his pupils shrunken to pinpricks, his face as weathered as an ancient burl.

Turtle bends again over her spelling work. Then she stops and turns to watch as two brown salamanders, speckled gold, crawl from the fire. They make their careful, clumsy way across the hearthstones, slow and seeming unharmed. Turtle looks once at Martin and then back down to the salamanders. She scoops them up and carries them in wet slithering handfuls out the door and through the fields to the woodpile battened with tarps. She stoops and lays them down among the logs, where they resume their crawling. All around her, in the gulch and in the field, the frogs are chorusing. She looks back at the house, where the firelight plays a dim glow across the window, and she looks out toward the dark ocean and the highway, hidden from her by the curve of the hill.

Eleven

TURTLE FINDS GRANDPA WAITING BY THE
side of the school office, leaning against the clapboard, wearing jeans and his little leather slippers
with their little leather tassels and his big Carhartt
jacket with a bagged bottle of Jack in the pocket.
A stream of middle schoolers is pushing past him
onto the front lawn, where the buses will arrive.
Rilke is making a dash from the library to the
bus, attended by cries of "Hey, sugar tits!" Turtle limps over to her grandpa. They stand in an
eddy between two buildings. He looks down at
her and wraps a hand around her shoulders and
pulls her to him. Turtle grimaces in pain, breathes
into his chest, his smoky flannel shirt, his long

johns. There is a coffee stain on his left breast. In his breast pocket, the butterscotch hard candies he likes. A week has passed since the beating, but the bruises are still there, and Turtle is ashamed of them. He is wearing a trucker's hat that reads VETERAN and she reaches up and pulls it off him and onto her own head.

"Well, hey, sweetpea," he says.

"Hey," she says, looking up at him, smiling, pulling the hat brim up and off to the side. She isn't surprised to see him, but still, it's bad. This is what he does when she doesn't come to the trailer. He goes to the little shingle-front Village Spirits at the base of the hill and then he drives up to the middle school and waits by the wall so she's got to come past him to get to the bus. He never lets her go very long.

He leads her to his rusted Chevy out in the teachers' lot. She is limping. Grandpa doesn't observe it. Rosy jumps up and shows her happy, stupid face in the driver's-side window. "Oh, you old girl," Grandpa says, opening the door while Rosy runs around on the bench seat, licking her own face. Turtle climbs in and sets her backpack in the footwell. In the drink holders, Grandpa has a Big Gulp cup of sunflower seeds and a bottle of Tabasco. Rosy scrambles awkwardly into Turtle's lap, wagging her tail in excitement. Her nails are dirty and untrimmed.

"How is school?" Grandpa asks.

"School's fine," she says. Grandpa puts the truck in gear and they pull out and go down Little Lake Road, beneath cypress hedgerows, make a left at the intersection, and start down the Shoreline Highway. Turtle bends forward under the seat and pulls out the jumper cables and old sweaters and under that a .357 revolver in a leather holster. She tosses open the cylinder, spins it, sights down the bore, and tosses the cylinder closed. Grandpa opens his coat and pulls out the Jack in a paper bag, seats it between his legs, unscrews the cap, and takes a drink.

"Did you ever get around to asking that boy out to the dance?"

"No," she says.

He looks back at her. "No?" he says.

"No," she says.

"That's not good," he says.

"I fucked up," she says.

They drive out of town, across Big River Bridge, and follow Highway 1 past Van Damme beach. They're going back to Buckhorn Cove. It's only four miles—a six-minute drive, but it will take them longer. Grandpa takes the turns slowly, the paper bag gripped between his legs. He always drives slowly when he's drunk. On the beach, a solitary girl in a wetsuit is dragging a kayak across the shingle and Turtle thinks of Anna.

"Fucked up how?" he says, looking at her.

"Spineless is all," she says.

"You're not spineless. You may be some other things, but you aren't spineless."

"Chickened out."

"Is there still time?"

Turtle leans out the window. The dance is in a week. Her hair whips and tangles and hangs back in streamers. She squeezes off three shots at a deer-crossing sign, putting two shots into the buck's black body and a third near it.

"Don't fire from the car, sweetpea," Grandpa says without heat.

"How was Martin when he was my age?" she asks.

"A wild child. Always getting in some trouble or other, and there was no stopping him. I tell you what, though. He loved your mother, **boy**, he loved her more than anything. This pasty scrap of a girl. Helena. Well, yes. **Helena**, and everybody called her Lena." Grandpa nips from the bottle.

They pull off onto a turnout just below Buck-horn Hill, just at the bottom of their driveway. Grandpa stomps the parking brake and shuts off the truck. He climbs out and holds the door open for Rosy, saying, "Come on, come on," while Rosy gapes at him and shakes herself excitedly every time he says "come."

Turtle fetches up an orange bucket from the truck bed and goes with Grandpa down the sandstone trail onto the beach, the cliffs forested in the thin, tilted stalks of columbines. Slaughterhouse Creek pours from a culvert into a muddy wallow where the trapped bull kelp is bleached colorless and soft as overcooked noodles. In the surf, the large round blue cobbles called bowling balls knock together.

Grandpa has to coax Rosy onto the beach, clapping his hands on his knees and saying, "Come on, girl!" Each time he claps, Rosy lurches forward, but thinks better of it. When finally she jumps off the trail and onto the sand, she runs a quick, excited circle around the two of them.

They labor through the sand together. Out in the cove is an island overgrown with buckwheat and paintbrush, undercut by sea caves, pierced by a blowhole that geysers white water high into the air. She and Grandpa have been coming to this beach ever since Turtle can remember. This is where her mother died, and somewhere out there her bones are grinding among the cobbles. Turtle looks back at Grandpa. The wind picks up his fine gray hair and tosses it in the air. He is frowning severely, not because he is unhappy, but because his jowls pull his face down this way.

They climb onto a stone causeway that runs out into the surf, standing just above the water. The stone is the pitted black of cast iron and old tide pools have left crusted rings of salt. Springs from the sandstone bluffs above leach out across it in trails of shaggy green algae, where minute frogs watch the ocean. At its tip, this long arm of rock is capped with a forest of knee-high sea palms. They walk until they come to a deep well in the rock filled with churning water, linked to the ocean by narrow subterranean passages.

The pool is six feet across, eighteen feet deep, shaggy with purple coralline algae and knobbed with mussels, the cracks crowded with crabs, the biggest of them six inches from elbow to elbow and the smallest dime-sized, black-striped and pink-clawed, their every knuckle and joint gristly yellow. When waves leave them exposed, they click their yellow-bearded jaws and burble water.

Grandpa and Turtle sit at the pool's edge and look down into its shady depth. Rosy hobbles around the rock for a moment and then, exhausted, flops down beside Turtle, showing her pink belly covered in bristly fur. Turtle begins to grub for fleas, picking them out and flicking them into the well, where they lie breaking dimples in the gin-blue surface and kicking tiny, spastic circles until a sculpin rises from the unseen dark and plucks them down. He looks as ancient as the world itself—with massive, frowning jaws, their joints standing out from the structure of his face, his eyes enormous and speculative, half hooded. Turtle wonders if he can feel the cold undertow from the caves below, and if so, whether he's ever followed those dark tunnels down into the black, where every anemone would reach out her sticky, gently-glowing tentacles and where he could see the whole awful and unlighted understructure of his world.

Grandpa holds out his hand. "How's that old knife, sweetpea? Is she taking care of you?"

Turtle looks sullenly down into the pool for a long moment. Finally she draws the knife, flips it to exchange her grip from hilt to blade, and extends it hilt-first to Grandpa. He leans over, takes it, and examines the steel blade scored from the grinder. He tests it with his thumb. He says, "Well, now. Well, now." There are rust pits along the spine.

She wants him to understand that she values the knife, and that she'd **meant** to take care of it. She wants him to know that. "I'm sorry about the edge," she says.

Grandpa shrugs, as if it's of no consequence, his face holding, in some subtle way, his hurt, a kind of resigned and complicated sense of injury and disillusionment, looking past her out at the waves, blinking like an old man.

She thinks about telling him how Martin took it away from her and put it to the grinder, but she says nothing, because there is nothing that she can say, and because excuses and explanations have never impressed her grandpa. She suspects that he can look at the knife and know more or less what happened. She goes on rubbing Rosy's stomach and Rosy lifts a leg to let her get into it better, the leg kicking faintly.

Grandpa says, "That old dog, oh Rosy, you have no dignity at all, do you? Look at her. Look at you, Rosy, you slut—turn back over." Rosy lifts her head up and rolls her eyes around to look at Turtle and twice tries to lick Turtle's arm before falling back.

Grandpa hands the knife back to her, hilt-first. Turtle sheaths it, thick with humiliation. Then she rises, picking up the bucket. Grandpa stays sitting, looking down into the pool, and says, "Listen, sweetpea, it doesn't matter, what matters is— My god, look at that **monster**."

Turtle turns and follows Grandpa's gaze. At the well's bottom, an enormous crab has emerged, as big as a dinner plate, struggling across the weedy bottom, waving his claws upright in the water.

"By god," Grandpa says, "you ever see a crab like that?"

Turtle brings her shirt up over her arms, un-buckles her pants, steps out of them, and dives into the cold water. She can hear Grandpa yelling at her, but she goes down into the gathering pressure and turbulence. She can feel the currents of cold water from sucking passages in the rock around her. Painfully, she kicks her legs, going down, and then she opens her eyes into the stinging green murk. She can just make the crab out, shadowed and dis-torted, trundling sideways across the rock, and she pursues it, kicking her feet to stay pressed down against the bottom, and then she lays her hands on the cold, crisp shell, somersaults in the water, and surges upward into her own plume of hair, up

along a passage of black rock, pitted and winding, gaping windows alternately fountaining water
or sucking it back, the weeds moving rhythmically in and out with this labored breathing, some
trick of the light making the pool's surface into
a shifting mirror, and though she should look
up and see her grandpa bent over the pool, she
cannot. She can only see the dark tunnel going
up and up and then opening as if into another
world, a hoop of heaving, splashing silver as alien
to her as the heart of a star. It is as if that reflective
hoop were a hatch, and she could burst through it
into another life.

She closes her eyes and gropes up with only the
remembrance of what she has seen, creating in
the mind that shifting pane of silver, and then she
heaves up through it, gasping in the bright day,
surrounded on all sides by black rock, and away
from her, the ocean booming against the cliffs and
the cobbles grinding in the surf. Above, Grandpa
and Rosy, side by side, lean over the edge, both
of them with identical expressions of surprise and
fear, raised eyebrows and open mouths, both of
them with wide, alertly darting eyes.

Grandpa says, "In here, sweetpea, in here," and
holds the bucket out for her. Turtle drops the
crab into the bucket, breathing hard, grinning
crookedly. "Well, look at him," Grandpa says,
stepping back, and Rosy, too, ducks away from the
edge. "That's a lot of crab right there, a hell of a lot

of crab." Turtle is neck-deep in the roiling water, her hair slicked to her head, as sleek as a seal. Her legs hurt. She holds on to the side of the pool and paddles as little as she can, staying deep enough to keep her purple and green shoulder underwater.

Grandpa looks back at her and says, "You get some mussels and we'll call that dinner." He hands her the knife and she takes it and passes it into her teeth, clenching down on the spine and holding it this way. She grips the mussels in one hand and cuts through the hairy holdfasts with the other. When the bucket is a quarter full, she passes it up to Grandpa, and then boosts herself out of the well, dripping water and rising to a stand in her pink panties, the knife in her teeth.

Grandpa gets unsteadily to his feet, knees popping, and says, "Julie, turn around."

Turtle says, "What?"

"Julie, what is this?" He comes toward her, touches her arm where the bruise from the fire poker is a black and green line, the first blow that Martin struck to knock her down.

"It's just a bruise, Grandpa," she says.

"Turn around," he says.

"Grandpa," she says.

"Turn around, sweetpea," he says.

She turns around, and he says, "Jesus Christ."

"They're just bruises."

"Jesus Christ. Jesus Christ," he says.

"Grandpa, it's nothing, it doesn't matter."

"Jesus Christ," he says, lowering himself shakily back down onto the rock.

She walks to her jeans, picks them up, and unfurls them. She begins pulling them on with rough jerks.

He says, "What are those bruises?"

"They're just bruises," she says.

"What from?"

"It's nothing," she says, "really."

"Christ, they look like they're from an iron rod."

"It doesn't matter."

"Jesus Christ," he says.

She buttons her jeans, zips them closed.

"Grandpa," she says, "I don't care, it doesn't matter. Really."

"What is that from?"

"Nothing," she says, "it doesn't matter. Really."

"All right, sweetpea," he says, getting up with difficulty, "let's take you home."

They walk back to the truck, Turtle limping badly, her wet legs sticking to her jeans, her panties standing in sodden outline through the denim, the sloshing bucket banging against her knees. Rosy gallops ahead and then galumphs back to stand stiff-legged before them, grinning sloppily.

"You old pooch," Grandpa says.

They follow the path back up to the highway, and Turtle sets the bucket into the footwell and gets in. The crab crawls around on top of the harvested mussels. Grandpa coaxes Rosy back into the truck with some difficulty, and then gets in himself. He starts the engine and then sits with it idling and leans back and wraps and rewraps his hands on the wheel and says, "Jesus Christ."

They pull onto the highway and drive fifteen feet and then turn up the rutted gravel drive to the house, the truck surging and lurching out of ruts, the crab clacking around in the bucket, while Rosy curls up, exhausted, watching Turtle with small supplicatory motions of her eyebrows. Grandpa takes a long draw on the Jack Daniel's and drives with one hand, sometimes looking over at Turtle, who sits with her hands clasped between her legs, looking out the passenger-side window at the field and the shore pines.

When they reach the Y where Grandpa's dirt road goes off just beneath the apple orchard to the raspberry fields and the other road goes up to the house, Grandpa stops. Turtle takes the bucket and gets out. Grandpa leans toward her and says, "Tell Martin I'm going to come to dinner." Turtle stands beside the truck. She cannot remember Grandpa ever coming for dinner. She just nods.

Then he drives away, and Turtle stands holding the bucket and watching him go. She picks up her boots, tied together at the laces, and yokes them over her neck. Then she limps away up the hill, the bucket bouncing against her leg, thinking, you cunt, you reckless, you reckless, reckless, reckless.

Twelve

THERE ARE GREEN TIDE LINES SCRAWLED on the porcelain of the tub, claw-footed and enormous. The copper fixtures and pipes are plumbed into crude holes in the redwood boards, ragged apertures gone to cobwebbed spider dens filled with cotton-ball egg sacs and the husks of spiders, haunted by one enormous black widow, so bloated that when she goes across the floor, she drags her bulk behind her and leaves trails in the dust, a creature Martin likes to call "that poisonous bitch Virginia Woolf."

Above the tub, a picture window looks down into Slaughterhouse Gulch, the pines hung with lichen, the blackberries clambering up from the sword ferns. The window is poorly sealed, the lintel pulpy and black with rot. Red mushrooms grow along the sill. Their caps are patched white from their broken cauls.

She hears him set the groceries on the kitchen table and then come into the bathroom. He sits on the wooden chair beside the sink with two bottles of Old Rasputin held loosely in one big hand. She settles into the tub so only her head is above the surface, hiding her purple and green shoulder.

He sighs and hooks the bottle caps over the chair's arm and bangs them open one after the other with the flat of his hand. Then he props his boots on the edge of the tub, looking past her and into the pines of Slaughterhouse Gulch, and seats one beer between his thighs and holds the other out to her. He nods encouragingly. She takes it and drinks from the bottle, looking at him sideways and resentful. He sits gathering his thoughts, raking the pads of his fingers across his stubble with a discontinuous rasping. He says, "Kibble, I fucked up. All right?"

She leans back deep in the tub and considers him.

He says, "Kibble . . . I am sometimes not a well person. You know, I try, for you." He clasps, unclasps his hands, displays his palms.

She says, "How are you not well?"

He says, "Well, kibble, it runs in the blood, I guess."

She drinks again from the beer, shovels wet strands of hair back from her face. She loves him. When he looks like this, and she can see how he tries for her, even his hurt has value to her. She cannot bear that anything should disappoint him, and if she could, she would wrap him up in her love. She sets the beer down among the mushrooms. She wants to tell him, but she doesn't have it in her.

Turtle says, "Grandpa says he wants to come for dinner."

"Oh, that's good, that's good," Martin says. "I brought home some cattle bones and I saw the mussels and that big goddamn crab. We have enough for a feast."

Turtle dollops shampoo into her palm. She lathers it into her hair.

"Kibble," he says, "you're just a goddamn beautiful human being. Look at you."

Turtle laughs, looking up at him with her mop of hair piled above her head, sudsy with shampoo. Daddy beckons her and she leans nearer and he puts his strong fingers in her hair and works the pads of them down her scalp. She closes her eyes, face presented up to the ceiling where cobwebs hang in sashes. "God, kibble," he says, lathering the shampoo, "you're the most beautiful thing in the world. I ever tell you that? Just the most beautiful thing." She extends her arms to the ceiling, stretching them, and the water goes in trembling drops down her forearms and into her armpits, and she thinks how good it is, the pleasure and the comfort.

Martin finishes lathering her hair and she lies

with her neck draped over the side of the tub looking up at the ceiling and he stoops over and kisses
first one eyelid, and then the other. He says, "I love
this eyelid, and this one." His kisses the bridge of
her nose. "And this nose." He kisses her cheek.
"And this face!" She wraps her sudsy arms over his
neck, his stubbly jaw against her naked one.

He pulls away and says, "Oh, kibble, I am so
sorry, so sorry."

"It's okay, Daddy," she says.

"You can forgive me?"

"Yes," she says, "I forgive you."

She sinks back into the water, thinking and recoiling inside about what will happen if Grandpa
tries to say what he's seen, and she knows she
should bring it up. Martin's every failing is a secret
between the two of them, and she feels that she's
violated that privacy. She can't bear that anyone
else should see something he's done wrong. She
rises out of the water, takes her hair in handfuls,
and wrings it.

She stands up out of the tub and sees her figure reflected in the picture window, Martin behind her, leaning forward in the chair, squinting,
scraping his thumb down the side of his jaw,
and both of them looking at her, long legs barred
black and green with bruises. She takes a towel
from the rack and wraps it around herself and
walks past him, her gait lopsided and short. He
turns to watch her go by, his left eye seeming sad-

der than the right, his face lined with love and sorrow, and she goes up the stairs to dress, filled in every pore with his love, big and happy with it, and thinking vengefully, come what may. She has to stoop to retrieve her clothing from the shelves, exhaling softly, painfully, and she dresses gingerly, taking a great deal of time, and when she is done she stands looking out her window, biting her lip. She thinks, no, it will come to nothing. Looking out at the hillside, in places a graceful sweep of timothy and wild oats, in others gone to pampas and weed trees, down by the road the blooming purple-white radishes. She cannot imagine how her life could change at all, she cannot imagine how this thing tonight could come to anything, she cannot imagine how it could go badly. Her whole life and its course, the people in it, it seems so immutable to her, and there may be difficulties and there may be words, but it will come to nothing.

She goes down the stairs and Martin is not in the kitchen. She finds him in the pantry, among the gun safes, the pegboard walls covered in tools, the steel shelves with crates of ammunition, boxes of shotshells, a pallet of clay pigeons stacked against the wall. She stands hipshot against the doorjamb. Martin plunges his hand into the dirty-pink water of the butcher's bucket, draws out the bloody cattle bones shedding water and sets them beside the table saw. He turns the saw on, and it rattles and then rises to a roar, and Martin feeds the bones into the saw blade one after another, pushing them gingerly through the course of the blade with thumb and forefinger, squinting into the spray of fine white dust and flecks of bloody water. The bones split apart and litter the tabletop and Martin keeps the saw running until he has cut each of the bones lengthwise. He carries them into the kitchen, rinses the bone dust off in the sink, lays them on a roasting pan, and slides them into the oven. Then he picks the live crab up with tongs and slides him in after. Turtle can hear the crab scuttling across the roasting pan. He empties the bucket of mussels into a blue enameled colander and begins to scrub their beards off, holding them in pairs and rak ing their sealed lips crosswise against one another, as if in some crude mimicry of kissing, his brow furrowed in repose. It is as happy as Turtle knows him to look, sometimes glancing at her and crinkling his eyes at her in pleasure. He pours cream and chicken stock into a skillet and sets it to simmering. He cuts scallions on the butcher block, grinds coarse black pepper with an ancient black pepper grinder, quarters and juices a lemon. He empties the colander of mussels into the skillet and leans against the counter and watches Turtle. He lays a second skillet over the top to steam the mussels open. They listen to the crab scrabbling inside the oven.

He finds a bread knife spotted with rust and then he stands, leaning against the counter, looking at it. "Well, goddamn," he says, "look at that, don't even use the damn thing and it's rusted." Turtle purses her lips. He toasts the bread in a stainless-steel frying pan. He preps a salad of radishes, garlic, scallions, and parsley, tossing them in lemon juice and olive oil and sea salt. They wait in silence, Daddy looking at the cooking mussels and Turtle cross-legged. After a while, he opens the oven and takes out the roasting pan and, with a pair of tongs, stacks the bones on the butcher block into a lattice, fetches the crab curled and dead from deep within the oven and sets it upside down beside the bones. He dishes the toast up and carries the butcher block to the middle of the table. Along the face cuts of the thighbones, the grease has seared into a gray-brown skin, while the marrow in the pipings is oily and liquid, boiling, making the skin ripple and crawl like something alive.

"Clean up this shit," he says to Turtle, and she rises and begins getting rid of the table's beer cans, shotshells, ashtrays, and the various books: **A Treatise Concerning the Principles of Human Knowledge, Being and Time**, and Barnes's **The Presocratic Philosophers**. In the kitchen, Martin pours the mussels into a deep bowl, and Turtle collects their mismatched silverware and deals it out, and Martin brings Bauer bowls and plates from a high shelf, thickly rimed with grease and dust. He cleans them with a rag, saying extravagantly, "Never let it be said that I didn't bring out the finest china for our learned patriarch, kibble, never let it be said!"

Turtle says, "That was a lot of cooking, Daddy."

"God knows," he says.

In another part of the house, a door opens. Not the sliding glass door that opens from the living room to the porch, the door through which Turtle and Martin come and go, but the huge oak front door with its cast-iron battens, which opens onto the foyer with the vaulted ceiling of dark redwood panels, the old chandelier, the walls hung with bear skulls. At the end of the hallway, an elk bust, one of the eyes fallen out. They listen to Grandpa walk through the foyer, turn down the hall, and then he appears in the doorway.

"Daniel," Daddy says, "I don't think you've ever used the front door before."

Grandpa says, "Listen, Martin—"

"Sit down," Daddy says, gesturing to a chair at the table. "I cooked those mussels for you. And next time—Dad, use the living room door, all right?"

Turtle doesn't think it's strange that Grandpa has come in through the front door. It's a formality that Turtle understands, and Martin understands, too, but has made a joke of it, as if it is a mistake and not a formality, and Turtle sits looking at him, hoping that he will not make a joke of Grandpa, seeing, too, that he wants this to go well, that he doesn't want Grandpa to be formal with them, and Turtle is afraid.

Grandpa looks from Daddy to Turtle, and Daddy shares a conspiratorial, joking expression with her. Turtle doesn't like how Grandpa looks there in the doorway. She thinks, come in. She thinks, don't be too hard, come in, Grandpa, and let it go. She knows that Grandpa doesn't have it in him to let it go, knows that he would lose everything in her eyes if he let it go, but that's all she wants from him. They would know that they were both of them spineless, but it would be okay at that. It's what Martin said was wrong with her, and it's what Anna said was wrong with her, that she's afraid of things, that she has hesitations, but even knowing this, Turtle is willing for that to be the way of it, let it be her failing and let Grandpa have the same spinelessness. Just let it be that way, the three of them eating dinner.

"Martin," Grandpa says.

"Good god, Dad, sit down and have something to eat," Martin says. "I thought these mussels were your favorite."

"You start without me." He says it grimly and reproachfully, and Turtle can see that he is letting nothing go.

"The hell—sit down, have some marrow."

Grandpa drags back a chair, sits in it. It seems to her that she has spent her entire life hoping that he was the man she believed he was, and not the man Martin believed him to be, and now she wants only for him to sit there and say nothing. Martin gestures to the lattice of bones, the grooved condyles like volute woodwork, the marrow crawling in the pipings, tendons glazed to the bone. "Have some marrow," he says again, shaving it up and spreading it across his toast. With a fork he lifts a small portion of radish and parsley, takes a shattering bite.

"Martin—listen," Grandpa says, leaning in, his arms on the table.

"No marrow? Can I get you a beer?"

"I don't want a beer."

"Let me get you a beer," her daddy says. "I always try and keep some of your beer around. I know you like that cheap tasteless shit. Good whiskey and shitty beer, that's Daniel Alveston."

"Sit down, goddamn it," Grandpa says. Martin goes to the fridge and opens it and stoops inside, looking for a beer. He comes back with a bottle of Bud Light and says, "See, I always keep some beer for you, Daniel." He bangs it open on the table's edge and Grandpa sits looking at him, hands crossed over his belly, his jowls deepening his frown into an impenetrable discontentment. Martin stands holding the beer out for Grandpa and the head runs over and down the sides of the bottle, but Grandpa will not take it. He says, "I don't want your beer, Martin."

Daddy puts the beer beside Grandpa's plate. He drags back his chair, sits. He says, "Well, the marrow isn't popular tonight, but you know, I tried."

"It's not the marrow," Grandpa says, looking at the crab with its dead legs in the air.

"I could make you a grilled cheese."

"I didn't come here to have dinner with you, Marty. Listen—"

"Listen—? Listen, hell. Drink your beer, Dad. You look silly with it just sitting there in front of you."

"Martin, you have to know, this is no way to raise a child."

"You motherfucker," Martin says, "you motherfucker. You think I don't know that? You **fuck**. You come **here**, to tell **me**, that **this**, **this** is no way to raise a child?"

Grandpa reaches for his beer and it pitches over, skitters across the table into Martin's lap with Martin snatching it up, saying, "What the—?" and fumbling the spuming bottle back into his lap, trying to stand and overturning his chair, almost going backward in it, then standing with beer dripping off his sleeves and off his shirt, the bottle rolling curlicues around the floor, knocking against the counter in time to the sloshing of its contents. Martin shakes off his wet hands, saying, "Christ! Christ!" He stalks to the kitchen, takes down the blue shop towels, spans them out, shears them off, pats at his sodden shirt, his soaking lap, pulls off his wet flannel and casts it across the dishes on the counter.

Grandpa says, "This is no way to raise a child, not like this."

"Christ," Martin says, looking down at himself.

"Martin," Grandpa says.

"What?" Martin says.

"This is no way to raise a child."

"Christ, Dad," Martin says, opening the fridge and taking out another beer. He bangs it open. "Christ," he says. "Tell me again, Dad. Tell me again how this is no way to raise a child."

"You've got to know it, Martin."

"I know it," Martin says, coming to the table, setting down the new beer. "Christ, Daddy," he says, still shaking foam off his hands, looking at his sodden shirt.

"Well, goddamn it, Martin," Grandpa says. "For fuck's sake, listen to me."

"I am doing the best that I can, Daniel. The best that I fucking can."

"Listen, Martin," Grandpa says, "it can't go on this way."

"Yeah?" Martin is composing himself. "Is that right, Dad?" He says it with some meaning Turtle does not understand, and Turtle looks quickly away from the table and says it again to herself, silent, framing his face, his expression, the tone, **Is that right, Dad?** wringing the meaning out of it, and then she looks quickly back to them.

Grandpa says, "And look at you, Marty. Just

look around you. You don't want your daughter to come up like this."

Martin looks at Grandpa, one of his eyes more lidded than the other.

"She could be a very fine young woman," Grandpa says.

Martin opens his mouth, looks aside, touching his jaw.

"Martin—"

"I know it, Dad."

"She can be—"

"Dad! I goddamn know it. Don't you think that's what I'm goddamn fighting for? Don't you think that's what I tell myself when I get up in the morning? Only take care of this girl and she will have more than you have, Martin, there will be more to her life. Her life will not be like yours. Only do right by her and it's all hers, the world, everything."

Grandpa sits scowling.

"You think I don't know that? You think I'm not fighting for that? With what meager fucking resources I have, Dad. With everything I've got, Dad. And I know it's not perfect, I know it's not even enough, it's not what she deserves, but I don't know what the hell you want me to do. I love her, and that is more than I ever, ever had from you."

Grandpa says, "Listen— There are bruises on that girl's thigh as deep as you please. Bruises. Black as you please. Bruises, Martin, that about look like you took to the girl with an iron rod. I ask you. I ask you, Martin."

"Shut up," Martin says.

Grandpa frowns severely, the flesh of his face yellowed, his jowls curtains of old-man flesh almost like rinds. He says, "I'm done letting you raise this girl, and if you know what's good for her, you are—"

"Shut **the fuck** up," Martin says. He scrapes at the table's edge with his thumb, and then he looks back at Grandpa. "You don't know what the **fuck**—"

Grandpa says, "There are bruises—"

"Shut the fuck up."

"It looks like you—"

"Go back to your trailer, old man." Martin gestures to Turtle. "You have no idea." He looks steadily at her. They all wait on his silence. "Apparently—neither do I. Nor she, I bet. Oh, she likes you. She loves you. Don't you, kibble?"

She is silent.

"Kibble—you love your grandpa?"

Turtle can hear the crab's legs creaking as they cool.

"Kibble?"

"I love him, Daddy."

"See—? See—? But you do not get to come here, reeking of whiskey, come here into my house and say she has bruises. You do not get to do that."

"Marty, you've got to want something different for Julia. Not this, Marty. Not this."

Martin sits raking his finger pads down his stubble. He says, "Well—**fuck**. I see kibble's got your knife now." He extends his hand and Turtle draws the knife off her belt and passes it to him. He hefts it. He says, "You know how many throats he slit with this knife?"

Turtle looks down at her plate.

"Forty-two, isn't that right?"

"Forty-two," Grandpa agrees.

"Korea, kibble. And at some point they put him to work in the DMZ tracking down infiltrators, and these poor fucks, these poor fucks had no idea that a bloodthirsty fucking psychopath from a wilderness a world away, a man whose forefathers hunted Indians in the American West, was out there just waiting in the weeds. How could you understand a thing like that? That was the most fun you ever had, I think."

Grandpa says nothing. His jaw tremors.

"He liked to come up behind some poor fuck, some fuck who's been forced into the war by governmental coercion and crushing socioeconomic pressure, and Daniel would come up behind him and just about take his head off with that knife. Isn't that right? Arm around the neck, raise the chin, and then right down through the big arteries on the left side. Isn't that right?"

"It was a war, Martin."

"And then they give you a shotgun and send you off to Vietnam. Isn't that right? This is a son of a bitch who likes to get up close and take you right low in the back with a twelve-gauge and watch you try and fucking crawl, and then kneel on you and cut your fucking throat. The M12, that was a good shotgun, wasn't it? An antique by then, but the best they ever made."

Grandpa says nothing.

Martin slaps his hands down on the table. "For what! A war for **what**? Did you give a fuck? Did you care or understand what you were fighting for? Fuck no. Fuck, fuck, fuck **no**. You just liked it."

"I understood why I was fighting, Martin."

"Maybe."

Martin sets the knife heavily on the table and Turtle picks it up. "A lot of blood in that leather handle that will never wash out, isn't that right?"

Grandpa lowers his head onto his chest as if resting, his jowls sagging away from his face and deepening his frown.

"Well," Martin says, "kibble must be proud to have that knife. A real family treasure. And, Daniel, you should maybe think that a hard streak runs in this family. You should maybe think about what that hard streak means in your granddaughter." Martin leans over and spits on the floor.

Turtle looks down at the pool of grease and cream on her plate.

"None of that matters," Grandpa says pon-
derously.

"None of that **matters**?" Daddy echoes in disbelief. "None of that matters? What I'm saying
is that, her whole life she's been loved. And that's
something I never had from you."

"I can't let you around that child. I can't do it."

"Let's talk about this," Daddy says. "Is it the
bruises that've got you worried?"

"It's the bruises, and this whole end-of-the-
world horseshit."

"It's not horseshit, Dad," Martin says.

"It's horseshit, and it's no way to raise a child,
pretending that the world is going to end, just because you'd prefer it did."

"No way to raise a child—? If you don't think
the world is in trouble, Dad, you aren't paying attention. The elk, the grizzlies, the wolves, they're
gone. The salmon, almost. The redwoods done
for. Pines dead in stands by the acre. Your bees
are dead. How did we bring Julia into this fucked-
up place? This dying, raped, rotting remnant of
what should've been? How exactly do you raise a
child into the company of the self-obsessed fuck-
offs who squandered and destroyed the world into
which she **should've** been raised? And what understanding can she ever have with such people?
There can be none. There is no negotiation. There
is no alternative. They are killing the world and
they will keep on killing the world and they will

never change and never stop. Nothing I can do, and nothing she can do, will change their minds, because they are incapable of thinking, of seeing the world as something outside of themselves. Insofar as they see it at all, they believe themselves entitled to it. And you tell me that my rage at such people, at such a society, is **horseshit**? You tell me this is no way to raise a child, and yes, I know it. But what else can I do?"

"Goddamn it, Marty, you can't keep—" He stops.

Martin says, "I can't keep **what**?" He gives Turtle a wild look. Grandpa jaws. He can't find the word. Turtle's mouth is open and she puts her palm into it and bites fiercely. She can feel the smile on her face like a dreadful thing.

Martin leans forward. He says, "Well, do you know what you want to say, Dad?"

"Yeah," Grandpa says. "Yeah."

"Well, what is it?"

"Well, I was saying—"

"**Yeah?**"

"Oh, never mind," Grandpa says.

"What?"

"Oh, well, I— I just meant—" Grandpa says.

Martin looks at Turtle. Grandpa is slurring his words.

"Dad?" Martin says.

"Never mind," Grandpa says. "Oh— Oh— Never mind."

"What? **What?**"

Grandpa looks from her to Martin with his one good eye, his right eye lidded, and he adjusts himself on his chair with dignity. He opens his mouth, and slurring badly he says, "I think . . . I was just saying that . . . this is no way to— to— to—" He stops.

"What, Dad?" Martin says.

"To—"

They wait.

"Oh, never mind," Grandpa says angrily, "never mind."

"To raise a child?" Martin says. "No way to raise a child?"

"Yes," Grandpa says, and he stops. He is spraying with every word. Turtle looks intently into his face. The right side seems to be going to sleep. The lid is closed. It opens once sleepily and shows the white crescent of the sclera and then lowers just as sleepily and stays closed. Daddy waits, leaning in, looking at Grandpa.

Grandpa says, "A— A—" and can't seem to find the word.

"A child?" Daddy says.

"Oh," Grandpa says, "oh never mind." He reaches one hand across the table to her, says, "I . . ." and whatever else he means to say, he can't find it. He says, "I . . ." and visibly searches painfully, mouthing.

"What the hell, Dad," Daddy says.

"I was going to . . ." Grandpa says. "I was . . ."

Martin says, "What in the **fuck**?"

Grandpa stands up, knocking his chair over, lists wildly to the side, and Martin lunges up, making a grab for Grandpa's shirt, and Grandpa goes down hard onto the floor.

"Kibble," Daddy says, "call an ambulance. Do it right now."

Turtle stays fixed in place, looking in horror at her grandfather lying half tangled in the chair. He struggles and rolls over onto his side. He looks up at Turtle. The right side of his face is slack, the skin hanging away in curtains of old flesh that looks like poured yellow wax. He says, "Sweetpea— Sweetpea—" He tries feebly to get his hand under himself.

"Call an ambulance, kibble." Martin comes around the table and kneels beside Grandpa. His boots creak.

Turtle rises and walks to the phone on the wall, picks it up, and dials. Martin is helping Grandpa out of the fallen chair. He says, "You fucking— You motherfucking— Goddamn you, Daniel. God-damn you."

Someone says, "911, what is your emergency, please?"

"Um," Turtle says. "What's our emergency, Daddy?"

"Stroke," he says.

"Wait— Wait— Wait, Julie—" Grandpa keeps saying. He jaws and searches for the word.

"Wait, **what**? Dad. Wait—**for what**?"

"Oh, never mind."

"What do you see?" Martin says.

Turtle uncovers the phone and she says, "Wait."

"Waiting," the operator says.

"Stroke!" Martin yells at her.

"Stroke," Turtle says.

"And are you at . . ." and the dispatcher gives their address.

"Yes," Turtle says.

"Oh, Martin," Grandpa says. "I was going to say— Say that . . . What I meant was . . ."

Daddy kneels, holding Grandpa's hands and looking down him, and he says, "What? Daniel? Tell me **what**? What is it?"

Turtle has never seen her father so desperate.

"Miss?" the dispatcher says. "Miss?"

"Wait," Turtle says. She wants everybody to stop. She wants everything to slow down. She just needs more time. "Wait," she says.

"Can you tell me exactly what happened?"

"Shut up!" Turtle says. "Just wait!"

"Miss—"

Turtle presses the phone to her chest and watches. Martin holds Grandpa's hand and says, "What is it, Daniel? What did you want to say? What do you see? Tell me what you see." She drops the phone and walks to the table and sits down beside Martin. He is kneeling over Grandpa, saying, "Tell me what's happening, Dad. Tell me what you see." In the corner, the phone hangs on its cord and the dispatcher says, "Miss? Miss? I need you to stay on the line."

Grandpa turns and looks at her, raising his head up from the floor. Turtle comes closer. He jaws, searching for her name, can't find it, opens and closes his mouth. He says, "Julie— I can't . . ."

"Goddamn it, Daniel! What is it? What? What?"

Martin grabs Grandpa's chin, and they look at each other.

"What did you— What were you—?" Martin says.

"Julie—" Grandpa says.

"Kibble, go upstairs," Martin says.

"I'm sorry," she says. She's looking right at Grandpa. "I'm so sorry. I'm sorry."

Grandpa is looking at her. Whatever he means to say is dark to her. The center is draining out of him, the substance, he is saying the things that it is his habit to say, but he is not saying what he means and he cannot get at what he means.

"Go!" Martin says, and she gets up and runs up the stairs, thinking, this will come to nothing. He will come back from this. She runs into her room, leans against the wall, gasping and listening. From below she hears Martin say, "Tell me what you see, Dad. Tell me what you meant." She waits in excruciating silence, trying to still her breathing. She is afraid that she will miss what Grandpa says for the sound of her heart, for the sound of her breathing, but she is hungry for air, starved for it. Downstairs, a rasp, the sound of movement, and Turtle stops breathing, listens. "Oh, I see . . . I see . . ." Grandpa says, slurring, and the sound of his feet scraping against the floor, shifting where he lies, and Martin says, "Daniel, look at me— I'm— It's me, Martin. It's Martin. Look at me." And Grandpa says, "Oh, never mind." Martin, in disbelief, says, "What? What?" There is a long silence, Turtle trying to calm her hitching breath, listening for any sound from downstairs, but there is no sound, and then Martin, his voice a low rasp, hushed with awe or with something else. "You bastard," he says. "You goddamn bastard." Then a long interval of silence, Turtle with her back to the door, listening, measuring out her breath to calm it. Then she hears the ambulance, watches it come up the drive. She listens to the strange men downstairs, talking. They are calling out numbers she does not understand, talking to one another, and Turtle walks back and forth in her room, crosses to the window and watches Grandpa carried out on a stretcher and loaded into an ambulance in the muddy yard. Daddy talks to the techs and afterward climbs into his truck and follows the ambulance down the drive. Turtle is left alone, leaning into the window well, roses and poison oak framing her in a tangled border.

Thirteen

LATE THAT NIGHT, MARTIN'S TRUCK COMES roaring up the gravel drive and Turtle stirs from her reverie in the window, hands clutched about goose-bumped shoulders. She climbs carefully out of the window well and goes down the stairs and stands out on the porch. Martin walks up to the steps and kicks them hard and then sits down. He takes out a pack of cigarettes, taps one into his hand, lights it. He draws on it. She comes to sit beside him, and he passes her the cigarette and taps a second into his hand. "Dead on arrival," he says. "DOA." He clears his throat, and in the doctor's hushed, affected tone, he says, "'Daniel has suffered a massive hemorrhagic stroke of the left

middle cerebral artery. It started as an ischemic
stroke, which means that a blood clot lodged in
the artery that profuses the left hemisphere of the
brain and the regions responsible for speech and
for movement. We do not know where the clot
came from. However, the blood vessels in an alcoholic's brain are very fragile, and he subsequently
ruptured and bled out into the brain tissue.' It was,
apparently, painful but fast. Not that he could tell
you. The first stroke, the ischemic one, that wasn't
painful. He didn't know what was happening.
But the second stroke, the hemorrhagic one, that
was painful, but by then he didn't have the words
to express it. Just locked in his own mind with
the mother of all goddamn headaches, however
briefly. The doctor said, 'Like a stroke from god.'"
Martin blows smoke out the side of his mouth.
"Motherfucker," he says. They sit side by side. He
picks gravel from between the deck boards and
flicks it into the driveway overgrown with chic-
ory and goosefoot. She sits in silence and thinks
of the ambulance going up the Shoreline Highway, passing bays and headlands in alternation,
and her here, waiting. She thinks, I killed him.
The thought comes so quickly, so painfully, that
it makes her shiver in disgust, grinding her teeth,
and she thinks again, I killed him. Her own insig-
nificance is oppressive to her—that she should be
the one who finally kills Grandpa, when so much
else had failed, and it seems to her that her own

relationship to Grandpa is shallow compared to his relationship with Martin, and if Grandpa's relationship with her had been less troubled, it was only because it had less depth. Grandpa was hard on Martin because Martin engaged his whole character in the way that Turtle engages Daddy's whole character. And there was something Martin had needed from his own father. Some question left unanswered.

Daddy rises and turns and kicks the porch step riser again. "Fuck!" he yells. He turns and looks down the hillside and yells, "Fuck!" Then he walks heavily back inside and Turtle sits alone on the dark porch until he returns with a five-gallon can of gasoline. He stands for a moment and then he begins to walk past her along the path through the orchard to Grandpa's trailer in the raspberry field.

"Wait," she says.

He turns and looks back, and his face softens, his brow furrowing with pain, standing there with the gas can in one hand, his shoulders slumping, his left eye squinting more than the right, and he says, very softly, with tremendous emphasis, "Oh, kibble. Oh, my absolute darling." He sets the gas can down and he walks toward her. She stands on the porch, utterly bereft. He takes her in his arms.

She says, "I want to die."

"Oh, kibble," he says.

She says, "I hate myself. I **hate** myself."

"Oh no," he says, clenching her in his arms. He

runs his fingertips between her ribs, following the grooves. They flex and give within his grasp. She feels herself small in his arms. Her face, she feels, fixes itself in some expression of pain and loss, and she says again, "I want to die."

"Oh, kibble," he says into her neck. He sucks air through his teeth, a painful sound, expressive of his regret. "He killed himself. I hope you see that. He killed himself and there was nothing either you or I could do. Fuck, I hate him for that."

"Don't," she says softly, her own voice surprising her with the strain.

He shudders, holding her. She is pressing her face into his shoulder, and he holds her this way, cupping his hand around the back of her head.

"I wish to hell it had been different," he says. "I wish you had had the grandpa you deserved and not the one you had. But it's just you and me now, kid. Come on."

He releases her, and takes her hand, and leads her through the orchard to the trailer, and when they get there, Rosy appears in the window, yapping and agitated. Martin opens the door and comes in and Rosy goes galumphing around the linoleum floor. Turtle climbs up the stairs after him and stands in the doorway. Looking around the trailer now, at Grandpa's things, they all have significance and meaning to her—they seem filled with his presence, and at the same time, they have shrunk, they are awful and painful in their shabbiness. She looks at the dinky foldout table with its cheap cribbage board, the plastic pegs still there from their last game, the deck of cards on the table, and she looks to the paper bag Grandpa used for his recycling, with bundles of frozen-pizza boxes folded there. There is the tiny oven, an ugly mustard color. She looks down the hall-way to the bedroom, the mildewed rayon sheets, black mold on the corroding aluminum window-sill with its pebbled plastic window. Christ, she thinks, has it always been this awful? She walks to the cabinets and opens one, and there is a bottle of Jack Daniel's and two rocks glasses and a plas-tic water cup and nothing else, the cabinet lining peeling up in places to show the cheap fiberboard beneath. Christ, she thinks. She opens the fridge, and there is a carton of half-and-half and some AA batteries. Christ, she thinks again with gath-ering painfulness. She leans against the counter. The pain comes on in dull waves, followed by the realization that he is dead, a realization that seems to have layers and depth, a realization she could go down and down into, as if into deeper and deeper water, mounting pressure. The pain is in her stomach and in her lungs, and it fills her with self-disgust and self-hate. Standing in the dingy trailer, she thinks, I want to die. I truly want to die. It is only my cowardice that keeps me from doing it.

She looks at Martin, shakes her head.

"He can't be gone," she says.

Martin tightens his jaw. He looks around, too. He gestures. "All my life," he says, "he was such a big man. He was my **father**. Look at this place, though. Always, he was bigger than life. Always, he told me I'd never live up to him. **Told me that**. Look at this." Martin has to stoop to go through the doorway, stands in the bedroom, toying with the cheap fiberboard door. He reaches up, plunges his hand into a gap between the wall and the ceiling, and peels the fiberboard panel aside, showing cheap insulation beneath. He heaves the torn board from the wall, drops his hands to his sides, looks over at Turtle. He says, "I don't know what all he told you, but you will outgrow us both. You will be more than he ever was. And more than me. Don't ever let anyone—not anyone, not me, not Grandpa, not yourself—tell you different. Look at this." He lifts the five-gallon gas can in his hands, unscrewing the cap.

"Don't," she says.

He looks at her, shakes his head, and pours gas over the bed. He walks backward, stooping, through the door, pouring gas along the carpet. He comes into the kitchen and dumps it across the table, the chairs, the cabinets and counters.

Turtle catches Rosy by the collar and carries the excited dog out of the trailer while Martin dumps more gasoline in the walkway. Turtle kneels in the raspberries, holding Rosy by the collar, and she watches Martin douse the place in gasoline. He steps down and stands beside her. He puts his hands in his pockets, digging for his lighter, and laughs, bitterly, quietly.

"What?"

"You know, kibble, I lived half my life in terror of that man. Christ." He gasps. The sound is strange and unexpected, like a hiccup. He finds his lighter and fetches it out, stands looking at it in his palm, and then looking around for something to light the fire with. He says, "Ah, but he was good to you, wasn't he?"

Turtle nods. "Yeah," she says, her guts squeezing at the inadequacy of her answer.

Martin stands shaking his head. "Christ. That's good, I guess. That's good. I don't know why I let you come down here to see him like I did. A girl should have her grandfather in her life, I guess. Christ. I would've said his capacity to hurt me was all run out, but it was something else, I tell you, to watch him with you. I tell you what. You come up as a child with such a man as that for a father and you have to spend a lot of your life persuading yourself that it was nothing to do with you, because I tell you—he was not so gentle with me. He was the most sadistic kind of fuck, kibble. So it takes some persuading. And it's hard, because it comes so natural to think that your father hates you for a reason. You almost want to think that. It's somehow easier than thinking his hate is inscrutable. That makes no kind of sense to a child. It is quite a thing, I tell you. And yet I have seen him be the most patient kind of man with you, kibble. I hated him for that. Isn't that strange? Years and years later. I would've said his capacity to hurt me was all done. Well."

He turns. He picks up a handful of grass, tosses open the lighter, and touches it to the grass, but the grass will not take. It smolders and blackens away from the flame, and does not burn. He looks around. Turtle stands there beside him. He says, "I should've taken some paper out with me."

Martin looks in at the carpet, sodden with gasoline. "Well," he says. He moves toward it, and the flame of his lighter goes out. Carefully, he leans into the trailer, planting one hand on the counter and extending the lighter down to the sodden carpet. He strikes the flint and then springs back, expecting the carpet to go up in a whoosh of flame. Nothing happens. Martin touches his jaw in frustration and annoyance, relights the Zippo, and tosses the burning lighter inside, onto a standing pool of gasoline. The lighter goes out, mid-flight, and lands with a splash.

"Well, shit," Martin says. He climbs back into the trailer, picks up the lighter, stands holding it between thumb and forefinger, shaking gasoline from it.

"I wouldn't use that lighter, Daddy," she says.

He shakes his head in muted, bitter comedy. "Fucking hilarious," he says.

He climbs down from the trailer, walks around back, and Turtle follows, bringing Rosy along. They stand in high raspberries behind the trailer, and Martin crawls into the undercarriage, and takes hold of a five-gallon propane tank attached to the trailer's gas hookup. He unscrews the propane from the gas assembly, hauls the tank around to the front, heaves it through the trailer's door. There are two more propane tanks stashed beneath the trailer, and he goes back for each, retrieving them, and lining them up in the trailer's hallway. He comes to stand beside her, draws the Colt .45 from his belt. He thumbs back the hammer and fires.

The propane tank **pings**, the bullet leaving a visible, gleaming scar in the white paint. Annoyed, Martin fires again, and then a third time, the shots throwing small, shiny dents into the steel. Martin stops firing. He looks at Turtle, who kneels in the raspberries holding Rosy.

He climbs back into the trailer, which groans under his weight. He walks to the propane, stepping around pools of gasoline, cranks the spigot open, but the propane tank makes no noise of escaping gas. He chews his lips. Then he smacks his head. "The valve," he says, referring to the valve that keeps the tank from venting gas unless it is assembled to a line. He climbs out and down, crawls back under the trailer, captures the gas hookup, and drawing his Daniel Winkler belt knife, severs the line in a single stroke. He walks back into the trailer and screws the gas hookup onto the propane tank, which begins to fountain propane from the severed line. He scrambles out, vaulting over the fountaining gas line, waving Turtle away. She can see the clouds of propane filling the trailer, rolling out the door.

The escaping gas begins to spread pools of frost across the floor in a funnel pattern from where the severed line lies on the carpet, and then the gas line heaves itself up into the air, sweeping across counters. Frost climbs up the cabinets, the cold wrinkling the skin off the ersatz wood, which buckles and heaves up from the fiberboard. Now Martin stands wiping his Zippo clean on his shirt, shaking gasoline off of it, and Turtle backs away, hauling on Rosy's collar. Rosy gives several excited barks and looks at Turtle, raising her eyebrows to points and smiling. Martin opens the Zippo, and the entire lighter goes up in flame. "Shit," he says, "shit!" and pitches it into the trailer and then turns and runs into the grass, shaking his burned hand.

For a moment, nothing happens. Propane pours out through the open door in visible white steam.

Martin says, "You're fucking kidding me."

Then fire flushes out the door and across the grass in a low wave. Martin claps his hands over his ears. The windows rupture out and strips of siding peel off the frame. Then there is a second explosion and fire lances up into the sky and something comes right out the open door and Turtle believes for a moment that it is a raven flying from the flames, flying right at her, and then Martin runs into her, hands over his ears, and throws her down to the ground as something whistles past. The flames collapse, and leave only the hulk of the trailer, burning steadily. Turtle can see a sheet of steel lying in the doorway—the unwrapped cylinder of a propane tank. Behind her, she can see the cylinder's head, launched off the tank like a cannonball. She can hear nothing. She looks at Martin. He is talking to her. Then, in her left ear, a hard, high ringing noise. Her right ear, nothing. She puts her hand to it. She looks to him again, holding her right ear, and he is talking. He laughs wildly. She looks down and sees Rosy barking frantically, stiff-legged, looking at the trailer and backing away from it. They stand together and watch it burn—the green raspberry canes curling and blackening away. The grass catches in fitful patches. Turtle looks to her daddy, then back to the burning trailer. The fire holds their attention for a long time. Over the ringing noise, she begins to hear him. She begins to hear the flames. She feels dizzy. She feels as if her right ear is empty, soundless, as if it has been permanently lost.

"I want to die," Turtle says, and she can hear herself speaking in a distorted, underwater way. She jaws open and closed, touching her jawbones beneath her ears, but there is nothing.

Martin moves to look away from the fire, but it is as if he cannot take his eyes from it. Turtle sits down, still holding her ears. The heat from the fire dries her skin. If the raspberries were not already so wet, they would burn. In places, the grass is aflame. Martin does not seem to care. There is the noxious smell of the burning cabinets, fiberboard panels, and insulation. They sit together in the grass. He talks, and she can hear him in some vague way, over the high, obnoxious single-tone ringing. Rosy barks, she runs in circles, she leaps up and down. She retreats and returns.

"Come here, kibble," he says.

She comes close to him. He looks at her, studying her. Whatever he says next is lost to her and she looks at him without comprehension. Sweat cuts runnels through the dust on his face. He says, "Are you **done** with your old man, kibble?"

"No," she says.

"You cunt," he says. He buries his fingertips into her jaw. "What are you thinking behind that little mask of yours?"

She has trouble making out his words. She watches his face, reading his lips. She feels sick to her stomach. There is a sensation in her skull, in her ear, very close to pain but not quite pain. She jaws open and closed.

"Goddamn," he says, looking intently down into her face. She cannot hear him say it exactly, but she sees his mouth form the word, **Goddamn.** He is fixed there in the firelight, as if looking down a well. "What are you? What **are** you, and what is in that little bitch mind of yours?" She just shakes her head, trembling against his restraining hands. He has her head in his grasp as if he can crush it, looking fixedly into her eyes. "What is in that little head of yours?" he says. "And how could I ever know?"

She closes her eyes. In the blackness, colors chase across her lids. She can see red adumbrations of the burning trailer. Smears of red and orange. Over everything, the high constant ringing tone. She could keep her eyes closed and lose herself in that monotone. It is emotionless and constant. Martin squeezes her neck and she opens her eyes to him.

"There is a terrible inwardness to you," he says. "Look at you. You are such a goddamn pretty little **thing**. Your goddamn eyes. I look at them and I don't see . . . anything. They say you can look into someone's eyes and know them, that the eyes are the window to the soul, but I look into your eyes and it's dark to me, kibble. They have always been dark to me. If there is anything in you, it cannot be read, it cannot be known. The truth of you, if it is there at all, exists beyond an unbridgeable and irreducible epistemological gap."

"I'm sorry, Daddy," she says. She strains to hear him over the high, constant tone. Inside, she is all hollowness. Out of her left ear, he sounds tinny, distant.

"I don't think you even know," he says, relaxing his grip, recoiling from her.

She feels gutted, with nothing inside of her and nothing to say, cannot think anything, cannot feel anything. If there is sorrow inside of her, she can't tell. She feels like something has been pulled out of her guts, roots and all, some alder tree, and where it was before, a nauseous emptiness, but that is all she can feel, no sorrow, nothing. She would be capable of terrible harm, if she only wanted. She could do anything and there is no limit to the hurt she could do, only now, she wants to close her eyes and run her mind around that emptiness like running your tongue over the socket of a pulled tooth. If she could, she would stop her ears to that terrible, constant ringing noise.

"I have given up everything for you," he says. "I would give you anything, kibble. But is that what you want? For them to hunt me down? Because they **will**. If that teacher ever catches on. If that fat fuck of a principal finds out, if anyone starts asking questions, if anyone ever finds out. Do you want that?"

She looks up at him and does not care. She can barely hear him, she isn't certain what he is saying. She watches his face and she knows that this is serious, but she cannot feel that seriousness and she cannot convince herself of it.

"I'm sorry, Daddy."

"Is that what you want?"

She says, "I want to die."

"And even if you tell no one, if you give no sign, if you never breathe a word, but someone, anyone, comes to me again and so much as suggests, I will open your little neck, and won't that be a goddamn beautiful thing. Then we'll find out if you can be had. Then we'll know. You think on that. You're along for the ride, you little bitch. We will see what light is in your eyes then, what ineffable little spark they might lose. Watch your goddamn little corneas drying up like fish scales."

She cannot follow him. Her mind is elsewhere. She thinks, is that what I meant, crawling up through the reflective mirror of the surface and out into this other world, did I mean to address him in some way he could not refuse and in some way for which it would be hard, terribly hard, to hold myself accountable? Is that what I wanted, and did I know, and if so—what part of myself is this, and who is she to me, sorting the rotten from the firm and guessing at these hollows of my mind, just guessing, is she still with me here?

She can barely hear him. If she looked away from him, she would not hear him. Painted across her vision, the afterimage of the burning trailer. The dark of her mind is lit with these things; alive, too, with the high constant ringing.

"Oh god," he says. "Kibble, I am sick for you. The unreachable truth in you. Just beneath the surface. And when I look at you—there are moments . . . when I almost, **almost**— God. God."

She waits there in the grass, feeling her every thought stored up and inarticulate within her. Martin gets up and walks away. She bows her head and lets the heat dry her skin, listening to the ringing, Rosy curled up beside her.

The breeze comes in the early morning and beads the sweet vernal grass with dew and she holds Rosy, both of them shivering with the cold and Turtle unwilling to rise, the dog's body enclosed in her arms. Rosy feels bony, her belly soft, her hair short, the trees around the clearing lit with a sullen red glow. When she rises, cramping, moving a sluggish Rosy off her lap and into the grass, Turtle smells like burnt plastic. She caps her hand over her right ear, uncaps it, can barely tell the difference.

"Hello?" she says. Her voice sounds distant and strange to her. "Hello?" She stands in the clearing, gaping her jaws, mouthing. Rosy looks up at her. She says, "Hello," and Rosy gives a little lurch, as if to launch into action, but then, not knowing what to do, stands looking up at Turtle, and Turtle cannot tell exactly how loud she is talking, but she can hear herself. She thinks, I have no idea how much is gone. Rosy watches her with her eyebrows raised to points. The dog stops, yawns, looks around, sits down, looks back at Turtle, who still stands in the clearing, watching the ravaged trailer, the line of the orchard, the forest, the glass blackened in a circle around the hulk. She looks up at the sky, clear and blue. She wants to die.

Turtle turns and slogs back through the dew-wet grass. She arrives at the house and with difficulty climbs the stairs onto the porch and opens the sliding glass door to find Martin sitting on the overstuffed chair, his feet flat on the floor, his arms flat on the chair's arms. He stares into the ashy fireplace, a book open on his lap. Turtle walks past, hoping for a moment that he will say something and she will gauge her hearing by his voice, but he says nothing. Rosy stands at the threshold as well. Turtle opens her mouth to ask him something, just to hear his voice, but thinks better of it.

She walks to the bathroom and Rosy comes in after her, hesitant, nails clicking on the floorboards, looking shyly around. Turtle turns on the shower and Rosy stands just outside the tub, and when she pulls the plastic wrap to encircle the tub, the dog whines. Turtle bows her head under the showerhead and listens to the water. She has the image of water trickling past her broken eardrum into the whorls of her inner ear. Rosy walks in a circle several times and then drops down onto the floor with her head on her forepaws and watches. Turtle thinks, did he really say all of those things? Or did I mishear him? She remembers him hunkering down over Grandpa, saying, **tell me what you see**. She thinks, did he really do that, did he say that or something like it? She can't remember. She stands with her hands by her sides, the water running over her head and she thinks, I wish I could feel something. She is covered in fleabites.

When she comes out of the shower, Martin is on the phone. She follows his mouth, he is saying "—for your concern. She will not be coming in today. Yes. Yes—" Then he says something that she cannot put together. He must be talking to the school. They must have called to report her absence. She stands there and mouths as he is mouthing, to figure out what he is saying, and Martin notices, stands up away from the wall in curiosity, his brow wrinkled, and now he mouths to her, **What the hell are you . . . ?** and she turns and gathers Rosy in her arms and walks away up the stairs, the dog fidgeting and kicking, Turtle feeling cold all over.

She lights a candle. She closes her door. She grubs Rosy for fleas, feeding them into the pool of hot wax with her pinched fingers. The wax burns her fingertips and the fleas float, immured black points, Rosy yawning hugely, showing yellowed teeth. Turtle wakes sometime in the night with Rosy whining and scraping on the door. She takes the dog downstairs and out into the yard, but Rosy goes on, through the orchard, her tail fidgeting nervously, laboring through the grass on her short legs, panting, until she comes out into the clearing and stands there, yawning, looking at Turtle, and Turtle says, "Oh, Rosy, oh, you old dog." She takes her in her arms and carries her back.

The next day, Rosy comes down the stairs with

her and stands in the kitchen as Turtle takes eggs from the carton and tosses them back. Martin comes out of his room, buttoning his flannel. She tosses him a beer and he catches it, bangs it open on the countertop. They walk together in twin ruts, Rosy trailing behind, wagging her tail and whining, and they stand at the gravel pull-out and watch the sea stacks and the horizon line. They say nothing. Finally, the exhausted gasping of the bus, the throwing open of the doors with the thwapping of rubber skirts, Martin saluting the bus driver, enormous in her coveralls and logger boots, Turtle sitting in class trying to listen and unable to listen but copying down everything that Anna writes on the board, every word, sitting at the edge of the field looking out at the trees, sounding herself for any feeling at all and finding none, and Turtle finally on the bus ride home, in the green vinyl pews, looking out at the ocean broken by kelp beds, the bulbs and fronds stirring the surface, wondering at its strangeness, which she sometimes loses track of because it is there, day in and day out, but Martin was right about this one thing, its strangeness. Turtle climbs the gravel drive at the end of the bus ride, and Rosy is not in the house and she walks through the grass and past the old claw-footed tub and through the orchard to the clearing beside the raspberries and there she finds Rosy lying in the grass, and she lifts the dog up and carries her back to the house.

Turtle sits across from Martin with the scraping of plates and Rosy whining in the corner and Martin looking at the dog and Turtle saying, "I'll pick up some dog food," and Martin still looking at the dog and finally saying, "No, I'll do it."

Every day, Turtle walks across the field, through the orchard, to find Rosy waiting in the clearing, and every day carries Rosy back, and eventually Martin comes from Mendocino with a bag of kibble and they fill a bowl, and Rosy stands hanging her head over the bowl and returns to Turtle and looks up at her sorrowfully, and walks back to the bowl and hangs her head over it sadly, and back to Turtle again, skulking, head low, peering up with the whites of her eyes showing, and Turtle saying, "What are we going to do with you, Rosy? What are we going to do with you?"

He brings home paperwork that absorbs his attention for the rest of dinner, touching one eyebrow with his thumb but not complaining, filling it out one line at a time, across the table from her in their firelit living room, a bleeding steak on a blue Bauer plate pushed out of reach, and one such night, Turtle asks, "Will he be buried, or cremated?" and he looks up from his paperwork, hands braced on the table, the span of his shoulders enormous, and he says, "All your grandpa wanted was to be dropped into a pit and then to rot there. So."

In the early morning, Turtle, roused by Rosy's

scratching, stands on the porch with the spotlights on, shooting skeet by the halogen glare, yarding ferociously on the pull cord for the skeet thrower and then raising the over-under skeet gun into the cup of her shoulder, the satisfying report of the gun and the skeet just gone to sparking orange dust in the halogen glare, turning around to see Martin leaning there in the doorway, his face unreadable, and realizing then and not sure how long it has been true, but the ringing in her left ear is gone. When Martin turns away and walks back to his bedroom, Turtle trudges through the cold high grass wet with dew and finds Rosy in the clearing by the burned hulk of the trailer and picks up the dog and carries her back to her room, and wakes again that night with Rosy scratching at the door, and Turtle will not take her down, and Rosy will not quit scratching and whining.

Then one day Martin picks Turtle up after school and drives her to the Little River graveyard. They park on the side of the road and walk in through the rusted gates and they watch as the casket is lowered into the ground. The sides are sandy coastal earth, rough as a shorn-open biscuit. The casket is simple. The crowns of her teeth ache with cold.

Martin says, "What I really wanted was a cardboard box."

The man, stooped, operating the winch that lowers the casket, looks up fractionally. Martin says, "The law says you have to choose a casket and they are none of them cheap." The casket is deeply varnished and Turtle is impressed with its somberness, but it looks nothing like Grandpa's coffin should look and she cannot and will not believe that Grandpa is in the coffin and she stands and watches the coffin go down into the grim black earth.

"They do not allow me," he says, "to make a coffin for my father. There is a process of accreditation to make a legal coffin, but how I wish I could have made one. They no longer bury people here. There is no more room, but your grandfather has had this plot for a long time. And that—" He nods to the black headstone beside it, and Turtle kneels and reads, VIRGINIA ALVESTON, and Martin says, "Kibble, meet your grandmother." The plot is covered in dandelions. The grass is scoured by the coastal wind and has the weedy look of all coastal grass, and Turtle waits by the headstone and can make no sense of it, and she looks up at Martin. He says, "Don't worry. You're nothing like her, and wouldn't've liked her if you'd've known her. She had a cast-iron heart, that woman. You're your mother, up and down, and if you have anything of Virginia in you, it's that streak of puritanism you have sometimes. She saved everything and would throw nothing away. She used to wash the floorboards by throwing a bucket of water across them. It rotted the legs of the tables out. She would've been proud of you, I guess, if she'd've known you ever."

She steps away from the headstone, looks down into Grandpa's grave. Martin puts his arm on her shoulder and she can feel the expansion and contraction of his ribs with his breathing, and she looks up and can see the arteries snaking the great trunk of his neck like cables, beating with his heartbeat. They are the only two at the funeral. Mist comes through the lines of trees at the cemetery's western edge. When the coffin has lowered, Turtle leans in and throws down the columbines she'd cut from the fence line and Martin looks at her and kneels carefully at the edge of the pit and casts down a handful of dirt and shakes his head and stands and takes her by the shoulder and they walk away together. Turtle cannot imagine Grandpa having a wife. He was always his own man, and Martin, too. She cannot imagine any women in the Alveston home except for herself. She wonders who these women were, what they were like. Virginia Alveston, she thinks, that's a good name, a woman with a cast-iron heart. She thinks, this is a woman who mopped the floors and kept the house clean. I didn't know who she was, and I've been eating off her plates.

Martin parks in the driveway and she gets out without a word and follows the path past the bathtub and through the orchard and finds Rosy again by the trailer. She is lying in the grass with her head on her paws, scratching sometimes at fleas, and Turtle sits down beside her and looks at the burned trailer and scratches under Rosy's collar. Rosy raises her eyebrows to points, not lifting her head but watching Turtle affectionately, and finally she does raise her head and opens her mouth and lolls her tongue and smiles at the girl and Turtle says, "What are we going to do with you, Rosy, you old dog?"

Then the last day of school comes, and after the promotion ceremony Turtle gets off the bus at the bottom of her driveway. She finds Rosy asleep in the field by the hulk of the trailer. Nearby, ravens gather in the trees, cawing to each other and watching the dog. Turtle kneels beside Rosy, who kicks and jerks in her sleep and then lies still. Her breath seems very fast to Turtle, and Turtle puts a hand on her side and looks out into the trees. She does not have the heart to carry the dog back and does not have the heart to wake her, and heads back to the house alone, to find Martin's truck gone. She walks through the empty living room and up to her room and sits down on her bed platform. She thinks, that old dog, she'll be okay there, for now.

Fourteen

SHE WAITS OUT THE EVENING. SHE RUBS
the instep of one foot with the arch of the other.
Her flesh is dry and leathery, and when she arches
her foot, the sole lays up in corrugations. The flesh
has grain, like a pine knot, and there are holes in
the callus like the holes along the tide line. She
succumbs to the quiet and when she wakes, it is
dark and he is still gone. He has come home every
other evening of her life and she understands, instinctively, that she has been abandoned. She killed
her grandpa with cowardice and self-obsession and
now her father has left her for those same reasons.
She sits with her back against the wall, chewing on
her knuckles, listening to the house, listening to

make sure of it, but she is sure. The breeze comes in through the open window and stirs the poison oak. Where the vines have stitched through the lintel, they are brown and knotted as blackbird feet. The wind eddies in the dark room where Turtle sits, shivering, afraid. She wants to rise and walk through the house, but she does not. She waits. Downstairs, the back door blows open and bangs against the side of the house. She can hear the alder leaves scuttling across the kitchen floor.

When Turtle was young and used to go on walks with her grandfather, she would ask him, "What is this?" and he would say, "You tell me what it is," and she would tell him about it. She would run a stalk of wild oats through her hand, the twin seeds each with a nib and a long, bent, black whisker. They had a lovely dartlike shape to them, bellying before the nib, tapering above. The lower half of each seed was clothed in a soft, golden down, deeply evocative, light as the fur of bumblebees but lying smoothly to the belly of the seed. The long black awns were coarse to the touch. She liked the way the chaff shelled in her hand. He used to say, "When a sweetpea knows something's name, she thinks she knows everything about it, and she stops looking at it. But there is nothing in a name, and to say you know a thing's name is to say that you know nothing, less than nothing." He liked to say, "Don't ever think the name is the thing, because there is only the thing itself, and the names are just tricks, just tricks to help you remember them." She thinks of the two of them, Turtle racing along, stopping and returning, as Grandpa labored through the grass and across the uneven ground. Only after she had her own way of telling him where it grew and what it was, then he would tell her about it, hulling it apart in his fingers, saying, "This, sweetpea, is the spikelet, and these the glumes, see how long they are? This is the awn. See how it's corkscrewed below and bent above? You keep looking just that carefully. You keep on like that, looking as if you didn't know, looking to find out what it is, really. That's what keeps a sweetpea nice and quiet as she goes through the grass. You look at a thing to find out what's there, sweetpea, always, always." He was wrong about names, though. Or half wrong. They mean something. It meant something when he called her sweetpea. That meant the world to her.

She thinks, I should go get that dog. Then she thinks, let her be. She waits, and her waiting and her silence is discipline in the stead of real sorrow, and still she goes down into it, her cheek to the floor, breathing slowly, hours passing and each hour like the first, each breath like the last, watching the silverfish wander the linty cracks between the boards, some sensitivity that she has long kept in abeyance awakening within her, and she can feel it, that gathering of pain, but it plays with her a game of red light/green light, and when she looks at it, it is far away and unmoving, but when she suspends her mind, lying there on the floor and gazing across the boards but not thinking, then she can feel it grow closer until it is all through her, the sorrow replete in the unattended emptiness of her mind like wild radishes blooming in an empty lot. It has found whole parts of her that she did not know she had.

In the morning Turtle walks falteringly through the empty hallways and rooms on legs painful with their returning circulation. Her back aches from sitting. She stands in the living room, looks at the couches, the kitchen's open door, the house silent, every object freighted with his presence. She goes out and leaves the door open behind her. The pines are tossing on the ridge and the apple trees in the orchard are quaking and the meadow grass is lying down in the gusts. She walks barefoot through the orchard and comes out into the clearing with the ashy trailer. The ravens have beaten out a place in the grass and Rosy is in the midst of them, back legs spread. When Turtle comes up to them, they caw and labor into the air ahead of her. They have been pulling the dog's intestines out through her asshole. Her fur is matted and ugly and the corpse swarms with flies. Her eyes are gone. Turtle kneels in the grass, covering her mouth with her bunched-up shirt. The ravens watch from the trees. Turtle feels gutted herself. Rosy's intestines are worm-colored ribbons drying in the sun.

That night, taking a can down from the cupboard, she finds a grass seed on the can top. She takes down cans covered in gobbets of newspaper insulation, their labels chewed off, stinking of piss. She stacks them on the counter. The nest is in the back corner of the cupboard. She washes the cans in the sink and opens one and sits spooning the beans straight from the can, miserable with hurt. She expects to hear the truck come up the drive at any moment, and each moment brings only the silence of the empty house. She waits in her bedroom, chin on her knees, hands wrapped around her shins, eyes closed. I want to die, she tells herself. I want to die.

She walks down the stairs and yells out to the dark house, "Daddy?" She yells it again, but he isn't there and she goes down the hall and throws open the door to his bedroom. She flicks on the light, stands in the doorway looking. The sheets are twisted. There are clothes strewn on the floor. She sits down on the bed. She is thinking of Grandpa's trailer aflame. She thinks, I blame you. I blame you for that. She is not sure what she means. It hadn't felt like a farewell. It had felt like an exorcism. The end table is covered with half-empty beer bottles and cigarettes crushed into bottle caps. She holds a bottle up to the light. There are dead flies floating in it. She thinks, you think you know a thing. You know someone's name and you think you know something about them, or they are familiar to you and so you stop looking because you think you've seen it before. That's blindness, sweetpea. You keep looking carefully. You keep on like that, looking as if you didn't know, looking to find out what it is, really. She sets the beer bottle down. Martin believed in names. They were both just fucking wrong. Both of them. She scrapes the bottles and bottle caps and the ashtray into the dustbin. She stands and pulls off the tangled sheets. The old stains like coffee stains dried to ragged outlines with their centers paled out. What reason there might be for this she does not know, perhaps the same reason tide pools leave their salt in concentric rings. Perhaps everything seeks its edge and flees its center and dies this way. The husks of bottles, of clothes strewn and ragged, of this silent bedroom, of this empty house. She drags the mattress off the bed. The beams are cobwebbed. She walks to the bookcase and levers a book out from the others, its top scummed with dust. She opens the foxed pages. Blackberries have taken root in her gut, alders, yarrow, and pig mint harrowed up from the black the way seeds can be, blackberry runners knitting through the latticework of her lungs, and if she were to open her mouth, she could disgorge the canes in a ropy tangle. A nameless wretchedness is on her. She thinks, you keep looking, sweetpea. You keep looking just that way as if you didn't know it. She begins pulling books off the shelf. She hauls on the bookcase and it will not move. She walks down the hall and brings back the wrecking bar and drives the bar behind the bookcase and levers it forward. The fasteners draw from the plaster like taproots, the galvanized nails bending and squealing. The bookcase falls forward in a wash of books.

She walks down the hallway into the pantry and picks up the chain saw from the floor, and coming into the bedroom starts it with a single, hard pull on the cord. She touches the saw blade to the bookshelf and then goes down through the lovely dark cherrywood, the long cherry ribbons thrown past her across the tangled sheets. She cuts through the beams into the piled books below. The air is filled with a lofted, fluttering confetti of shredded paper. She carries the smoking chain saw to Daddy's bed and touches the blade to the runner and the bed splits and collapses, and holding the chain saw in one hand she drags the headboard away from the wall. She goes down through it. The phone rings and she walks to it and pulls it from the wall. She stands in the bedroom breathing hard and looking at the ruined furniture, the tangled sheets. She kills the saw and sets it at her feet.

She retrieves a shovel and a pick mattock from the basement. She carries them through the foyer, out the door. The perimeter spotlights switch on with a clicking sound. She walks out through alders and the elderberries, spotlights switching on as she comes into each new tract of darkness, lighting everything up with halogen glare. She digs a pit among the pines, whole branches and trees gone dead with some unknown blight. She cuts through the knotted roots with the pick mattock, digging steadily and carefully, taking breaks to prop herself up on her knees. She digs for a long time. It only needs to be big enough for whatever will be left, the ruins, the ashes, the fused remainder of springs and screws. She stops sometimes to roll her shoulders and to knead the meat of one hand with the fingers of the other. Then she returns to it. When she is done, she sits on the edge stirring habanero sauce into a can of refried beans with her knife and eating straight from the blade. She wipes the knife on the thigh of her pants and pitches the can into the pit.

She drags out the sheets and the mattress. She drags out the sectioned runners and the headboard. She drags out the desk and the cherry bookshelves. The face cuts shine in the gloom. She opens the footlocker and it is full of pictures of her and her mother. She overturns it and stirs through them with the knife blade. She heaps them back into the locker and carries it out. In a drawer, she finds a checkbook with $205 left in the ledger and three envelopes full of cash, stacks of hundreds, fifties, twenties. She counts it out as $4,620 and leaves it beside the checkbooks on the kitchen counter. The bills, the bank statements, the documents, she carries all these out into the pit. She fetches a red wheelbarrow out of the high grass and pumps up the tire and wheels it into the kitchen and shovels dishes from the counter and empties each drawer and props them empty against the wall. She retrieves the skillets and the Dutch oven and carries them to the fireplace and banks them into the ash and tears out the pages of **The Brothers Karamazov**, crumpling them and piling them and teepeeing the kindling. Then she leans in and blows the coals to life.

She walks to the couch by the fireplace, lies down on it, slides her palms across the upholstery. Then she climbs out of it and takes the axe off the floor and stands glossed with sweat, the sandy soil stuck to her jeans and to her boots, and brings the axe hard down into the spine of the couch. She works with rhythmic deliberation until it splits, and she passes the knife through the upholstery. She cuts and tears, lifting it from its staples until the frame of the couch becomes clear. In the shed she pumps up ten gallons of gas from the underground tank and carries it out and climbs high up onto the pile and, standing on his crumpled mattress, empties the steel gas cans, treading back and forth across ruined shelves, the remains of the footlocker and the bed. She sets the pile on fire, and it burns huge and greasy black while she watches.

She works all night. In the morning, kneeling before the river stone hearth, she drags the skillets from the fireplace with the poker. They are caked in a scabrous red ash and look ruined, fire-ravaged and rusted out. Fishing through the hot ash and dragging each onto the hearthstones, she is afraid that the fire has oxidized them. She carries out a Griswold number 14 skillet and lays it down on the porch and picks up the hose and blasts the skillet with water. The burned grease sheds in clots. Beneath, the bare steel is shining and clean, unmarked and unwarped, as good as the day it was cast. She holds it up to catch the light.

Fifteen

IT IS FOUR MILES NORTH ALONG THE Shoreline Highway from Turtle's house to Mendocino, where she goes each day to look for Jacob. She walks on the embankment above the road, eating dandelions and curly dock. She rips up thistles and, handling them with the skirts of her flannel, pares off the thorns and chews the stalks speculatively, polishing dirt from their twisted taproots with her thumb. People pull over to ask if she's okay, to ask if she needs a ride, and she stands raking one boot against the blacktop and cracking her knuckles and says that she's going to meet her friends and that she likes to walk. One guy, leaning over to talk to her through his passenger-side

window, says, "Are you . . . eating a thistle?" Turtle
looks at him. He says, "Is there any meat on that
thing at all?" She shakes her head no, not really.
He is looking at her intently. Turtle straightens
up away from his truck door and mounts up the
embankment into the woods. He calls something
after her, but she doesn't catch it.

Crossing the Big River Bridge into Mendocino,
she stops and looks across the beach for them.
Clear eddies have carved sandy pits against the
river's stony south bank and deep in these wells
the water reposes gel-thick and sapphire-blue beneath the shifting top layers. A few people walk
the tideline, but the boys are not there. She follows the road into town and stands on the high
concrete sidewalk in front of the Gallery Bookshop, looking up the street. Main Street fronts the
headlands, where blackberries sprawl up against
the fence, and beyond which the velvet grass is
blooming in the softest, gentlest purple she can
imagine, white umbels of angelica floating in the
field. She stands, going up onto her toes and down
onto her heels, looking up the street.

In the evening she returns home and sets her
stinging nettle to boiling in the copper pot, the
leaves rafting together, and sits cross-legged on
the porch eating strands of kelp that she has hauled
up from the beach in crates, hosed down, and left
to dry on stainless-steel laundry racks. With a pair
of chopsticks, she shepherds a nettle leaf out from

the others, rolls it slowly in the water, working with the chopsticks, and then lifts it dripping out of the pot. Cross-legged on the counter, she blows on the steaming leaf, waits, passes it into her mouth.

In the quiet of the house, the timbers creaking, the wind keening in the shingles, the roses itching at the window, her mind is entirely empty, and when it is not and when she cannot empty it, she repeats small phrases to herself, over and over, to drown out thought. Grin and bear it, she thinks, over and over, until the words no longer have meaning. She hinges open her Noveske and drags out the bolt carrier, her hands oily as a mechanic's. The firing pin is muddy with powder residue and she stows it in her cheek, sucking the steel clean, dipping a rag in whiskey-colored solvent and taking up the powder-black bolt, thinking: grin and bear it, grin and bear it, grinandbearit, grinandbarret, grinenbarret. The well pump goes out. Then one night, the lights flicker. She looks up. They go out. There is a crackling screech like an arc welder. Turtle picks up her shotgun and, triggering the weapon light, goes down the dark hallway to the pantry. She opens the electrical box and pans the weapon light across it. Most of the fuses have been replaced with blackened, corroded pennies. They are ancient, caked in thick white concretion. One is smoking, molten copper running from it in long drips. She throws the main, cutting off all power. Then she picks up the fire extinguisher and walks back into the dark living room and stands waiting, wondering what she will do if the insulation catches fire. She spends long hours in the pump house with its two green water-storage tanks, pumping water by hand with the pump's aluminum lever, bringing it up from the well down in the gulch to the tanks that feed the gravity lines in the house. She sits alone, bare feet on the concrete floor, levering and levering. She sits on rocks on Buckhorn Beach, cracking urchins open and picking out their viscera, barefoot, eyeing the ocean, rinsing their orange gonads in a sieve. She rolls handfuls of sea snails like dice, holding one poised between thumb and forefinger, waiting for it to relax, and when it does, she slides the firing pin past the black waferlike foot, through the muscular body, and draws it recoiling from the shell. She brings the others up to the house, pocketed in a fold of her shirt, stopping and unsheathing the knife to dig up a big white fennel root. Boiling, the shells rattle against the bottom of the pot. Some nights when she wakes in the coolest part of the evening and crawls out of her sleeping bag to sit before the window, she is sick with dread, telling herself, the solitude is good for you, girl, telling herself, this is not even solitude, this is something else. She sits cross-legged in the window and the cool breeze off the ocean eats into the dead parts.

After a week of looking for them, she walks out to Portuguese Beach, at the west end of Main Street in Mendocino, and they are there. Jacob is wading in the surf while Brett watches from the tide line, taking hits of whipped cream from the can. Turtle follows the staircase down to the beach beside Park Service signs warning of rogue waves. The beetling sandstone cliffs are overgrown with wild cabbage and hung in garlands of nasturtiums that braid with springwater. Turtle walks up the beach following a wavering tide line of dead jellyfish and sits down beside Brett. "Hey," she says.

"Holy shit!" Brett says in delight.

Jacob turns to look and says, "Holy shit!"

"It's Beaver!"

"It's Turtle!" Jacob says.

"Turtle!" Brett lunges across at her, and Turtle laughs as he tackles her, saying, "You! You!" He bears her to the sand. "You!" he says.

Jacob says, "Where have you been?"

"Did the Avengers call you?"

"You look **great**!"

"Skinny, though!"

"How's your summer?"

"We've missed you!"

"Seriously, dude, we **have**."

"Home," she says, "I've just been home."

They are both in board shorts, barefoot, shirtless. Brett's nose and cheeks and ears are sunburned. Sand sticks to their shins in patches, their hair is mussed. She can see their shoes on a log farther up the beach, their books, their shirts.

"Come on," Jacob says, slogging up out of the water. "How long has it been?"

Turtle doesn't know.

Brett says, "Dude! Like—mid- or late April to whatever today is."

"July seventh."

She says, "Can we not talk about it?"

"Sure. Like when we saw Brett's mother, sitting on a pedestal, naked."

"And we **never** talked about it."

"Which might've been the right move."

"Because what is there to say?"

Jacob lights a joint and draws on it and passes it to Brett. They sit down against a sandy, splintery redwood log looking out at the ocean. It is bright and there is a glare off the water and they are all squinting. The air is clear and it looks like they can see entirely across the Pacific.

"So how are you?" Brett holds the smoke in his lungs, nodding, and passes it to her. She looks down at it.

She says, "Good. I've been good."

"Do you want to talk about it?" Jacob says.

"Dude! She **just** said."

"Are you all right, though? Can I ask that?"

"Yeah," she says.

Jacob receives the joint and squints at her. "You eating at all?"

"Hey," she says.

"Hey," Brett agrees.

"I'm just asking."

"Come away with us, Turtle," Brett says.

"What?"

"Turtle. This high school thing is somewhat . . . a little bit . . . just a tiny bit lame."

"No . . ." Jacob says, scandalized.

"Yes," Brett says. "Profoundly lame."

Turtle says nothing.

"High school is **awesome**," Jacob says.

"Mmm . . ." Brett says. "Mmm . . . Is it, though?"

"Brett wants to go away and become pirates."

"Dude! You're not saying it right."

"How am I not saying it?"

"It sounds dumb when you say it like that."

"Okay, so how should one say it?"

"Not like that! It sounds childish. Turtle's gonna think I'm childish."

"How do you say it?"

"I want to go away **and become pirates**!"

"You're right. That sounds way less childish."

"What do you think, Turtle?"

"No," Turtle says.

"Harsh, guys. Harsh."

"I like it here," Turtle says.

"Jacob, tell her about the thing."

"You tell her."

"What thing?" Turtle says.

"Tell her, please, Jacob?"

"What thing?" she says again.

"Out in the Pacific Ocean," Jacob says, "is a vast floating island of trash as big as Texas. A vortex of plastic bottles, Styrofoam coolers, packing peanuts, plastic bags mounded up on the hulks of half-sunk ships. Brett wants to go there and become pirates."

"You're not saying it right."

"Brett wants to go there **and become pirates**!"

"Tell me that doesn't sound **awesome**."

"It doesn't sound awesome," Turtle says. Turtle doesn't know why anyone would want to leave Mendocino. She has never understood the tourists, either. She doesn't know what the point of it is.

"Although . . ." Jacob says.

"Here it comes," Brett says.

"**Nation building**," Jacob says, "has a certain appeal. Doesn't it?"

"No," Turtle says, "it doesn't."

"Founding a glorious republic," Jacob says.

"Hmm," Turtle says doubtfully. "Probably hard."

"Reclaiming the flotsam and jetsam of a failing civilization, and from the ashes building a Utopia."

"My parents were Utopians," Brett says. "Now they're divorced and my mom is tired all the time. She says she's just plain worn out. She says, 'Brett, honey, I'm worn out.' Her hands hurt her. She's a massage therapist. But she has arthritis. I'm telling you, that is not the way. **Pirates**. That is the way."

"We could farm mealworms," Jacob says, warming to the idea, "in our Styrofoam deserts. They can subsist entirely on plastic. I can see us now: farming our mealworms by day, and by night reading Plato aloud to one another beneath the constellations of a foreign sky, accompanied by the vast grind of an entire continent of plastic bottles churning in the current and by the ethereal whisperings of grocery bags saltating across the mounded plastic dunes."

Turtle says, "I think you're imagining the garbage island to be more interesting than it is."

Brett says, "If you really did have a hundred miles of mealworms, I bet you'd hear them at night. Chewing. And chewing."

"We could farm fish in vast nets made from knit-together plastic bags."

"I can see us now: a wild and savage tribe of sword-wielding eco-irates, as ruggedly handsome as we are visionary, crossing the mealworm barrens astride our giant war iguanas."

"War iguanas?"

"**Obviously** war iguanas."

"If you think about it, there are probably iguanas there already, resident in that barren and postmodern Galápagos, each generation more shopping-bag-colored than the last."

"**Dude.**"

"And if we used rhizofiltration, we could recapture nuclear waste from the ocean and sequester it in giant laminated-glass tetrahedrons that would slowly warm the waters around our island so we could farm more fish."

"Imagine the fecund, uranium-warmed lagoons, bounteous with farmed lobsters and kelp, patrolled by shoals of salmon, and lit from deep within by mysterious, glowing green pyramids, hung on vast, creaking anchor chains, while on the plastic shores above bask our noble if tempestuous reptilian steeds."

The wind lifts stray hairs from her ponytail and whips them across her face. They stick to her chapped lips. She pulls them away, tucks them behind an ear. If there really is an island of trash out there the size of Texas, it's just a shitty place and there's no salvaging it. But she doesn't need to tell them that.

They walk back up to Main Street discussing whether you could ride an iguana if it was big enough and if it would be appropriate to carry a trident and if giant laminated-glass tetrahedrons filled with nuclear waste could disrupt the currents of the entire ocean and cause a mass extinction event. They go into Lipinski's Juice Joint and when Turtle sees the prices chalked on the board, she begins cracking her knuckles. Jacob pulls out his wallet and unfurling the bills, says, "It's okay, Turtle," and Brett says, "The movie about us could be called **A Fistful of Mealworms**," and Jacob says, "Hey, Dean, we're starting our own republic, are you interested at all?" and the bearded, gauged barista says, "Will there be tourists?" and Brett says, "No," and the barista says, "Will there be weed?" and Brett says, "As pirates, our primary intoxicant will obviously be rum, but yes," and Jacob says, "We're going to farm psychotropic sea toads in shallow lagoons warmed by nuclear waste and you can lick those to get high," and Dean says, "What?" and Turtle won't order, so Jacob says, "She'll have the falafel. At least I think so. She's been struck mute by capitalism," and Dean says, "It's the damn tourists. It's always been bad, of course, but we were featured again in the **New York Times**. I read that, in Mendocino, a hundred dollars only buys you, like, eighty-two dollars' worth of stuff," and Brett says, "That literally makes no sense. By definition, a hundred dollars buys you a hundred dollars' worth of stuff," and Dean says, "It's the damn tourists," and Brett says, "Okay, Dean, I get it that you don't like the tourists, but they cannot be blamed for ills that are, by very definition, impossible."

They sit at a wooden table out on the deck in the shadow of a water tower. The fence is overgrown in morning glory. Dean brings out three mocha glaciers, holding the glasses all together and all of them sweating chips of ice with the blended mocha mounded as thick as ice cream. They eat the messy cucumber and falafel pitas, discussing if you could really farm salmon in giant tanks of welded-together plastic bottles and if you could feed them mealworms raised entirely on plastic. The hard thing, Jacob keeps saying, is that mealworms should be fine, but they mature into poisonous beetles. Turtle has never had coffee and it makes her hands shake. Her pita falls apart and she keeps having to lick her fingers clean, looking at the boys to follow the conversation.

Jacob looks at Turtle. "Want to come over?"

"Yeah," she says.

"Need to call your dad?"

"Not really," she says.

"Yeah?" Jacob says.

"Yeah," she says.

At five o'clock they meet Jacob's sister, Imogen, who works at a coffee shop in town, and she drives them to Jacob's house. Their feet and shins are still covered in thin layers of sand. Both boys get in the back. Turtle rides shotgun with Imogen, who looks curiously at her. Jacob leans forward between the seats to introduce them. "Turtle, Imogen. Imogen, this is the chain-saw-wielding, shotgun-toting, Zen Buddhist, once-and-future queen of postapocalyptic America."

"Charmed," Imogen says, pulling out of the parking space.

"Her reign will be hard but fair."

"In our advisory roles, we will council fairness."

"But no one can entirely temper the stoical hardness that is her essential nature."

"And how did you meet my stupid brother?"

Turtle says nothing.

"Oh, come on, how'd you meet?"

Turtle looks back at Jacob. Both boys are reading, Brett leaning against the passenger-side door with **A Rage for Revenge**, Jacob sitting upright with **The Iliad.**

They drive in silence for a while.

"So, Jacob—is this the chick that saved your dumb, lost life when you were lost in the woods?"

"We weren't lost."

"It sounded like you were lost, though. Like, **super** lost."

"We weren't. We knew where we were. We didn't know where the road was."

"So—lost, then."

"We weren't lost."

Imogen says, "So, uh—Turtle, how do you like school?"

"Fine."

"Where do you live?"

"Little River."

"Oh, so just south of here! Inland, or by the coast?"

"Coast."

"Do you like it?"

Turtle doesn't answer.

They cross the Noyo and go through Fort Bragg, the town ten miles north of Mendocino. They go on past MacKerricher State Park and across the Ten Mile River and they turn off the highway.

They are a long day's walk from Buckhorn Hill. Jacob's house is a contemporary redwood structure at the end of a long, winding black drive. It overlooks the north bank of the river and is surrounded by coastal prairie.

"You live in a **mansion**?" Turtle says.

"It's not a mansion," Imogen says.

"Hey!" Brett says. "Hey, Turtle. I live in a double-wide trailer. So check your privilege, homeslice."

"My what?"

"It's, like, five bedrooms, guys."

"What did you call me?"

"Shut up, Jacob. It's a mansion."

"Did you just call me homeslice?"

Brett says, "We looked you up, missy. Several years ago, a property adjoining yours with a third of an acre sold for one-point-eight-million dollars. You own **sixty acres** of ocean-view property in one of the most expensive real estate markets in the U.S."

"It's not technically one of the most expensive—" Jacob says.

"But it's the best!" Brett says. "The best!"

"But—" Turtle says.

"Shut up!"

"**Yeah**," Jacob says. "Yeah. And **this** is not a mansion."

"Shut up, Jacob."

They pull into a large, clean, empty four-car garage.

"Okay," Imogen says, getting out, "you kids have fun with . . . whatever this is."

Jacob shows Turtle the house. It is nothing to him. It is all familiar. To Turtle, it is incredible. In every room, floor-to-ceiling windows look out on windswept bluffs and the Ten Mile estuary. In the kitchen, there are black-granite counters and a black-granite kitchen island, ceiling racks hung with stainless-steel cookware, maple butcher blocks. It is all very clean. Turtle wants all of it.

"Where are your tools and things?"

There had been none in the garage.

"Tools?"

"You know—tools," she says.

"Oh, there's a whole bunch of tools in Mom's workshop. Acetylene torches and things."

She says, "So what do you do when something breaks?"

Jacob looks at her smiling, as if waiting for the rest of that sentence. Then he says, "You mean, like—are you asking, like, which plumber do we call? I could ask Dad."

Turtle stands looking at him.

They go through a hallway with a floor-to-ceiling glass case of Pomo baskets.

Turtle stands looking at the small, tightly woven brindled baskets until Brett and Jacob reach the end of the hallway and turn and wait for her. In the living room, a huge spiral staircase with oak treads bolted directly to a varnished pine trunk leads to Jacob's and Imogen's rooms. A bookshelf takes up an entire wall of his room, with a ladder for reaching the top shelves. More books are stacked against the walls and heaped on the end tables, some of them open, dog-eared, and heavily annotated. The beige carpet shows the pattern of light-and-dark nap from being vacuumed that morning.

Turtle sits on the bed looking around.

"I know, right?" Brett says.

"Yeah," Turtle says.

"What?" Jacob says.

"Yeah," Turtle says meaningfully.

"His dad patented a process of detecting errors in silicon microchips."

"What are silicon microchips?"

"You know—your phone." Jacob holds up his phone.

"Oh."

"His mom makes naked chicks."

"What?"

Jacob says, "She casts nudes. They're reminiscent of Rodin in their pronounced corporality and in the exaggeration of their human idiosyncrasies. In some, she has replaced the vascular system with clematis."

"They're gone all the time. Brandon to Utah, where they make the silicon wafers—I don't know why, because no one gives a shit about Utah, I guess—and Isobel to artsy places all over the world."

"They're not gone **all** the time."

"They think Imogen looks after him."

"Imogen **does** look after me."

"She doesn't. She lets him drive to school. He doesn't have a license. He has to cook for himself. Weak gruel and porridge. He's basically Oliver Twist."

"She drives me sometimes."

"They go to the same school and she won't even take him."

"Well, her classes start later than mine on Tuesdays and Thursdays."

"It's child abuse."

"Lies. All lies."

"Imogen makes him sit at intersections with a cardboard sign that says, 'Abandoned Child. Anything Helps.' Then at night, she takes all the money and buys lip gloss and music."

Jacob rolls his eyes.

Later they eat dinner with his parents around a claw-footed mahogany table. Windows look out on the beach, where a circle of gulls rises and collapses and bull kelp tangles in the surf. Brett sits with one leg folded under the other, about half out of his seat, looking ready to get up and wander off in search of something. Turtle keeps looking at Brandon and Isobel Learner and then down at her food. Brandon is a thin, quiet man wearing a white dress shirt and slacks. At the beginning of dinner, he carefully rolls up his sleeves. Turtle puts her hair up, draws the firing pin out of her mouth, and skewers it in her ponytail. Isobel Learner is looking critically into her glass of red wine, wearing a robe belted around her jeans and T-shirt. She has black hair streaked with gray and wears small silver earrings with blue stones.

"So, Turtle," Isobel says. "How are you liking your summer?"

They are eating ahi on a bed of wild rice with grilled broccolini.

"It's okay," Turtle says.

Isobel has a gentle, wine-drinking, leaning-back curiosity, with all the work and all the thinking done for the day. Her hands are stained black as if with gunpowder residue, but it's something else.

"What is it your father does?"

"What?" Turtle leans forward to hear.

"Your dad—does he have a profession?"

"Say that again?"

"Mom," Jacob says, "you're mumbling and hiding your mouth with your glass."

"Ah"—setting her glass down—"what does your father do, Turtle?"

"He, uh—" Turtle says. "He works as a carpenter. But he reads a lot."

Isobel tilts the wineglass forward, comparing the red wine to the white of her napkin. "Look at this," she says. "Turtle, honey," she says. "Come

here. You see that? The meniscus? The meniscus
is— Have you done physics? Well, do you see
the thinnest ring where the wine clings to the
glass?"

The wine is a deep dark red. Along the edge, a
razor-thin oval slivers out across the glass, like the
thinnest, sandy edge of a pond, and where it at-
tenuates, the ring is tea-colored. Turtle is looking
at Isobel carefully to see what she is saying.

"You see how it's just sort of off-brown the way
that white apple flesh turns brown when you leave
it out?"

"Yes," Turtle says.

"That's the oxidation. It's a product of the age of
the wine."

"It's rust?"

"Like rust, yes."

Isobel sets the wine down, abruptly rises, and returns from the kitchen with more wineglasses, the
stems slotted through her fingers. She sets them
out and pours into each.

"Honey," Brandon says, "is this a good idea?"

"Yes." Isobel pushes a glass to Brett, then to Turtle, Jacob, and Imogen. Turtle lifts hers, compares
it to the white tablecloth. She looks over at Isobel
and Isobel demonstrates swirling and then putting
her nose to the wine. "What do you think?" she
asks.

"About what?" Turtle says, smelling the wine.

"What kind of fruit?" Isobel smiles at Turtle,

leans in. She has a snaggletooth, and when she smiles, it shows.

"Ah," Jacob says, swirling his own glass. "Big, ripe summer blackberries leaning against a white picket fence in Napa with the vintner just come out onto his porch holding a cup of French roast—"

"**Nyet!**" Isobel says, cutting him off. "I know what you're doing, mister. Well, she can look after herself." She swings her impressive gaze to Turtle, who sits with the glass in front of her, and then to Brett. "What do you think, Turtle? I love that name. Turtle? Turtle! Great. Come to you in a spirit quest, or born to it?"

"Uh," Turtle says.

"That's okay. Swirl that glass, honey."

Turtle swirls the glass.

"What do you smell?"

"I don't know."

"Orchard fruit—apples, pears, stone fruit? Black fruit—blackberries? Red fruit—raspberries, strawberries? Cherries? Leather? The forest floor? Gaminess?"

"She doesn't like being put on the spot," Jacob says.

"She's not on the spot. Blue fruit—blueberries? Tart? Fruit-stand fresh? Sitting on the counter a couple of days? Or jammy—baked into a pie?"

Isobel is hanging on her answer. There is no menace in her at all.

"Grapes," Brett says, "fermented grapes."

"Black fruit," Turtle says, "but fresh. Fresh blackberries. Black cherries. A little of that—like, a nasturtium blossom," Turtle says.

"Pepper! Yes! Black fruit and spice," Isobel says, leaning back in her chair, "a little cherrywood, do you get that—? As if you were to bite into a fresh cherry woodchip." She buries her face in the wine and inhales. Expressions chase themselves subtly around her eyes and eyebrows, a dry comedienne expression, she knows exactly how funny she's being, and she's enjoying herself.

"All right," Brandon says, reaching for Turtle's glass, "we can take that wine away."

Jacob tosses his back before Brandon can get to it.

"Oh, let the girl try it, Brandon," Isobel says. Brandon lets his hands down, looks at Isobel. Turtle has always known that other people grew up differently than she did. But she had, she thinks, no idea **how** differently. She lifts the glass, tastes it. It is sharper than it smells. It seems to fill her mouth. Isobel is watching her intently. Turtle wrinkles her nose. She gets the blackberry there, in the middle, then she gets a texture off it, like Isobel said, as if she'd bitten into the edge of a cherry bookcase.

"On the palate?" Isobel asks.

"Ugh," Turtle says, "ych."

"Well," Isobel says, leaning back, smiling, "she has time."

That night, Brandon shows her to her room, which has a king-size mahogany bed with a linen duvet. He shows her into the attached bathroom and stoops over the bathtub showing her how to work the shower and where to find the shampoo and toothpaste. Down the hall, they can hear the boys beating each other with pillows and laughing.

"Jacob says you've told your dad you're here?" Brandon asks.

"Yeah," Turtle says. "Of course."

"Good. Good."

They wait in silence. Brandon says, "You're quiet, aren't you?"

Turtle doesn't know.

"That's good." He smiles.

Turtle crinkles her eyes at him.

"Jacob said that your home situation might be a little, ah, liberal," he says, leading her out of the attached bath. Turtle has no idea what he means. "What he said was, well, he said we shouldn't bother you about it, because you were an Ishmael upon the broad blue seas of these, your teenage years. And I just wanted to say that this bedroom is, you know, always here, just in case you need a Queequeg's coffin to keep you afloat, you know."

She may not understand Brandon's words, but she can parse his every intention just by framing his expression in her mind.

"It's not like that," she says.

"Oh, well. Of course," Brandon says. He's embarrassed. He pats the bed. "It's memory foam. The best, supposedly. And you're, uh, always welcome here, anyway. We all do the best we can, I guess."

Turtle lies in bed that night, listening to the house. Downstairs, some machine cycles on, the water softener or the refrigerator. She looks at the spackled ceiling. She guesses that the boys will still be up talking, but she cannot hear them. She pulls the duvet off the bed and onto the floor. She can't stand a bed. She lies on the carpet with her head pillowed in the crook of her arm.

In the morning, Imogen drives them into Mendocino and they spend the day at the beach. They go to Lipinski's and lunch on the porch, passing around a joint and drinking mocha glaciers. Days go by this way, Turtle walking back home or being driven back by Imogen, meeting them at Big River Beach or Portuguese Beach in the morning. Sometimes they catch a ride with Caroline from Mendocino to Brett's double-wide trailer on Flynn Creek Road, where the plastic sinks, the shower, and the toilets are crusted with mineral grime and the water reeks of sulfur and calcium. In the living room there is an aviary where three parrots shoulder together, watching the humans eat dinner at a Formica table heaped with bills and junk mail and an old sewing machine and a single mason jar filled with buttons.

Caroline keeps staring at Turtle as they eat.

"Mom, quit staring," Brett says.

"I'm not staring," Caroline says.

They are eating some kind of casserole.

"I'm just happy she's here," Caroline says. Then, leaning forward, "So, how's Martin?"

"He's all right," Turtle says.

"Any projects?"

"Um," Turtle says, "no, not really."

"He **always** seemed to have a project. Used to be. Build something. Research something. What's he been up to?"

Turtle bites her lip, looks around. "Reading, mostly."

"Well, he **always** was a reader. You know, I'm glad you're here. I was beginning to think we'd never see you again. He never called. That night after we dropped you off, he said he would call, but I haven't heard from him," Caroline says, "and his old number is disconnected."

"Is it?" Turtle says. She knows it is.

"Yeah," Caroline says. "Did you guys change the number?"

"The phone lines," Turtle says, "run up through the orchard, sometimes a branch messes them up, or sometimes water gets into the line."

"Oh," Caroline says. "Has he talked to the phone company about that?"

"It's intermittent," Turtle says.

"What **is** he feeding you these days?"

"Mom," Brett says.

"A lot of nettle tea," Turtle says, "and dandelions."

"Nettle tea," Caroline says, "is chock-full of vitamins and minerals, and of course it's also a mild abortifacient, but I suppose you're not too worried about that. Well, now, is he still growing?"

"Growing?" Turtle says. "No."

"Wait," Jacob says, "a mild **what**?"

"Growing?" she repeats.

"Is he taking care of you?" Caroline asks. "Everything is all right?"

"Wait— **Was** he growing?" Turtle asks.

"No, of course not— I was, no," Caroline says. "I just meant— Where has he been? If you're going to be coming over here, I'd like to talk to him, at least. There must be a way of getting ahold of him. Have you talked about what classes you're going to be taking next year?"

Turtle shakes her head.

She likes the rides home in the evening with Imogen and Jacob. It is always the end of a long day and she is tired. She goes home most nights. Isobel is oblivious. She is too involved in other things. She cares very much for Turtle's opinion on things, for talking to Turtle about things, but she has not noticed or seemed to notice anything unusual in Turtle's home life and she does not care if Turtle goes home or not. But Brandon is paying a quiet attention. Caroline, too. And also, the boys wear her out. It is good to sit over the pot with the tea roiling and to be alone with the thoughts that surface there. She likes them, but she is exhausted by their company. She's never spent so much time with other people. They feed off one another's enthusiasm. But Turtle is very worn out by them. She is not entirely sure how she feels, climbing up the steps alone, back to her darkened house, returning to solace, in some way, and to comfort— but also to regret. There is a way the house feels to her when she comes home. It is the same house and she knows it, but it looks different than it has ever looked before. She will sit cross-legged on the hearthstones, building up the fire, eating strips of dried kelp, and listening to the silence as the firelight rises before her and drains across the empty living room floor.

Sixteen

WHEN SHE HEARS THE 4RUNNER COMING up the drive the next day, she pulls on her jeans, threads the knife onto the belt, slips into a T-shirt and flannel. Then she folds up her blankets and sets them by the hearthstones and opens the door. It is Jacob, without Imogen this time. Standing on the porch, he looks past her, and she watches him take in the scrubbed floorboards and clean counters, the scoured fireplace, frying pans hanging on hooks along the wall in the kitchen. The living room smells of powder solvent and oil.

He says, "I like the place. Spare."

"It's not spare," she says.

"All right," he says, "a little minimalist."

"This is just how the living room is," she says.

"All right," he says, "I like it."

"You should."

"Where's Captain Ahab?"

"Out."

He lifts a paper grocery bag, rolled down at the top, and says, "My parents think I'm at Brett's. Brett is at his dad's in Modesto. I brought picnic things."

"You ever have eel?"

"I didn't know we had eels, but now that I know, I'm wondering why we're not eating eels **right now**."

In the kitchen she takes down a skillet and a stick of butter from the warm fridge. Then she walks past him out onto the porch and picks up a can of lighter fluid and a bucket. They go down the hill together beside a deep-cut seam in the grass running with clear water, overhung with currants and thimbleberries. Frogs leap from the grass to the water. They walk through a stand of alders and Jacob reaches up to capture an alder leaf in his fingers and his shirt rises and shows his tawny stomach. Inside the crests of his hip bones, two alluvial hollows, the top of a trim and boyish V going down into his pants. These hollows fill her with excruciating want, a sensation of almost happening, like stepping down from one stair to the next. For a moment she cannot look away.

They duck through the barbwire fence, cross the

highway, and climb down to Buckhorn Beach, a broad crescent of black shingle and white foam, blue-stone causeways diked with quartz, green waves among gardens of the large, round cobbles. Buckhorn Island sits a hundred feet from the tide line, out between the two hooks of land that form the cove, and the backwash of the retreating waves funnels through the island's cave and there meets the incoming set, booming the island like a drum, lofting slurries of white water through the blow-hole, hanging foam into the island's pines, the water slapping down onto the rock. On the south-ern arm of the cove, there is a redwood mansion and a gardener going back and forth with a lawn mower. These would be Turtle's closest neighbors, within a fifteen-minute walk of her house. She's never seen them. The sky is blustery. Beyond the safety of the cove, the surf breaks white on the bare, rocky islands that litter the coast here.

They set their picnic bag behind a driftwood log and Jacob takes off his shoes and rolls up his pants and carries the bucket out to the rocks. When the waves break against the island, the water surges into the tide pools, rises up, and retreats. The tide is not low enough for good tide pooling. When-ever they lift a stone up, the eels careen through channels, pools, fields of sea grass, Turtle and Jacob plunging their hands into the turban-snail-filled bottle necks. When Jacob pulls his first eel out, its head pushing from between his fingers, jaw open, it slithers free of his right hand and he catches it with the left and it slithers from his fist and is gone, winding madly across the rock, Jacob lunging after it, and then the creature is under the next stone. He braces his shoulder to it, and Turtle helps him. They heave the stone aside and the placid pool below is split by ripples as eels flee in every direction, Turtle lifting them by handfuls into the bucket and Jacob trapping one in a dead end. It is an oily-black monster, twenty inches long, thick as a garden hose. He lifts it out of the pool and it squirts out of his fist and he goes hard down on his knees, lunging, lifting it and again losing it. The creature flashes once across the slick blue rock and is gone beneath a wine barrel-sized stone. Jacob puts a shoulder to the stone, but cannot move it.

The eels are black with kelp-brown tiger stripes and doglike faces, jutting jaws. Turtle already has a dozen in the bucket. She and Jacob find iridescent-green centipedes, horned sea lemons with lacy gills unfurled, porcelain incrustations of spiral tube worms. They shift more cobbles. Sometimes, the water beneath will be still, the snails clattering across the mother-of-pearl carpets, the hermit crabs lifting their blue-pink clutch of limbs back into their blue-pink turban shells, the sullen-looking clingfish suckered against the stone, stone-colored themselves. Other times, the tide pool erupts with the spiny backs of the eels. Jacob follows one down a channel, groping through the sea lettuce, trapping it against the wall and losing it, lifting it in one hand, losing it into a knee-deep pool full of urchins.

"Okay," Turtle tells him, "you're going to get one this time."

"It's like the glee grave robbers must feel, cracking open caskets to see what's in them."

Turtle says, "What?"

"You know, lifting aside the stones is like—it's like opening a hatch that goes into the unknown. We could lift aside one of these rocks and find—anything."

"What?" Turtle says. "No. You stand there, I'll push them to you."

"What is it like for them?"

"It's not like anything for them," Turtle says, "they're eels."

"They may not be, technically, eels."

"They're obviously eels."

"That's true."

Jacob kneels down beside one inlet and Turtle pulls a stone aside. Beneath, the eels split in every direction and Turtle herds them, flashing, slithering, toward Jacob. They boil into his inlet, Jacob trying to block them off, and then he catches one, brings it out of the water in one hand, its head lashing. Then, with a sucking gurgle, all the water drains out of their tide pool.

They both look down at it, stumped. They stand,

Jacob brandishing the eel, Turtle thinking, what just happened? Then a bad feeling hits her and she looks up. The ocean around them is gone. It has retreated out past the island, the kelp beds and tide pools crackling and naked. Every pothole and every stand of bowling balls issues a long slurping noise as the water is pulled back into the ocean.

Jacob says, "Turtle—!" and then he boosts up and runs. Turtle, barefoot, goes after him, slips on a wet cobble and falls onto hands and knees. Jacob stops, turns, and looks at her. He looks up. Then she is underwater, being poured across the rocky bottom. Her overwhelming feeling is of surprise. Every effort and thought shrinks to nothing. She is unlocked from her body and becomes vast, enormous, and boundless, while around her kelp strands unfurl and hang upward. Rays of light break through the surface far above. The water looks motionless, uniform and blue, but in the slanting bars of sunlight, she can see grit and kelp crabs streaming past.

Turtle's forward rush slows. The pressure mounts in her ears. The light dims. She is held in the slackening current. She feels it begin to change as water drains from the flooded cove back out to sea. The undertow peels sand from the bottom in long, undulate ribbons. Turtle thinks, swim, you bitch. Then she is dragged backward, helpless, raked along the rocky floor, bowling balls lurching up from their sockets and bounding after her.

The roar is so grindingly vast that every individual sound is lost.

She climbs desperately toward the surface, breaks among creamy heaps of white water, and takes a lungful of air. The black wall of Buckhorn Island is hard beside her, terrifyingly close, shining blue mussels knurled to the rock like so many porcelain razors. Brush that wall, she knows, and she may not make it. She cannot see Jacob anywhere, but ahead of her the beach is flooded, the driftwood thundering against the cliffs. No way he escaped. He is here somewhere, only she cannot see him. The water is still draining backward, even as more waves are pushing onto shore, so the entire cove is filled with muddled, complicated currents. It tosses and heaves like water carried in a bucket.

She dives. The cobbled bottom is right there—they are in ten, fifteen feet of water. She can see Jacob against the surface. He is drifting, limp, blood falling from him in streamers. She grabs him by the hair and hauls him up.

"Breathe!" she yells. "Breathe!" He takes a breath and immediately pukes. She holds on to him. Buckhorn Island is close beside them. They are being dragged toward it. A tremendous amount of water has washed up into the cove and all of it is now pouring back out to sea, funneling past the island, through the narrow, rocky channels that usually protect the cove. She and Jacob have to reach the beach. If they are pulled out with the tide, they will find themselves in the unsheltered sculpture garden of twisted black rocks that litter the coast here.

Above them, on that well-groomed hook with its redwood mansion, the gardener is still going back and forth with the lawn mower.

"Jacob, can you swim?"

He nods. She dives and he follows. Together they kick hard across the blue-cobbled bottom, great whips of seaweed winging past. They make no headway against the current. She breaks the surface, choking. Then a backwashing wave crashes over them, and Jacob is sucked, screaming, into the island's gorging stone tunnel. She delves under the surface and follows him into the cave beneath the island. They breach together. The chop throws water over their faces. Turtle gasps. She sucks air. They lull up and down, the lapping water and their breathing echoing, and Turtle looks up. They are in the tide-hollowed chamber inside the island.

She can see the bright demi-circles of the entrances to either side, blocked by intermittent swells. One side looks toward the beach. The other fronts open ocean. Water eddies off the walls and drips, echoing, from the vaulted ceiling. It is waist-deep, the color of old glass. The mouth of the blowhole is open above them and garlands of nasturtiums hang through it, the flowers a burnt red. The floor is carpeted with brown feathers of kelp, and huge orange starfish cling everywhere to the rock. The kelp fronds plume forward and back with the opposing currents.

"Shit," Jacob says, and she turns. A wall of water is sweeping in through the cave's mouth.

"No," she says. She turns and looks behind them. A second wall of water is rising in through the opposite entrance, and the two walls are converging. One is the wave coming in off the ocean and the other is the backwash draining from the beach. "No, no, no," she says. Her thoughts are green and yellow with terror. She thinks, we are going to die, her diaphragm hitching with sobs. He grabs her by the waist. She puts her chin on his shoulder. She thinks, we are going to die, we are going to die right now. The water swells around them, lifts to their chests, and then the wave hits her and she goes slip-sliding through the kelp and is miraculously swung up into the air among lofted chandeliers of water and great, hanging tresses of blooming nasturtium. Her brain and her guts hurt with terror. She puts her hand out to brace against the impact and she is clapped against the wall. Her fingers break, her arms fold, and she is keelhauled across thirty feet of rock, rolling side over side, covering her face with her forearms and going hard into the stone with the rupturing bursts of shattering mussel shells. Something is talking to her, someone right behind her is whispering into her ear, you are not going to die, hold on, you are not going to die, and Turtle herself thinks, you bitch, you slit, you just hold on, do not let go, never let go.

Then they are out of the cave. Turtle is swimming hard. The water tosses above her head and the chop breaks around her. The beach, the cove, and Buckhorn Island are behind her. Around them, the sea is worked into green mounds that funnel and break on crooked black rocks. Kelp fronds rise out of the indecipherable green, broader than her hands, painted in lustrous brushstrokes dark and golden brown. She and Jacob have been drawn into the maze of small islands and black rock that lie just off the coast. She fights hand over hand through the water. There is no pain, no sense of effort. She catches a glimpse of sand, shingle, blue walls of rock. It is an island, some nameless piece of rock a hundred yards from the bluffs with a small, sandy notch cut into the western face. She fights through the surf and a swell drags her up onto the rough blue stones of the sea stack's small beach. She pitches forward and claws out of the draining water, then turns and wades back in to help Jacob up.

Seventeen

TOGETHER THEY SLOSH UP THE BEACH to the stone foot of the island and clamber desperately away from the water, a climb of twenty or twenty-five feet, the damp blue rock shearing away beneath them, the cracks grouted with swarms of quivering roaches. She mounts into a swash of spongy, tightly grown weeds and lies puking. The top of the island is thirty feet of scrubby grass filled with the small, bleached bones of birds. She crawls on her elbows to the edge and looks out. The island is of a height with the bluffs. Between here and there, three hundred feet of black rocks awash in the surf and the shadow of rock sprawled beneath the blue-green water. Between the sets, it looks almost as if they could swim to shore, but when the waves break into those channels, it is something else. She lies in the grass thinking, we're fucked. Then she thinks, we're not fucked. If anybody knows how to handle this, it's you. Where are your guts?

Jacob is lying beside her, facedown, hands clenched together beneath his chest, shivering and vomiting. He has a concussion, she is sure of it. She has had a few herself and knows the feeling. He is bleeding copiously into his hair. There is blood on his face and in the grass all around him. It's the outsized bleeding she associates with scalp wounds. He is going to be fine. She cannot say the same for herself.

"Can we swim there?"

She looks at him. She does not know if she can even stand.

"Yeah, I didn't think so."

There is a single cloud high above, attenuated into white threads. She peels her hands from bloody folds of her shirt and looks at them. Her nails are cracked away from their pulpy beds. Her right hand is cut deeply across the palm. She's broken the smallest three fingers of her left hand. All but the index. She puts her hands in her armpits and lies with them held securely against her. It hurts to breathe.

"What do we do, Turtle?"

Sand is stuck to half his face, his teeth rimmed with blood. He has vomited all over himself.

"Turtle?"

"Yeah?"

"Are we okay?"

Her mouth is full of sand. She says, "We've got to traction my fucking motherfucking goddamn fingers."

He begins vomiting again. She lies in the grass and watches the single cloud turn and shift. At last he says, "That sounds like something better left to a doctor."

She doesn't say anything to this.

The wind blows across the island's top. He's trying out his objections in his mind. She can see him doing it. He shivers in tight bursts.

"Okay," he says at last.

"Okay?"

"Okay."

"We need sticks to splint them," she says. "Wide cotton ties, an inch wide, eight to twelve inches long."

Jacob staggers to his feet. Turtle lies holding very still and grimacing. Jacob paces around the island. He is unsteady on his feet. At last, he says, "Not a lot of sticks here." She can hear him trying several of the small bones scattered in the grass, but they are bleached and fragile. At last he says, "How about a pen? I've got one in my pocket."

"Still?"

"Well, I started with three."

"Get my knife."

He comes over to her. She lies very still. He un-snaps the clasp and drags the knife from the wet sheath. He cuts the pen in two. He says, "That was my lucky pen. I wrote a very good essay on Angela Carter with that pen."

"Now we're going to need several cotton ties." She eases herself up and they cut the ties from her wet flannel.

She carefully extracts her broken hand from her armpit and holds it out.

"Jesus Christ," Jacob says.

The bones make angular protrusions in the skin. Her ring finger is visibly dislocated from its socket.

"How are you not freaking out?"

"What?"

"Aren't you, like, flipping out?"

"Jacob."

"You need a doctor."

"Pull steadily and firmly, in line with the finger."

"Oh god."

"Don't go easy. Pull firmly on that bitch."

Taking hold of her broken pinkie finger, he says, "Oh god it's bad, oh god it's real bad, it feels real, real bad."

Turtle looks up at the sky. Her body flushes with anticipation, and she can feel her hair prickling and standing up.

"Now?"

"Yes, now."

"Okay," he says.

"Wait!" she says.

He looks at her. She takes a deep breath. She is quivering with fear.

"Don't limp-wrist it, Jacob," she says.

"I don't know what that means."

"Just do it right the first time."

"I'm gonna try."

She blows air through her pursed lips, shuddering and shaking.

"Okay: now."

Jacob pulls traction and the finger straightens with the audible grinding of bones. Turtle hisses through gritted teeth. Jacob shrieks as the finger straightens. "Motherfucker!" she says. She gasps, sweating. "Motherfucker!" she says again, looking at him almost with needfulness. Jacob places the trimmed pen half against the straightened finger and wraps it carefully with a wide flannel band and ties it off.

"You're lucky you didn't die."

"I know it."

"I'm serious, Turtle."

She looks at him flatly, trying to see how she could be anything else but serious.

"The way you got dragged across those rocks."

"I know."

"I can't believe you're alive."

She says nothing.

"You might be kind of a tough person."

Afterward, Turtle lies in the grass getting her mind back. With the pain from splinting the fingers it felt like the thinking part of her had gone away and she needs it back. Jacob says, "So I've been looking down into that little beach below us. I think it's mostly safe. I think we could go down there. The waves aren't really coming up very far. There are driftwood logs down there and fishing floats with little bits of nylon rope and seaweed and there are a few plastic bottles. I think we can make a raft."

"The tide's still coming in," she says.

"We better wait, then."

She closes her eyes with pain.

"I'm kind of leery." He's eyeing the stretch of water. "If we do make a raft, we'll have a tough decision."

Turtle says, "I was thinking that. If we head straight toward the bluffs, right there ahead of us, we won't be able to beach the raft at high tide because the beach is flooded and we'll be broken on the cliffs. But at low tide, we can't get across the rocks. So, we'll have to try and make it back into Buckhorn Cove. Past the island."

Jacob pauses. "Sure—there's that. But also, like, are you Jim and I'm Huck? Are you like Huck and I'm Jim? Those parallels are just kind of tangly and might be hard to sort out. Because, like, in a certain way, I'm the captive of a delimiting and coercive capitalist mind-set, but also you might be like a literal and actual captive. So it's hard to say. We're gonna have to talk that one out."

"What?"

"Well, I'm just saying that— Never mind."

"What are you talking about?"

"Nothing. I was being childish and naive. This is why I don't have Twitter."

"**What?**"

"Just— I'm gonna shut up now."

When the tide goes out that afternoon, they pick their way down to the beach and Turtle sits on a log looking west. The beach is coarse sand fretted with cobble, set back into a little notch in the island's western cliff face and enclosed on three sides by leaning, blue sandstone walls, twenty feet high. The beach is only ten or so feet wide. It ramps steeply out of the water. In each retreating wave, the beach cobbles lurch from their beds and roll over one another with a sound like the world grinding its teeth. The wind cuts crosswise to the mouth of the notch and eddies against the rock walls. In gusts, these eddies reel foam up into the air and churn it into spindly twisters that go staggering across the tide line. Set into the graywacke sandstone wall that forms the back of the notch, there is a triangular crack, the mouth of a cave. It must go entirely through the island, because sometimes it burbles startling washes of seawater. Jacob kicks through the piled driftwood, calling out his finds to Turtle. "A Sprite can!" Then, "Turtle! A two-liter Coke bottle!"

He comes over and sits beside her. He is shivering. His teeth chatter. For all the sun, they can't shake off the cold, which seems to have gotten in their bones. They are both still wet.

"What can we do?"

"I don't know."

"What can we make with this?"

"I don't know," she says.

"Well, what do we need to do next?"

"We need to make a fire."

"Okay. Why?"

"Well, we're not getting home tonight. Not unless someone comes to get us, and no one's coming for us, I don't think. And if we're gonna make it through the night, we need a fire."

"You don't think we'll make it through the night?"

"Not comfortably. We need water, Jacob. And with a fire we can make fresh water. Plus, as exposed as we are, we're going to get cold. Not cold enough to die, but cold enough to be miserable."

"Can't we make fire by rubbing two sticks together?"

"Everything's wet."

"Could we use the knife and strike sparks from these rocks?"

"We could maybe start a fire with a bow drill."

"What are the chances it would work?"

"Low," she says.

"Let's try!"

"We need to think. We need to be sure. Before we do anything, we need to be sure."

"I'm excited about this."

She is silent.

"We've got to try **something**. And since your plodding literalness will not allow us to strike sparks from your flinty heartstrings, we should try a real and actual solution."

"Okay."

"Great."

"I'm not ploddingly literal."

"I know."

Turtle sits in a crescent of sunlight on the beach, her hands clamped in her armpits, and explains what they need to make a bow drill while Jacob brings driftwood for her examination. "We'll need a pliant rod for the bow itself and we'll string it with a strap from your shirt. Then wood of matching hardness for a spindle and fireboard. Then a handboard—the handboard matters less." She coaches him on the clove hitches for tying off the bow, saying, "Looser. Looser yet. There. The bowstring will roll a loop around the spindle, and you rotate the spindle by sawing the bow forward and back."

"Okay—?"

"So the bow should be bent **well** shy of breaking."

"Here?"

"There. Now tie it off with another clove hitch."

Some tine of bone shifts in her ring finger and she sucks her teeth, sweating.

"You okay?"

"We need a spindle. Something dry."

She watches him sorting through the driftwood.

"I can't tell if they're dry," he says, looking at his own hands, too scraped up and too sandy to feel the damp.

"Test them against your face."

He tests a wood scrap against his face, looks at her blankly—he doesn't know.

"You're useless," she says, raising her chin.

He holds it against her cheek, saying, "I am **not** useless."

She closes her eyes with attention. "Too wet. But everything's wet."

"How about this?" he says, picking up another.

"It's redwood."

"And?"

"You want a fine, tight grain. Lay dents in it with your fingernails. There, see how soft that motherfucker is? Useless."

"Okay. This is good. Keep talking."

She nods to a piece she's picked out. "The spindle is held between the fireboard and the handboard. The top end of the spindle is a sharp point that turns freely against the handboard, like the point of a top. And the bottom end should be a round joint that fits the fireboard's socket as tightly as possible. That rounded point of the spindle, which pivots forward and back in the fireboard's socket as you saw the bow, is what makes the coals."

He picks up the spindle and begins to work at it.

"Slivers," she tells him. "More like paring fingernails than carpentry."

Jacob wipes blood from his eyes.

"There. Like that."

"This is awesome," he says.

"Shut up and focus."

She watches him whittle the spindle and auger a hole into the fireboard with the point of the knife. He lays the remains of his T-shirt and her flannel across a driftwood log and, rasping the knife blade across the fabric, brings up trundles of lint for tinder. He prizes splinters from the logs for kindling and props them up to dry. By the time he is done, it is getting late in the afternoon, the light slanting into their little notch of beach, jellyfish and kelp suspended in the clear blue waves and silhouetted against the horizon. The tide has continued to rise. A single wave swishes past the rest and climbs, crackling, up the beach to her feet. Turtle's guts squeeze, even as she watches it dissolve into the sand.

"The tide?"

"The tide."

They climb back to the island's top and huddle together in the scrubby grass. The top of the island is exposed and the wind cuts right through their damp clothes. It is six p.m., she would guess, or thereabouts, and the tide will likely peak just after sunset, around nine or ten. They are both shivering. It is going to be a very high tide. The biggest waves make Turtle very nervous. Jacob says, "Should we try to start the fire now?"

"Not in this wind."

"I think we need to make a raft."

"Maybe," she says.

The sun melts into the horizon, the moon cresting up in the southeast, waxing gibbous, a day or two shy of full, sitting nearly opposite the sun in the sky. It is cold. The wind gutters at sundown, and then it picks up. Jacob falls into a fitful sleep, gasping and shaking, and Turtle clings to him for warmth, breathing the hot wet air he exhales, her hands aching, but she cannot sleep. The wind sucks all the warmth out of her and she lies in silent, bitter endurance of each moment with her hand sometimes cupped over her ear, the ache seeping nauseously down into her very cochlea, into her jawbones. She cannot sleep, but her mind descends to fevered imaginings that do not deliver her from the torment of the cold. Clamped tight and fetally about herself, her back throbbing and the cold seeping through her, she feels stripped of everything, bereft. She crawls through the grass and looks down at the beach. The dark water's rise has swallowed the sand. The driftwood logs rolling-pin against the cliffs. She can catch the spray where the waves break against the island. She lies cursing to herself. Her back, deeply cut where the waves broke her against the mussel beds, is throbbing and engorged. The feeling is familiar to her, the distinctive swelling of a wound not getting better but worse. The cuts must be dirty, packed with bits of cotton, mussel shells, something. She needs to get out of the cold, out of the wind, into some clean, warm, firelit room. She crawls back to Jacob and, drawing against him, soaks up what warmth she can. Hours pass like this. Finally, when Turtle hears the sound of the waves change from the booming, breaking crash against the bluffs to the swish and grind, she wakes him.

"Jacob."

"What?" he says.

"We have to get out of the wind."

"Turtle," he says, "what if another wave—?"

"I can't," she says, her teeth chattering. She leads him, Jacob holding her elbow as they pick their way with numb, bloody feet down to the beach. The tide is still terrifyingly high. The sand is wet.

"Jacob," she says, "I'm fucking **cold**."

"It's the wind," he says. "I could stand it if it weren't for the wind and the spray."

"We need to make a fire."

He is silent for a long time. Turtle is on her haunches with her arms wrapped around herself. She can read his face as he tries and discards his own questions.

"Okay," he says. "Tell me what to do."

She shows Jacob how to hold the fireboard in place with his toe, how to hold the spindle between the fireboard and the handboard, pressing carefully and steadily with the handboard, how to saw the spindle with the bow so that it turns, forward and back, forward and back. Then she sits up with him, coaching him. "Slower—patient, steady. Don't speed up and don't slow down. Just go even strokes, forward and back, forward and back. Like that." He breathes rhythmically with the drawing of the bow, forward and back, and she warns him, "Steady, steady."

With a misstroke, he jumps the spindle from the socket.

"Goddamn it," she says, shivering. "Listen, Jacob: Slowly. **Carefully**. You have to do this right."

Coolly, he reassembles the drill and begins to work.

Turtle says, "Don't think about it. If you think about it, you kill it. Pay attention, but don't think about it, put your brain in your lunch box and just go to work, there's a part of you that knows how to do this, and you have to let that part do it."

She lies in the wet sand, suffering with cold, but sheltered now from the wind. She can feel her heartbeat in her swollen back and in her broken fingers, which are cemented into her armpit with blood and salt. She opens her mouth and her lips come apart with a cracking noise. Her tongue wallows audibly in her mouth. Her eyes are gummy and she blinks with difficulty to clear her vision. Her face is numb. The moon is still in the southeast, hidden by the island. She tells herself, it may hurt, but you're a long way from dead yet, girl. When you stop shivering, then you'll know. But you've still got it yet. The clouds above her are lit eerie and silver, and she can make out their smoky, wispy texture. Where the waves lap up, she can see the silver on their faces, the beach itself black and lightless in the shadow of the island. Jacob is bent intently over the bow.

"Jacob," she says.

He says nothing.

"Jacob, I need you to do this."

"I'll try."

"Don't fuck this up."

The cold and her own uselessness are on her like a panic. If she had the use of her hands, she could do it. God, she thinks, shivering, why do you have to start to lose it now, Turtle?

He wavers again and she hisses, "God fucking damn it. **Concentrate.** Pay attention, you spoiled useless spineless—"

She watches with wretched urgency.

"I'm sorry," he says.

"Fuck, fuck, fuck," she says. Her voice is hoarse, bitter. "Jacob, you have to carry some weight here."

"I'm sorry."

"Oh," she says, "you're sorry? Fuck, Jacob. Fuck."

She could die. She could die here on this island, broken, dehydrated, sapped by the wind, and, finally, awfully finished by the cold and the wet. She could die because of his incompetence. She needs him to understand that, and at the same time, she does not want to scare him and so, seething, she watches him, her throat throttled with rage. "You pathetic piece of shit," she says, wracked by shivering. The words are disgorging from some deep pit inside of her.

"I think it's too wet," he says.

"You useless, useless little bitch," she says.

"I'm sorry."

"**Sorry**. You're sorry? You have to be a hell of a lot more than sorry." Turtle thinks, he doesn't know how to do this and he needs you. If you cannot see that, you are useless to him and to yourself. If you cannot tell him, cannot explain it to him. She lies shivering in the sand.

"Listen," she says. "Jacob, you have to do this. No choice, Jacob."

"I'm trying," he says.

"'I'm trying,'" she bleats back at him.

What am I doing? she thinks nightmarishly.

"Do you suck this badly at your entire life, or is it only the important things?"

"I think, like you said, it may be too wet."

She thinks, he's right. Of course he's right. She

thinks, you need to coach him. She says, "Your tools aren't the problem. Being a useless piece of shit—that's the problem."

"Turtle. I got to tell you, it doesn't look like it's going to work. It's not just that the wet keeps it from making coals. It's like, because the wood is wet, it crumbles before you can get enough friction."

"It sounds," she says, "like you're gonna have to stop fucking it up."

She thinks, what is wrong with you? She lies on the cold sand and responses come to her and she throttles them down, thinking, you have to do this and you have to do this carefully. She thinks, this one is on you, it really is on you, you have to tell him something and it has to be the right thing and it might save your life. She says, "One time, my daddy had me do pull-ups off the rafter and he—" Her voice fails her, hitches, she doesn't know what to say, can't believe she's saying he—what? She doesn't know herself. She says, "He put that knife between my legs. So that if I fell from the rafter—" Again, she doesn't know, if she fell from the rafter **what**. "And he— He—" There is a horror, almost a disbelief in the telling, like she can't believe she's doing it, as if she can't believe it's even possible to talk about it. "And he, he asked me to do pull-ups, and I did them. You reach a point where the next pull-up hurts so **bad**. You'd think you could do pull-ups until you just **couldn't** anymore. You wouldn't have to **make** yourself do pull-ups. Because, well, there's a knife between your legs. But that's not how it is. Every pull-up is still a choice, and to do them, it takes discipline and it takes courage. You think, I don't have to do this pull-up. You **want** to give up. And you start thinking maybe it's a good idea, because the pain of holding on to the rafter becomes greater than the threat of death. Because then it wouldn't hurt anymore. Because holding steady is—is— There is this bad, really **bad**, sense of uncertainty, an uncertainty so painful, so asshole-clenching, that it becomes— It's an awful thing to say, but it's easier to let go and be split in fucking half than it is to try and hold on, suffering and **not knowing** what is going to happen. That's courage. Taking your own fucking life in your own fucking hands when that is the hardest thing you can do. No one thinks of it. Everybody thinks they'd do the right thing, but that's not true. They don't understand how scary it is. How hard it is. No one understands unless they've been there. We're there now, Jacob, and you're gonna do the right thing **despite** the fear and **despite** the hurt."

He is listening to her, sawing carefully back and forth, the bow turning the spindle.

"Hold on to it," she says.

He is silent, breathing in time to the steady working of the bow, back and forth. She can hear from his breathing how exhausted he is. His right hand works forward and back while his left bears steadily down on the handboard. She watches him for a long time. She is cut loose, adrift in her mind. She thinks, stay awake. Stay awake. She feels staked to the sand. The waves rise and retreat on the beach, and despite herself, and despite the cold eating into her bones, she falls asleep, and wakes feeling herself half dead, the moon cresting the island, the light crept up from the waterline like a pale tide, crept over her, and not yet climbed onto Jacob, who crouches in the dark. The knife, stuck in the sand, casts a long shadow. She can hear, above the ocean's swish and grind, a kind of panting susurration in Jacob's breathing, and she realizes that he is whispering, **come on, come on**, over and over, and that the raggedness of his intonation matches his breathing and matches the working of the bow. An orange glow expands and retreats with the working of the spindle and lights him from beneath, his whole body bent with the power of his will. Blood drips from the points of his hair, and the blood-slick hollows and panes of his face catch the cinder's nascent light. Turtle, looking deep into these shadowed features, finds a color, a red that is as dark as black, like the after-image of a color. She has never seen another person this way, and has no words for it. It's as if he has quenched down within himself every doubt, filled his mind only with the possibility of fire, the spindle smoking in the socket, and glowing orange powder falling from the socket's notch into the tinder. Turtle's guts seize with anticipation.

Then, with a crack, the wooden bow breaks and Jacob's susurration changes to a no, no, no, and he throws aside the broken bow and takes the spindle in two open palms and rolls it, forward and back, breathing but not saying, come on baby, come on baby, and then she sees what he sees: the tinder has begun to smolder. He tosses the spindle aside, takes up a wad of smoldering grass and lint and he turns it over, raising it into the cold air of the cove. The glow ekes across the sand, enclosing the both of them in its burbling red light, Jacob in the privacy of utter preoccupation, stooped over the tinder and blowing it into life, and Turtle lying with her hands trapped in her armpits. There is a moment where she knows that the tinder will catch and quicken to flame, and she opens her mouth in painful excitement, thinking, oh my god, oh my god, and then, in the wet ocean air, the tinder bleeds out to dull orange, the coals attenuated along the lint, smoking and going white, and then the fire dies. Jacob holds the dead tinder cupped in his hands, rocked back onto his butt in astonishment, and she draws him toward herself and takes him in her arms, and she sinks her good fingers into his flesh, digging into him, and he allows her to hold him, and they wait out the cold night this way.

Eighteen

TURTLE WAKES WITH WATER BEADED ON
her eyelashes. She blinks it away and sits up
from her wallow of cold sand. Her back throbs,
swollen and sick-feeling. Her hands are scabbed
to her shirt. Everything is swallowed in fog. She
can hear the waves netting the cobbles in and hauling them out again, and she can make out the dark
line of the tide and nothing else. There is no sun,
only a diffuse gray light, the sand slick and black
except for the sand dollars. The dew condenses on
the leaning cliff face above them and drips steadily
around them. Turtle's hair is wet with it.

She climbs up to the island's top. The weeds are
frosted with dew. She lays herself facedown in the

dewy grass and it wets her skin. Shivering and shaking, she brings her dry mouth to the grass stalks and sucks the moisture from the blades. The water is delicious. She rolls over onto her back in the cold wet grass. "Jacob!" she croaks. "Jacob!" Her voice will not carry, so she crawls to the island's edge and croaks down at him until he wakes, looking wildly around before he looks up. She grins for him. Blood from her lips runs down her chin.

"Wow," he says, his voice breaking. "That is the sound of nightmares." He gathers their things and climbs up toward her.

They lie bending grass stalks into their mouths, sucking dew from the blades. Below, the tide climbs onto the beach. Turtle finds a small, oily black scat filled with broken crab shells.

"Jacob," she says.

He crawls through the grass toward her.

"What is that?"

She prizes her hand from out of the bloody, sand-crusted rind of her shirt and teases the scat with a bird bone.

"Raccoon scat."

"Are there raccoons on this island?"

She buries her face in it, inhaling deeply, closing her eyes against the must.

"Blue fruit?" Jacob says. "Notes of leather? Gaminess?"

"It's moist," she says, filled with a big, pleasurable, hopeful delight.

"Medium tannins?" Jacob says.

"Day before yesterday. The moon was waxing gibbous. Almost full."

"People don't know this about you, but you have a strange, poetical, and associative intelligence. Now I'm imagining this raccoon laying a deuce beneath a waxing gibbous moon while waves break on the rocks."

"Full moon tonight. Or almost."

"I wish I understood what you were talking about."

"I know how we're going to get home."

They crawl to the island's landward edge and lie in the grass looking out into the fog. Stalky, blooming succulents nest in the sandstone, their scales powdered blue. The surf is gentler than the day before. The island is the tip of a long, underwater ridge of rock. Several such run out through the shallows. They are very black with green-blue kelp-choked furrows between them.

"Do you remember the tides yesterday?" Turtle says. She turns over in the grass, lies looking up at the clouds, counts the tides off on her fingers. "You got to my house a little before seven a.m. By nine-ish, we'd gotten ourselves here. The tide was coming in and it peaked around eleven, and it wasn't very big. We stayed up on top of the island because we were afraid. Then sometime that afternoon, let's say around three p.m., it went out. It was down to about two feet. That's when we went down to the beach. We collected stuff to make the bow drill. Then we had to come back onto the island because a real big tide came in. It was five or six feet high, it peaked around ten last night. Maybe as late as midnight. That's three tides. After midnight, the tide began going out again. That's when I woke you up. We went back down to the beach and you tried to work the bow drill, and when it didn't work, we fell asleep down on the beach. But what we didn't know was that the tide kept going out all night. It was the biggest of the set, a very, very low tide, and it would've been at its lowest just before sunrise. It was probably a foot down past zero, a foot and a half down. That's about five feet down from where you see it now."

Jacob is staring out at the rocks. "Most of those rocks aren't but a foot underwater."

"Yeah."

"You could—you could walk across all that rock to shore. Hell, you could wade out through the shallows."

Dry, mucusy pleats on her lips crack and weep.

"So you're saying that while we slept, a land bridge appeared between us and the mainland and we missed it? We were lying on the beach, cold, suffering, dying, but we could've just gotten up and walked home?"

"We couldn't've seen it from here, because this beach faces the ocean, and probably deep water. We would've had to be looking towards shore, on the other side of the island. But yeah—we weren't looking, we didn't know, we didn't think, and we missed it."

"You barely made it through the night, Turtle."

She nods. It was a simple mistake and it almost killed them.

"And this low, low tide will happen again tonight?"

"Yes."

They wait in the wet grass together until the fog lifts. Turtle's face begins to burn and she can see the skin on her arms glazed white and crackled. She covers her face with her flannel and stares out through a nook. The sun is high above them and a little to the southwest. The light flashes and glitters off the ocean. Turtle watches.

"Hey," she says. "Did you say you found a soda can?"

"Yeah?"

"Bring it over here?"

"Sure," he says.

She takes the Sprite can and begins polishing the shiny, concave bottom with the edge of her shirt. She dabs a little soil onto her wet forefinger and uses that to polish it to a mirror shine. She holds the can upside down in the crook of her knee, the bottom angled at the sun. Then she takes up their bird's nest of tinder and hovers the scraps above the concave mirror. A bright bead of light appears, vibrating with Turtle's shaking hands, throwing off crisscrossing loops of glare, and she works the tinder closer to the concave mirror until the spark contracts to a needlepoint of white-hot light. Within fifteen minutes, the tinder is smoking. Bright red cinders appear among the threads. She lifts it up and blows the fire into life. She sets the flaming bundle in the grass and begins to take up the wooden kindling they'd prized from the driftwood.

Jacob says, "Damn."

She grins hugely. Jacob drags up driftwood from the cove before it is covered by the tide and hacks it to kindling with the bowie knife. She shows him how to hammer the blade down with a driftwood club, essentially using the knife as a splitting wedge. Working steadily, Jacob splits whole logs into kindling and when the fire is going big enough, she has Jacob fill the Sprite can with water. She connects it to a soda bottle with a long, hollow strand of bull kelp, cutting away the kelp bulb to make a nozzle that fits over the can. She puts the can in the fire. The steam rises into the flexible hose and condenses into the plastic soda bottle. The first capfuls are salty. Then it's good. They lie, tending their fire, absorbed in the meditative distillation of water.

"Just wait," Jacob says. "When you're stranded, alone and fearful, upon the bleak, windswept island that is your freshman English class, broken on the rocks that are **The Scarlet Letter**, I will take your hand and say, 'Be not afraid. The moon is waxing gibbous. The scat is moist and smells of manzanita berries.' And you will be amazed."

Turtle is careful to smile only very fractionally.

"I feel pretty sunburned. How do I look?"

She crinkles her eyes at him.

"Bad, huh?"

"Bad, yeah."

"This escape plan better work. The parental units will expect me back from Brett's on Monday."

"They won't be mad?"

"Yeah, probably. When they see my face. My mom will be all, 'Do you want to die of skin cancer?!'"

"You'll be safe, though?"

He laughs. Then he quits laughing.

"What is it?" she asks.

"Nothing."

"Tell me."

He just shakes his head. They sleep most of the day. They tend the fire and drink water by the cupful. The ocean swallows the beach and retreats. Smoky ramparts of clouds appear on the horizon and the sun sets beneath them, a faraway, bloodred fist.

"Do you think your dad is right," he says, "to withdraw from the social contract?"

"I don't know."

"But what do you **think**?"

"If it happens, if it really happens, the house can't be defended."

Jacob is silent at this. After a long time, he lies down beside the fire and goes to sleep. Turtle, sitting on the island, feels level with the setting sun. The moon hangs in the east, breaking above the mainland, a deeper, smokier red. Swells of wine-dark water rise around her and sweep past, gathering as the coastal shelf inclines beneath them, their great bent backs glossed red and purple. They break against the bluffs and raise and collapse spuming towers of a height with the moon. She stands guard as night falls and as the moon climbs into the sky.

Sometime that night, in the dark, she hears the beginning of the low tide by the swish and grind of the freshly revealed cobbles. Jacob sleeps his exhausted sleep. She is cross-legged, waiting out the moon. It will arc across the sky and begin to set in the west before they can go. Exhaustion rises and falls through her mind like a tide itself and she thinks, you are still and you watch and you wait. She thinks, wait. You wait, you bitch, and you watch and you do not miss the moment. She thinks, you have this at least: you have yourself and you can do with that what you will, Turtle. The smoky red moon wheels through the night, and when it lights the island slantwise from the southwest, casting a long silver path across the water, she rises and walks to the landward edge. Stone spurs stand up from the ocean floor in long, diagonal slashes, wet and glossed with moonlight. The island sits like a castle on the end of its causeway, the landward side too steep to climb, the western face slanting down to the small cove, which fronts deep water. She wakes Jacob gently, touching his face and saying his name.

They descend to the beach. The island is footed in a vast black tide pool. The sand ramps down into that cold, unmoving water. Jacob is afraid. From within its depth, faint glimmers. Across its surface, the dappled reflections of the starry vault. They wade out into the water holding hands, shivering with cold, and then release each other and plunge forward and swim, both of them wounded, floundering. Jacob clambers gasping onto the next stand of rocks. Turtle begins to climb out after him, stops, stands arrested. A ridge of black flesh breaks the surface, and she reaches out and puts her good hand on a scaled flank. It turns, drops beneath the surface, and Turtle cannot guess the size of the thing. She waits, and the flank lays out of the water again, and she puts her hands on it and feels an enormous strength there, a firm muscled body beneath the scales. Jacob stands on the rock behind her, looking on, and Turtle takes a step back down into the water. The darkness and the moonlight move in slippery patterns across its surface.

"Turtle," Jacob says warningly.

She looks into the dark water. She takes a second step down off the rock and something brushes against her leg, something circles, and she feels the passage of its flank—six feet, maybe more.

"What are you doing?" he says.

She looks up at him as if breaking from a spell, and climbs back out. The rocks themselves are slippery and hard to climb, so Turtle and Jacob keep to the sandy passageways among the out-croppings, hip-deep in water. Crabs move atop the rocks on either side, the creatures silhouetted against the blue-black sky, turning themselves cautiously sideways, lifting their claws into the air, their legs clicking on the stone. The water grows shallower and rockier. Holding hands, Turtle and Jacob move haltingly, they feel their way, they are careful of urchins.

Even so, it takes less than twenty minutes to find their way up onto a small, private beach be-neath Turtle's neighbors' house. There is a red-wood staircase that climbs onto a wide lawn with Monterey cypresses and a large mermaid fountain lit by underwater lights. Near them, the neigh-bors' redwood mansion, with its wall-to-wall pic-ture windows, an empty room, empty couches, a table, light slanting from the kitchen.

They follow a gravel driveway out onto the high-way and a single car slows as it passes them, the headlights cutting across rattlesnake grass and wild oats, lighting them brilliantly, then going past. They walk along the road, listening to the quiet ocean. They limp up her driveway, sticking to its grassy median, and in through the door, Jacob leaving bloody heel prints on the boards. They sleep on the floor of her room, on wool blankets and under her sleeping bag, holding each other, exhausted, waking, each as the other rises to drink more water, glugging it down their dry throats and sighing and then standing, listening to the creaking of the old house.

Nineteen

JACOB WAKES THEM EARLY. "COME ON, come on, come on," he says, rousting her up off the floor where she lies facedown, protesting into the blankets. "Come on," he says. "We gotta get you clean and fed and I got to get home. Come on, come on. You're excited, I can tell. My parents'll be home from the airport soon, and seriously, I best be there." He gets her up. He has made oatmeal pancakes. They are on a platter on the counter. "The power's out," he says, "but I guess you know that. I checked the eggs in a glass of water. They seemed to be okay, if not ideal. You haven't been to buy groceries in a while, have you? Though you're not exactly strapped for nonperishables."

She sits on a towel on the bathroom floor with her left hand lying out in front of her, curled and broken like a crab left at the tide line. Jacob has found the first aid supplies under the sink and has boiled a basin of water and has laid out the wound sponges, irrigation syringes, splints, and gauze. He reads the directions on each sponge and ointment, Turtle watching with deadpan incredulity. "Okay, okay," he says, rubbing his hands together, psyching himself up. He puts on latex examination gloves and begins to cut away the sand-crusted flannel-shirt bandages. Her pinkie finger comes into view. He says, "Whoa. Oh—okay. So. **Wow**."

"I'm fine," she says around the thermometer.

He pulls out the thermometer and frowns at it. "Ninety-nine two. You have a fever."

"I run hot," she says. Jacob has put peanut butter on some of the pancakes. She takes one off the platter, folds it in two, and takes a bite.

"Ninety-nine two is not normal."

"Hmm," she says, taking another bite. "For me it is."

"We need to go to the hospital, Turtle."

"These pancakes aren't bad," she says.

Jacob fills the syringe from a copper pot of hot soapy water and begins irrigating the wound. The water drains pink into the basin.

"So—what do you have against hospitals?"

"My daddy doesn't like them."

"Where is he?"

She selects another pancake with her free hand.

"Marlow hasn't found him yet, then," he says. "And you're afraid that if Child Protective Services gets wind of that, they'll take you away."

She has nothing to say. There's a little too much peanut butter on her pancake and it's giving her trouble. She chews mightily.

"Maybe they **should** take you away."

"You don't think that," she says after a heroic swallow.

"No," he says. "I think that the system is probably completely fucked and Kafkaesque. I think you don't want to be part of it. But I do think you need a doctor."

"No doctors," she says.

"If I don't trust you to make your own decisions, I don't know who I would trust. But please— Turtle. Let's go to the hospital."

"No."

"I'm begging you."

She is silent.

"**Begging**."

There is nothing to say.

"The sum total of all your trust in me; does that prevail on you at all?"

She says nothing.

"Do you know Bethany?" he says. "Her parents are into meth. So Will, the philosophy teacher at the high school, took her in and she lived with them for a little while and now she lives up Lit-

tle Lake Road with a friend from school. This is
Mendo. Everybody hates the system. Half of us
are growers and the other half are aging hippies,
right? And then some are like my parents, Silicon
Valley transplants who believe in social services,
but who deplore their present underfunded, stag-
nantly bureaucratic iteration and want them to
be run by Google and financed by Scandinavians.
What I'm saying is: Nobody's gonna turn you in.
Nobody wants you to go into a state- or federally
run institution. People will take care of you. Caroline would, in an instant. My parents would. So
what I'm saying is that, if we call Will, that's the
teacher I'm talking about—or hell, any teacher, if
you have someone you trust—and they take you
into the hospital and tell the doctor you're their
student, nobody's gonna call CPS. You'll be in and
out of the hospital just fine."

"And they'd let me come back here?"

Jacob hesitates.

"I don't want to get away from my daddy," she
says. "And I don't think he would let it happen,
either."

"You need to get away, Turtle."

"He's my daddy."

"That was a pretty serious story you told."

"Not that serious."

"You could tell any teacher that story and you'd
be done with this."

She is silent.

"You could tell any teacher that story and in a **moment** you'd be living with me, giving my sister scathing looks at the dinner table every night and learning all about wine and hearing about Dad's **fascinating** trips to Lehi, Utah—where there's always some riveting drama about defect analysis in silicon wafers, complete with intradepartmental romance, misbehaving chemical engineers, you know, just an intricate story about how such and such an error got missed. We've got that bedroom for you, and Isobel would pay you to help in the studio. It sounds kind of good, right?"

She chews her lip.

"He could've hurt you badly."

"He didn't," she says, "he won't."

"I think he will."

"You don't know what the fuck you're talking about. He doesn't want to hurt me. He loves me more than life itself. He's not a perfect person sometimes. Sometimes he's not the person he wants to be. But he loves me more than anybody else has ever been loved. I think that counts for everything."

"'Not a perfect person sometimes'?" Jacob echoes. "Turtle, your dad is a vast— A titanic— A **colossal** douchebag, among the worst to ever sail the lemon verbena seas, a primordial ur-douche the depth and profundity of whose douchism staggers the mind and beggars the imagination. Though, of course, Marcus Aurelius says that we should not despise others for hurting us. He says we should recognize that they act out of ignorance—against their will, even—that you'll both be dead before long, and that this person hasn't really hurt you, because they haven't diminished your ability to choose. And I think he's right. You don't have to hate him. But you might probably should really possibly think about leaving. By which I mean you should go to the hospital. Because only some kind of narcissistic sociopath could possibly object to you seeing a doctor right now. Anyone who cared about you—that'd be their top concern, if they could see what I see. Everyone else, they'd be like, 'Fuck it, my daughter's in pain, she has compound fractures in three fingers, we're going to the hospital.'"

He is done with her pinkie finger, applying antibiotic ointment and wrapping it in gauze. Then he traps the aluminum splint down over it and tapes it in place. He looks up at her. "Next finger," he says. "You ready?"

"You don't know what you're talking about."

"I think I have some idea."

"You don't."

He cuts away the cotton wrappings and reveals her left ring finger, swollen, the nail black. With the irrigation syringe, he blasts a thin jet of water and, to their surprise, the nail lifts from the bed, held fast by a few pale threads of flesh.

"Fucking motherfucking fucker fucking **fuck**," Turtle says.

"What do you want me to do?"

"Rip it off."

"Shoot, I can't rip it off."

"Rip the fucking thing off."

He seizes the nail with forceps, cuts it free with surgical scissors, and drops it into the water.

"Motherfucker," she says.

"Keep talking. It seems like the talking helps."

"Fuck," Turtle says. "Fuck, fuck, fuck."

"Great! Now try sentences."

"You don't know him."

"Turtle. This looks really bad."

"Jacob, you've only met him the once, and briefly."

"You mean when Caroline dropped you off?"

"Of course that's what I mean. What do **you** mean?"

He tapes down the final splint.

"I kept expecting to see your finger bones sticking out, but I think the breaks are all closed and these cuts are superficial. Which is good. I think. I don't know. You know who would know? A **doctor**."

"Jacob—did you meet him another time?"

"That's it for your hands. Let's see your back."

"Jacob?"

She tries to pull her shirt up and over her head, but it's stuck to her. Wincing, she lies down on the towel. Jacob picks up the trauma shears and begins to cut away the shirt. He cuts from the hem to her neckline and tries to lift it, but it is fastened to her in bloody badges, and he takes his time, irrigating to soften the scabs and then pulling it away.

"You **need** a hospital. The shirt has been pushed into the wound."

"You've never even spoken with him."

"I did speak to him. He never told you? I walked here from Mendocino after school. Your dad was on the porch, drinking beer and reading Descartes. I came up, and I said I was looking for you."

Turtle is silent.

"He said you were away at your grandfather's house, and I asked him about Descartes, and he said he was reading the ontological proof for god's existence. He had a strange, an interesting take on the proof—"

"When was this?"

"Shortly after we met. Late April. Early May. Something like that. Prom was coming up and I thought—"

"Did you tell him your name?"

"Yes."

"He asked how to spell it?"

"Some of these cuts are deep, Turtle."

"Did he ask where you live?"

"Yes, he did."

"Why didn't you say this before?"

"Did I get you in trouble?"

"No," she says.

"These look awful, Turtle. How were you— How did you not mention that you were this hurt?"

She lies on the floor and lets him irrigate the wounds and extract bits of shell. Late April, she is thinking. Early May. It must have been when she was out with Grandpa and Grandpa told her how to ask for the dress. His timing had been so bad. And her own. She almost cannot believe it. Jacob is drawing long strips of cotton out of the wounds on her back. She thinks, he came here and he spoke to Martin and I never knew. Christ, she thinks.

After he leaves, she goes into Martin's room and picks up the phone book. She finds a single dog-eared page. There are Larners and Lerners, but only one Learner. **Learner, Brandon & Isobel, 266 Sea Urchin Drive.** The name has a tick by it, a single blue pen stroke in the margin. Turtle stands holding the phone book. Jacob had talked to Martin. He had been talking to Martin on the day when Grandpa had been telling her how to ask about the dress. Perhaps Jacob asked Martin about prom. Then, when she'd asked about the dance, Martin had understood and he had pretended not to. He had waited for a sign from her. He'd gone up to her room, and she'd twisted away in his hands. He'd taken it seriously then, goddamn, and how prescient he had seemed. How it had surprised her, lying on the mud out in the yard and Martin bringing the iron poker down again and again. It had seemed that he could see into her heart, but that hadn't been it; he had known. He had met Jacob, talked to him, and hidden that fact from her. Grandpa had wanted her to go to the dance. Jacob talks to Martin, Martin understands, and when Turtle hesitates, when she pulls back, he knows what to do. Then the tidal pool in Buckhorn Cove. Grandpa's death. Martin's disappearance. And all because of what? she thinks. A boy, she thinks. No, she thinks, because of what a boy represents.

Turtle walks through the hall and down into the basement. Opening the cabinets she takes down the most familiar bottle, SMZ/TMP. She stands looking up at the drugs. She has taken veterinary sulfamethoxazole/trimethoprim before, for urinary tract infections. She is looking at it. She cannot quite come to grips with what has happened. Martin's single blue tick mark by the address, it was meant for her. She knows what it means: If you cannot be controlled, he can. Jacob is nothing to him; only her doubts, only her straying—that is real. She takes down the card with Martin's notes on the SMZ/TMP. She reads it for a third time. She takes three of the 80 mg tablets. She will take them twice a day. Then she takes down the Levaquin box. His note reads, **Anthrax inhalation 500mg 60ds; for blck plague, othrs 250–750mg q 24 hrs.** She dispenses the foil sheets with the 250 mg red tablets in their extruded plastic bubbles and takes two. She climbs back up the stairs carrying the antibiotics. You cannot see Jacob again, she thinks. You cannot involve him in this, you cannot get him hurt. Her grandfather died for a mistake like this.

And now Jacob wants her to leave. It is all useless. All this talking, all Jacob's talking, all of her thinking, it is all useless, and what matters is already set in her and it will not change and she cannot be persuaded. She lies on her stomach across a wool blanket by the fireplace. Her thoughts rise through the murk of her mind like bubbles. She watches her little finger in its foam-lined aluminum splint pulse with her heartbeat, her back an old half-rotted sponge taking on achingly hot water. She thinks, when he'd found out, when he'd had the proof of her even thinking, even hesitating, he had pinned her to the muddy ground. She remembers the helplessness of it. That is the measure of his seriousness. She thinks, you cannot keep Jacob safe. Then she thinks: no, the truth is that you can, but you're not willing to.

When she wakes, she stands by the counter eating Jacob's pancakes from the platter. She takes the tablets, drinks a glass of water. Sunlight pours in the windows and she leans against the counter watching the revolving motes of dust, each mote leaving a blurred trail like a comet. She goes into the bathroom, sits against the wall sucking on the thermometer, and when she checks it, her temperature is again 99.2. She puts her fist against her forehead. You're okay, Turtle, she thinks. You're just worn-out.

She takes her antibiotics as regularly as she is able. In the mornings, she brews herself stinging nettle tea and goes out on the porch with her tea to watch the ocean. Several days a week, Jacob arrives with paper sacks brimming with food, piled under his arms, hanging from his wrists, and Turtle, sitting cross-legged on the floor in front of the fireplace, hands wrapped around a cup of tea, will look up and admire him. The first time was just a day or two after their return home, and he came with news: "My parents **freaked** when they saw my face! You should've seen them! They were like, 'Whaaaat haaaaaaappennnnned?!' And when I told them that I was washed out to sea and you came and rescued me, my mom said, 'It's very dangerous to go into the surf to rescue a drowning person,' and I said that you weren't afraid of danger, that danger was afraid of you, and they asked where Brett was in all this, and I said he was washed out, too, only he had his Easy Cheese can, and he just triggered the nozzle and jetted away to safety."

"So you lied," Turtle says.

"I told Brett the whole story over the phone—he was **pissed**! He was like, 'I miss everything!'— I told him how we were washed out to sea and how it was like making furious love to a clash of orgiastic rhinos in a swimming pool filled with broken glass, and how you made a fire by staring balefully down into the reflective bottom of an aluminum can until your immense force of will was concentrated and magnified by the parabolic mirror into a white-hot spark of pure Turtle rage that could light anything on fire, even the hearts of unwary high schoolers."

"What did he say?"

"He had to admit that it might work."

"I wish you wouldn't lie."

"And then I said how you waited until the darkest part of the second night, just before the dawn, and as the moon touched the horizon, you spread your arms and commanded the seas to part, and they parted as quickly and as widely as his mom's legs, and we walked back across the ocean floor with sea monsters basking in the pools and how they called out to you with a siren song and how you wanted to descend into the black and join them until I took your hand and led you away. It seemed almost like he didn't believe me."

When her back has scarred into thick pink keels, she goes shopping with Jacob's family, slouching uncomfortably around the fronts of stores while Isobel picks out summer dresses, saying, "Oh, but you'd look so **good**! Oh, but you have the perfect figure for a dress. Oh, look at this! Oh, please, please, Turtle! I'll buy you ice cream! Anything!" and Turtle massaging her knobby fingers while Isobel appeals to Jacob, saying, "Jacob, tell her to try it on!" and Jacob putting up his hands, saying, "I have no power over her, and if I **did**, I wouldn't squander it on clothes," and Imogen saying, "I know where you'd squander it," and Isobel saying, "Imogen!"

And later, going shop to shop, Imogen announces, "I'm taking her to Understuff. Home-slice needs a bra."

"You're not," Jacob says.

"I am, too, dingus," Imogen says.

"I am not a dingus," Jacob says.

"Social media is gonna ban all photos of her and she won't have any friends and then she will die alone drinking wine from a box and her hundreds of cats will close in and eat her face. That's not what you want for her, Jacob."

Turtle says, "What?"

In the end, Turtle stands by herself in the changing room of the lingerie store. It all feels too posh. The room is uncomfortably large and the carpet unfamiliar. The walls are hung with silks. Imogen and Isobel throw bras over the door at her and Turtle stands inside holding them and setting them on the chair while they describe, through the door, how the bra should fit. She takes off her shirt but cannot work the clasps. Her left hand is still clumsy. She is embarrassed that either of them should see her ruined back. She doesn't like her lean, ugly face in the mirror. She has slashes for cheekbones, squinty eyes. Her long blond hair has the thick, wild texture of fur, partially dreaded. She stands stark and grimacing. Outside, she can hear Imogen and Isobel appealing to Jacob, and Jacob saying, "She's **shy**, guys!" She stands in the dressing room. She holds the bra up. None of this matters, she thinks. They are preoccupied by things that do not matter, they do not see what it is and they do not see what is important. She thinks, if this is what other people have, I don't envy it.

When Isobel finally knocks, she calls, "Just a minute!"

Alone in her ancestral home, she waits beside the fire with an oil lamp and she watches the flames, listening to the wind, imagining the blackberry canes creeping up between the floorboards to cast their green runners across her shoulders. Every day of it is good and any day could be the last, though it feels as if he might never return. It feels as if this could be her life. Each day, she puts off telling Jacob. She is aware that it is the wrong thing, and it is a selfish thing. But it has been the same wrong, selfish thing since she met the boys above the Albion. She has always known it put them in danger. She is almost comfortable, knowing what she needs to do and not doing it. She rubs olive oil into the pink wounds. Her joy is full and aimless. It accretes in layers under her skin and knits her pores tight. She sleeps folded in wool blankets in front of the fire. One night, her breasts aching and sore, she gets up and goes into the bathroom and sits there on the toilet, and she looks down to where a clue of blood unspools into the basin. She touches the pads of her fingers to her pussy and brings them up, daubed with her menarche. She puts them in her mouth and sucks them clean and then puts her fist against her forehead and cries for herself and for Martin. It is the end of something. She has been too skinny, her body has had too few resources. She hunches over her naked knees and sobs. She does not want anything to change. She wants nothing lost.

"You're making me fat," she tells Jacob the next day. He grins, putting the groceries in the cabinets. He is carefree. He thinks she's joking. He thinks they will go on like this forever. He is excited to help with her college applications. He stands in the kitchen, groceries laid out across the counter, a slab of lamb bleeding on the butcher block, the Dutch oven heating on the stove, with him crushing garlic cloves with the flat of the knife, shelling them, mincing them with an easiness and a calm domestic competence utterly alien to her, a kind of miracle. He is saying, "I am in love with George Eliot! My god! **Middlemarch**! That is a motherfucking **book** right there! Such a book—! She has a wonderful, broad, **generous** style; she writes the way I want my letters to Congress to sound, you know?" As she watches him, she can imagine Isobel instructing him how to do it, a glass of wine on the counter and all of them, Isobel and Jacob and Brandon and Imogen, in the kitchen cooking some meal, which Jacob is cooking for her now, and Turtle can see in the patient serenity with which he wheels around the kitchen a whole inheritance of love. When Jacob is here, with her, the desire to touch him grows, becoming a kind of need, and she lets each moment of need pass her by, sitting there next to him, cross-legged, unable to do anything but look until sheer inactivity carries her through the unendurable moment. After he leaves, she will sit watching her fire, in love with wanting and not having, and sometimes, thinking of something he'd said, she'll grin and lie back on the blankets in front of the fire, still grinning.

Her moments of happiness occur right at the margin of the unbearable. She knows it will not last and she thinks, you can never forget, Turtle, what it was like, here, without him. You have to hold tight on to it, how good it is. Remember the way everything felt clean, and good. There was no rottenness in any of it. But also, she thinks, how hard. Nothing is as difficult as a sustained and unremitting contact with your own mind. She thinks, does it matter if it is difficult? It doesn't matter. It is still better. Turtle Alveston, do you take this nothingness and this emptiness and this solitude? She thinks, do you take all these nights alone and will you have this and only this for the rest of your life?

Twenty

ONE MORNING SHE WALKS DOWN TO BUCK-
horn Beach with a bag of small, bitter apples from
the orchard. She sits in the lee of a driftwood
log. The tide is out and the bay is roiled. The wind
comes stiff from the north and raises foot-deep
slurries of sand that make every current visible.
Seagulls huddle together in the lee of the northern
cliffs. Where driftwood logs lay crosswise to the
wind, eddies of sand collect in their wind shadows
and mound up into ramps that match the log's
silhouette. There is a constant, scouring hiss.

Behind each kelp heap, the wind cuts a V, leaving
a gore where bark chips and bits of dried eelgrass
accumulate, gyring and collapsing, toying together

into balls. Sometimes, long strands of seaweed or sticks of driftwood spin up out of the eddy and go winging end over end across the cove and away to the south. She looks up the beach, and Martin is walking toward her, wearing jungle boots, 501 jeans, and a flannel shirt, shading his eyes against the wind, the gusts plastering the flannel to his chest. The light comes slantwise from behind him. The beach is sandy blue, the cliffs are dun brown, and Martin's footsteps throw gouts of sand into the wind. He comes within ten yards of her, spreads his arms wide, his presence here a terrible trespass, and she loves this about him, sits looking at him, the wind whipping his long hair around his big, handsome face, him broad-shouldered and enormous as ever. She stands, dusts the sand off her butt, and walks into his arms. He smells like cigars and engine oil. They stand holding each other. Then Martin takes her by the arm and everything is like before. He leads her away up the beach and they follow the dirt track up the bluffs. Martin's truck is parked beside the highway at the bottom of the drive.

He pulls out onto the highway and drives toward town with gear-shifting recklessness, taking the turns far out of his lane, looking over at her, chewing on his lower lip. There is a short-barreled AR-15 in the footwell, propped against the vinyl seat. The receiver has been milled out by hand for full auto. The vent holes in the exposed bolt carrier are streaked with filth. She sits beside it and beside him and she thinks of those moments of solitude that had given her such pleasure and knitted her pores tight, but which had been so painful, so unendurable that she could not choose them for herself, given the choice. In the closed cab, she can smell him, feel him invested with tremendous weight, a presence like a well beside her in the truck cab with its own sweet smell of WD-40 and of bad cigars crushed out in the ashtray.

"Kibble," he says, "I fucked up. God, I know it." Jaw set. Driving recklessly fast but paying attention, shifting, punching the accelerator, passing a car on a blind turn, roar of the engine, back into his lane, shifting, waiting, looking at her almost angrily, and then out at the road, gripping the wheel, gripping the stick shift, another glance at her, lopsided smile full of regret, Turtle catching flashes of him in her peripheral, there beside her and absorbing all of her attention, and he says, "Fuck, it's not your fault. It was— Christ, do you remember the way he looked?"

"No," Turtle says.

"**Awe**. A look of awe. Do you remember it?"

"No."

"You look like him. Do you know that?" She stares ahead, cliffs, guardrail, huge sparking blue ocean, a kelp bed, then the bluffs run out west of her and the ocean is hidden by houses, inns, and the hanging, wooden signs for inns, redwood fences, beautiful old cypress trees. He downshifts, climbing a hill past a stand of eucalyptus, snatches a look at her. "I lost it, kibble. I **lost** it. The look in his eye, Christ, that look. I can still see it. Painful, the doctor said, painful and fast, but that's not what it looked like. He looked like he understood something, and not something good, kibble, not something good, but something like— I have run it through my head a hundred times. A thousand times, more, and I don't know what I can get out of it. He was my **father**, and he looked up at me, and there is a way he must have felt, the specific, unquantifiable way that it feels to be extinguished into the godless dark, and it is— Christ, kibble. I watched him die. I **killed** him, kibble. If I had handled it differently—spoken to him differently, more gently."

Turtle can still not look up at his face, his hands wrapping and rewrapping around the steering wheel, fixed over the gearshift, huge stained thighs of his Levi's, splits in the vinyl, yellow insulation, rusted springs, brown rubber mats in the footwells, fir needles in the mats' ridge-and-groove detailing. He looks at her and he says, "I lost it and I left, and **fuck**, kibble. I mean—for all the contempt I felt for him, for all of that contempt I had for his failures—I **left.** With my old man . . . he had one chance with me, I think. I really only **gave** him one chance. I never understood—**who** he was. I don't think he loved me, or if he did, it was in some crippled way. All the mistakes he made, I held that against him and thought, I will **never** make his mistakes. His life is not life, and the mistakes he made, he made because he was cowardly and hard-hearted, a wretched, bigoted, hateful, impatient, dithering— Kibble, the **things my father was**. A fuck-off, an alcoholic son of a bitch, a murderer. And me, I was young and I had **no** compassion, I was never **never** going to make those mistakes. I wanted to repudiate everything he was, and more, I believed I could. There was no salvage—I was not like you, I did not listen, I didn't care. No understanding. And fuck me, kibble, because for all of his failings, and for everything he got wrong there at the end, he came to you, he was worried about you, he was willing to give everything, and where was I?"

She looks at his shoulder, the flannel, his belt, his Daniel Winkler belt knife, the seat, the ashtray, out at the road ahead of them, then up, his jaw, working side to side with anger. "I was scared and I **fucked it** and I don't know how— Christ! How have I become this man I am now, set in my ways, scared like he was, set like he was, uncompromising **like he was**, and I hate this, I never wanted to be this man, and I thought—Fuck! I saw him go down into the godless dark, and I saw you—saw you, and do you know what you are? The only numinous thing in a dark and profane world, and without you, nihilism. Do you see?"

He looks at her. She watches the ocean, watches the riffled red fescue on the bluffs. No, she thinks. No, it cannot be that in the end of it all, I am like you. That cannot be. Those parts of you I turn from, I will turn from forever and I will not at the end of it find that I am like you. She makes a wedge of her hands, fits it between her thighs, sits clenching them.

They eat breakfast on the porch of the MacCallum House, above the windswept Mendocino Bay. The server brings out breakfast burritos heaped with salmon caviar and garnished with nasturtium flowers and pea shoots. Martin's face fills with an expression she cannot read and cannot reproduce in her own mind. He holds his fork in one hand and his knife in the other with his forearms against the table, leaning in toward her, his attention fixed on her, and he says, "Just look at you. Jesus Christ." She doesn't say anything. Women near them are wearing summer dresses; the men are in white dress shirts. Turtle does not know if they are tourists or Silicon Valley transplants with summerhouses here. Martin has no attention for any of it but her. Turtle is wearing old combat boots, olive drab fatigues, a black sports bra, and a wifebeater. Tangles of hair keep blowing across her face and sticking to her lips. Martin examines her like a man probing his mouth for canker sores. "Go on," he says, "try your breakfast burrito." She picks up her fork, looks at the heaped orange caviar. "You are the most beautiful thing," he says, "that's what I think. Everything about you, kibble, is perfect. Every detail. You are the platonic ideal of yourself. Your every blemish, every scratch, is inimitable elaboration on your beauty and your wildness. You look like a naiad. You look like a girl raised by wolves. You know that?" She cuts into her burrito, spills its home fries and scrambled egg, rakes them across the plate with the tines.

"You know about Actaeon?"

"No," she says.

"Actaeon was a young hunter who went out into the wilderness and came upon a forest pool where the virgin goddess and her handmaidens were bathing." He looks out at the ocean, chewing on his lip, and then he looks at her, his whole face lit with pleasure, and he sighs through his nose, expressive of that contentment. "Artemis, that bitch. Artemis. In punishment for him seeing her, Artemis turned Actaeon into a stag, and he was hunted down and torn apart by his own hounds. Goddamn; you look just like she must have looked. Give me your hand." She leans forward, and he takes her hand, clenches it in his own. "Goddamn but it's good to see you. Goddamn it's good."

Turtle waits for him to see the broken fingers, but he does not see them. With his thumb, he strokes the meat of her palm, looking carefully at her, his eyes blue, irises tangled with white threads, thick black hair pulled into a ponytail, still wild, but thinning now, seams of his scalp visible, the flesh around his eyes chinked like splintery wood, deep smears beneath his eyes, still a big man but smaller now, diminished and stooping, the physical presence of him still invested with a tremendous and specific gravity, but less awe-inspiring, as if he were retreating inside of himself, no longer quite the man who could stand in front of a doorway almost spanning it with his shoulders. They wait, him stroking her hand and looking at her, and she does not know what he sees in her face, but he sits searching it and it seems to pain him and he looks out at the ocean and she can see him gathering his patience, can see him reasoning with himself, can see him saying, **Give her a minute**, and he looks back at her and he says, "Kibble?"

"Yeah," she says. She thinks, you will trust in your discipline and your courage and you will never leave them and never abandon them and you will be stronger, grim and courageous and hard, and you will never sit as he sits, looking at your life as he looks at it, you will be strong and pure and cold for the rest of your goddamn life and these are lessons that you will never forget.

He is waiting on her to say something and she doesn't know what to say. He wants something from her, some reply. She cannot remember what he has said. He releases her hand and sits back, almost angrily, almost impatiently, and she picks up the nasturtium flower on her plate and spins it between her fingertips, not knowing what he wants from her.

"Why?" she says, because she doesn't understand. "**Why** were you scared?"

He looks out at Mendocino Bay. "I don't know if I can really articulate it, even to myself. The death of a parent, kibble, god, it can get under your skin."

She nods at this, but still she doesn't get it, knows what it has done to her, the grief of it, the way it ate into her bones, but there had been no fear, and she does not understand—fear of what?—and looks at him and knows, really knows, how little she understands him.

"Where did you go?"

He nods to her burrito. "You going to eat that?" She picks her fork back up and eats and then, embarrassed to be chewing, looks down. He says, "North. I went north. I went into eastern Oregon and Washington, and then out into Idaho and Wyoming."

"What did you see?"

"Nothing," he says.

"Why, then?"

He shakes his head. "I **fucked** up."

"Oh," she says.

"Will you take me back?"

She looks down at the burrito on her plate, severed open, spilling its contents, doesn't want to

eat, sick to her stomach with dread and excitement both. She wants him back so **badly**. There
is so much to him, so much depth, and she wants
that again, the heft and the weight of him, and
everything he takes from her, but still she mourns
the loss, the girl who was alone in that house, who
cut apart his bookshelves and burned his clothes,
and she doesn't think that it is her place to say yes
or no, it is his house, she is his girl, he could always
come back, she knows it and he knows it.

"Well," he says, nods again to her. "How is that?"

"It's good," she says.

They pay the bill and walk back to the truck.
They drive back to the house and park in the
driveway. There is a child on the porch, face in
her hands, black hair in tangles, matchstick arms
tiger-striped with bruises. The girl is nine or ten,
maybe seventy pounds. When Martin gets out
of the truck, the girl looks up and runs to him.
He picks her up by the armpits and swings her
around, laughing. Then, with his arm around her
shoulders, he walks her back to Turtle.

"Kibble," he says, "this is Cayenne."

Cayenne peeks out from under her hair. She
scratches one shin with a callused heel.

Turtle looks her up and down. "Who are you?"
she asks.

The girl looks away, nervous.

Turtle says, "Who is this?"

"This is Cayenne," Martin says again.

"Where's she from?"

"She's from Yakima."

Turtle cracks her knuckles. That's not what she meant.

"It's in Washington," Martin says.

"Get out of here," Turtle says to the girl. She hesitates, and Turtle says, "Get—the **fuck**—out of here." Cayenne flashes Turtle a horrible little scowl, then bolts for the sliding glass doors and into the house.

"Where'd she come from?"

"We're looking after her for a little while."

"Why?"

"Come here," Martin says.

Turtle comes closer, and he puts his arms around her and puts his face against her neck and breathes in her scent.

"God, the way you smell," he says. "Are you glad I'm back?"

"Yes, Daddy," she says, "yes I am."

"Are you still my little girl?" he says. She looks up at him, and he smiles lopsidedly. "Look at that goddamn face. You are, aren't you?"

She studies him. There is something in her as hard as the cobbles in the surf and she thinks, there is a part of me that you will never, ever get at.

He says, "Look at you." He wraps his hands around her throat, cupping her hair demurely to her neck, and there is almost a hatred of her in his eyes, and she thinks, do it. Fucking do it. I want you to do it.

"Just looking at you," he says, "is hurtful. That's how beautiful you are. You hurt to look at." His hands tighten and relax around her neck. She thinks of walking along the ocean floor with Jacob, of the way the anemones battened down like knuckles to wait out the tide, and of that sunken pool with its circling, unseen creature. She wants to be his girl, Jacob's girl, and she wants that to be taken from her. She stands looking up at Martin, and she thinks, take everything from me. Take away my dignity and everything else, leave me with nothing.

That evening, Turtle carries her blankets up the stairs and she stands in her old doorway and looks at her old room. She walks to her plywood bed and can see her own residual shadow, painted in sweat and grease. She unrolls her blankets across the floorboards, kneels at the foot, and smooths them out. Turtle walks back out of the bedroom, slams the door, stands just outside of it.

She goes down the stairs into the unlighted living room, where Cayenne is sitting cross-legged on the kitchen counter. Martin is hefting her frying pan, turning it this way and that in the light.

"Cured the shit out of this, didn't you," he says.

"Yes," she says.

"Doesn't look any different."

She comes to stand beside him, runs her finger-tips across the surface, black as if painted, and she says, "Before, the curing was laid on too thick and it flaked. I buried them in coals and burned all that old Crisco grease off them. Recured them with organic lard. You take your time, and this is how it looks."

He shakes his head and reaches up to the open-faced cherrywood cabinets, takes down the canola oil and pours it across the pan in long curlicues, and then picks up the skillet and tilts it slowly this way and that to spread the oil across it, places it back on the flame.

Cayenne watches silently. She looks sometimes at Turtle, sometimes at Martin. In the dark, her expression is nearly unreadable—if anything, pensive. She has a blocky oval face, a jutting jaw, rounded, clunky cheekbones, **Twilight** open on her lap. Turtle feels nothing looking at the girl. Nothing. It is like the socket where a tooth should be. She thinks, his mistakes are not your mistakes. You will never be the way he is. You will never.

Martin opens up a cooler he's set on the floor, takes out two steaks wrapped in butcher paper, slaps them down onto the cast iron, and then stares fixedly at them. He reaches into his pocket and pulls out a handful of change, sorts through it with his thumb, separates out a fifty-cent piece, and flicks it to Cayenne, who plucks it from the air. He replaces the rest of the change in his pocket and walks out of the kitchen, across the living room, and stands against the wall.

"Come here," he says to Turtle.

Turtle walks to him. He unholsters his Colt 1911 and hands it to her. He says, "You've been keeping up?"

"No," Turtle says.

"You should've kept up."

Turtle looks across the room to the girl holding the coin. She looks at Martin. She'd made a mistake with the skillet, said a little too much.

"I don't want to do this," Cayenne says.

"Look at you," Martin says, smirking. "You don't even know what we're doing! Hold that up higher." Cayenne raises the coin, framed between thumb and forefinger, and she looks from the one to the other of them.

"You can't be serious," Turtle says.

She looks at him.

"I don't want to do this," Cayenne says again.

"You're gonna be fine, sweetheart," Martin says. "This is gonna be fun."

"I haven't been keeping up," Turtle says.

"It's all right," he says, "Daddy's here," and he laughs at her expression.

"You can't be serious," Turtle says again. She looks to the girl sitting cross-legged on the kitchen counter. A single wisp of black hair lies across Cayenne's face and the girl does nothing to remove it.

Behind her, the only light in the kitchen comes from the blue flame in spreading horizon across the underside of the skillet.

Turtle says, "You're not serious." She drops the magazine and locks the slide back. In the gloom, the exposed barrel glitters with brass fouling, and that's a bad sign. She has known him to carry cheap range ammo and reloads, so she thumbs out the first round in the magazine stack. It is Federal HST .45 auto +P 230 grain. It's much too powerful.

She looks to him, to see if he's still serious, and he is. She seats the magazine, drops the slide, steps into her stance. Martin comes around behind her and puts his hands on her arms. He adjusts her hips and then her shoulders. Into her ear, he says, "Loosen up a little bit. Relax. There. Steady."

Turtle lines up the sight post and notch, then runs her focus out from the sight picture to the coin, framed between Cayenne's small thumb and forefinger; it looks unimaginably tiny, a bare spark of silver in the dark, the girl looking right back at her and then closing her eyes, her chest rising with steadying inhalations, the coin moving slightly up and down with every breath. Cayenne has set her book down on the counter and her fingers stray toward it, find the book's hardbound edge, and stay there, touching it as if for protection.

Behind the coin, Turtle can see the kitchen door, with its blue paint peeling away in ribbons, and in the vacant circle where the knob should go, a single blue-bellied lizard with its head cocked up, blue throat just visible and tagged with deer ticks like blue sesame seeds, the keeled scales of the neck standing up like thorns, the spiny crests of the brow silhouetted perfectly in that keyhole of evening light.

Turtle breathes and draws her attention back into the sight picture, blurring the girl out of focus, bringing the sight post into perfect relief, and focusing on the top edge of that post, placing that edge on the unfocused silver spark of the coin. Nowhere is she more aware of the shallow depth of field of the human gaze. She cannot keep both the girl and her sight post in focus. Martin says into her ear, "Don't think, just put your brain in your lunch box and go to work. Don't think. Just aim. Just shoot."

Turtle pans the gun aside, finds a chip of paint on the door, six inches up and six inches left of the coin, and she fires. The Federal HST 230 grain is explosively loud and kicks hard, throwing a divot of wood off the door. Cayenne flinches but does not drop the coin, and Turtle brings the barrel into perfect control, breathes and finds that bullet mark and fires again, throwing up a second divot an inch to the left of the first, Cayenne flinching again and gasping, the coin jumping involuntarily in her hand, her brows screwed together, little lines laying up between them, the coin quivering.

Turtle brings the gun to bear on her third shot, pulls the trigger, and nothing happens.

She looks at the top of the gun and sees a shell stovepiped in the ejection port. Usually, when the slide doesn't close, she feels the difference in the recoil and hears the different, flatter note of the gunshot. She isn't paying attention. She isn't focused.

"The gun is dirty," she says to Martin.

"You're limp-wristing," he says, meaning that her grip isn't firm enough for the action to work properly.

"No," she says. "It may be fouling, it may be the magazine, it might even be a defective extractor."

"Or it's your limp wrist."

She lowers the gun and lets Martin observe her bullet marks in the door, noting their spread, about an inch. He takes her point. "Well," he says, "that would've been fucked up, wouldn't it?"

"Yeah," Turtle says.

"She missed," Cayenne says. Turtle can tell the girl is trying to keep her voice calm, but it is tight and nervous nonetheless. When neither reacts, she says again, "She missed."

Turtle walks to the counter, beside the girl. She ejects the magazine and drops the jammed casing, lets the rack spring forward. Then she reloads the gun and slivers back the slide to show the bright brass casing seated correctly in the chamber. She sets the gun down. This close to Cayenne, she can hear the raggedness in the girl's breathing. She has put on a pair of pink socks since Turtle saw her in the driveway. Perhaps the wood floor is too cold for her. The socks are large on Cayenne, the baggy heels at the girl's ankles, the toe boxes pushed out irregularly. Turtle turns back to Martin. "I'll clean that gun for you later. It's dirty."

"Nah," he says, walking back to the kitchen, "it's not dirty."

"I've seen dogs," she says, "with assholes cleaner than that gun."

Martin walks laughing back to the skillet, tests the pliancy of the steaks with the pad of his finger, and compares it to the meat of his own palm, touching thumb and forefinger together to match the pliancy of rare steak. He draws his belt knife and flips them with the broadside of the blade, shaking his head. The steak comes gorgeously off the black curing. "You bitch," he says, squinting down into the skillet, his mouth half open, half grinning, wiping the knife blade across the thigh of his Levi's and sheathing it.

Cayenne takes conspicuous, steadying breaths. Turtle can smell the girl; her unwashed body, her childish sweat, the smoke of Martin's Swisher Sweets in her clothes.

Cayenne brushes a wisp of hair snagging on her eyelashes, her hand shaking. Her shirt clings to her sternum with sweat. "She missed," she says again, watching them for a reaction. Father and daughter wait in the darkening kitchen, attentive to each other.

"She didn't miss," he says. "She hit what she was aiming at, and what she meant to show," Martin explains, as if speaking to an idiot, "is that she has too much spread. She can't place her shots close enough to the target." He walks to the door, measures the distance between shots with thumb and forefinger, a little more than an inch.

"Oh," Cayenne says, clearly still confused.

"Pick that shit up," Martin says, turning around, annoyed.

"I thought—" Cayenne says.

"Pick that shit up," he says.

Cayenne picks up the coin.

"Kibble just has to do better." He turns and looks at Turtle. "Kibble," he says to her, meaning that she should try again.

"I'll miss," Turtle says.

"Nah," Martin says. "You'll be fine."

Cayenne looks from one to the other. "I thought, I thought she had too much spread," she says.

"Don't you worry," Martin says, "don't you worry. Kibble has a genius for this. She'll do just fine." He looks at Turtle, says, "Kibble? Don't choke."

"Daddy," Turtle says, "you can't mean it."

"One more try," he says, holding up a finger.

"But—" Turtle says.

"No 'buts,'" Martin says. He walks across the room, steaks hissing on the skillet.

"I have a Sig Sauer," she says, "a nine mil, clean and greased, with Hornady 115 grain FTX." The round weighs half as much as the 230-grain .45 round.

"This gun is fine," he says, hefting the Colt.

"It's not fine. It's dirty. I don't trust the extractor."

"Where's your backbone? Positive mental attitude, kibble."

"Christ," Turtle says.

"Kibble," he says, warning her.

Turtle walks across the room. He stands beside her, holds out the gun. She takes it, unloads it, thumbs back the hammer, and takes aim. She pulls the trigger, watching the front sight post carefully for movement. The gun dry-fires, the sight post remains as fixed as if held by a vise. "I have my doubts about this gun," she says, although she is reassured by her own steadiness and the lightness of the trigger pull. She returns the magazine and chambers a bullet. She wraps her hands around the grip, marrying one to the other, her thumbs spooning like two lovers beneath the slide. She brings the gun to bear on the coin, and exhales.

"Is that what you wear these days?" Martin says.

Turtle stops, looks over at him.

"A black bra," he says, "and a white undershirt? You've got to have better clothes than that."

Cayenne, expecting the shot, gasps nervously when it does not come. She squeezes her eyes closed.

"Where'd you get that bra? I never bought you that bra."

"No," she says.

"Where'd you buy it, then?" he says.

"Can we talk about this later?"

"Tell me how you got that bra," he says.

"I bought it," she says.

"Well, it's terrible."

"I needed a bra," she says. "What was I supposed to do?"

"Well, that's a terrible bra."

"I never saw you stepping up to get me a bra."

"That's because you never had tits."

"That's not true."

"It is true. Do you know how I know that it's true? Because if you'd've had tits, I would've bought you a bra. That's how I know."

"I had tits."

"No. Because if you **had** had tits, I would've bought you a bra."

"Well, I have them now," Turtle says.

"If you can call those tits."

Turtle looks at him.

He says, "Are you going to pull that trigger, or what is this?"

"I don't want to do this, Daddy," she says.

"You have this, sweetheart. My love. My absolute darling. You have this. Take your time, and do it right; just put your brain in your lunch box and let your body relax; roll the trigger without tugging, let the action engage smoothly; know that the recoil is coming, and then forget it; do not surrender your attention until the heartbeat **after** you have fired. What are you thinking about?"

"Nothing," she says, though it's not true.

"That's right," he says, "nothing."

Turtle empties her mind. Her focus is intent. Bullets don't follow a flat trajectory. They arch, just slightly, before descending. Turtle zeros her sights for twenty-five yards, so at this range she can expect to be shooting a little low. But if he's zeroed the sights for fifty yards, she'll be shooting an inch high. It is also possible he's zeroed his sights for seven yards. She cannot ask. The best she can do is guess. She takes all the slack out of the trigger, places the top edge of the front sight exactly on the top edge of the coin. It goes minutely up and down, less than a quarter of an inch variation, but Turtle sights at the top of the coin's cycle, and then waits for the girl's inhalation to lift the coin again.

"Don't blow it," Martin says warningly.

"I can't do this," she says.

He says, "My absolute darling."

Across the room from her, Cayenne's eyes are clenched shut and she cries silently, snot running down her lip. Wisps of hair stick to her face. Turtle puts all of that out of her mind, takes the girl out of her focus, and all that she can see clearly is the front sight post, a flat steel horizon, and she places it exactly on the out-of-focus coin, knowing in her bones that she has this shot, even with the unfamiliar and dirty gun, its barrel sparking like streambed gold with shaved brass, even with the hot ammo, even with Martin breathing down her neck. All the old habits are coming back to her and the sight post is unwavering and obedient to her intention. The coin rises to the top of its cycle, Turtle draws the trigger, and Cayenne pitches off the counter, screaming.

"Fuck!" Martin says in surprise. A chill of disbelief goes over Turtle's body. She and Martin stand watching Cayenne flop across the kitchen floor, clutching her hand to her chest. Turtle thinks over and over again, oh shit. The girl's shrieks are broken by ragged gasps for breath.

Martin stands in place and Turtle walks into the kitchen. Cayenne is lying on the floor, on her belly, with the injured hand trapped to her chest, shaking her head furiously. Her screams subside into panting. Turtle thinks, oh shit. Oh shit.

Martin follows. Cayenne, whining and panting, curls slowly onto her side. Martin casts about for the fifty-cent piece. It is in the frying pan. He walks over, plucks it out, and sets it on the counter.

Turtle and Martin wait with the huddled Cayenne in between them. The girl is wordless, one hand clutched to her chest, the other extended, the fingers grasping at the splintery floor. A high-pitched keening comes from her.

Turtle takes two steps across the kitchen, seizes the

edge of the sink, bends over it, thinking that she will throw up. Martin touches Cayenne with the tip of his boot. "Are you all right?" he says. Nothing comes from the girl except for gasps. Turtle turns around and looks at the child. The sight of her small, shivering rib cage fills Turtle with torment. In the gap between the girl's hair and the neck of her shirt, Turtle can see the articulated knobs of her vertebrae, and the fine, small hair at the nape of her neck. Martin squats down, his knees popping, the leather of his boots creaking, and puts a hand on her shoulder.

"Hey, sweetheart, you okay?" he says.

Cayenne shakes her head, which is folded into the crook of one arm.

"Tell me what happened," he says.

Cayenne shakes her head again.

"Where'd she hit you?"

Cayenne shudders. A wracking quiver runs down her body. Turtle grips the edge of the sink, white-knuckled.

"Your finger?" Martin guesses. "She shot your finger?"

Then, as if suddenly finding that she can speak, the girl heaves up and thrusts her face at him, jaw out, eyes bulging, and screams, "I want my mom!"

"Sweetheart," he says, reaching for her.

"I want my mom!" she yells, ribs trembling and heaving, but she allows him to take her hand. There are red dabs on her shirt. Martin enfolds her injured hand in his two, and Turtle can see that the first joint of the pointer finger has been shot off, leaving a meaty stub.

"I want my mom!" Cayenne screams at him, searching his face for any reply. She seems to be gripped both by agony and complete perplexity that Martin and Turtle are remaining silent. But Turtle has nothing to say. Cayenne's screams embarrass her.

Martin says, "Kibble, look around, see if you can find her finger."

At this, Cayenne howls, and then yells again, "I want my mom!" She gasps and trembles. Her brows draw together angrily.

Turtle looks around the kitchen. She gets down on her stomach and looks slantwise across the floorboards, under the overhung edges of the cabinets. The finger has perhaps simply ceased to exist.

Martin says, "You're going to be fine, sweetheart."

The girl wraps a fist around her finger. Blood leaks out between the knuckles and drips down her wrist. She is silent, her mouth spasming, her eyes sealed shut, shaking her head. A single line wanders down her forearm, and Turtle, looking at it, is astonished at how slender the forearm is. She could encircle it with thumb and forefinger.

Martin says, "That's right, just hold the pressure on it, just hold pressure on it and we'll let it bleed for a little while, you're going to be fine, that's nothing, you don't need that little bit of finger, you're going to be fine. Kibble? Those steaks are probably about burned. Would you take them off for me?"

Turtle walks to the counter. Cayenne is keening. Turtle takes two plates down. She draws her knife, skewers each steak, and drops them in turn onto the plates.

Cayenne screams again, "I want my mom!" and Turtle pauses, mid-action, listening, and then continues as if Cayenne hadn't spoken. She turns off the burner. She looks at Cayenne, sitting upright, rocking back and forth. The girl's eyes are swollen, tears wetting her neckline. Martin says, "You were so **brave**, you were so **good**, you're going to be **fine**."

Turtle walks out onto the porch, carrying both plates. The hillside is there, and the ocean. She stands in the gathering dark. In the kitchen, the girl's high-pitched whine rises to a scream. Martin is trying to bandage the wound. Turtle sets the plates down on the arms of the Adirondack chairs and sits down herself. She notices a speck on Martin's steak, dots it on the tip of her finger, and looks at it. It is like a frangible, cloudy bit of a plastic bottle. She flicks it off her finger.

When Martin comes out, he sets the fifty-cent piece on the arm of her chair. It is bent, with a single black pockmark just off center, rimmed with grease from the skillet. Turtle picks it up, looks at him. He shrugs, to indicate that he doesn't know exactly how that worked. He picks up his plate, holds it, looking out at the ocean. Then he says, "Maybe, maybe, it hit the coin and glanced up into her finger."

Turtle nods.

He says, "Just unlucky."

Turtle looks at him.

He says, "No way to've seen that coming."

"What?"

He shakes his head. "Couldn't have seen that coming."

"Really?"

He looks at her. "You hit the coin dead-on."

"No way to have seen that coming?" Turtle repeats.

Martin seems to marvel at her anger. He says, "It should've been plucked right out of her fingers. She isn't a **vise**. She can't hold a coin so hard it **ricochets**. It should've been plucked right out of her grasp."

"No way," Turtle says, "to have seen this coming?"

"Why are you mad at me?" he says, as if it's inscrutable. "You hit the coin. Dead-on. It should've been plucked right out of her fingers. There is no way, no way that she held that coin tight enough for it to ricochet up into her finger."

Turtle opens her mouth to say something. She closes her mouth, returns her attention to the ocean. She says, "You didn't seem bothered in there."

"Why?" he says.

She says, "That girl is in pain."

Martin says, "You know, some people think pain is the solution to solipsism."

"What?"

"The problem is that we have no evidence that other people are conscious and alive, like us. We know that we are conscious because we have direct experience of our own thoughts, our emotions, the unquantifiable way that it **feels** to be alive, but we have no experience of others' consciousness, and so—and so, we do not know for sure that they are alive, **really alive**, experiencing their life as we experience ours. Perhaps we are the only real person, surrounded by hollow shells who act like people, but who have no interior life as we do.

"The idea, so say the philosophers, is that you sit yourself down across from someone, and begin breaking his fingers with a hammer. You see how he reacts. He screams. He clutches his hand to his chest. You infer that he acts this way because he is **in pain**.

"But what really happens, when you are face-to-face with someone in pain, what really happens is that the gulf between you and them is made apparent. Their pain is utterly inaccessible to you. It might as well be a pantomime.

"When they are not in pain—when you two are just talking about Hume or Kant—you can believe that there exists, between you, an intercourse of ideas and emotions. But to see someone in pain like that, once you get past the surprise, is to make apparent the unbridgeable gulf that separates your own human mind from all other, alien personalities. It illuminates the true and actual—not the **social** and the **imagined**—state of human intercourse. Communication is a thin veneer, kibble."

Turtle looks down at her steak. She cuts into it, puts a piece into her mouth, and begins to chew. Martin eats with silent thoughtfulness, looking grimly out at the slivered sunset and the darkening ocean, the sweep of the hillside, the shore pines turning to black-green in the twilight.

"People condemn this observation, kibble. They believe that to insist on the profound isolation of the human mind is madness. But in practice, everybody accepts the fact. We wouldn't permit social stratification unless, on a basic level, we understood that we are insulated from the hardships of other people. And we are: it affects us not at all. These assholes discourse as if they care, but that's a social lie, and if you're paying attention you'll see—you're on your fucking own. Society will never help you. That principal, that teacher of yours, they'll look out for you insofar as it's their job, but they don't really give a fuck, kibble. You're invisible to them. As an individual person, with thoughts and hardships and a mind of your own, invisible."

Turtle's steak is bloody red in its interior. Amazing, how it parts before the knife. Blood and grease pool across the plate. The meat has a powerful, gamy taste. For Turtle, Cayenne's pain had eclipsed everything else in its importance and mind-bending immediacy.

"What's the matter?" Martin says.

"Nothing," she says.

He sits looking at her, chewing.

"You don't like it?" he says.

"No, I like it," she says.

He looks down at his plate. He cuts off a piece, spears it on the knifepoint, holds it out to her. She looks at it.

"Aw," he says, "come on."

"No," Turtle says, "I'm not hungry."

"Oh come on, you're hungry."

"I'm fine," Turtle says.

"She'll be okay. It was hardly anything. A scratch off the tip."

"Fuck."

"Nah, don't sweat it. It's just the very tip."

"Fuck."

"Eat your steak."

"I feel sick," Turtle says.

"No you don't," he says.

She opens her mouth and he puts the knifepoint within the cage of her teeth. She closes her mouth on the blade and looks at him, the knifepoint against her wet tongue, and he draws the blade slowly from her mouth, teeth scraping the steel. She begins to chew, looking at him.

"I don't understand it," he says. He picks up the bent coin between thumb and forefinger, holds it framed as Cayenne had. With pointer finger, he indicates the black pockmark. He says, "You hit the coin. I knew you would hit it, and you did. I just don't understand what happened. Just—just one of those things."

Turtle watches him in silence.

He turns the coin over in his hand, shaking his head. "Just one of those things," he says at last.

After dinner, she goes up to her room and curls into her roll of blankets. The girl is downstairs, lying on her sleeping bag in front of the fireplace, her finger wrapped in gauze. How this house must seem to her. Turtle listens to Martin pace from room to room, and sometime in the early morning, he climbs the stairs and opens her door.

"Come take a walk with me," he says.

She lies there quietly.

"I know you're not asleep," he says.

She sits up and he says, "Just the same old kibble."

She pulls on her fatigues and she is acutely aware of him, slipping her pale white thighs down into the legs of the fatigues and hitching them up over her hips. He leans in the door, expressionless, his eyes hidden in the dark. They walk together down the stairs and past where Cayenne is lying in her sleeping bag in front of the fireplace, holding her injured hand to her chest as if it were a bird. They go out through the sliding glass door and off the porch and down into the fields, wet with dew. He seems in the grip of some wordless awe. As they walk, the grass wets their pants to the hip. They come to the doors that stand open and ajar in the middle of the field, without structure, three of them broken open, four of them intact, forming a rough circle. Martin walks to a doorpost, leans against it, swings the door on its rusted hinges. They look back up the hill to the house, impressive and gloomy, the white clapboard besieged by roses and poison oak. Turtle can see her own window, the rose canes risen up about the frame and reaching inside. She can see the great picture windows of the master bedroom. Out west of them, the ocean buckles and heaves. She looks up to Martin, and he leans against the door, toying with the knob, looking away into the middle distance.

"How is she?" Turtle says.

"She's all right," Martin says. "She'll be okay, give her a couple of days. She's not like you were. Christ. You could chew on nails."

Turtle walks into the middle of the circle, stands on all sides surrounded by the doors. Martin toys with the antique glass knob, swings the door open and then closed, engages the deadlock. This silence goes on for a long time. The wind sweeps across them and the culms wend together among themselves in quiet, lonely congregation, and down on the beach the breakers fold onto the cobbles, and Turtle, her hair stirring, looks toward her father.

He says, "Well, fuck."

Turtle thinks, he left and you had time to gather the pieces of yourself, and you did some of it, you did enough of it. You have a choice now, and don't tell yourself that you don't. You may never get that moment again and there may not be very many such moments in your life, but you could do it now. You maybe did not get very long, maybe not so many nights alone as you could wish, but it was all you needed and now you have a choice. Walk away, Turtle. Just walk away from him, and if he follows after and if he will not let you go, you kill him. He's given you everything and all you need to do is walk away. Do you remember when blood ran in your veins like cool, clear water? You could find that place again and it would be hard but it would be good. Nothing and no one can keep you away from it; only you can take yourself back into the dark, only you can do that. He can't do it to you, and don't lie about that. So walk away, Turtle. Think about your soul, and walk away.

He strides over to her and hits her hard in the jaw and she reels back in a plume of blood and her overwhelming feeling is one of relief. He grabs her by her hair and hauls her up and swings her into the closed door and she grabs the doorpost with one hand and the knob with the other, holding on to it for purchase, her face pressed into the beam as he yards her pants down, and she thinks, oh thank fucking god, and he pulls her fatigues down around her thighs and, unbuckling his jeans, there is a moment where she waits on him, clinging to the doorpost, her pants tangled around her thighs and her cunt bare to him and he stands behind her, his hot breath on her neck, and she turns to look at him over her shoulder, eyes so narrowed that his face is shadowed by the tusks of her lashes, looking at him with love, real love, and Martin, with his fist knotted in her hair, drives her forward into the door, the grain of the wood laying weals against her cheek.

She feels in his movement something straining, something reaching too much, his fingers raking at her hair, clutching and rending. His face is fixed in concentration as if he is trying to direct his attention through her to some principle beyond her, grinding her against the closed door in desperation, every movement a continuous, repetitive contempt. He would annihilate her if he could. He pulls at her arms, her hair, as if he wants to pull her apart, repeating over and over, "You bitch, you cunt," and something about the words is meaningless and chantlike. Turtle turns her face into the wood, closing her eyes, her hand between her legs, grinning with the pain, two fingers framing his cock, his ballsack contracted into a wrinkled lime against her fingers, and Turtle seeming larger than herself, outside herself, willing to die at that moment, willing to be undone, feeling his hatred of her, a straining unendurable compulsion, and Turtle surrendering to it, opening to it, her every thought seizing and black. He bucks and spasms, he clutches at the back of her head, at her shoulder, sinking his fingers in deep, and Turtle closes her eyes, her whole body clenched up. She turns her face away from the door, plants it in her own biceps, and cries out, hair plastered to her cheeks. Martin steps away from her and his spunk runs out of her and down her leg and she catches some of it in her cupped hand and straightens, staggers with her fatigues still knotted around her thighs, and hitches them half up, still unbuckled but around her hips now, flapping open, and she turns to look at him. He is stooped, breathing hard, his eyes open as if in astonishment at what has happened. Turtle is cold and resolved, her flesh stripped of warmth, her very heart inside her cool and wild and unconquerable. Martin drags out the gun and puts it beneath her chin, his breath ragged and steaming through his open jaws.

He says, "This could be it. Just you and me, and then, nothing—nothing—" It's as if he cannot fasten on her eyes; he looks past her and then at her mouth and he does not meet her stare. He runs his tongue across his lips, some unconscious gesture of pain or relish, and then he flashes her a grimace, showing her all of his teeth, his lips pulled back.

He raises her chin with the gun, and she allows it to be raised, her eyes moving to follow him as he angles her face upward. He says, "I need you. I need you so badly. And this, this could be our world, kibble. Fuck the rest of it. That would be it. I would do you and then I'd do myself. Burn the fucking house down. Burn it all fucking down, and be done with it. Goddamn, I am so tired, kibble. I want to end it like this, kibble, you and me, a perfect ending. Have you down to your bones, once and for all. You know, right now, that there's no going back. We're too far into this thing, and I've gotten nowhere. I spent three months away from you and I knew, every day, I knew that I was doing the wrong thing. There's no running away from this, and there's no going on with it. So we end it together. Right here. Right now."

He moves the gun from her chin to her forehead, he looks fixedly down into some point between her eyes, and she gazes back at him, trembling now, quivers that come in tight succession and then recede, and the grass stirs all around them like an ocean.

"You want to kill me," she says, just to say it.

At this, he shudders. He steps away from her and he puts his hands to his temples, one of them holding the gun. Then he stoops in the grass as if he might throw up. "Fuck!" he says, shaking his head. "Fuck!" he says. "Fuck!"

He puts the gun under his own chin, looks up at

the dark sky with the silver-lit undersides of clouds. Then, because he forgets that there is a round in the chamber, or because he wants the drama, he racks the slide noisily and Turtle hears the round jam. He makes an aggrieved noise, looks at the gun, inspecting it in the dark. "Fuck," he says in disbelief, banging on the gun's frame with the heel of his hand.

"You needed to clean it, that's all."

He shakes his head. "Don't talk to me like that," he says, "don't you be a little bitch. Not right now. Not **now**."

Turtle says nothing.

"Fuck," Martin says. He looks in through the ejection port. Turtle can tell, just from the sound, that the gun has fed another round into the chamber without extracting the first. She knows that she can fix the jam, but she makes no move to help. Martin probes the round half lodged in the chamber, trying to rack the fixed slide, grimacing. "It's fucking jammed," he says, as if he can't believe it. Turtle is embarrassed for him. Martin bangs the gun with the heel of his hand, trying to make something give. "Okay," he says, looking around. "Fuck. Okay." He looks up, nodding now, reappraising, biting his lower lip, breathing hard in frustration. "We go on like we always have."

Turtle spits into the grass, and walks away through the field up toward the house sitting lonely and dark at the top of its black hill.

Twenty-one

TURTLE LIES THAT NIGHT ON HER FLOOR, belly-down, chin on her hands, looking into the flame of her oil lamp, spooning one foot against the other, thinking, he came back and everything left you. All the dreams about the girl you could be. Gone. You always thought it was him. But you wanted him back. You're in this, too. You were a child once but not anymore and what could be excused in a child will not be and cannot be excused in you. You should've, she thinks, used a fucking condom. She doesn't know exactly how it works, but things have changed. She thinks, maybe it was you all along. Maybe there is something in you. Something rotten. You asked for it, or you wanted it. Of course you did. You brought him into this when you were just a child and your mother understood and when she understood, she killed herself, and now he cannot get away. He looks into your eyes and he wants to die.

Turtle could smash to pieces. It is bad thinking, sloppy thinking. When you look at the thing like it is, she thinks, you see that Martin spent his life reaching out toward Grandpa, groping for some sign, and Grandpa just fucking hated him. Your father was raised in total, annihilating, self-hating destitution, and that is how he lives. But he loved you. Loved the hell out of you. How he found that in him, you might never know. All the strength in you, that came from him. The spark in you, whatever faith you have in yourself, everything in you that resists the rot, all of that came from him. He never had it for himself, but he found it for you. And you have to think he had some idea what he might be preparing you for and what he might have to give up. She is shaking. And you might, she thinks. You might be okay. And if that happens, she thinks, it'll be because he gave you everything. That is the best of him.

In the morning, she comes down the creaking stairs and finds Cayenne still asleep in front of the fire, curled on her side, hunched a little, knees drawn up, heels pulled almost to her butt, her hands folded around one another and clutched to her chest. Turtle walks quietly into the kitchen.

She doesn't want to wake the girl, and so takes down her copper pot from its meat hook as silently as she can, and instead of running the tap, takes up the water glasses left on the counter and pours them down the side of the pot. She strikes the match on her thumbnail, lights the stove. She hitches herself up onto the counter, sits there cross-legged to wait. She is looking at the girl. She thinks, goddamn. The worst interpretation is that Martin picked the girl because it is about children. But Turtle doesn't think so.

When the water begins to boil, Cayenne stirs and wakes, pushes herself against the wall. She sits hunched, holding her finger in her other hand. She watches Turtle silently. After a moment, she picks up her book, opens it, sits bent over it. Turtle hates her little cunt face.

Turtle says, "Whatcha reading?"

The girl looks up at her, blank, sullen.

"What are you reading?" Turtle says.

"**Twilight**."

"I see that."

"Oh." The girl stares.

"I mean, what's it about?"

She riffles through the pages to her own, marked page, as if trying to remember. "Just . . ." she says.

Turtle ladles up tea from the pot into her cast-iron teacup.

"You know," Cayenne says. "I didn't need my

mother. Not really. I was just so pissed off. I just said that because I was so pissed off."

Turtle thinks, **I was just so pissed off.** The girl is copying someone, some man in her life, her mother's boyfriend, somebody, who said that. I didn't mean it. **I was just so pissed off**.

Turtle says, "Yeah."

Martin comes out of his bedroom into the kitchen and stands at the counter beside her. He looks down into her copper pot of nettle leaves and then picks up a kettle and fills it with water. He begins looking around in the cabinets for coffee but there is no coffee and finally he goes to the grocery bags he has left on the floor and takes out a blue tub of Maxwell House and decants it into the French press. Turtle waits for someone to speak but no one does. His kettle boils and he pours it into the French press and waits, staring fixedly down into the thick, black, crackling crust of grounds at the top of the beaker. Cayenne turns the pages of her book. Turtle looks back at the girl and wants to say something but there doesn't seem to be anything she can say.

Martin places both hands down on the counter and leans forward onto it. "I've been thinking about it," he says, "and I think we've got to open her back up."

"What?" Turtle says. Martin goes into living room and kneels down beside Cayenne, holds out his hands. She gives him her hurt one. He turns it over.

"I got a good look at it when I bandaged it, and the bone inside was crushed to shards and the meat around it was badly bruised and maybe even burned, and I don't think the skin can close over the wound. I think we've got to cut that finger open and clip the bone down to the first knuckle and then sew it back closed so that the skin can heal across the tip."

"No," Cayenne says. She takes her hand and holds it to her chest. "No. You can't."

Martin doesn't appear to hear her.

"All right," Turtle says.

Cayenne pushes herself back with her heels, scooting across the floorboards until she is against the wall. She holds the wounded hand to her chest. She says, "No. No. No. No. No. No. No."

"Watch her," he says to Turtle, and rises and walks away.

The girl is shaking all over. She says, "You're not going to let him, are you?"

Turtle looks away, embarrassed for the girl. Then, rather than stay in the living room with her, Turtle follows Martin down the hallway to the pantry. He says, "They have some kind of surgical tool for trimming bone, I just don't know what it is and I don't have one. You know, I always meant to get more medical implements, but there just is never enough goddamn time or enough money, kibble, and now look at this, I'm looking at wire cutters and diagonal pliers and things."

"Is this necessary?"

"Yes it's necessary. I was thinking on it last night. Unless we can stitch the flaps of skin together over the end of the finger, it won't heal. There's a diagram in one of the books I had downstairs—it's called a fish-mouth amputation because you trim the end of the finger like a fish mouth. You have to trim all the interior tissue, apparently, or the amputation bulges or 'mushrooms' at the tip. All we've got to do is make two deep cuts on either side of the finger and peel them open and dig the bone out, pare out the extra tissue, and stitch it closed. I have a suture set, so we can do that just fine."

Turtle says, "Is it really going to be that easy?"

He looks at her. "Why wouldn't it?"

"What if there's something we don't know about the anatomy? Or just something we're not thinking of?"

"Look, kibble, it's a finger. It's not trivial, but it's not rocket science, either." Martin picks up a flashlight and throws open the hatch to the basement and she follows him down the spiral staircase and among the tarped-up pallets of five-gallon buckets. He opens the aluminum cabinets and stands casting the flashlight beam across the ranks of glass blister caps and prescription bottles, and takes down a glass ten-milliliter single-dose bottle of .25% lidocaine HCI, turns it over, stands looking at the expiration date. "Expired," he says,

shaking the bottle, "but we'll see. Plain. No epi-
nephrine, which is good. This will work."

"What about something more general?"

"Knock her out, you mean?"

"Yeah," Turtle says.

"She doesn't need that. I don't have anything
like that and she doesn't need it. We could get
some veterinary ketamine, maybe, but it would
take time and with a kid that size, more dangerous anyway."

"Will this really work?"

"Yes," he says.

"You're sure?"

"Yes," he says.

They climb up together. He goes into the bathroom and comes out with the bucket of first aid
supplies. The scalpel and the sutures are in sterile
packaging, but the diagonal pliers, the hemostatic
forceps, the tweezers, and the surgical scissors are
all loose and he drops them into the boiling tea.
He opens the freezer for ice, but there is no power
and the freezer does not run and he takes out the
ice cube tray with its rows of water and throws it
into the sink and he looks at Turtle morosely. Cayenne watches without speaking, holding her hand
to her chest.

"I don't want to," she says.

Martin turns to a cooler on the floor, now full
of stagnant water, and takes out a beer with the
label soaked off, bangs it open on the countertop.

He leans back against the counter and looks at the child, holding the dripping beer loosely slung between thumb and forefinger, taking drinks. The boiling implements rattle against the bottom of the pot.

"I don't want to," Cayenne says again. "I don't want to."

He empties the pot of tea into a colander. The implements are steaming. He carries the colander over to Cayenne.

"Is the colander clean?" Turtle asks.

"Sure. It's clean."

"Have you ever injected lidocaine?"

"Hell no," he says.

"And is ten milliliters enough?"

"It's a whole bottle. I'm sure it's enough."

"We don't know what it does, after its expiration."

"Kibble, you're making her more nervous than she needs to be."

"It's expired?" Cayenne asks from the living room.

"No, sweetheart, it's sort of a 'best by' date. It's not really expired. That's all just legal stuff."

Turtle says, "I'd like to do this the right way. If we're going to do it, we should do it right. What about veterinary ketamine?"

"Hell," Martin says, "we **will** do it right. Ketamine, that shit is expensive. We don't want to accidentally euthanize the girl and we don't need to put her entirely under when it's just her goddamn finger. If we had ice we could just numb it with cold, but we don't have ice. The lidocaine is perfect. The lidocaine will be fine."

"What's 'euthanize'?" Cayenne asks.

"Kibble, let's have a towel to work on, a basin of water, and an irrigation syringe." When Turtle has gathered the things, Martin looks over at her and says, "You know, we really could use a table right about now." Turtle says nothing. Martin says, "Give me your hand, Cayenne."

Cayenne holds it to her chest. "No," she says.

Martin says, "Come on, sweetheart."

The girl shakes her head. Martin sighs and looks at Turtle. Turtle does not know what to do.

The girl says, "I don't want to."

"You have to."

"It'll heal on its own."

"Some things, maybe, but not this. Give it here."

"I promise it will," she says. "I **know** it will."

"Cayenne," he says.

"I promise promise promise," she says.

"I'm warning you, girl."

Turtle thinks, I'm warning you, girl. She bites her lip. The phrase goes through her and fills her guts with pleasurable anguish.

"Cayenne," Martin says.

"No, I won't," she says. "You can't do it. You **can't**. No! No! No!"

"I'm going to count to three," Martin says.

"I won't do it," Cayenne says. She is crying. "I'm afraid. I'm afraid, Marty."

"One."

Her eyes are crumpled shut. Her face is red. She is sobbing, shaking her head. "You're scaring me," she says. "You're **scaring** me."

Someday, Turtle will have to explain how she let this happen.

"Two," Martin says.

Cayenne and Martin hesitate. Cayenne's look is terrified. She seems to not know herself what she will do. Martin is implacable. It is like neither of them wants to find out what happens when he gets to three.

"Three," Martin says, and Cayenne throws her hand forward. Martin grasps her by the wrist and sticks the hypodermic full of lidocaine into the webbing between index and middle fingers. Cayenne cries out and Turtle sees his hand constrict painfully around the girl's wrist as he depresses the plunger. He withdraws the needle, sticks it into the other side of the knuckle, and depresses the plunger all the way.

"There," he says, "that wasn't so bad."

There are tears in Cayenne's eyes. She is gritting her teeth.

"Toughen up," he says. "Look at you. Not like kibble," Martin says.

"Not like kibble?" Cayenne says. She doesn't understand.

"The devil took her soul," Martin says. "And left her empty inside."

"Shut up," Turtle says, "you're confusing her."

"I'm not confused," Cayenne says, and now she looks at Turtle as if to see if she really is empty inside. Martin begins to cut away the gauze padding. Beneath, the fingertip is a ragged stump cut short right at the edge of the nail bed. The meat is pink and ringed with blackish-red scabbing. He begins washing it, and Cayenne murmurs and complains, trying to pull away, Martin pulling her hand back. When he is done washing it, he takes the hair tie out of Cayenne's hair and wraps it around the base of the finger for a tourniquet, turning loops of it around a pair of hemostatic forceps until the finger begins to drain white.

"It **hurts**, Marty," she says.

"This will cut into the bleeding. You want me to see what I'm doing, don't you? Well."

"Marty, it **hurts**."

"So," Martin says, "how are things, kibble?"

Turtle examines his expression, unable to reply.

"Couldn't get it together to pay the electricity bill, though, could you?"

"It's turned off at the main. There's a short somewhere."

"Well. I'll get it fixed."

Cayenne's finger is waxy and drained of blood from the tourniquet. "Okay," he says. "Hold her hand down." Turtle pushes the girl's hand down onto a towel.

"I'm scared," Cayenne says. "You're scaring me."

"Close your eyes and think of England," Martin says.

"What?" Cayenne says, confounded. "What?"

"What is wrong with you?" Turtle says, holding the girl's hand clamped to the floor by the wrist.

Martin begins cutting away at the remains of the fingernail, and Cayenne opens her mouth and screams. The scream is unbearably high-pitched and goes on and on. Her body goes rigid and she heaves against Turtle, and Turtle, for all that she is bigger, cannot hold her. "Shut up," Martin says. "Kibble, shut her up! For christsakes, Cayenne, shut the fuck up." Cayenne stops and gasps for breath. Her hand is writhing. Turtle cannot keep it pinned in place. "You can't feel it," Martin says.

"I can," Cayenne says. "I can feel it."

"She can't feel it," Martin says. "Shut your fucking eyes. You can't feel it."

"I can, I can feel it."

"Listen—" Martin says, and stops. "Listen," he says, "I know you're scared, sweetheart. I know you are. And I know that this may look really, really bad. But we have to do this. Do you hear me?"

The girl is looking up at him.

"Do you hear me, Cayenne?"

"Yes."

"We have to do this, and you're going to help. Because if we can't do this, we're going to have to drive you back to that gas station where I found you and give you back."

"No," Cayenne says.

"Well then, you're going to need to be very brave. All right?"

Cayenne closes her eyes tight. Her small face screws up in concentration. Her nose wrinkles. He plunges the scalpel into the flesh and cuts from the right side of the finger, across the top, and down onto the left side. Cayenne struggles weakly. Turtle holds the girl's hand planted fast to the towel.

Martin slips the scalpel beneath the flap of the skin. Because of the tourniquet, it bleeds only weakly, like the latex that weeps out of broken milkweed. "This," Martin says, levering the scalpel to expose a crescent of flat, pinkish tissue slicked with thin blood, "is the keratogenous membrane, kibble. It's the germinal matrix that produces the nail." He snips it away.

Cayenne lashes frantically. "No no no no no," she says. Her words are broken by ragged, sobbing gasps. Snot is running out of her nose. Hair is stuck to her face. Her eyes are squeezed shut. The girl's finger is so small that the movements involved are tiny, delicate. He slips the scalpel into the bloody yellow mess, working carefully around some submerged object.

"Easy, easy," Martin says. "Easy, girl."

"Stop! Stop! I can feel it," Cayenne cries.

"Shut up."

"Maybe we should wait," Turtle says.

"She's being hysterical. She can't feel shit."

"Even so," Turtle says, "maybe ketamine."

"Well, it's started now," Martin says. He brings out a bone, shorn at one end, small as a bit of pencil lead. Cayenne's eyes are closed and veins stand out on her forehead. She's gasping quickly and shallowly. Turtle glimpses the joint of the next bone lower down. Martin peels the top half of the skin away to expose it. "Clip that," he says.

"You're not serious," Turtle says.

Cayenne is whimpering.

"Clip it," Martin says. "Clip that thing."

Turtle looks at the tiny, yellowish-white knob. "Cut it, kibble," Martin says.

"I can't," she says.

"Clip it," he says. "Don't look at her. I told you, she can't feel shit."

Turtle picks up the diagonal pliers and opens the beveled jaws and closes them over the bone end. She lifts them away and drops the severed bit of bone on the towel. Then Turtle hears car tires coming up the gravel drive.

"Motherfucker, not now," Martin says. "Who the fuck is that?"

"I don't know," Turtle says. "How would I know?"

"Well, who's been coming over?"

"No one," Turtle lies.

"Don't fuck with me, kibble, who's been coming over? Oh," he says. "Oh, tell me it's that little boyfriend of yours. Oh, just let him come on in here. Just let him come on in here and see this, and he and I will have the kind of discussion he won't ever forget."

Turtle rises and walks toward the sliding glass door. She catches a glimpse of Jacob's 4Runner coming up the drive. Martin is plucking up the flesh and snipping it back with scissors. "Shit," she says. She can hear his music roaring from the speakers, the Black Keys' "Psychotic Girl." She hears him park outside and the squelch of the parking brake. She feels paralyzed. All she can think is, not like this. Not now and not like this. She throws open the sliding glass door and steps out onto the porch and slams it closed behind her. Jacob is parked in the graveled lot beside Martin's truck. Martin and Cayenne are not visible from his angle. But if he walks up onto the porch, he'll see them. Jacob kills the engine and the music stops and he walks around the front of the truck and leans against the hood. Turtle climbs down off the porch and out into the driveway. She feels hollow.

"So," he says.

"So," she says.

"Missed you at registration today."

"What?"

"Registration for high school. It's today. Everybody signs up for classes and the teachers and upperclassmen welcome freshmen to the school. We play icebreaker games. It's a holdover from our hippie roots. It's not exactly awesome, but I thought you'd be there. I'm guessing this is not a coincidence." He gestures to Martin's truck.

She stares at him.

"I'm not the only person who missed you," he says.

She stands in silence. He looks like a paper cut-out of himself.

"It's not gonna work," he says.

She has no idea what he's talking about.

He spreads his arms as if to encompass the idiocy of something, as if to incite her to reason-ableness. "Didn't you think how excited Caroline was to see you at registration? She was looking forward to it for weeks. She wants you and Brett to sign up for the same elective classes. She thinks you'd like woodshop. And now you're transferring to some school in Malta, Idaho? Idaho? What the hell, Turtle?"

Turtle walks toward him. He is like a fragment of a life she had to leave behind a long time ago, his whole presence invested with strangeness and inadequacy.

"I mean," Jacob says, "come on. All of a sudden, it's like—Brandon, Isobel, Caroline, they're like, 'Where's Turtle?' and I'm just like, 'I have no idea.' What's—" He spreads his arms again. "What's going on?"

"Jacob, you can't come back here."

"What?"

"Leave, Jacob. You have to leave and you can't come back. I have some things I need to take care of here. You can't help me and I don't want you to help. If you love me, and if you trust me, you will leave."

He gestures, seems to have no idea how to answer her. "What? What are you talking about?"

"Jacob," she says.

"What?"

"I want you to go."

"That's not good enough." He gestures again to Martin's truck. "I mean—are you really planning on going to Idaho? Are you really transferring there? Is your dad moving you out there? Or did your dad just transfer you there, hoping that the paperwork would get lost and no one would notice? Because that's just not gonna fly. And you know why it's not gonna fly? Because there are people who give a fuck, Turtle."

"Jacob, I told you. There are things I need to take care of here."

"I mean, what's the plan?"

"You're not listening to me."

"Come on," Jacob says. "This is stupid. I mean, just get in the truck with me and come get registered. Because we both know you're not leaving Mendocino."

"Jacob, you need to go."

"No."

"Jacob," she says. "Listen to me."

"No, Turtle. This is simple! I mean—this is stupid! Let's go and—"

"You spoiled fuck," she says. She grabs his shirt and jerks him toward her. "I don't know what the hell you're talking about, but it's not simple. It's not at all simple, and you better fucking **leave**. Are you listening? I don't want you pretending you know anything about it when you **know nothing**. I don't want you telling me what to do. Now get the fuck off my property." She shoves him back against the truck and says, "Go back to your pathetic, bloodless little life. I'll be here living mine. And don't you ever tell me what to do, not like that, not ever again."

"Okay," he says. "Okay, I'm leaving. But if you think I'm never coming back—"

She spits into the gravel between them. He slowly gets into the truck and starts the engine, watching her through the windshield. He turns the truck around and roars away down the drive. She stands for a moment longer. You just keep giving things up. You just keep giving them up like that. What you want, she thinks, is to have no choices. But, she thinks, he's right. He's right about you, which is why you can never see him again. He is right about Martin, and if you could ask him about Cayenne he would know what to do. Hell, she thinks. Right? You think he is right? He doesn't know anything about it. I'm all Martin has, and I can't leave him alone with that. I can't. She thinks, when your daddy sees clearly, then he wants everything for you, and when he doesn't, when he can't see that you are your own person, then he wants to bring you down with him. How could Jacob know anything about that, how could Jacob be right about Martin? Martin has more hurt in him, and more courage in him, than Jacob could ever understand. They look at you, and they see what you need to do. Go, he'd say. Run. But they don't see it from where you stand. They don't see who you'd be leaving behind and what all of that meant to you. They can't. They only see it their way. And Jacob is only right in that he would say what anyone else would say, as if it weren't complicated, but he doesn't get it. Profoundly doesn't fucking get it, will never get it, and that world, Turtle thinks, has not done so well by you that you owe it anything. Just because everybody believes something, just because everybody but you believes it, that doesn't make you wrong.

Inside, Martin is crouching awkwardly over Cayenne's splayed hand and stitching the wound closed. "Christ," he says. "Was that your little boyfriend? I'd relish the chance to meet him, you know." Cayenne is leaning back against the wall, her mouth stuffed full of her shirt, her face clenched. One eye opens, rolls, and fastens on Turtle, the skin around the eye crumpled in pain.

"Shut up," she says. "I know you've met him."

She watches his face harden, thinking, if you ever hurt him, I will open you like a fucking fish and pull out your entrails in fucking handfuls and I will fucking leave you that way. Martin is dragging the needle through the bloody, puckering edge of the wound.

Twenty-two

TURTLE LIES IN A COLD BATH AND LOOKS up at the boards of the ceiling. It has been a week since the amputation. School has started without her. She puts her hands on the bathtub's sides and raises herself up, walks to the sink and kneels there, going through the things beneath the sink until she comes back with a disposable razor. Her legs are near hairless but she runs the razor up her shin, and then stops and looks at the blade, and she thinks, what are you doing, Turtle, what are you doing, and then she goes to the sink and picks up Martin's shaving cream and dispenses it into her hand and stands there, dripping water, lathering her pubic hair and then gently parting it from her skin. When she is done, she walks to the toilet and sits down and throws the razor on the floor and puts her head in her hands.

She comes out of the bath into the kitchen. Martin has torn open the wall and exposed old newspaper insulation, blackened wiring. He is sitting on an overturned five-gallon bucket, tearing out the boards along the floor with a cat's paw, smoking a cigar. Long ropes of rat-eaten wiring lie on the floor with an ohmmeter. A pair of kitchen tongs leans up against his bucket. The back door is propped open with a Skilsaw. Turtle, in 501s and a T-shirt, stands toweling her hair. In the living room, Cayenne has the belt sander turned faceup and is sharpening sticks on it for some purpose all her own. She works with one hand, holding the other, wounded hand close to herself. She seems utterly absorbed. What the hell she's doing, Turtle doesn't know.

"Oh, kibble," Martin says, "I'm going to be having the guys over for a game of poker. I think it's better if they don't hang out with Cayenne. I think you should take Grandpa's truck, go into town, show her around Mendocino for a couple of hours. Come back around eleven, when the guys are gone."

"She hates me," Turtle says.

"She doesn't hate you," Martin says. Picking up the kitchen tongs, he reaches into the wall and draws out a dead rat and wings it out the open door into the gulch.

"She hates me, and she's right to hate me."

"She'll come around."

Turtle looks at Cayenne, who cannot hear them over the sander. The girl should be wearing earplugs. More boards have been torn out in the living room. They are stacked on the floor near Cayenne with the heaps of hacked-out newspaper insulation blackened and charred from the short. Martin has been furniture shopping. A new bed in the bedroom, and a new table in the living room, covered now in spools of wire and beer bottles and cigars and old plates. There is a stack of bills and the letter from the district. Martin has not bothered to answer it. Turtle is sure that someone will follow up on her absence from school. Martin has done nothing. He does not seem to care. She looks back at him. She hates him with such intensity it is hard to look at him. He is bent forward into the wall, wrenching the wiring up from where it is tacked to the studs.

Turtle spends the day shooting skeet on the porch. In the evening, she walks up through the orchard with Grandpa's keys, the Remington 870, and a jump starter. She comes to where the ashen remains of the trailer are succumbing to the raspberry brambles. She unlocks the truck and sits on the old vinyl bench seat, looking at the burned black trailer through the cracked windshield. In the drink holder there is a Big Gulp cup full of sunflower seeds, and in the other a bottle of Tabasco. She is overcome for a moment, thinking of Grandpa, of the cribbage games, of how he used to put Tabasco on his pizza. She wraps and rewraps her hands on the steering wheel, tries the ignition. The engine turns over and over without starting, and then it catches, and she throws the truck into reverse, turns around in the grassy field, and drives back to the house, not looking back, touching her jaw with two fingers as if it were sore. She knows how to drive, but she has never driven without Martin there in the cab with her, and she just eases along. She parks Grandpa's truck beside Daddy's and, leaving it running, goes into the unlit house. Cayenne is reading in front of the fire. She stirs the girl with her foot. "Come on," she says.

Cayenne does not look up. Her pointer finger is tightly wrapped in gauze and buddy-taped to her middle finger to keep her from using it. She lies on her stomach, intent on her book. She swings her feet through the air, ignoring Turtle.

Turtle touches the girl's bare shoulder with the toe of her boot. The girl looks up, her face stiff and sullen.

"You're coming with me."

"What?" Cayenne says. This is how she always replies. Turtle can look right at the girl and say

something and the girl will look back and say,
"What?"

"For fuck's sake, get up."

The girl dog-ears her page, heaves herself up.
She does everything one-handed.

"What are you reading?"

"What?"

"It's a different book, right?"

The girl closes it, looks at the cover.

"Did he buy you that book?"

"So?"

"Come on," Turtle says, and grabs the girl by
the upper arm, the girl coming along more like
a puppet than a child, and she pushes her into
the passenger seat of the truck. Turtle gets in on the
driver's side.

"Where are we going?"

"I don't know," Turtle says, "but we can't stay
here." She wants to take the girl by the hair and
dash her into the window for hating her. She wants
to reach into that cunt's small mind and crush that
hate out like crushing out a candlewick, and she
thinks, you cannot hate me, you cannot think the
things you think about me.

"All right." The girl says it sullenly, as if she did
not really consent, says it with a bitter, hateful,
passive-aggressive resignation, the way her mom,
or her aunt, or someone, said it in the face of each
new circumstance.

"Hey," Turtle says. "Hey, don't you be a little cunt with me."

The girl sits, looking down at her book.

"You have somewhere you want to go?"

Cayenne shakes her head.

"That's what I thought," Turtle says.

Turtle shifts the truck into gear and pulls back onto the road. She turns north onto the coast highway with no clear idea of where they are going. Jacob has not been to see her in the last week. To keep herself from going north, toward Jacob's, she turns east onto the Comptche Ukiah Road by the Stanford Inn and the Ravens Restaurant. On their left, the slopes cut away to Big River. The light comes purple-green through the trees. Turtle still has no clear idea of where she is taking them. The girl is silent beside her in the cab. They come to a set of warning signs posted by the road, and then a long section of road where the left-hand lane has sheared away. They can see strewn plates of blacktop among the trees below. The road becomes a single lane that Turtle threads slowly, both of them looking at the ragged edge of blacktop. Then through the town of Comptche, a handful of houses fronting the road, a redwood schoolhouse with a couple of basketball hoops, a general store, and the junction with Flynn Creek Road. Turtle keeps them on the Comptche road and they climb into the hills, winding past ranches, into narrower and more difficult roads. She drives slowly. The only way she knows to think about this problem is to imagine she is reaching out to herself some years ago. It is a bad idea, but she can turn up nothing else in her mind. They turn off onto a deeply rutted track of orange clay covered in oak leaves. They follow it for a quarter of a mile until they come to a yellow Forest Service gate, where Turtle parks.

She gets out, stops. She pockets Grandpa's Tabasco, checks the shotgun's magazine, and slings it. Then she walks around to the girl's door, opens it, says, "Come on. We walk from here."

Cayenne stares at her.

"Come on," Turtle says.

The girl does not move. She makes no expression.

"Christ," Turtle says. "Jesus Christ."

She walks away, leaving the door open and the headlights on. After a moment, the girl hops out of the cab and follows. Turtle turns, waits, and they continue together. Dead branches are strewn across the road. Saplings grow in the median. They come to a wide pullout where heaps of scrap lumber and stacks of tar paper shingles stand rotting underneath towering redwoods, and they can see down a boggy slope above a creek, a single cottage in the clearing, the eaves hung with lichen, the shingles chinked with moss and scattered by ravens, leaving bare spots of patchy tar paper. Jacob and Brett showed her this place. Some building project abandoned by its owners.

"Julia," Cayenne says. "What are we doing?"

"Come on."

Turtle walks over to a heap of lumber, old clapboard siding of some kind, covered now in redwood needles. She squats down, slips her fingertips beneath a board, and lifts it aside. The board beneath is covered in rotting duff, marked with the paths of some crawling creature. Centipedes go snaking for cover. Cayenne comes over, stares down with sullen, stifled interest. Turtle lifts aside the next board, and this one, too, is empty, except for a single copper-gold California slender salamander, four inches long, its skin as supple and moist as the flesh of an eye, with tiny, almost vestigial, legs. Turtle indicates the slender salamander, and Cayenne purses her lips. Turtle lifts this board aside, sets it carefully down. There are dirt and leaves crushed between these boards, and creeping white roots, and Turtle is about to lift this board up when she sees the scorpion: big, with yellow jointed legs, her body like a scab blackened with age, holding the same depth of color. On her back, heaped scorplings, each as white and moist as ant eggs, with the small black dots for lateral eyes and the small, single black dots for median eyes.

Turtle picks the creature up by the barbed tail. She draws her knife and straight-razors it down the scorpion's back, shaving the scorplings into the leaf litter. They salt the board, crawling in every direction, bright white against the duff. The scorpion lashes and twists under the knife, arching her back and reaching desperately with her claws, her ocher mouthpieces flaring and closing.

Cayenne gasps. "Careful!" she says.

Turtle holds the scorpion up to the headlights, and the light shines through the coil of her guts. Cayenne draws closer. The scorpion strains, reaching through the air, curling and falling back to her full length. Turtle lowers the lashing scorpion into her mouth and tears off the tail and discards it among the scattered, swarming scorplings. She chews, passing the lashing arachnid from one line of molars to the other, the integument cracking apart. Turtle swallows.

"Oh my god!" Cayenne says.

"You want to try?"

"Oh my god!" Cayenne says again.

"Come on."

"No!"

"Give it a try."

"No!" Cayenne says.

"You sure?"

"I don't know."

"Don't be a pussy," Turtle says.

"Okay, okay," Cayenne says. "Maybe."

The next scorpion is larger, his armor a pitted rust color. He turns in confusion from right to left, and then arches his body, displaying claws and tail. The bulb is pus-yellow, and the stinger itself is a thin black hook. Where plates of his rust-color armor abut, the integument is textured with chitinous warts.

Turtle takes the Tabasco from her back pocket, shakes a dash out onto the scorpion, which flinches. She says, "You like hot sauce?"

"This is gross," Cayenne says, knocking her knees together, touching her fingertips together.

"Yeah?" Turtle says.

"I can't believe we're doing this," Cayenne says, but she says it excitedly, almost urgently.

"Puts hair on your ovaries," Turtle says.

Cayenne gives a startled, nervous laugh. Then she says, "I like hot sauce."

"All right," Turtle says. She dashes more Tabasco onto the scorpion, which swings its claws, opening and closing them, and moves to strike with its tail. The Tabasco is very bright in the headlights.

"You want to pick it up or should I?"

"You do it."

Turtle catches the scorpion by the tail and swings it lashing into the air. It claws at her, dripping Tabasco, jointed, cricket-yellow legs spidering in the air, descending one after another in some reflexive movement of walking. He throws off flecks of Tabasco with his urgent twitchings. Turtle holds it out.

Cayenne says, "Oh god!"

Turtle says, "You got this."

"Oh god." She dances away nervously and excitedly, comes back.

"Do it," Turtle says. The scorpion strains his claws up, trying to curl back on himself and reach Turtle's fingers. His eyes are small black points set in his rusty-red armature. Their gloss catches the headlights.

"I can't!" Cayenne says, hopping up and down.

The scorpion strains for Turtle and then drops to full extension, dripping, the red droplets running from his claws. Cayenne opens her mouth, comes up from underneath the scorpion, and closes her mouth on it.

"Bite the tail," Turtle says. "Bite the thing off."

Cayenne gnashes her teeth and the tail peels away in Turtle's fingers, and Turtle flicks it into the duff. Cayenne hesitates, mouth locked closed.

"Chew!" Turtle says. "Chew!"

Cayenne's eyes bulge. She chews hard, and then swallows. Turtle claps her on the shoulder. The girl puts her hands on her knees, gasping and distraught.

"You okay?" Turtle says.

"Christ!" she says, grasping at her heart with the fingertips of her unwounded hand. "I'm so nervous my heart hurts! It does!"

Turtle laughs, and then Cayenne laughs, too.

"That was so gross!"

"Nah. Nah. It was fine."

"Let's bring one back for Martin!"

"All right," Turtle says. They lift aside boards until they find another scorpion, and this one Turtle carries back to the truck and drops into the Big Gulp cup. They drive back in the dark, the road now deserted, the headlights cutting across the forest. Cayenne sucks on her thumb. They pull onto Highway 1, and turn north. Buckhorn Hill is south. They are going toward town.

"Where are we going?"

"I need to pick up something," Turtle says.

"Okay," Cayenne says.

"Just something I thought of."

"What?" Cayenne says.

"It's nothing," Turtle says.

"Julia, have you ever been stung?"

"No."

"Never?"

"Never."

"Oh."

They drive in silence.

"Julia?"

"Yes?"

"Nothing."

"What?"

"**I've** been bitten before, though."

"Yeah?"

"Yeah. There are these bugs that bite you and lay eggs in your skin. Then all the little bugs hatch under your skin."

"Really?" Turtle has never heard of such a thing.

"Yeah, and I had a big bite, and so what my stepdad, really my mom's boyfriend, I guess, but kind of my stepdad, what he did is, he had, like, a beer bottle and he heated it up on the stove, with, you know—he heated it up until it was, like—**really** hot and the air inside of it was really hot, and then he put it on my arm, and it sucked onto my arm, and when it cooled, it, like, suctioned out all the spider eggs. Like a vacuum. Like they were all white and stringy. He sucked them all out and it was okay after that."

"Christ."

"What?"

"Just— Christ. I guess."

"Have you ever had that happen, Julia?"

"No."

"Really?"

"I've never even heard of that."

"It happens all the time. You don't have that here?"

"All the time?"

"Yeah. That people get, like, the bugs in their skin? Yeah."

"Would that even work?" Turtle is having trouble imagining the bottle trick.

"Yeah, it works. You've never had those bugs?"

"No."

"They're—you know." The girl scratches at her arm. "You know—under your skin."

"No," Turtle says, "I didn't know that was even possible."

"Oh yeah. And, like, the people at the hospital, they don't even believe you."

"You went to the hospital?"

"Yeah. Oh yeah, all the time. Like, if you can't pay for a doctor, you can just go to the ER. They have to take you. It's the law. That's what my step-dad says. But you go in and the doctor won't even look at it. They just pretend like it's not happening. They won't CT scan it or anything."

"Huh."

They drive through Mendocino, and up into Fort Bragg, where Turtle pulls off the highway and into the parking lot of the Rite Aid. She leaves Cayenne in the car and walks through the sliding doors. There are no other customers in the store. The lights are bleakly bright, and there is a single checker at the counter. Turtle walks to the back, to the closed pharmacy. She walks along the aisles until she finds the pregnancy tests. She kneels down in front of these, picks up a pink box, and walks quickly back to the front, where she pays with cash, peeling the bills off with shaking hands. The checker is an old woman with reddish, curled hair, and she does not look at Turtle, but says, "You all right, honey?"

Turtle picks up the box and stuffs it into her pocket. She says, "Yeah, I'm fine."

The checker says, "Honey, you sure? You need anything?"

Turtle is about to turn and walk away, and the woman says, "You got somewhere to stay for tonight?"

Turtle turns back. She says, "I'm fine. Yeah, I've got somewhere to stay."

The woman keeps looking down, not directly at Turtle. She says, "All right, sweetheart. Be safe. Have a nice night."

Turtle turns and walks out to the truck.

When she gets in the truck, Cayenne says, "What was that?"

"Nothing."

"What did you buy?"

"I didn't buy anything."

"Oh."

"Cayenne—how long have you been with Martin?"

Cayenne chews her lip. She is so small. Her feet do not reach the floor of the cab. She swings them a little. She is flat-chested and all elbows. For one moment, Turtle looks at her and thinks, I could drop this girl off at Anna's house. Go to a phone book, find Anna's address, and just drop her off. Tell Martin she ran away.

"How long, Cayenne?"

"Like, a little more than two weeks."

Turtle cracks her knuckles.

"What, Julie?"

"I'm just losing my fucking mind, is all."

Turtle is looking out at the parking lot.

"What?"

"What was it like, with him?"

"Good," Cayenne says.

"What does that mean?"

"Really, really good," Cayenne says.

"Good?"

"Yeah."

"It was good?"

"Why, Julie?"

"Do you need to see, I don't know, a doctor?"

"For my finger? It still hurts, but it's less painful now than before, Julie."

"Where are you from, Cayenne?"

"Washington. Like, eastern Washington."

"I know, but what happened?"

Cayenne slips her thumb into her mouth, turns to study her own dark reflection in the window. Turtle sits awkwardly beside her in the cab. She starts the truck and swings around in the empty parking lot and out onto the road. She drives slowly, waiting for Cayenne to say more, but she doesn't. They are silent, except for the scorpion knocking against the edges of the Big Gulp cup, and Turtle is reminded of her grandfather and the time they had driven back home with that big crab knocking against the sides of its bucket. She thinks, I wish to hell he was here, he would know what to do. But Turtle thinks then, maybe he wouldn't, maybe he'd be just as useless all over again. There is so much of her life she doesn't understand. She knows what happened, but why it happened and what it meant, she doesn't know.

They pull back onto the highway. He hasn't touched Cayenne, she is sure. But Christ, she thinks, what's wrong here is that you think you'd know. Grandpa can't have known, and maybe you wouldn't know, either. Maybe he fucks her all the time and you can't tell, just like no one could tell with you. She's eating out of his goddamn hand. Well, Turtle thinks. He can be pretty fucking persuasive. And what if she came from somewhere that no one cared about her, and all of a sudden there's Martin. What would you do, if you'd never had that in your life? If you were a child. You'd do a lot, she thinks. You'd put up with a lot. Just for that attention. Just to be close to that big, towering, sometimes generous, sometimes terrifying mind. Turtle is looking out at the dark road. There are no other cars out. No matter who this girl is, Turtle can't help her. Turtle has her own problems.

Twenty-three

THEY PULL UP THE DRIVE, LURCHING IN and out of ruts. It is late, but Jim Macklemore's truck and Wallace McPherson's VW Bug are still parked beside Martin's truck. Turtle parks in the grass and she and Cayenne get out, Turtle reaching into the cup and retrieving the scorpion. She walks to the house with the shotgun slung on one shoulder, holding the scorpion by its tail. The girl follows, carrying her book. The electricity is back on, but the house is dark. The men are playing cards by the light of a single lamp.

They go up the porch and in through the sliding glass door. Cayenne bursts into the house and runs ahead to where the men are gathered around the newly purchased table.

"Martin!" Cayenne says. "I ate a scorpion!"

Martin scoffs and does not look up.

Jim Macklemore turns, fat and blond, with thinning hair pulled back from his blushed-red face, his Hawaiian shirt unbuttoned to show his greasy chest and thick blond chest hair with a small silver cross. He has two little sapphire ear studs. Wallace McPherson sits opposite, in a white dress shirt, a black silk vest, and X-wing fighter cuff links, a bowler hat beside him on the table, arms sleeved with tattoos.

"We ate a scorpion," Cayenne insists.

Martin says, "Cayenne, not now. Go to kibble's room."

"Why, Julia, how you've **grown**," Jim says, smiling and holding out his hand.

Turtle shoulders past him and drops the scorpion onto the poker table. It lands on a mound of quarters, tail raised, claws moving reflexively through the air.

"Holy shit," Wallace says, "holy shit."

Martin lights a cigarette.

"There is a scorpion," Wallace says, "on the table."

"I did," Cayenne insists. "I ate a scorpion."

"Nah," Martin says patiently, taking the cigarette out of his mouth to lean forward and inspect the creature.

"She did," Turtle says, "and we brought this one back. Thought you might be hungry."

Martin makes no expression, but waits before exhaling the smoke, and then he blows it out raggedly.

"Try it, Marty," Cayenne says.

Wallace says, "You're not really going to eat that, are you?"

Putting his hand on her shoulder, Jim Macklemore says to Turtle, "What are you studying now in school? I myself was always interested in politics."

Turtle ducks out from under his hand and asks Martin, "You gonna eat this?"

Martin holds his burning cigarette upright. The cherry is just barely visible in the dark; above it, the tower of ash. He turns it slowly, inspecting it from all angles. He says, "You want me to eat that scorpion?"

"Try it!" Cayenne says.

Turtle can see that the girl wants to share this with him. She wants this to be something they've all done together. But Turtle doesn't want him to do it. She wants to show Cayenne something important here, about her own substance and about Martin's, because Martin, Turtle thinks, is afraid.

Martin says, "You didn't eat a scorpion."

"Why would we make this shit up?" Turtle says.

Martin draws on the cigarette, squints at them through the smoke.

"It was fucking delicious," Turtle says.

"You're not **really** going to eat the scorpion," Wallace says. "That would be crazy. To eat the scorpion. That can't be healthy. Aren't they full of poison?"

"Nah," Turtle says. "Nah, it's fine."

"Come on, Marty!" Cayenne says.

"Yeah," Turtle says, "come on, Marty."

"If I can do it, you can do it," Cayenne says.

"The girls have a point," Jim says.

"Don't be a little bitch, Marty," Turtle says.

Martin chews his lip. At last, he says, "You really want to see me eat this scorpion, huh?"

"Yeah, Marty," Cayenne says. "Julia ate one."

"This is the thing we're all doing, huh?"

"Yes!" Cayenne says.

"Okay," he says. He leans forward, rubs his hands together in prefatory consideration. The scorpion hunkers on the pile of coins, tail raised, claws spread.

Martin opens thumb and forefinger, reaches out, withdraws his hand. He rubs his forefinger to his thumb as if preparing for the creature's texture.

"Just like that," Turtle says. "Just like that." She indicates picking up the scorpion by the tail. "Come on," she says.

Martin extends his hand again. Wallace leans forward, smoking a cigar, to get a better look. He's still holding his cards, shaking his head in wonder. Martin spreads thumb and forefinger, hesitates just above the scorpion, which raises its tail and spreads its open pincers. Small expressions, too fast to read, chase themselves across his face.

"You didn't eat a scorpion," he says. He draws his Daniel Winkler belt knife and drives the point down into the scorpion. The creature twists, arching its back painfully, its tail striking the spine of the knife. Its claws are outstretched, straining open with visible and painful urgency. Martin lifts the knife, the scorpion skewered on the tip, and then he reaches down and plants the knife against the floor, and with his heel, scrapes the scorpion's twisted, straining body from the blade and grinds it under his boot. He wipes the flat of the blade on the table edge and throws the blade down among the coins and cards and beer cans.

Cayenne mews in surprise, putting her hand to her mouth. Turtle pulls up a chair and sits down. Martin considers her. In his **let's be serious** tone of voice, dry, slightly affectionate, forgiving, he says, "Come on, you didn't eat a scorpion."

Turtle looks at him levelly.

From their places at the table, Jim and Wallace exchange glances.

"We did," Cayenne says. "I told you we did."

Martin laughs, his laugh sharpening almost into a titter, and he collects the cards and begins shuffling them. "Oh right," he says, laughing again. "It's some fucked-up bonding thing, and now I fucked it. Well. Well. You cunts. Christ. Always

getting in some fucking trouble for some fucking **bullshit**. Never anything right." He talks in
an aggrieved tone, racking the cards hard against
the table's edge, then breaking them and bridging
them and striking the deck against the table's edge
and breaking and bridging them again. Everyone
else sits in silence. He says, "The **fuck**, the **fuck**
if I'm gonna be in trouble for not eating some
fucking **bug**. The **fuck**. Isn't that always the way?
Christ, you bitches. All the same, with your bitter,
female minds."

Martin deals out another hand of cards, and
the game gets going again, the lovely handmade
Daniel Winkler knife sitting on the table, the
blade still with bits of shell and smears of guts.
After that hand, with the girls sitting there, the
game winds down. When the men are packing up,
Turtle grabs Wallace's arm and says, "I'll walk you
out." Wallace nods, closes the lid down on his yo-
gurt container full of change, and then walks away
to the door, Turtle beside him. Cayenne sits on the
counter, holding her injured hand and watching
the departing poker players.

Turtle walks with Wallace out to his VW Bug.
Wallace, Turtle knows, has a philosophy degree
from some college up north, she doesn't know
much about it, but she knows that he's different
from the others, a decade younger, closer to Jacob
in his worldview than to Martin. Wallace opens
the car door, and stands just inside of it. Turtle

says, "Wallace, I don't think Cayenne is here of her own consent. I think she shouldn't be here. I don't think it's safe for her here."

Wallace gives a startled laugh. He says, "You think she's been kidnapped?" He laughs again. "Julia! Listen. If she was kidnapped, wouldn't she be like, 'Help me! Help me!'? I mean—**come on**. The girl is obviously okay." He squints at her, then he looks toward where Martin is laughing, helping Jim into his truck, banging the roof of the cab joyously, saying, "Bitches! Am I right? You never fucking know!"

Turtle leans in to him. She says, "You can tell someone, can't you?"

Wallace says, "Oh come on, Julia. It's really none of my business. He's probably just taking care of her because her parents are drug addicts or some shit like that. He's a good guy. He got a little unhinged in there, sure, but he's all right. Besides, sweetheart, it's none of my business, is it? And who would I tell? Child Protective Services? Come on. She's better off here. I **know** Martin. He's an odd guy, but he'd never **hurt** someone. You came up good, didn't you? A forceful young woman, you've become."

"Tell someone, tell the cops, I don't care, anyone," Turtle says.

Wallace laughs, putting his hands up. "Yeah," he says. "Yeah, right!"

"Please."

"Right. Call the police! And then I'd answer the door in the middle of the night and he'd be there with an M16, right?" Wallace laughs again, at the idea of it. Turtle is staring. He will not believe it, she thinks. He will not. He does not want to believe it. "And maybe a bottle of Jim Beam? No," he says, still chuckling, "No, Julia. No one's a **prisoner**."

He pulls his car door closed, looks at her through the window, and Turtle puts her palm against it. She wants to scream at him. She wants to yell. She stands in the high grass while Wallace pulls away, throws the VW Bug into drive, and goes down the road.

Turtle walks back into the house and goes up to her room. There, she stands in front of the window, the moonlight slanting in around her, and she turns the pink box over in her hands. It reads, FIRST RESPONSE PREGNANCY: **Only test that tells you 6 DAYS before your missed period.** She turns her back to the window, sits on the ledge, chewing her lip. She thinks, can Grandpa have known, and can he have let it slip him by, and how could a man I loved do that? She thinks, no, Turtle, you're thinking about this all wrong. If he ever overlooked something, it's because he knew your daddy loved the ever-living shit out of you, that whatever harm he might ever have done to you, it was a drop in the ocean of his love. Grandpa knew that, so stop thinking to yourself about him, because it means nothing, and what he decided to do at the end, that wasn't something he'd been putting off, that was something he should never have done, not earlier and not then.

She listens until Martin comes back into the house. She hears him talk with Cayenne. Their voices murmur and rise. Then he goes into his room and he paces. Turtle listens for Cayenne, but the girl lies in front of the fireplace, reading her book, making no noise at all. Turtle opens the box and dispenses the three small, pink plastic packages into her hand. She rolls them forward and back. She thinks, it's not possible. It is not possible that it could happen to me. Turtle could tear the walls down. She is choked, throttled, replete with rage. She thinks, it cannot be.

She hears Martin's bedroom door open. She hears him come down the hallway. She hears his footsteps on the stairs. Fucking bastard, she thinks. We can't keep doing this. This is too fucking dangerous. This is an entirely different game now. He stands outside the door. She depresses the release, draws the Sig Sauer half out of the holster. He opens the door, stands in the doorway. She is still. She feels fixed in place. The world rotates around her. She is looking at his boots. Tremors chase themselves up her thighs. She has her right hand on the Sig in the small of her back, tightening on the polymer grip.

He comes into the room. He raises her chin up

with his knuckle and she puts her arms around him and breathes in his scent, wool and cigarettes and gun grease. The Sig Sauer is still in her hand. He carries her back to his room, and she feels for him a terrible neediness. He is so massive that to be in his arms is skin-crawlingly good, like returning home, like going back to being a child. Martin cradles her in one arm to work the cut-glass knob with the other and kicks open the door and carries her into the bedroom with his clothes strewn on the floor and a new bed with new sheets and a new bedside table. The shadows of the alder leaves and the alder catkins play across the wounds on the walls where she prized out the screws and pulled down his bookshelves. There is still the old familiar gap between the drywall and the floor, and this dark line bounds the room, an unbridgeable gap where the two meet, a gap opening into the dark of the foundation that breathes up its cold mineral and female scent, and Turtle can imagine the great beams of the foundation resting right on the sandstone and the dirt beneath the house, beneath the floorboards, the dark places sashed with spiderwebs. He walks her to the bed and he throws her into the air and she hangs suspended in the room's silver light and dappled shadows, and then she drops onto the bed, into the feather duvet, the knotted sheets with his tobacco-scented sweat, lying there where she has been thrown as if she cannot move, as if she is a puppet and not a girl, her head cocked up and her eyes open and looking at that drywall, Martin dragging off her pants and throwing them aside, and then lifting away her panties and discarding these, too, the leaves coming in and out of focus on the wall. She wants in some way to quench her loneliness. She wants to lie here and be wrung clean of all personhood. He kneels down between her thighs and she puts one hand in his hair and cries aloud with grief and with self-hatred and with some suspended and awful pleasure. When it is done she lies in the tangled sheets unwinded and unmoved while Martin sits at the bed's edge, propping himself up on a knee, gasping, sobbing almost—all she needs to do is wait silently with the fan of her ribs opening and closing, laboring until everything that she held sacred about him will be gone, and then, she doesn't know what. They wait in the darkness in the long moments after what they have done, and it is different than it was before and Turtle will not speak and will not move. It feels as if she can hold still, can relax all vestiges of herself from her limbs. She will not spend long nights in contact with her own mind, she will not have to rise from this bed or admit how she came into it, she can do nothing and be nothing and there will be no pain. She can feel it, though, everywhere in the room, climbing up the walls, in the shadows of the sheets, breathing from the dark gap between the floorboards and the drywall, a brooding pain that gathers and accretes and waits for her, the pain of being herself, each moment long and particular and awful.

"Goddamn," he says from the edge of the bed. She does not look at him. "Goddamn. Your fucking guts, kibble." Turtle says nothing. "Into that gutsack full of hate, into slick wet filth, and again into hatred and into filth and into nothing."

"Shut up," Turtle says.

"Into hatred and into filth and into nothing," Martin says.

"Shut the fuck up," Turtle says, sitting up.

Martin says, "Your rot-filled guts, kibble."

Turtle rises and he watches her. She stands in the middle of the room and looks for her panties, but she cannot find them, and she walks back and forth while he sits stooped and big-shouldered and sullen and dappled with shadows from the alders, his form enormous and silent and bent as he studies her picking up dark pieces of clothing and toying them apart to see what they are, and finally her pants, and she pulls her pants on while he watches her and she looks levelly and hatefully at him as she pulls them on, and she thinks, I thought at least you could give me this, you could at least do that, but the truth is that you give me nothing, she thinks, pulling up her pants and sashaying them on to her hips and holstering the gun as Martin watches her dress, and she thinks, go ahead and watch, asshole. I don't know how to get away, and I don't know if I can get away, so we will find out, I guess. Go ahead and watch, she thinks, because there is something wrong with me that I would take this risk, that I would allow you to do this to me. He watches and she buckles her pants and then pauses, standing upright and allowing him to admire her, and walks from the room and down the hallway and stands at the poker table. There is a rule, she thinks, that life has taught you, that Martin has taught you, a rule that every wet-thighed slit like you gets what's coming to her. Dim light comes in from the windows and from the smoldering fire. Cayenne is crying softly, in front of the fire, and Turtle thinks, fuck.

It had not occurred to her that the girl would hear and she cannot explain to the girl, so she stands at the poker table thinking of everything that Cayenne has heard and thinking, fuck, fuck, fuck. She cannot bear that Cayenne has heard her go into that room, she cannot bear that Cayenne has heard her consent to it. It has always been private. Turtle stands listening to Cayenne cry and cry. She thinks, I will walk to my room and leave the bitch to cry. You think I give a shit about her? You think she matters to me? She is a bitch like all the others and her femaleness eats holes through her mind. I have nothing in me for her, she can't have me and I have nothing to give and no one could expect me to, no one could expect me to give a shit for the girl.

Well, she thinks, Jacob would expect you to help. Jacob wouldn't even doubt that you'd help. But Jacob is an entitled piece of shit who doesn't understand the depth that things can have sometimes. How bad they can be and how deep-down the rot can go. Just walk to your room, Turtle, because that girl is nothing to you. But thinking of Jacob, she walks to the girl and sits down beside her and gathers the child into her arms. She feels nothing, and she does not know why she does it except for that. She holds the little girl and thinks, she is nothing to me. The bitch is nothing to me. I could kill her if he asked me to. I could do that and it would weigh me down some, but it wouldn't be the end of me. She shushes her, and Cayenne says, "I'm afraid, Julie, I want my mom. I **really**, **really** want my mom." She says it over and over again, as if hoping that Turtle will reply to it, but Turtle can only squeeze the girl harder.

Finally, Turtle says, "Hey, Cayenne."

"Yeah?"

"Don't call me Julie."

"Really?"

"Really," Turtle says.

"You don't like it?"

"It makes me want to puke."

"Why?"

"I don't know. That's my mom's name for me."

"What, then?"

"Turtle."

"Turtle?" Cayenne says.

"Yeah."

Cayenne is sniffling, but she is a little tickled, too. She sucks and tucks her snotty hair behind her ears and snuffs and peers at Turtle, lines appearing and disappearing on her forehead with her amusement and her anger.

"But," she says, "that's— No, that's silly. No."

"No?"

"You can't be **Turtle**."

"Why?"

"You're so pretty."

Turtle laughs.

"You are. You are **so** pretty."

"Cayenne," Turtle says. "There are some things I care about. But you know what I don't give a fuck about?"

"What?"

"Prettiness."

"Oh."

"What?"

The girl shakes her head.

"What's wrong?"

The girl feels chided. Turtle holds her and rocks her back and forth and feels something fierce, some emotion she cannot place at all. Something very like willingness.

"It's all right. I'm just teasing you."

Cayenne nods. She still looks chided.

"I don't mean you shouldn't care. I don't mean

it's a bad thing to care about or that you're wrong. I just mean. You know. I've got other things."

"Okay," Cayenne says. Her voice is small and high, and there is nothing grudging in it. Turtle holds the girl and she thinks, I will never let anything hurt you. The thought comes unbidden, and she knows it's untrue. But she likes it, she likes that she could be such a person—and she thinks it again, suspending her own disbelief and putting her cheek to the girl's hair and saying, "I will never let anything hurt you."

Cayenne cries and cries. She says, "Why did you do it?"

"I don't know," Turtle says.

Cayenne says, "Why did you let him?"

"I don't know," Turtle says.

"Turtle?"

"I don't think anyone knows why they do things. They just think they know it."

"Really?"

"It isn't until things get hard and you see yourself doing the wrong thing."

Cayenne sobs. She says, "Aren't you afraid?"

"Yes," Turtle says, and she knows that it's true only after she hears herself say it.

It makes Cayenne cry harder, trembling and heaving, and Turtle gathers the child into her arms, pulls the girl into her lap. The girl bites into Turtle's shoulder and Turtle smiles. Cayenne shakes her head like a dog worrying a rat. Turtle holds the girl in her arms, and the girl is small, with slender shins and small bony feet, and her hair is rough and coarse on Turtle's cheek. It sticks to Turtle's lips and the girl reaches up and puts her arms around Turtle's neck and Turtle says nothing, but holds her, and holding her, she thinks, this is a thing I can take care of, and if I couldn't show the girl any love, I could show her care, I can do that much, maybe. I am not like him, and I can take care of things and can take care of her, too, maybe, even if I don't know if it's real and even if I don't mean it more than that, I can salvage something maybe by just doing that, by just caring for the bitch. She holds her and hums a little, her chin on Cayenne's head, the girl's legs tucked up in Turtle's arms.

Twenty-four

TURTLE WAKES WHEN THE SPOTLIGHTS
come on. She lifts the shotgun off its wall pegs
and pulls on jeans and a white T-shirt. She puts
on a mesh-back cap to keep her hair out of her
face and pads out of her room and down the
stairs. Martin is standing in the living room with
his modified AR-15, looking through the sliding
glass door out into the field. He turns, squints at
her as she comes down the stairs. Cayenne is sitting up, in front of the bare and lightless hearth,
still wrapped in her blankets. Turtle climbs down.
Martin scrapes his thumb across his stubble. He
gestures with one hand at the picture window,

the fields lit up with a halogen glare. He says, "You think something's out there?"

"No," Turtle says.

"No?" he repeats. "But you don't know. We don't know what's in that field. Do we?"

"No," she says, "we don't know."

He shakes his head slowly, grinning.

"It's a deer," she tells him.

"Isn't this great?" He walks up to the wall of glass, puts his hand against it, leans against it, the field beyond crooked mismatched shadows and the glare off the grass stalks. "We stand," he says, "at the limit of an uncertainty and we inquire not only into the particularities of this moment, but to all such moments; what lurks beyond the visible. What is in the grass, kibble? What is out there?"

"Nothing, Daddy," she says.

"'Nothing, Daddy,'" he repeats in annoyance, and then laughs at her, still braced against the glass door and looking past his own reflection into the field, and from where she stands, he seems to be confronting this washed-out image of himself, canted forward and exhausted against the glass. "This is the problem with you, you little cunt: You think you know what's out there. But you don't know. There is a terrible poverty in you, a poverty of mind, of imagination, of **heart**. The truth is that, because we do not know—for us, there both is, and there is not, anything in the field. It is Schrödinger's intruder. The world is rich with potential, kibble, and both states exist for us at this moment; there is nothing in the field; and at the same time, there is out there something unknown. Most likely, some bastard who is about to die. Perhaps that boy of yours, and perhaps he's out there right now, there in the grass, shitting himself with fear. He figured he'd come by and say hi, give you succor in your time of need. Well. We just don't fucking know until we find out. For the moment, nothing is true, it is all up for grabs, and what you believe says nothing about the world and everything about you. Here you chart your course through life."

Turtle walks to the window. Father and daughter, side by side, present against their twinned and partial reflections. Beyond, the spotlights light up the grass, a wickerwork of shadows and golden stalks shuffling together. There does seem to be a fertile potential just beyond the window. She can feel the pregnancy test against her thigh, still in its packaging.

The lights shut off. He ruffles her hair. Without a word, he walks away. She can see nothing except her breath fogging the glass in front of her. She opens the door and walks out onto the cold, wet porch and crosses to the balustrade and breathes in the scent of the field, listens to the grass moving, the soft and distant sighs of the ocean. The night feels bereft to her. She hopes almost, with a kind of bitterness, for something to come. She begs for it, wills it.

Fuck it, she thinks. Fuck it. There's nothing out there. She walks down the porch steps and the lights come back on with a click. She walks across the gravel drive and out to the edge of the field. She thinks that Martin must be watching from the window and she thinks of how she must appear, lit up by floodlights, a girl holding a shotgun by the receiver, waist-deep in grass, wearing a white T-shirt and a mesh-back cap, looking over an unbroken hillside, turning in patient surveillance.

She wades out, the sharp smells of the crushed vegetation coming up to her, the wild mustard and radishes. She goes down to the highway and she stands at the margin of the blacktop. Beside her, Slaughterhouse Creek runs in a steep-sided gully so thicketed with fuchsias that the creek is invisible, the sides orange sandstone. She climbs down, steps into the knee-deep water. She has to sweep the fuchsias aside with her hands, following the stream, her feet numbing with cold. She comes to a culvert that goes beneath the road, big enough to walk through, the water echoing through the tunnel.

On the other side of that tunnel, the ocean folds into the shingle. The tide is out; there is a black expanse of cobbles, and each cobble holds an eye of moonlight, and each looks soft and wet like flesh, stretched out before her in a multitude. The beach draws breath like a living thing, and she can smell the muddy stink of the estuary. These waters begin at the wellspring of Slaughterhouse Creek, in the great stone drum, and they end here.

At the tunnel's mouth, she strips out of her clothes. Then, naked, holding the shotgun, she climbs into the algae-slick culvert, touching one corrugated steel side, the bottom sandy. The tunnel smells of iron and hard water, the creek throws strange and crisscrossing ribbons of moonlight across the ceiling. She parts the curtains of blooming orange nasturtiums, and jumps down into the catch pool. The mud at the bottom is cold clay and it molds to her feet. The water is chest-deep, breathing around her, the eelgrass pluming in and out around her legs. Turtle yokes the shotgun over her shoulders. Her feet make warm places in the mud. She pushes aside floating driftwood and climbs out onto a shelf of gritty stone constellated with the dark bowling balls. The white apron of surf advances and retreats in the dark. When the waves lie out, they push the foam to her feet. She is covered in the estuary mud. Bits of eelgrass stick to her legs. The ocean is as rich, as pungent, as an open mouth around her.

She thinks, Turtle Alveston, he raped you and you went back for more. You are either pregnant or you will be soon. If you leave, he will go into the living room and kill Cayenne. Then he will drive to 266 Sea Urchin Drive and he will kill

Jacob. You have to recognize where you are. You've got to really goddamn look at it without lying to yourself.

She ejects a shell from the chamber into her hand and weighs it, rolls it forward and back. It is a trim green cylinder of corrugated plastic with a low brass rim, heavy for its size. She drops the shell back into the breach and slides the pump all the way forward, feeling the bolt lock closed, the shotshell firmly seated in the chamber. She sits cross-legged on the cold wet stone and she places the barrel in her mouth, tastes the powder residue, threads her thumb through the trigger guard and angles the gun barrel up into her palate. She imagines pressing the trigger down. The gun will fire. A hot load of double-aught buckshot and granulated plastic buffer will travel up the barrel, contained in its plastic shot cup. The shot cup will hit her palate and split apart into a fan of plastic fingers, the buckshot pellets disgorged. She imagines herself sitting rigid and erect as her mind unfurls from the cloven, yawning bud of her skull, blooming vast, red, wet, expanding for one deep momentary breath.

Turtle thinks, pull the trigger. She can imagine no other way forward. She thinks, pull the trigger. But if you do not pull the trigger, walk back up that creek and in through the door and take possession of your mind, because your inaction is killing you. She sits looking out at the beach, and

she thinks, I want to survive this. She is surprised
by the depth and clarity of her desire. Her throat
tightens and she takes the gun out of her mouth
and strings of saliva come with it and she brushes
them away. She rises and stands looking out at the
waves, overcome with the beauty. Her whole mind
feels raw and receptive. She experiences a searing,
wide-open thankfulness, an unmediated wonder
at the world.

She wades back through the eelgrass and boosts
herself up and into the culvert, the shotgun tilted
back against a shoulder. She goes through the
pockets of her folded jeans, tears open the pink
packaging one-handedly and draws out the pregnancy test. Leaning back against the culvert wall,
and triggering the shotgun's weapon light up at
the top of the culvert, she reads the directions,
reads them again. Her face is numb. Her lips are
numb. She puts her closed fist to her forehead,
shaking all over, and she thinks, if it is, if it's in
there, then you can handle that, too. She flicks the
light off and squats naked in the culvert with the
crisscrossing silver light thrown back at her from
the creek and pisses on the flimsy plastic stick,
barefoot and ankle-deep in the cold water. Then
she sits in the dark with her back braced against
the corrugated wall, touching the shotgun barrel
self-comfortingly to her face, to her forehead, letting the time run, waiting for the two pink lines
of the positive response to fade slowly into being,

putting one fist in her mouth. She feels a dead weight of certainty.

It doesn't happen. The small, oval result window shows a single pink line. The test is negative. She triggers the shotgun's weapon light again and pans it over the test. The light is so bright, so harsh, that it is hard to see. It's the same. Negative. She feels no relief. It may not even be true, it may just be too early. But if it is true, she thinks, if it could've happened to me and it did not— She stops. You got lucky, she thinks. Don't squander that. She is shaking. Her face is clenching into an expression she does not understand. She lowers herself until she is sitting, splay-legged in the cold water, her hands grasped around herself, broken-feeling and empty.

Twenty-five

TURTLE IS SITTING CROSS-LEGGED ON THE
floor cleaning the Remington 870 when Martin
comes out of the bathroom and says, "Goddamn
it, kibble," and then he stops and looks at her as
if seeing her for the first time. He says, "You're
cleaning the gun again?"

Turtle doesn't look up.

"You could fire that thing all day every day for
years before it would fail," he says. "That thing is
clean enough. Besides. When have you even fired
that thing last? It's not dirty. You can't've gotten it
dirty."

Turtle still doesn't look up.

"It's like a fixation with you, isn't it," he says, and Turtle sighs and looks up.

"Don't you look at me like that," he says.

She says, "What do you care?"

"I don't give a shit," he says, "it's just you're always cleaning, cleaning, cleaning, and it's like, Jesus, there's no point. Just let it be. Guns get dirty, that's just how it is."

"What were you going to say?"

He walks into the kitchen and takes a beer from the fridge. He seems to want to say something and to be unable to say it, or perhaps unable to frame it in his own mind.

"It doesn't bother me," he says, "I don't care. It's just—"

Turtle waits.

Martin gestures angrily to the bathroom. He says, "I don't know what the problem is, but will you please tell Cayenne to get her ass in the tub?"

Turtle rises, collects her cleaning kit and gun and throws the towel over her shoulder and walks to the bathroom and finds Cayenne in the middle of the room, arms crossed, scowling ferociously, the bathtub filling with green-blue water, the porcelain bottom laddered with silt.

"I don't want to take a bath," she tells Turtle.

"Yeah?" Turtle says, and glances at the black widow in her web behind the shower fixtures, near the recessed water heater. She is almost the color of black leather, with a bulbous abdomen and slender, jointed needles for legs, stomping on her web menacingly, making the whole structure tremble. The red hourglass is clearly visible. Her web is tangled and haphazard, filled with the husks of dead creatures. Turtle sets her things on the floor. She walks to the wall and reaches into the hole, breaking the web strands with a soft crackling sound like carbonation. Cayenne says, "No, Turtle! Wait! Don't!"

Turtle draws her hand out of the hole. Her fingers are netted with old spider silk. Cayenne puts her hands to her face and says, "Leave her, please leave her."

The spider races around her broken web.

Cayenne says, "Leave her."

Turtle sits down beside the gun.

"Stay here?" Cayenne says.

In answer, Turtle lays out the towel and the gun across it, opens the wooden chest of the cleaning kit. She dismounts the barrel and lays it across the towel.

"I thought you were worried about her," Turtle says.

"Yeah," Cayenne says, cranking on the hot water. "Yeah, I am. How old is she?"

"Almost two years," Turtle says. "They don't usually live this close to the coast. She came in some oak firewood Marty bought from Comptche."

"Martin's really fond of her," Cayenne says.

"Maybe 'fond' is not the word."

Cayenne goes nervously to the tub and cranks on the hot water. Then, looking sometimes at the agitated spider, she begins taking off her pants. Turtle starts to clean the barrel with a copper twelve-gauge brush.

"Turtle," Cayenne says.

"Hm?" Turtle drives the plunger through the barrel.

"Turtle?"

"Yeah?" Turtle looks up.

"Nothing," Cayenne says, shaking her head. She climbs into the tub and sits down in it, puts her chin over the edge and stares at Turtle.

"Turtle," Cayenne says.

"Hm?" Turtle says.

"What are these mushrooms called?"

Turtle sits, the barrel spanning her lap. Cayenne is studying the mushrooms growing on the windowsill.

"Tell me about them," Turtle says.

"But what are they called?"

"What does it matter what they're called?"

The girl sits thinking for a long time, hmming and hawing to herself, making small conspicuous noises of observation, and then she turns to Turtle, and then to the mushrooms again. Turtle works the plunger through the barrel.

"Maybe I want to write a book about you," Cayenne says, "and I want to say how you had a bathroom, and the window was covered in mushrooms, and they were such-and-such mushrooms, and then I'd need to know the name of them."

Turtle says, "You're not writing a book."

"But I **might**."

"It doesn't matter, their name," Turtle says.

"They have little shutters," Cayenne says.

"Hm," Turtle says.

"What are those called?" Cayenne tries.

"Little shutters."

"That's not what they're called."

"What does it matter what they're called?"

"It matters to me," Cayenne says. "Are they called blinds?"

"You and I, we can call them blinds."

"Louvers," Cayenne says.

"Did you just make that up?"

"It's a kind of blind," Cayenne says. "They have them in castles."

"Ah."

"But what's their **name**?"

"Well, what else do they look like? What are they for?"

Cayenne scowls in annoyance. She pushes up her nose and sticks out her tongue at Turtle and Turtle bends again over the barrel.

"Are they toadstools?" Cayenne asks. "Can you eat them?"

Turtle shakes her head.

"I thought people ate mushrooms, in case of survival."

"It's not usually worth eating mushrooms," Turtle says. "They're the same stuff as grass. It'd be like eating fingernails, and wouldn't do you any good, there are a very few that would be some good, but many more are poisonous and hard to tell apart."

"But if you were dying," Cayenne says.

"Only if you really knew what you were doing."

"Tell me about mushrooms," Cayenne says. "About eating them to stay alive."

Turtle says nothing to this.

"Tell me about what mushrooms you'd eat if you had to," Cayenne says.

Again, Turtle says nothing. Cayenne gazes at Turtle, seeming unsure how to solicit a response.

"Turtle," she says.

"Hm?"

"Turtle," Cayenne says.

"Yes?"

"Turtle, tell me about what mushrooms you'd eat if you had to, to survive."

"I wouldn't," she says, driving the brush through the bore.

"Turtle," Cayenne says.

"Someone might. I never learned them."

"Turtle," Cayenne says urgently. "I just didn't want you to kill her."

Turtle picks up **New Moon** from the floor and opens to a blank page and sights the clean white paper to backlight the barrel. The bore is clean, the steel unpitted and darkly reflective, bending the light along its curvature.

"Do you know why?" Cayenne says.

"No," Turtle says.

"Ask me why," Cayenne says.

"Why?"

"I think she's kind of beautiful. Do you ever think so? That Virginia Woolf is kind of beautiful? And also kind of scary?"

"Hm," Turtle says.

"Turtle?"

"Yes?"

"Do you know what I mean? That you wouldn't need to kill her, not really?"

Turtle looks over at Cayenne. She says, "Yes, I can see that."

"Would you have killed her like that? Just barehanded?"

"Yes," Turtle says.

"Why haven't you done it before?"

Turtle doesn't say anything.

"Turtle?"

"Hmmm?"

"Turtle?"

"Yes."

"Why haven't you killed her before, if you would've? If it would be that easy. Why haven't you just done it before?"

"I guess I never worried about her until she bothered you."

"So you'd kill her for me?"

"Yes."

"Turtle?" Cayenne says.

"Christ," Turtle says. "What?"

"Nothing," Cayenne says, embarrassed. She lowers herself down into the tub and out of view. Turtle finishes cleaning the gun and begins to re-assemble it. The phone rings.

"Turtle," Cayenne says gently, sitting up out of the tub.

The phone rings again.

"Go get that," Cayenne says.

"Why?" Turtle says.

"Because," Cayenne says, "I want to know who keeps calling."

"It's no one," Turtle says.

"Turtle," Cayenne says.

"What?"

"I know who it is." She says it slyly, teasingly.

Out in the living room, the phone rings again.

"I think you should get it," Cayenne says. "Since Martin got the new phone it rings all the time now."

"He's on a shopping spree," Turtle says. "Table, chairs, new bed, new phone."

The phone rings and rings.

"You threw the old phone away," Cayenne says meaningfully.

Turtle sits, cleaning.

"Martin says it's your **secret lover**." Cayenne is

very interested in Jacob. Turtle gets up and walks into the living room. Martin is at the counter with a beer, and he nods to the phone on the wall.

Turtle walks to the phone and picks it up off the cradle.

"Turtle?" Jacob's voice is a clean, tightly fitted copper brush plunged through her throat and into her guts. She braces the heel of her hand against the wall.

"I can't talk to you," she says.

"Listen," he says.

"You listen," she says. Turtle cannot stop hating him and start needing him, not now, and she doesn't know what that would mean for her, to need one more thing that she isn't able to reach for, and she cannot bear to think of Jacob while she lies slicked with sweat and watches the shadows of alder leaves come in and out of focus against the drywall.

Jacob says, "Turtle, I—"

"No."

"Turtle—"

"No."

"I love you," he says. "I don't know what—"

Turtle hangs up. Martin touches the counter's wood grain with a finger pad. Invested in him are all of the things she understands to be true and which she cannot look at him without seeing.

She walks back into the bathroom, where Cayenne is soaping up with Dr. Bronner's. Turtle sits down at the edge of the tub. The room smells of peppermint. She looks at the mushrooms growing on the windowsill, and then she looks at Cayenne, really looking at her, and she finds herself loving the set of the girl's shoulders, the ridge of her scapula moving beneath her reddish-brown skin, the hairless cups of her armpits as she raises her arms. Her finger is still covered in its splint and bandage, wrapped now in a plastic bag. Turtle thinks, I hope nothing ever happens to you. I hope you stay exactly this way, and thinking this, she sits there, regretting it all, thinking, Christ, that harm could ever come to a girl like this, and look at her. Just look at her.

Cayenne points to the mushrooms on the windowsill, and says, "What would it be like to be really small, Turtle? All those mushrooms would be just like trees, wouldn't they?"

Turtle smiles and doesn't know what to say, just shakes her head, and thinks better of it and says, "You'd live in fear of the black-tailed weasel."

"That lives under the kitchen floor?"

"The same."

At this, Cayenne nods very somberly—not having thought of the dangers, but accepting them now. Then she says, "I think we should name the weasel. It's wrong that he doesn't have a name."

"What would you name him?"

"Dilbert," Cayenne says.

"Dilbert?"

"Or else Rodrigo."

The two girls sit in silence. Turtle picks up the gun and begins going over it with a rag.

"I don't know what kind they are," Turtle says.

"Oh," Cayenne says.

She waits on Turtle's every movement.

"Turtle," she says.

"Gills," Turtle says.

"Ah," the girl says. "But I like 'louvers' better."

"So do I," Turtle says. "Isn't that a museum, though? The Louver?"

"No," Cayenne says.

"Oh," Turtle says, "I thought it was. Some place."

"Like where, Turtle?"

"I don't know."

"Where, Turtle?"

"San Francisco?"

"Do you think San Francisco is bigger than Wenatchee?" Cayenne asks.

"I don't know," Turtle says. "I've never been there."

"To Wenatchee?" Cayenne says.

"To either."

After dinner, she and Martin sit out on the porch and talk, Martin smoking a cigar, inspecting the ash for the cherry in the dark. Cayenne is inside, reading. The sun has set. He drinks, pitching the empty bottles sidehand out over the field. Turtle sits with the stock of the skeet gun balanced against her thigh and shoots each bottle at the apex of its flight. In the dark, the struck bottles seem to vanish, their glittering passage simply arrested.

"You ever hear of a bug that lays eggs in people?"

He takes his cigar from the arm of the chair, seems to settle into himself.

"Daddy?"

"Well, now," he says. "I don't know."

"You never heard of that?"

"Well, I don't know."

"What?"

"Where'd you hear that?"

Turtle is silent.

"Meth heads, kibble, hallucinate bugs under their skin. They pick wounds all over their arms, their thighs, in their cheeks. Sometimes they pick at their eyes. Is that what you mean?"

"Nothing else?"

He is silent.

"Could Cayenne have been on meth, do you think?"

"No, kibble. I don't think so."

He drinks from his bottle. Turtle breaks the shotgun over her arm, shucks away the hull casings. She chambers two bird-shot loads, locks the gun closed.

"Hell," he says. "Maybe."

Just inside of him are all the things she needs to know.

"If she wasn't on the drug, if only someone that was on the drug told her that there were bugs under her skin, she wouldn't believe that," Turtle says. "If they went to the hospital and the doctors told her it wasn't true. She'd know it was wrong. That whoever it was, they were wrong."

Martin runs his thumb around the lip of the bottle.

"You've got it all figured out, kibble," he says.

"I don't," she says.

He says, "Try this one." He rises, wings the bottle out over the field like a discus thrower. Turtle shoots without rising, without shouldering the gun. The bottle arches away against the blue-black sky, and then it is simply gone.

He grins. Sits down grinning. "Uncanny," he says.

"You haven't written to the school district."

"No."

She hates to ask him.

"That's the sort of thing you have to take care of, or somebody notices."

He chews his lip.

It is possible that he has not filled out the paperwork because he does not believe they will go on like this much longer, or it is possible that he has not filled out the paperwork in the hope that someone will take her away. If he is being purposefully reckless, she needs to know.

"Daddy."

"You think I'm running out the clock."

"Are you?"

"No."

She waits for more. She thinks, I will not talk before he talks.

She says, "What if they send someone to the house?"

"Well."

"Well what?"

"No one cares, kibble. You think someone's out there, keeping tabs on you?" He runs his tongue across his lips, slowly, as if looking for a split. "We'll get your enrollment figured out. Something."

No, she thinks. They care.

"What were you doing with Cayenne?" she says.

She turns. He is staring out over the hillside toward Buckhorn Bay.

"Well?"

"What the hell, kibble?"

"Before you got here. Why did you have her with you?"

"That's a hell of a thing to ask."

"Well?"

"Christ. Jesus Christ."

She waits.

"Jesus fucking Christ, kibble."

"What, then?"

"Fuck, I don't know."

"You don't know? That's all? You don't know?"

"I just picked her up. That's all. Just found her and took her along."

"How?"

"How what?"

"How did you pick her up?"

He gestures mutely, as if to suggest that he'd come by her the way you usually find ten-year-old girls. She wants to wait him out. There is a way it feels to ask him things. To need things from him. A specific way that feels.

"How did you find her, Martin?"

"Christ."

"How?"

She waits. She can't believe he's going to leave it at this. For a while, she's determined not to ask.

"How?" she says.

"Christ. If it means all that fucking much to you."

He pitches his beer bottle out into the dark.

"Yeah," she says. "It does."

"It was nothing. I was at a gas station and went around back to take a leak and some guy's got Cayenne by her arm and he's talking to her. He's holding her by the arm and talking. Nobody else there. You should've heard him. Two a.m. and the things he is saying. Kinds of things remind you of your old buddy, Grandpa. I thought, well, this is just not going to fucking fly."

He gestures. That's the end of the story.

"You just—?"

"We tooled down all these old, overgrown back roads in Washington and into Idaho. She'd ask about things. How do cars work? How are coins made? Who invented money? Who would win in a fight, so-and-so or so-and-so? We'd pull over, lift up rocks by the side of the road, find skinks and things, toads. Go fishing, and fry up the fish for dinner. Just go a few miles each day, and camp. And that's when it hit me. I'd done the wrong thing, abandoning you. What I couldn't figure was why I'd done it. I was about out of my head."

"What's gonna happen to us?" she says.

"I don't know."

"You don't know."

"Hell. We're gonna be all right, kibble."

"You think so?"

"Hell."

"That's all you've got. 'Hell'? That's all?"

He is silent for a long time.

She thinks, we have never been all right and we aren't ever going to be all right. She thinks, I don't even know what all right would look like. I don't know what that would mean. At his best, we are more than all right. At his best he rises above all of it and he is more than any of them. But there is something in him. A flaw that poisons all the rest. What is going to happen to us.

Twenty-six

SHE STOPS GOING DOWN TO HIM. EACH night, she wakes with the breeze coming in through the window, her mind hot and alive, water slithering down the window's black pane. Downstairs there is a room where everything ends. She lets the earth turn slowly around her and she thinks, you are doing this for a reason, and if you can't see what comes next, you take each moment as it comes. In the mornings she sits cross-legged over her tea with the fresh leaves beside her on the counter. They are like huge, toothy, green spear blades fuzzed with silica needles. She ladles tea into her cast-iron teacup and Martin comes up the gravel road from his morning walk down to the beach.

He comes in through the sliding glass door with the wet flowers of rattlesnake grass stuck to his jeans and he holds up a padded postal service envelope. "Package," he says, "for **Turtle Alveston**. No return address. What do you think, kibble?" He tears away the strip and extracts a book and a letter. "Marcus Aurelius," he says, "**Meditations**." He thumbs through it. "Hell of a book. **Hell** of a fucking book. You should read that instead of **Lysistrata** or whatever the fuck you've picked up." He laughs bitterly, licking his lips, touching them with his thumb, and begins sorting through the letter. He folds it and tears it into strips and discards it into the fire. Turtle ladles tea from her teapot. Martin walks away down the hall and slams the door.

Cayenne says, "Turtle?"

"Yeah?"

"I didn't know you were reading something, Turtle."

"He's an asshole."

"Oh."

Turtle drinks her tea.

"Are you, though?"

"No."

She strips and cleans the Sig Sauer by the light of the oil lamp. She taps the magazine in and racks the slide and puts the gun to her temple just to remind herself that she is never so trapped that she cannot escape. She thinks, you have lost your guts, lost your courage, you are disgraced, but you are still here.

It has been a week since she's been down to his room. When she comes down the stairs in the morning, Martin is making pancakes in a chipped Bauer bowl, hipshot against the counter with the bowl under his arm, tipping his beer into the batter, gesturing with the spatula. She looks slowly away from the window to Martin, who is smirking, who has asked her a question. She blows across her teacup and watches the steam diffuse and reform. She picks up the shotgun from the counter and jumps to the floor and walks away. She sits on the toilet, her pants about her ankles, holding an unwrapped, urine-soaked pregnancy test, turning it between thumb and forefinger, watching the negative result fade slowly into the little plastic window. Speculative about what it means. Turning it slowly.

That evening, she has the gun stripped and laid out when she hears Martin come out of his room. Turtle pauses and seems to hang above her guts and the world to rise around her, to lift, and she listens to him climb the burl treads of the staircase. She assembles the gun, barrel into the slide, spring onto the recoil rod, recoil rod tensioned against the barrel, slide locked back on the frame, slide release engaged, magazine into the well, then she drops the slide to chamber a round, letting him hear. He pauses outside the door. She waits on him. The knob turns. He walks in and seems confounded to find her there, cross-legged before the oil lamp, bottles of powder solvent, degreaser, and the oil arrayed around her.

"Clean in here," he says.

She says nothing.

"Okay, kibble," he says. "Okay."

She closes the door after him and sits down with her back to it, hating him. He will punish me for this, she thinks. He means to teach me a lesson about this, about what I'm doing, and I'm sure I'll learn it.

Turtle boils her tea and sits on the counter and watches Cayenne stir from her sleeping bag. She has finished her vampire books and is reading **Deliverance**.

"How is that?" Turtle says.

Cayenne wrinkles her nose. "It's **weird**."

"How so?"

"Just"—screwing up her whole face—"**weird**."

That night Turtle sits sharpening her knife, listening to the hush of the polishing stone, regretting it all. She thinks: come up. I want you to come up. I'm sorry, I'm sorry, and I'm sorry, and if you come up it'll all be okay. It'll be just like it was before. She knows what she should do. She should go down into his room. She can't do it to herself, though.

In the morning there is something grim and sad and self-hating in his face and he opens the fridge and takes his beer and bangs it open and he walks out and down the porch steps and she looks at his retreating back, and she thinks, I will take what comes.

He is out there, staring at Buckhorn Cove, for a long time. Turtle waits that night, dissembling the Sig Sauer and reassembling it, the shotgun laid beside her with a fifty-five-round bandolier of shells, picking up Marcus Aurelius and opening the page and reading by the light of the oil lamp and then tossing the book away and picking up the gun, taking the slide from the frame and sitting with the two paired in her hands and staring at them.

Then she hears Martin's bedroom door open, hears Martin cross the long hallway to the living room where the stairs to her room begin. Turtle's whole body prickles. She listens. He walks into the living room and stands at the foot of her stairs and she waits, thinking, come on up, you bastard. You might hurt me but you can never break me, so come on up the stairs, motherfucker, and let's see what you have. Turtle's scalp prickles. It feels like the skin is tightening. The fear grows on her. She hears him whisper to Cayenne, and the rustling noise as he picks her up, still in her blankets, and then his heavy, uneven footsteps going down the hallway as he carries the girl back to his room.

Turtle thinks, thank god it's her and not me. Then she stands up and grabs her hair. She walks to her door and puts the heel of her fist against it. This is not your fault, she thinks. This is not on you. You owe that girl nothing. You can't do anything about this. She walks back to the window, sits down, chewing on her knuckles. Though Jacob would have no doubt that you could stop this, and that's how little he knows about you and that's how little he knows about life. She picks up the Sig Sauer and holsters it and picks up the shotgun and shoulders the bandolier and then she opens the door and she thinks, motherfucker, what are you doing, Turtle, what are you doing.

She walks down the hall, her boots soft and worn. She stops, listening for any sound, and she can hear nothing over her own breathing and over her heart, and she thinks, Christ, girl, breathe steady. She descends into the living room. Turtle stands holding the shotgun. Down the hall, the new bed creaks, and creaks again. Turtle passes the bathroom on the left, and then the foyer on the right with its twenty-two bear skulls, and then the pantry on the left, and she comes to Martin's lightless door at the end of the hallway, the cut-glass knob.

She is acutely aware of her own smell in the dark. Her knees are loose; she puts her forehead against the wood panel. On the other side, a painful gasp, the hitching of breath. A protracted silence, and then another gasp of breath, half-stifled. Turtle stands there and she thinks, you can turn around now because you have no plan and there is nothing you can do and there is nowhere you can take that girl. You can't take her away and you can't keep her safe and it is blindness to think otherwise. Think about who he is. How much bigger he is than you. How much stronger and smarter, how much more experienced. She thinks, you will die. You will fail and you will die, and for what. The moment you take that girl out of this house, he will drive up the coast and go to Jacob's house and kill Jacob. That is what you are hazarding, Jacob's life, and your own. And he won't do that girl all that much harm. He will do to her what he did to you night after night for years, and you're still here.

Then she thinks, but if I go back up the stairs, there will be a whole tract of myself I will have to keep half lit by remembering, and I will never come to peace with it, but if I go in there now and I do just the best that I can, that is a story I can tell myself, however it ends. More than anything, more than life itself, she wants Jacob Learner back, she wants her dignity back. She thinks, okay, you cunt, put your brain in your lunch box and go to work. She thinks, if you're going to do this, you have to do it exactly right.

She tries the door. Then she trips the slide release and draws the pump back to expose the yawning maw of the chamber and she drops in the breaching round and slides the pump forward and feels the breech bolt crunch closed. She shoulders the gun and blows the lock. Her hearing, sensitized by the silence, is instantly gone. She kicks the door open, racking the shotgun as she steps through. Martin lurches up from the covers and lunges toward the side table, sweeping aside bottles and magazines, reaching for the Colt, and Turtle shoots it off the table, the shotgun throwing a lance of flame, a beer bottle tossing its glass neck, spuming, the ejected shotshell hanging in the air beside her, revolving as it arches into the dark. Martin sweeps the covers off himself and steps out of bed and takes a single step toward her, huge and naked, his thighs immense and shining in the dark, his chest deep and black with hair, and Turtle brings the shotgun up.

"Wait—" she says.

Then he is on her. He backhands her across the face. She strikes her head on the doorjamb and lands sprawled in the hallway. He looms out of the darkness, huge, kneeling over her, and takes her neck in both hands and forces her to the floor. She makes a choking, throttled noise and then all sound is cut off. She seizes him by the wrist and cannot break his grasp any more than if she were fixed in place by a railroad spike.

"Shoot at **me**?" he says. "Shoot at **me**? I made you. You are **mine**."

They do not lash or even move, but strain against each other there in the hallway. His face is a murderous rictus. Turtle's mind fills with a silent agony. She can feel his fingers sinking wells into her neck, the flesh strained almost to shearing. Her face is thickening into a crust like a mask. She is aware of this beneath the howling, mind-bending air hunger, and aware, too, of the roof of her mouth **itching**, and her eyes **itching** as blood vessels bleed into her skin.

Turtle clutches at his fingers. They are lapped into folds of her flesh. It is like trying to pry roots from stony ground. She claws up gouts of her own skin. His palm gaps up and she chisels her thumb beneath it, her thumbnail cutting a deep, bloody groove in her throat. Desperately, she works her thumb along his palm toward the smallest finger of his left hand. Her mouth strains for air. Her face is swollen, engorged with blood, her vision narrowing, going gray-black and losing all depth, inky black vessels unfurling across the left-hand side.

He heaves her up and slams her back down against the floor, Turtle desperately intent, prying at the smallest finger of his left hand, tearing at it, her thumb hooked beneath it. Slowly, torturously, she begins to lever his littlest finger away from the others. She fights for leverage. "Shoot at me, bitch?" he says. "I **made** you." He lifts her up and slams her back into the floor, trying to knock her unconscious, trying to shake her grasp. Her vision swims with sparks. She gets her entire fist around his finger, drags it back, and tears his hand away. He lurches to a stand before she can break any of the small bones of his hand.

Even released, Turtle sprawls. She cannot get up. She cannot breathe. She does not know why. Even with him no longer there, she cannot take a breath. There is no gurgle, no sound of air. It makes no sense. She rolls onto her stomach and scrabbles across the floor. I'm going to die, she thinks. I am going to die right fucking here. In this hallway. She wants to cry out for help, but she cannot. Something has been crushed in her neck. She wallows, fights for air, and then Martin walks up behind her and kicks her in the groin.

She rears up silently and then collapses. "Fucking **bitch**," he says. "Fucking—fucking—**fucking bitch**. You are mine. Mine. Mine," he rasps raggedly. He does not seem to understand why she is on the floor. He pauses, perplexed. She still cannot breathe. Her air hunger has an all-consuming urgency. He kicks her again. In agony she rends at the floorboards. Her diaphragm convulses violently. She props herself up and can feel the air in her mouth—a cold mouthful of air, cold against her teeth. She takes hold of the half-open pantry door. She thinks, get up, Turtle. You have to get up. You have to get up.

He says, "You bitch. You **whore**."

She staggers to her knees, takes a great bloody suck of air, grabs at the knob of the pantry door to steady herself. She thinks, all right, you cunt. Let's see what you have. She sucks air again. Cold and painful and good. All right, she thinks. No more fucking around.

Martin picks up the shotgun and walks toward her, saying, "Mine, you are mine." He walks right up to her and he brings the gun up into her face. He is too close to her. He never could do anything right. Turtle looks up into the shotgun's great black bore like looking into a pupil, thinking, he was never careful of you, he never believed in you. Everything falls away, each gesture, each thing collapsing into itself, stripped of doubt and hesitation. She reaches out and latches the shotgun's barrel just behind the front sight. Then she pulls the gun down toward herself like it is a railing and she is helping herself up the stairs, angling the barrel away from herself. There is no effort or sense of effort. Her intentions simply unfold into action.

The gun goes off. It throws a white-hot lance of sound and fire past her hip into the wall. Martin has not let go of the stock and he comes forward with it, stumbling, off balance, his mouth gaping and appalled. It is happening too fast for him and he can do nothing. She drags him down to where she wants him. Then she sets her feet and drives her elbow up into his jaw.

There is no pain, but she feels the blow all the way down to her heels. Martin reels back. He hits the wall and goes down.

Turtle exchanges her grip on the gun and racks it. The shell ejects and clatters across the boards, smoking. She stands where she is. With each breath, the world around her draws color, draws depth. She does not walk toward him. There is a backsplash of blood on the wall. She tries to speak but produces only a painful rasp. Something has been damaged in her throat. Her vocal cords, something. Martin lies facedown.

Kill him, she thinks. He will never let you go. He levers himself up and casts around. A bit of tooth is on the floor and his eyes fasten on it. Blood is falling from his mouth in drippy strings. His pupils are blown to hoops. His legs work uselessly. Turtle thinks, just pull the trigger. She could do it if she needed to, but it is the need she doubts. He pushes himself up, sits back against the wall, his legs stuck out straight before him, staring. His hands lie uselessly at his side. His chest heaves. He seems stunned.

She opens her mouth to ask him something and produces a chapped and bloody sound. He looks up from the floor and she tries to weigh his look, but it is blank, almost expressionless. She wraps and rewraps her hands around the shotgun's ringtailed pump. His shoulders cabled with tendons, knotted with great fistfuls of muscle. His body knobbed and trenched with shadows. Muscles stand out in sashes across his ribs, which heave open and closed with his labored breathing. In this stooped posture, his powerful stomach is lapped into folds. He has drawn his legs up and his bare feet rest flat on the boards, snaked with veins, a fan of bones standing out from them, the arch high, his gigantic, stubby toes clutching at the boards. He does not look away from her.

She staggers past him along the wall to where Cayenne is huddled in the bed, grasping at the rucked sheets. Turtle holds out her left hand with its crooked fingers and the girl stares into the dark. Turtle can barely stand. She points the shotgun at the girl, swings the barrel to indicate that she should move, and Cayenne screams, bringing her hands to her face, then cutting off abruptly. Turtle climbs up onto the bed and takes the girl by the hair and hauls her back through the hallway, trying to keep her from looking at Martin, pulling her into the foyer. The bear skulls shine yellow in the dark, the chandelier looms from out of the cobwebbed rafters, the great brass goosenecks catching the light. Turtle pans the shotgun one handed, hauling the girl with the other hand.

He clears his throat, hacks. "Don't go," he says. His voice is thick and slurred.

Turtle levels the shotgun at him and Cayenne cleaves to her, burying her face in Turtle's stomach, wrapping her hands around Turtle's back and gripping the wifebeater and the flannel with her small fingers. He spreads his hands, holds them out in mute appeal. Turtle opens the huge oak foyer door and shoves Cayenne out into the driveway. She walks to Grandpa's truck and opens the passenger-side door and the girl climbs in, clumsy and naked, holding her arms around herself. She turns back and gives Turtle a single frightened look, her hair in tangles. Turtle slams the door, turns back around. She can see Martin through the open door of the foyer. She tries to see it in him, what he will do. If he knows, himself, he makes no sign. He seems to be staring at the floor or at his own, open hands. Just don't follow me, she thinks. Don't follow me, you son of a bitch.

She walks around the front of the truck and gets in. She could shoot the wheels out on his truck, but if he's going to come after her, she wants him to do it now and she wants him in a vehicle she'll recognize. The keys are in the ignition. She wrenches the headlights on and throws the truck into gear and roars down the driveway. Cayenne crawls across the vinyl seat and puts her cheek in Turtle's lap, her eyes sealed shut, jerking and spasming, and Turtle puts a hand on the girl's hair, on the side of her cheek. The truck fishtails out onto the black and familiar highway, and at the sight of this clean expanse of tarmac, the yellow dividing line, the mailboxes, the hummocks of torch lily, she gasps with relief. She reaches up with one hand and touches the divots torn in her neck by her own fingernails. She moves the rearview mirror. In it, her face is mottled with black capillary bleeds from the strangulation. When she opens her mouth, it is purple-black inside, her teeth rimmed pink.

Turtle tries to say something and cannot; her mouth opens and closes with a clicking sound. Cayenne reaches out with one hand, grabs ahold of the thigh of Turtle's jeans, slowly closing her hand into a fist, and Turtle looks down at the girl. Cayenne draws her thighs together, one hand wrapped around her own stomach. With the dome light off, the cab is near lightless, but Turtle catches silver-lit adumbrations of the girl in the headlights of passing cars. Turtle can see the half silhouette of a silver cheek, the crescent of an eye socket, her gaping half-mouth, planes of her face catching the light and her black hair soaking it up.

Twenty-seven

A MILE OR TWO MILES OUT, TURTLE STOPS
the truck just past a blind turn. They are on the
winding, dark, cliffside highway south of Mendocino. Cayenne sits up wordlessly. Turtle reverses
and backtracks through the curve. She watches
her rearview mirror carefully. She cannot turn her
neck enough to look over her shoulder. The embankment on the right is in the dark. On the left,
her headlights light the guardrail, the cliff. They
spear out above the ocean. Turtle changes gears
and takes the turn again, slowly, watching the embankment, watching the guardrail, watching the
road ahead as it comes into view. The headlights
catch the guardrail but not the forested slope on

the right. She drives a hundred yards farther and pulls off on the left side of the road and sits in the cab, listening to the ticking of the engine.

"What, Turtle? What is it?" Cayenne says.

Turtle cannot quite shake her head. She moves it fractionally right, fractionally left.

"What is it, Turtle?"

"Wait here," Turtle says.

"What?"

"Wait here."

"Turtle, I can't— What?" She is crying, shaking her head.

I won't let him hurt anybody, Turtle thinks. I won't let him go after Jacob or Cayenne to punish me. But I won't hurt him unless I have to. She knows he has Jacob's address. She expects that is where he will go next, to look for her. She can't go anywhere else anyway, for fear that he will go to Jacob's house without her. He has effectively narrowed her options down to one.

"Turtle?"

Turtle leans back into the vinyl seat. She's exhausted. Her neck is stiffening up. Her mouth is full of blood from her cut lips. She's having trouble swallowing. She opens her mouth to speak and blood runs out and drains down her shirt. She tries to shake her head but her neck is too tight. She kicks open the door and gets out and stands leaning against the quarter panel, kneading a muscle in her groin.

"Don't leave," Cayenne says. "No no no, don't leave."

Turtle reaches for the bandolier and finds that she's lost it. She has four rounds in the shotgun, five in the sidesaddle, and fifteen 9mm hollow points in the Sig Sauer. She slams the door, walks across the road sliding the waxy, corrugated shotshells out of the sidesaddle and into the spring-loaded resistance of the magazine, feeling each click into place. She mounts up onto the embankment and lays herself down into the coyote brush so that she will have a clear shot through the windshield into the cab. She is on the inside of the turn. The angle is not good but she will be out of the headlights and Martin will be looking ahead and left. She expects him to hit the brakes when Grandpa's truck comes into view. She will get one shot. Maybe two. Then she'll unload on the wheels. She cannot prop herself on her elbow. It is bruised black. She cannot remember it hurting at all. It had felt so effortless. But now the entire arm is seizing up. She thinks, as soon as he comes around the corner, if he comes around the corner, don't even think. Right through the windshield. If he gives you the chance, put a second into him. Her whole face aches. She can't feel her lips. He'd backhanded her hard enough to lift her off her feet. She'd been trying to say something. She had the drop on him and she thought he would stop. She had thought he would step back, put his hands up. But he'd gone right into her. No hesitation. She looks over the shotgun's sights, out at the empty road, shivering in the breeze. She almost died for that mistake. She had come very fucking close. Luck, she thinks. Pure luck that she started breathing again. You crush your windpipe like that, and it doesn't necessarily open back up. That had been a near thing. People die from a hell of a lot less.

God, she wishes she had her .308. Well, she'll just have to work with what she has. With the shotgun and a sidearm, she is more or less confined to the up close and personal. She waits, the night getting colder, the breeze wetting the grass around her, and she thinks, maybe, maybe. There are no cars. It is possible, just possible, that he has let them go. She hears a car coming. She waits. Not him, she says to herself. It's not him, because he has cut us loose. It has been two hours, going on three. She waits, shivering. She can see Grandpa's truck farther up the road, but she cannot see Cayenne. She hopes the girl is okay. She must be terrified, waiting in the truck alone, but she will survive that.

A green Subaru comes around the turn. The headlights hit the truck and the car slows just as they come into Turtle's sights. Turtle looks down the shotgun at the woman behind the wheel. A child in the back is looking out at the forest. His breath mists the window, and then they're gone.

She hurts all over. She thinks, where do you go next? What do you do next? But there is only one place she can go. Turtle lies in the grass waiting for him to come around the turn. Come on, you bastard, she thinks. He doesn't come. After hours of waiting, she eases herself up, careful of her bruised neck, and limps back to the truck.

Cayenne has found Grandpa's barn coat and put it on. She is lying curled on the seat, shaking all over, quivering like a dog. At first, Turtle thinks the girl is asleep, but getting in the truck, careful and doing her best not to turn her head, she can see the gleam of a sclera in the dark. Turtle puts her hand on the ignition. Maybe, she thinks. Maybe. She leans over and spits into Grandpa's Big Gulp cup. Maybe. She turns the key.

They drive north through Mendocino. Then through Caspar. Fort Bragg. Empty parking lots flash by, dark buildings. They wait at a streetlight with no other cars in sight. Then head on north. The green digital clock blinks **00:00** but it must be almost morning. The dunes encroach on the winding dark road, just visible through stands of eucalyptus. The bluffs fall away beneath and they cross the Ten Mile Bridge, the estuary below dark and weed choked, with the posts of rotting piers extending from the reedy shores and the great, wallowing gloss of the river. Then Turtle and Cayenne are past the bridge and they follow a newly poured tarmac road along redwood clapboard houses with decorative walls of stacked shale, concrete driveways unmarked by tire tracks, small gardens of rockroses and weeping pines mulched with freshly cut woodchips.

They make a turn and almost run over a girl in a ruched red dress. She is riding on the back of a tuxedoed boy, her dress hitched up, the boy struggling to crawl with a beer in one hand. They're squinting against the headlights. Cayenne and Turtle wait in silence as the girl, laughing so hard she can barely move, struggles up off the boy's back and falls to the pavement. She is holding her high heels in one hand and she waves the shoes at them in apology. Cayenne and Turtle wait. A boy in a baggy, bell-bottom white tuxedo runs out of the bushes, pursued by a goose. He stops to help the fallen girl and the goose spreads her wings and hisses. The boy hauls the girl to her feet and struggles off to the side of the road, the goose following. Turtle looks once at Cayenne, and then she takes her foot off the brake and the truck pulls away from the teenagers.

The road unwinds ahead of them, the headlights slicing across the high, golden, breeze-riffled grass. They round a bend and Jacob's house comes into view, close to fifteen cars in the driveway. Turtle turns off the headlights and eases down the drive. A tall redheaded girl in a tiara is standing on the deck with her hands on the balustrade, looking out over the parked cars. Her silver sash reads HOMECOMING. A thin stub of cigarette is fitted between two fingers. What the hell, Turtle thinks. What the hell? Whatever it is, it seems to be winding down.

Turtle parks behind a big van covered in bumper stickers that read REPUBLICANS FOR VOLDEMORT, MY OTHER CAR IS A MAGIC MUSHROOM, and GUNS DON'T KILL PEOPLE/GAPING HOLES IN VITAL ORGANS KILL PEOPLE. High schoolers are sleeping inside. She kicks the parking brake on, shuts the truck off. Cayenne hunches forward, the barn coat pulled around her shoulders, sucking her thumb, looking up over the dash at the redheaded girl. Turtle opens the door, drops one leg out. Some muscle in her groin has tightened up. She waits there, getting her breath back from the pain, then drops out and stands leaning against the truck, kneading her hip joint with her knuckles. She walks with difficulty around the hood of the truck to Cayenne's door and opens it and sets the shotgun on the hood and puts her hands under the girl's armpits and swings her out and picks up the shotgun and leads the girl by the hand past the line of cars, rusted Subarus and Volvos, the western moon bending off-white and crater-pocked across the black windows. Just inside, the colorless shadows of sleepers. The redhead watches them come up onto the deck. Turtle opens the double doors onto an entrance hall. On the wall, two portraits of weathered men with gnarled beards, one holding a Civil War–era rifle and the other holding a double-barreled shotgun. The caption reads EEL

RIVER INDIAN HUNTERS. Their eyes are glazed. A couple leans against the wall, necking, the girl in a giant, green dinosaur onesie. Across the floor, boots and dress shoes, tennis shoes, heels. They go through the T intersection into the hallway lined with its floor-to-ceiling glass case of Pomo baskets. A fan of light comes through the half-open door ahead of them. They can see the walls lined with books, a glimpse of white carpeting, the red silk puddle of a dress on the floor. Turtle eases the door open with the shotgun and they step into the living room. In the middle, a half-dozen high schoolers are playing Monopoly. Brett is among them, lying on the floor in a brown corduroy suit with leather elbow patches. The other boys are in borrowed suits, the girls in dresses. Money is scattered on the floor and stuck under the edges of the board. Picture windows look onto the wraparound deck and the hot tub, where two naked girls sit at the candled edge, their dresses draped on the deck railing, their ballet slippers side by side, their pale spines arching, ridges of their scapulae moving with their arms. In a corner of the room, a grand piano, and on top of the piano, a pair of red pumps and a red clutch.

One of the girls on the floor sits up. It's Rilke, from Anna's long-ago classroom, from long-ago bus rides. Her hair has been worked into curls that hang around her oval face. She is wearing a pink strapless dress and tights, barefoot. She stares at

Turtle, her mouth gradually opening into a lip-glossed O of surprise. Turtle leads Cayenne into the room. Brett looks up, stops.

Into the shocked silence, Turtle gasps out Jacob's name. Even to her, it is an appalling sound.

Rilke says, "Oh god."

Brett says, "Turtle—?"

"Oh god."

Turtle gestures with the shotgun. All of them, they all need to leave. She doesn't know how to go about that. She needs to find him. Everything else comes after finding Jacob. She is making that plan in her mind—find Jacob. Get everyone out of the house. Bunker down. Martin will come or he won't. But, she thinks, he won't. If he was going to come, he would've made that move already. He wouldn't wait nearly four hours to pursue her. He would pursue her immediately. She thinks so anyway. And she can keep Jacob safe. She is sure of that. The two of them together, they can do this.

"Is she—?" one of the girls says.

"Turtle," Brett says. "Turtle. You look like you were **hung**."

She says, "Jacob—" Her voice cracks and fails.

"What?"

"Christ, **listen** to her."

"Oh my god."

"Turtle, I can't hear you," Brett says. "You need Jacob? Is that what you said? What—what happened? What's going on?"

Cayenne is hiding behind Turtle, holding on to Turtle's hand and grasping at her flannel. Rilke has risen to a stand and is staring at Cayenne, slowly raising her hands to cover her mouth in shock. "Oh my god," she says. Turtle ignores her. "Brett," Rilke says, speaking through her cupped hands. When he doesn't respond, she says it again. "**Brett**."

One of the girls says, "Somebody find a land-line. Somebody call the cops."

Cell phones, Turtle remembers, don't work here.

"Where," Turtle says with difficulty, "is Jacob?"

Jacob will know what to do. He'll get everyone out of here. Then they'll get through this together.

"Um—" Brett says, biting his lip and looking around as if he might be in the room. "I mean, he could be anywhere. But where? I mean—I don't know?"

"Brett," Rilke says softly, emphatically. Brett looks at her. "Brett, the girl," she says. Turtle looks down at Cayenne. At first she doesn't see anything. Then she sees it. There is blood on Cayenne's legs. It has run down the insides of her knees and down her shins and it is dry and scabbed. It does not look like much.

"Oh my god," Rilke says. She sinks to her knees. She does not seem to know what to do with her hands. She reaches out to touch Cayenne and then brings her hands back and cups them over her mouth as if to keep herself from crying out. Cayenne shies away. "Oh god, oh god," Rilke says.

Turtle grabs Brett, jerks him forward. "I need Jacob." Her voice is harsh and chapped.

Brett says, "Turtle—it looks like you're bleeding into the whites of your eyes—are you all right?"

"Jacob," she repeats. It's all she can say.

Brett raises his arms, lets them drop. "I'm telling you, Turtle. I don't know! He's not in his room. He's not here. All I know is that when Imogen decided to have this party, he said he wouldn't come. He tried to get me to go hiking with him out to Inglenook Fen and I said, 'Fuck that, I'ma party.' I thought you'd dumped him. Hell—**he** thinks you've dumped him."

Turtle stands. Jacob isn't here. She has no idea what to do. With that impossibility, she can feel all of her momentum draining out of her. The world goes gray and flat with stress, her vision closing in from the sides as if the room were drawing back from her, and in this retraction, the scene, these people, this house, it grows stranger, darker, impenetrable and unnavigable. The floor wheels and she is afraid, for a moment, that she will go down.

"Turtle?" Brett says.

She gapes at them. Brett is talking to her, and Rilke is on her knees in front of Cayenne, patting Cayenne uncontrollably in a stymied impulse at more effective comforting. People are talking. It's on her, Turtle realizes. To get all of these people out of here. To get them to safety in case Martin is coming. It is dawning on her what a colossal mistake she's made, and she is, with a throttling and rising panic, trying to figure out what to do.

"Turtle?" Brett says again.

She just stands there.

"Turtle—what's **happening**?"

She walks to the bookshelf. Set beside a book-end is a clay jar full of pens and she upends it and taking out a Sharpie walks to the wall and writes:

Get everybody out of here

"What?" Brett says. He stands staring at the words. "What?"

She writes:

Run

A semicircle of strangers stares at her.

"Oh no," Rilke says.

"Like, **now**?" Brett says.

"This is bad," Rilke says.

Turtle gestures them out with the shotgun.

"Wait," Brett says. "Why? **How?** We took every-body's keys—"

She gestures again with the shotgun and even as she does it, she recognizes the futility. The house is full of sleeping people. Cars are choked in the driveway. She changes her mind. "I need to go," she says. "I need to get out of here."

"Turtle—I can't . . . I can't understand you."

She turns and drags Cayenne toward the door. If she hurries, she can set another ambush. Just before the bridge.

"Stop," Rilke says.

Turtle looks at her.

"You can't take her," Rilke says.

Turtle puts her finger to her mouth. Everybody hesitates.

"Brett, she's been—"

Turtle gestures with the shotgun. Rilke cuts off.

"Turtle, what the hell? Where are you going?" Brett says.

Turtle is dead silent. She can hear a truck out in the driveway. She hears it shut off, and she hears him kick the door open, hears the door slam. A numbness starts in her gut, a sucking, squelching, pins-and-needles awfulness as if those goopy coils were rags being wrung of blood. Rilke is talking, her words meaningless and warped, and Brett, too, and the others, all of them talking, and Turtle is thinking, he didn't let me go. He hasn't cut me loose. He waited for me to come back, like he did after he found out about Jacob. He gave me the opportunity to repent, because what he really wants is for me to come back on my own. But now he's come here. She has seconds to do the right thing and if she does it wrong, people are going to die. Shit, she thinks. Shit.

Twenty-eight

TURTLE SHOVES THE GIRL TOWARD RILKE.
"Stay," she says. Cayenne shakes her head. Turtle
takes a knee, level with the girl. "I'll come back."
Her voice is a chapped rasp. The girl shakes her
head.

Promise, Turtle mouths.

"You promise?"

Turtle nods slowly, painfully.

To the others, she gestures up the stairs.

"Uh-uh," Brett says. "No way. I'm not leaving
you."

"**Brett**," Rilke says. "Someone tried to kill her
and that person is **here**. That person is **here** right
now."

"I don't care," Brett says. "I'm not leaving her."

"Brett—!" Rilke is holding on to Cayenne. "Brett, we need to go—"

Turtle leaves them talking and crosses the living room and goes into the hallway, closing the door quietly behind her. She can hear Martin's footsteps coming up the deck. The hallway meets the entranceway at the T intersection and she gets down on her belly so as not to be backlit by the hallway's display case, slithers across the carpet, noses the shotgun around the corner into the entranceway. The necking couple is still there, leaned up against the wall. The girl in the dinosaur onesie looks over at Turtle. She moves to brush a strand of hair from her face and then, recognizing the gun, freezes, opening her mouth. Turtle puts a finger to her lips. They stare at her. Turtle raises her eyebrows, looks to the door. They follow her gaze.

Martin must be just on the other side of the door, standing on the deck. She hears the boards creak. The girl turns very quietly and looks back at Turtle. The shotgun is clearly not aimed at her, but there are some people who believe a shotgun can fill an entire hallway with buckshot. Turtle puts up her hand: **Don't move.** She is trying to say: **Stay where you are.** She wants them to know she won't hurt them. The boy does not look away from the door. They wait. The low-recoil rounds Turtle is using have about a third of an inch of spread per yard of distance. She's five yards from the door. Turtle thinks, come on. Come on. She waits, her guts uncoiling within her, tucked hard against the wall, looking around the corner with the gun laid out and herself half hidden beneath the end table. She welds her cheek to the stock. The carpet smells of some kind of shampoo. In the kitchen, the refrigerator cycles on. Turtle can see no shadow of him, but knows that he is just beyond the doors and she waits, thinking, come to me now, you bastard.

The doorknob turns, and the door swings open, a soft toss. The girl jerks in surprise, and stays silent. Turtle's finger tightens on the trigger, but there is no shadow in the doorway, no sign of him, and she can imagine him hard against the edge of the open door, trying to draw her out. He seems to be deliberating. Come on, she thinks. Come on. The stock is slicked with sweat where it lies against her cheek. The sight bead glints. Dim yellow light from the deck fans across the tiles of the entranceway. Her mouth is dry with fear. She tries to swallow and cannot.

The boy pushes away from the girl, takes a step toward Turtle, and Turtle shakes her head, mouthing at him, and he stops. Martin is capable of shooting through the door into the hallway, and he will, if he hears footsteps. He knows that Turtle might be waiting for him, and he will be sensitive to the dangers of trying to come in through the door. The boy hesitates. A silence drags on.

The girl stands holding herself, shaking. The boy is partially in her line of fire, but she does not want him to move. The deck boards creak, and Turtle unwraps and rewraps her left hand where it lies on the pump.

She is beginning to think she's missed something. The silence drags on too long. Turtle puts the shotgun stock against the floor and crutches herself up with it, thinking, no, no, no. She limps back toward the living room, supporting herself against the glass case, and as she comes to the living room door, a slash of light cuts beneath it. She knows what it is: Martin has walked around the side of the house and climbed up onto the deck and is panning his weapon light across the room, looking for another way in, and then she hears the hiss of the glass deck doors on their sliders and the double kiss of their seal and Turtle thinks, shit, shit, shit. In the other room, just beyond the door, Cayenne screams, and Turtle can hear Martin's voice dimly through Cayenne's protracted, gasp-broken shrieking, but she stays where she is. Go through that door and die, she thinks. Go through that door and you'll just fucking die. Cayenne's screams cut off.

"Kibble," Martin says.

Turtle walks through the door. Martin is standing in the middle of the room. He is carrying his short-barreled AR-15, modified for full auto. Two thirty-round magazines are duct-taped end to end. More magazines will be stuck behind his belt. His lips are broken open. Rilke is holding Cayenne.

"What did you do?" he says. He spreads his hands. This occurs to her only now. There is no going back from this. Not with witnesses.

Turtle opens her mouth, cannot talk.

"Kibble," he says, pursing his lips. He holds his arms out.

Turtle stands.

"Right now, kibble," he says. He spits blood onto the white carpet. When Turtle does not speak, Martin looks around at them. He says, "Why doesn't everybody give us a minute?"

The other high schoolers bolt for the door. Brett and Rilke stay where they are, Brett with his hands up, Rilke holding Cayenne. One of the others will be calling the cops. Perhaps somebody already has. Turtle is wondering, if she goes with him, what happens to Cayenne?

Turtle tries to speak, cannot. She swallows, tries again. "The girl?"

Martin says, "Leave her."

"No no no no," Cayenne says. "No no no, he'll kill you. He's gonna kill her."

Turtle is holding the shotgun one-handed, down by her leg.

"Kibble," Martin says. He walks toward her. He kicks the Monopoly board out of the way. He spreads his hands reasonably, the gun hung loosely from one, saying, "Listen, kibble. Listen. You have to come with me."

Cayenne is whimpering, "No no no no no no no."

Martin says, "I love you too much to ever let you go. You made a mistake. You maybe forgot that we tried this already." He smiles, falls silent, then gestures, run up against some mute extremity of language. "We tried it and what we found is that we are nothing, apart. There is no going through that again. There just isn't. You have to see that. And these others—" He gestures again. Set pieces. Objects. That is her mistake. To believe in a world outside of him. He takes his last step toward her and pitches out onto his knees and wraps his arms around her, pressing his cheek to her pelvis. Brett and Rilke watch silently, Cayenne closing her eyes. Turtle lifts her arms like a girl waist-deep in cold water. She thinks, kill him. Kill him right now. Do it before he kills you or Cayenne or Jacob or Brett. But she does not have it in her to kill him here on his knees, and she thinks, what would Brett think of you then, what would Cayenne think of you, a murderer, an executioner, and is this where it ends, because, she knows, it doesn't have to. He is talking, at least.

Martin's shoulders jerk. He clenches her, closing his eyes so tightly that the corners crease, and he says, "I love you. Hell." He tightens his grip even more. She doesn't know what to say. She looks over him at Brett in mute appeal, but Brett will not go. Martin's face is furrowed with intensity and Turtle opens her mouth to speak and cannot. "Fuck!" Martin yells. "Fuck! Look at you! Fuck! Fuck!" He pauses, and in the silence he watches her. Then he rises. "Come with me, kibble."

She stands in place.

"Everybody," he says. "Get out."

No one moves.

"Everybody," he says again. "Get **the fuck** out!"

Brett says, "No, man. No, I don't think so."

Martin turns to him. He says, "You're Caroline's boy, right?"

"That's right," Brett says.

"You better go ahead and get the fuck out"— Martin gestures with the gun—"before you get yourself shot."

Brett stands still, his hands up. "I can't. Sorry. She's my friend."

"You and me, kibble. What do you say?"

Turtle spreads her arms, empty, helpless. "Okay."

"Okay?"

"Don't go, Turtle," Brett says. "We aren't letting this asshole take you anywhere."

Martin considers her, one eye squinting more than the other.

"I'll go," she says. She does not know what she

means. She will go with him or she will take him out into the hallway and kill him there. She needs to get him away from Brett and Cayenne.

He weighs her, nods to the shotgun. "Drop it."

She hesitates. She tries to speak. Her voice breaks. She is weighing the chance that she drops the shotgun and he kills all of them.

He turns away from her. He looks at the wall. He looks at the room. He purses his lips into a kind of speculative grimace and runs his hand down his face. He is trying to decide what to do.

She says, "I'll come."

He smirks at her, knowingly, shaking his head, his smirk souring into something hateful, something bitter, jaw-clenching and darkly speculative. He runs his thumb along his lips. He must see some expression in her face then, or he must make some decision.

"Put it down, kibble."

Turtle unslings the shotgun, pitches it to the floor.

Brett steps forward. He says, "You're not taking her anywhere."

Martin ignores him. He's looking at Turtle. He says, "Come on, kibble."

Brett steps between them, puts his hand on Martin's chest. "No," he says, "I won't let—"

Turtle sees Martin's face. She goes for the Sig Sauer. Her right arm isn't working like it should. She bids for the gun desperately, and for one awful moment her shirt is in the way, bunching up over the holster's trigger release, and she can't get the gun up and clear, scrabbling disbelievingly, watching Martin step back to make distance between himself and Brett, Brett's hands up and out, and then the bright muzzle flash. Brett arches forward, stooping, his back bowed out behind and the bullet bellying his shirt like a sail. Martin looks past Brett at Turtle. She sees the second muzzle flash and the bullet hits her like a sledgehammer to the cheek. She falls, seeing stars, blind in the left eye, her face white with pain, lying right on top of her shotgun. Cayenne is screaming, breaking across the carpet toward her. Then Turtle is up and running, the shotgun in her hand. Something hits her low in the back and she sees the mist of blood projected ahead of her onto the wall, the puckered bullet hole appearing at its center, small as a cigarette burn. She crashes through the doorway, and slews down the hall, her mind yellow and green with terror. She casts a look over her shoulder and she sees a flare of light, like someone striking a match, her vision patterning with green and red dots, a splattering of afterimages, and something smacks her just beneath the right shoulder blade. She hears the **pock** of gunfire; it seems smaller and less consequential than it should, and the sound follows after the blow. She falls onto hands and knees out into the kitchen. She grabs at her belly, the hot squirt of blood in her hands. She can hear the **pock pock** of more gunfire, but it is utterly disorienting. She does not know where the bullets are striking or if they are striking her. She cannot draw a deep breath.

She crawls across the kitchen floor, thinking, you have to get up. She is gasping shallowly. Cayenne is pulling on her. Turtle plants her hand in a slick of blood and it goes out from under her. She lies with her face on the granite tile. The girl drags at Turtle's shirt. Turtle can see the shotgun beside her on the floor. She rolls over on her back, pulls her knees up, drags the Sig Sauer out from its holster and brings it up. Her aim is drifting all over the place, her vision swims, her left eye is full of blood and she closes it. She braces her wrists between her thighs just as Martin comes into view. She fires and he dives back behind the wall. She fires through drywall to drive him deeper into the hallway.

Cayenne grabs Turtle by the arm and tries to haul her across the floor and Turtle heaves herself up, boots and hands slipping on the blood-slick tiles, picks up the shotgun, and hobbles toward the door, which opens onto the back deck. Then she stops. She looks at the kitchen counter, and then lurches toward it, supporting herself one-handed along the kitchen island, the other holding on to her stomach like a runner with a stitch, the shotgun slung, the blood glugging out through her squelching fingers. Her shirt is sopping. It makes an ugly smacking sound when it swings into her stomach. She can't take a deep breath.

"We have to go!" Cayenne is screaming. "Turtle! Let's go!"

Turtle pulls the drawer open, and it's right there: lightbulbs, screwdrivers, finishing hammer, nails, duct tape. Blood is falling from her face into the drawer. She keeps blinking it out of her left eye. It is just a scratch, she tells herself. It doesn't feel like a scratch. She pulls her shirt up. It's okay, she's telling herself. All you have to do is do everything right. And that's just fine.

Martin comes around the corner. Turtle lifts up the bloody shotgun one-handed and blows a hole in the wall just as he falls back. He sticks the gun around the corner and fires blindly into the kitchen, hosing the walls with automatic fire, and Turtle aims and fires again. The buckshot goes through the tile, exposing studs and electrical wires, insulation, exits out the wall, and she hears the shattering of the glass case, hears him scrabbling through the glass away from her. She swings the gun up and shoots out the kitchen light. They plunge into darkness. Then Turtle thumbs on the shotgun's weapon-mounted strobe. The room fills with blinding, flickering illumination. It flattens all the shadows into harsh, depthless lines and all color into white sheets of glare. She knows from experience just how hard it is to shoot into that strobe. The weapon light is mounted on the bar-

rel with quick-release tabs and she dismounts it
and rolls it across the kitchen island, ten feet away
from her and aimed at the hallway door.

In the nauseous, flashing light, she hitches her
shirt back up. She can see the wound in her belly.
The blood has sheeted down her stomach and
her jeans are sodden with it and it sloshes in her
boots. She tears off a strip of her shirt, wads it
over the hole, and begins duct-taping over it. She
is lucky Martin is using a short-barreled rifle. By
the look of the exit wound, she's been skewered
right through, the bullet not fragmenting or yaw-
ing at all. With longer barrels, and higher veloci-
ties, those 5.56 bullets can peel apart or tumble.
He's careless, she thinks. He's careless of these
details and he always was. Martin is firing at the
flashlight. Turtle ignores him. The duct tape is not
going to do much good, but it'll do something.
That's not true. Where she's going, it's going to
save her life.

"Turtle!" Cayenne screams.

Turtle ignores her, taping up around her stomach
and up around her chest, a tight, duct-tape girdle.
Something flashes and Turtle looks up. The granite
backsplash beside her ejects and lifts from the wall
in shards. In the strobe there is no movement. Just
single, bright white flashes. He's no longer shooting from the doorway. He's in the adjacent room,
shooting through the wall right beside her. Turtle
dives, bears Cayenne to the ground. Above them,

splinters of tile and glass are constellated in the air. A scroll of particulate grit blooms outward. The girls huddle on the floor behind the island, Cayenne screaming and screaming, face to the tile. The kitchen island isn't actually cover. The 5.56 rounds may be small, no bigger and only slightly heavier than a .22 rimfire, but they'll still go right through it. Turtle sits up, braces herself against the cabinet, and continues wrapping the duct tape around herself. She doesn't want to try firing back at him through the wall. She just doesn't have enough ammunition and she doesn't know who might be in the room with him. Then the firing stops and Turtle hears him drop the magazine, the sound of the new mag loaded into the well, the steel-on-steel sound of the bolt released forward, but something goes wrong. It is a jam. You motherfucker, she thinks, you incompetent fuck. Probably, he'd done a shitty job of retooling the gun for full auto and it's jamming up on him. Cayenne is plastered to the floor, eyes clenched tight, convulsing wordlessly, and clawing at the tile. Turtle grabs her by the hair and heaves her up and the girl seizes Turtle's wrist in both hands and they stagger to the deck door. The strobe destroys all depth perception and so they reel half blind through the room and Turtle fires into the doorframe ahead of them and kicks it open and steps out. More fire searches the kitchen and they pitch out on the deck and crawl awkwardly out toward the stairs. The strobe will hold him for another few seconds. Turtle grabs the railing and drags herself down onto the stairs and they descend into a rocky notch of beach covered in dried bull kelp that cracks hollowly underfoot. A stiff wind comes from the north and it picks up their hair and pulls it in streamers across their faces.

Twenty-nine

TURTLE WALKS WITH DIFFICULTY, HER footsteps wringing water from the wet sand into shining halos. Ahead of her, the river is lined with sleeping geese. There look to be hundreds. Turtle blunders forward, leaning on the girl, lurch and step, lurch and step. The duct tape is squeezing in time to her heartbeat and, she realizes, the roll is still attached to her, hung on a long tail of tape. She runs several more passes around her stomach, tears the roll off and drops it to the sand. She is breathing in quick, hard pants and cannot seem to get enough air.

The bluffs are not high. The river runs beneath them for another twenty-five yards and then the bluffs fall back. Beyond the bluffs, the river's shallow estuary is strewn with driftwood logs, sandbars, and stranded heaps of bull kelp, forty yards to the tide line, where three sea stacks stand in black outline, the breakers shattering white and rolling in across an expanse of beach that spans the horizon from north to south, each wave barreling a freight of water and sand that shakes the air. Above her, Jacob's house, sitting on the corner of the bluffs, overlooks both the river and the beach. Turtle and Cayenne stagger forward, and the flock begins to take flight all around them. Turtle reaches the river's edge and drags the girl forward into the cold water, slogging thigh-deep through a confusion of beating wings, and pitching into the current. Then Turtle lets go and swims hard across the sandy bottom. The river is only six or eight feet deep, but it carries her along with surprising force. She breaks the surface for air once, geese still taking flight all across the river, the house obscured from view, and she dives and swims again. She swims out past the bluffs, reaches a driftwood log that juts from the bank into the water, grabs ahold of it, and comes up behind it. She drags the girl out of the current and into the leaning, chiseled face of the riverbank behind the log.

Forty yards away, Martin comes out onto the deck and pans the weapon light across the beach, the light cutting slant through the river's surface. Dappled reflections carousel across the cliff face.

Turtle and Cayenne lie behind the log, chin-deep in water, sheltered against the sandy bank. He has a small height advantage—the deck is twenty, thirty feet up and overlooks the entire beach.

She has nothing in the shotgun but buckshot. He is right at the limit of her range. If she had a slug, she could reach out to him on those steps and end his life just like that. Her thoughts are coming to her slowly, the edges of her vision closing in, the world hollow and drained of sensation. She grabs the girl and points her downriver and Cayenne shakes her head. It's another twenty or twenty-five yards to where the river meets the ocean. She wants the girl to follow the river to the sea and then strike south along the tide line. It's her best chance. Turtle holds up three fingers— **In three**—looking at the girl meaningfully and the girl shaking her head and Turtle drawing her close and kissing her hair and then pushing her away and both of them breathing ragged and the sound of their breathing seeming magnified by the water and by the chiseled sandbank and Turtle turns and draws the Sig Sauer with water draining from the magazine and from the barrel, lays it across the log, finds the glowing tritium sights, picks out Martin with his light searching the beach, and she fires.

Martin must see her muzzle flash because the weapon light swings across the beach toward her and he begins firing back. Waterspouts jump into the air and flare black and nebulous against the weapon light's sunlike apparition and wood chips geyser from the log and are raptured into the dark. Turtle aims right back into that annihilating glare. The shadows of her gunsights sundial across the gun's slide and across her arm and the Sig Sauer eclipses the light and casts its slim shadow back onto Turtle's right eye, the sights themselves haloed in shining white light, and she pulls the trigger. The light blinks out. Turtle continues firing, minutely attentive to the click of the trigger reset, her vision washed with afterimages. The Sig Sauer locks open and she drops it into the river, the gun hissing and then gone. She closes her eyes, consciousness slippery in her hands, and she thinks, you have to get up, Turtle. You have to get up.

Cayenne is gone. That, at least, had worked. The girl got away. Turtle crawls on elbows and knees through the water along the sandy bank, barely able to remember what she is doing, the river shallowing out around her as it broadens. Ahead of her, a mound of bull kelp lies islanded in the river course. Turtle slithers toward it, belly-down. There is a sandbar here, heaped with kelp and driftwood. She crawls up into kelp. Flies and sand fleas startle up from it around her. It smells of salt and of rot. She is taking fast, uncontrollable gasps, dragging the shotgun on its sling. She lies shaking with cold and with fear. Beside her, a crumpled jellyfish with purple skirts, limbs in ropy tangles, the hollows crawling with sand fleas swollen and magnified by the lenslike flesh. The water is brackish. The river current trades with the waves, changing direction back and forth. The surf rolls on toward her with a cacophonous grind palpable in the water and in the sandy bed below, palpable in her guts, which wallow in their ruptured and mucilaginous sack, each breaking wave sending a swash of water that rises around her and then drains. She lies scooping after oily thoughts like raking through seaweed for eels, thinking, I could close my eyes and this, all of this, would be over. Then she thinks, no, fuck that—you had your chance, you cunt, and you're in it now.

Turtle eases up and looks through the kelp at him. Martin is limping down the beach beside the rivercourse and Turtle experiences a terrible surge of joy. She'd hit him, the fuck, at however many yards, and her with a 9mm and him with the AR-15, on higher ground and with the flashlight blinding her, and she'd hit him. She'd hit the flashlight, too, or else he'd be using it. Come to me, she thinks. Come to me in the dark, you fuck. Come to me and die. She eases into the water, which rises up around her eyes, and she pulls herself deeper into the heavy, oily tangle of kelp.

It takes him a long time to make his way down the beach and she lies unmoving, her heart clenching her whole body with its beat, panting, dizzy, and she thinks, just a little bit longer now, Turtle.

Hold tight to the world and do not let go and do not fuck this up.

Martin is following the river's edge. It must appear to him that there is no hiding on this vast, flat expanse of beach. He stops abreast of where she lies in her kelp heap. He, like her, is waiting for his eyes to adjust to the dark. He watches the river for any movement, peering in the attitude of people who cannot see well in the dark. The gun is up against his shoulder. The shotgun is trapped underneath her. She doesn't want to move to pull it free. She wants him to walk by. She will move if she needs to, but she doesn't like her odds. She wants him to walk past. He keeps looking away toward the river's mouth, where the three islands stand in the surf. Still, he doesn't want to have the kelp heap at his back. Turtle closes her eyes. No, she thinks. He raises the gun and fires, searching the kelp heap with automatic fire, Turtle lying with eyes closed, teeth gritted, the wet smack of the bullets into the kelp, but nothing happens. He doesn't hit her. He stops firing and studies the kelp heap. Then he makes his decision. He swings the gun toward the surf and walks by.

Turtle exhales hard, putting her knuckles to her mouth to keep from sobbing. Then she pulls herself slithering from under the kelp, the sandy shotgun dragging free, and she rises to her feet and limps after him through the shallowing rivercourse, thinking, not much farther, Turtle, all you have to do is keep your feet under you, you bitch. It is lurch and step through the shin-deep water, lurch and step, and it feels like god has taken her by the abdomen and is squeezing her, the beach drained of color, drained of smell and of sound, a black and white sheet, the white of the waves, the silhouettes of the islands, and Martin.

Ahead of her, he approaches a narrow corridor between two islands, cavelike and winding. He thinks she is there, holed up ahead of him. Turtle's vision is tunneling down to a single determined thought. He stands at the margin of the tide, knee-deep in water, facing the ocean. The moon is ahead of him and backlights him. It is touching the horizon's edge. She lifts the shotgun, shedding water from the magazine tube, and does not know if it will fire.

"Daddy," she says softly from behind him, and he swings around and the night dials apart with the helicoptering strobe of the muzzle flash. Turtle pulls the trigger. Her own muzzle flash makes a three-quarter corona of light broken by the silhouette of the shotgun and a great lance of fire reaches out to him and she sees his shape and then darkness. She never sees him fall. The sound of the shotgun rolls across the beach, everything extinguished, gone, the afterimages white and green and red, each retaining the impression of color, but each of them as dark as black. She pitches onto hands and knees and crawls toward him, puts her hand on his leg. His jeans are soaked and crusted with sand and she takes hold of his shoulder and drags him toward her.

His hand, enormous, calloused, covered in sand, clenches at her and his strength is just like she remembers it. She hauls him into her lap and sits stooped over him, hot and alive in the cold water, his labored breathing twinned with a suckering squelch. Turtle puts a hand on his face and holds his jaw. His mouth opens spasmodically, and she thinks he will talk, he will say something now, but he just gasps, sucking air through a pit in his chest, and she covers it with her hand and feels the wound draw flush against her palm, and he drags in a breath. She thinks that he will speak, but he does not speak. She says, "I love you."

His legs kick in the sand, some reflexive twitching motion, and when the wave breaks over them, his body lifts in her arms, the water dragging at their clothes, sucking the sand out from under her, leaving them half buried in the wet dregs. His jaw moves and then he says over and over again, "I— I— I—" but he cannot get past this first word and she can see the enormous tendons of his neck, the grain of the flesh, dark freckles, stubble, snaking veins thick as her fingerprints, the apple of his throat like a hard knot, the two cords that stand out like cables on either side of the hollow, and whatever else he would say is swallowed in the roar of the tide and he wraps his hands around her wrists to fight her and she drives the blade down through the leathery skin. The coarse white strings of tendons flash once and a spume of blood is thrown up and across her face and his back tightens and he arches up, his hips rising off the sand, his trachea gaping black beneath the blade, and then another wave breaks over them and she can feel the hot underwater jets of blood. The blade lodges against some hard knot of bone and she drags the knife forward and back and it breaks through his neck and down into her own thigh and she is sitting now in a hot pool of blood in the slack moment before the wave retreats, the moon shining through the gap between the islands, holding Martin still underwater, his fingers opening and closing convulsively as he struggles. The hot, arterial pumping stirs the surface. She tries to draw the knife from his neck and cannot. She hauls on it, gritting her teeth, and still cannot pull it free. Then the wave retreats and she can see his blood running in great black ropes across the wet sand. She bends over him and he is irretrievably gone. It is his same body in her arms and she takes hold of his flannel shirt, and it is his flannel shirt, his sodden jeans, his boots sticking up out of the sand, but he is gone from her. Cayenne comes toward her from the dark alley between the islands and drapes her arms around Turtle's neck and puts her cheek against Turtle's shoulder and Turtle lets her but will not and cannot take her hands off him. Cayenne pulls at Turtle's shirt and Turtle looks up, out at the beach. The waves fold onto the sand and the moon touches the water's surface, and she thinks, the hell, isn't that something.

Thirty

TURTLE SITS ON THE EDGE OF A RAISED garden bed, the forest quiet around her, the redwoods eighteen to thirty-six inches through the centers, second growth from the burls of huge, duff-filled stumps, the biggest of which were long ago burned to ash-scaled cauldrons fifteen feet across. Indian pipe, sword fern, and madrone grow at the edge of the clearing. Above it sits Anna's cottage, big south-facing windows, homemade stained glass in the kitchen and a dream catcher in the second-story bedroom, roof covered in solar panels, the building and land inherited from Anna's grandmother. The forest has been crowding in closer and darker since the house was built.

Sitting on the deck's balustrade, Anna's cat, Zaki, looks down at Turtle and lids and opens her pale blue eyes approvingly.

Turtle digs her gloved hand into the soil of the raised bed, rich and black from a recent rain. She doesn't have to dig far before she finds the roots. She gets down on all fours. The bed is on six-inch concrete risers. A crooked finger of feeder roots has climbed out of the earth, following the trail of the dripping water, crossed the open gap between the earth and the bed, and snuck in through one of the drainage holes.

Turtle began gardening eight months ago, hampered in every movement by pain and by her ileostomy bag. One of the bullets took her low in the back, passed between two intercostal arteries, perforated her jejunum, and exited out her lower left side, another scraped her left cheekbone, and the third glanced off her seventh rib on the right side, just below the scapula. The rib punctured the pleural sac around her lungs, and as that pleural space filled with air, her right lung began to collapse. "Just a small pneumothorax," Dr. Russell had said, thumb and forefinger minutely apart to indicate its size. "Just a **small** one." Dr. Russell was a thin man, with pale skin blotched with blemishes, balding, quiet and careful. He'd lean in while he talked, pinching thumb and forefinger together as if capturing the texture of her voice, and he'd ask again, "Why'd you think to tape up like that, Turtle?" and Turtle would shake her head, because she didn't know, and he'd smile and lean back. He was excited by her case and by her injuries, which Turtle liked. He loved this part of his job, she could tell. The contents of her small intestine had spilled into her abdominal cavity and after the first stabilizing operation, there had been two major surgical procedures to clean out infection. If her duct-tape bandage hadn't held, Turtle might not have survived at all. Seawater, Dr. Russell liked to say, is nasty stuff. Her survival amazed him.

The surgeons brought a loop of gut up to the skin on her right side, above her groin, which made a puckering red asshole in her hip, and for six months, she shit out of that, or really, dibbled through it. A flexible adhesive patch with a gasket was placed over the stoma, and the ostomy pouches snapped onto it. Turtle would wake up in the middle of the night clawing at the flange where the pouch met the baseplate, and one night she'd almost succeeded in pulling it off, woke up just in time and staggered out to the bathroom and stood at the sink, imagining herself yarding out a foot of pink intestine through a keyhole in her side, stood clutching the bathroom counter, panting with pain, looking in the mirror and shaking her head, and she'd thought, Martin tried to tell you, he tried to tell you that one day you would need to be more than just a scared little bitch with good aim, that one day you would need to be absolute in your conviction, that you would need to fight like a fucking angel, fallen to fucking earth, with your heart absolute, and you never got there. You were full of hesitation and prevarication right down to the end. She stood at the sink thinking, you were never enough and you never will be enough. That day she'd waited for Anna to come home, and when Anna opened her car door, Turtle said, "I want to make a garden," and Anna had stood, holding her bankers box of tests to grade, slack with exhaustion, leaning back against the Saturn, and then she'd put the box back inside and Turtle had gotten in the passenger door and closed it with the bungee cord.

Together, they'd lifted redwood two-by-twelve boards out in Rossi's lumberyard and inspected them for knots and turned them on edge to look for warp, and set aside the boards that they liked, and then a big-bellied man with jeans and a flannel shirt and measuring-tape suspenders cut the boards into eight-foot and four-foot lengths, and still looking at Turtle, he'd taken off his gloves, slapping them into his left palm, and he'd extended his right hand. The man's ungloved hand was very large, and he gripped hers firmly, almost painfully.

They went inside to the hardware desk to pay for the boards and for the galvanized nails and for the potting soil they'd purchased and there had been a woman behind the desk with her hands planted on the counter, chewing gum impressively, bleached blond with dark brown roots and wearing a fluorescent orange vest. CINDY, her name tag read. She stared at them. Anna had toted up their board feet in a small notepad she carried in her back pocket, carried everywhere because she was making notes for a novel she meant to write and never knew when an idea would come. Taking out the notebook now, she said, "Eight twelve-foot redwood two-by-twelves."

"Uh-huh," the woman said, punching it in.

"Eight bags premium potting soil."

"Uh-huh," the woman said.

"One pound galvanized nails."

"Uh-huh," the woman said, and the way she said it made Anna look up at her, every time, curious if the woman was hostile.

"That's it," Anna said.

"Uh-huh," the woman said. She put her hands down on the counter and leaned forward.

"Well," Anna said, taking out her wallet, "how much do I owe you?"

"No charge," the woman said.

"No charge?" Anna repeated.

"Uh-huh," the woman said.

"For the redwood boards?"

"Uh-huh," the woman said. There was nothing inviting or kind about the way she said it.

"I'd like to pay," Anna said. She held her wallet open in her hands.

"Uh-huh," the woman said, and nodded.

"So how much do I owe you?"

"No charge," the woman said.

"I don't understand."

"Uh-huh," the woman said.

"You can see that I **want to pay**, right?"

"Uh-huh," the woman said.

"So," Anna said, "I insist. How much do I owe you?"

The woman leaned her bulk forward onto the counter. Propped her elbows up. She was broad through the shoulders. Her cleavage was leathery red and suntanned. She said, "This is still a small town. It don't always feel like it, but it is. You aren't paying for that lumber."

"Well, thank you," Anna said.

"Nuh-uh," the woman said, "don't thank me. She'll need more soil than that and it won't all be free."

"Well, thanks anyway," Anna said.

Cindy watched Turtle and Anna on their way out the door. Anna just shook her head.

They'd arrived at North Star nursery as it was closing. The place was locked up and a young man in a green sweater and jeans and muddy work boots was walking to his truck when they pulled in. He watched them and then approached Anna's Saturn as she parked and got out. "Anna?" he'd said, and Anna had said, "Tim," and they'd hugged and then he looked at Turtle and he said,

"So this is her," and Turtle looked out west, to the clouds above the ocean. She wondered where Cayenne was right now, and if she was safe. The girl had gone to live with her aunt. Turtle had spoken to the woman on the phone, had said, "I want to talk to that girl every week and I want to hear in her fucking voice that she is okay, and I will know if she isn't," and the woman had paused and then she'd said "All right . . ." said it mockingly and sullenly both, dragging the word out with a passive-aggressive resignation, and there was something muted and superior at the end there, as if she thought Turtle were ridiculous. It was just the way Cayenne had said it, when the girl had been at her most sullen, and the shock of recognition had gone right through Turtle, had taken her right back to standing above the girl, with Cayenne lying on the floor reading, trying to get her to go out looking for scorpions. She knew that it was a bad home the girl was growing up in, but what could she do. It was not as if Cayenne had been safe with her.

Tim let them back into the nursery, and Turtle took a little red wagon and dragged it around while Tim and Anna stood beside the gate, talking. The nursery had a fenced yard with slat-topped tables covered in black plastic seeding trays and containers. It was early evening and the sky was purple. Turtle rolled her little red wagon through the nursery's gravel walkways. Tim wanted to come over and talk to her, it was in his posture, but he stood with Anna by the fence and watched. People expected that she would not like to talk to men, but that wasn't true. She lifted the black plastic trays of sugar pod snow peas, loving their rich green leaves, the black soil. Holding them to her chest and looking over the tables and tables of plants, it felt like anything was possible. There was an entire table of lettuces in four-cell packs, drunken woman frizzy-headed lettuce, butter-crunch, mascara, flashy butter oak. She wanted kale and chard and the sugar snaps and garlic and artichokes and she wanted beds of strawberries. She wanted it all. It was mid-February and still cold, but Anna thought you could plant lettuce year-round where she lived. Artichokes or snow peas would do well. Any of the crucifers. Better to wait if she wanted to plant tomatoes.

They paid for the plants inside, Tim squinting over Turtle's red wagon and, with difficulty, keying the numbers into a register, sometimes consulting sheets of laminated paper. Turtle had a scar across her left cheek. A thick keel of numb tissue, and she touched it absently when she was speculative. There were decorative plants and water features inside, but all the pumps and lights were off. Anna and Turtle stood together by the register. On the counter in front of them was a black-and-white flyer of Turtle walking out of the waves, leaning on Cayenne and holding the shotgun. Turtle did not remember walking off the beach.

This one read SUPPORT TURTLE ALVESTON. The picture was taken by one of the paramedics. The poster
was curling, stained by some freshly watered plant
that had dripped down the counter. She had been
shot, people liked to tell her, three times, saved
everybody at the house that night, and walked off
the beach of her own power. She was a hero. They
loved that about her. You **walked** off that beach,
people told her, doctors, nurses, techs, strangers.
Brett, when he'd visited her, had said it. **You're
a hero, Turtle.** In his hospital gown, sitting in a
wheelchair with the nurse there. He'd been shot
in the chest. But unlike her own pneumothorax,
his had been serious. The right lung had entirely
collapsed and there had been sucking wounds on
both sides. "You're like—a **hero**," Brett had said.
"I mean, **dude**—how were you still on your feet? I
don't know how you walked off that beach." Smiling at her, marveling. She'd missed this. She'd
missed him. He said, "When the end comes, you
come get me. You come get me, okay?"

"Okay," Turtle said. She was lying in bed, the
chest tube taped to her side, the tubes dribbling
serosanguineous fluid. "Okay. I'll come get you."
She didn't think any of it was true. She wanted
to know what his long-term prognosis was. How
his life would be affected. She wasn't a hero.
She'd failed Cayenne, failed herself, failed Martin,
she'd endangered everybody there, failed again
and again, blundering from room to room mak-

ing one stupid mistake after another, trying and failing to control a situation that could not be controlled, and she didn't remember walking off the beach, and all for what, a life without him that she did not want, that she did not understand. If they knew how she'd kicked open the door and found him with Cayenne and how she'd had the chance to end it before it ever came to anything, how she hadn't pulled the trigger. She'd looked at Brett, unable to explain any of it. His life would never be the same. Not ever. Train yourself, Martin had said, to an absolute singularity of purpose, and she hadn't done it.

"All right," Tim said. "That will be twenty-two dollars."

Anna said, "Really? That seems a little low."

"Does it?" he said, looking at the plants.

She began the garden that same night, running into the house and plugging in the battery charger for Anna's cordless drill. Anna had a whole tool set that she had bought when she first decided she would live alone in Comptche, but she had never used it because she was afraid of the power tools. She said, "You're going to use the drill?" and Turtle nodded, pulling Carhartts over her Smartwool long underwear, and Anna said, "Do you know how?" and Turtle nodded, and Anna said, "You'll be careful?" and Turtle said, "I'll be careful," and Anna said, "You won't drill a hole through your finger or anything?" and Turtle said, "No, I will not do that." She wore a headlamp and her wool sweater and her old jungle boots, and she looked at Anna dead-on and guileless because Anna was embarrassed and anxious, and Turtle wanted to show Anna that she could ask whatever question she wanted.

"Okay," Anna said a little bashfully. "Okay."

Turtle had told Dr. Russell about the surgery they'd done on Cayenne's finger, drawing it out on a sheet of paper. Dr. Russell said that the amputation made sense in a sterile environment, but that it made no sense to do it on your living room floor. Though it was, he said, an operation he performed all the time, it wasn't necessary. The skin would epithelialize—it would grow back over the tip of the finger if you just kept changing the dressings. And when Turtle said that they'd gone past the knuckle, had clipped back the next bone, Dr. Russell had paused, very fractionally, tilting his head to the side, and said, "Well—maybe that made sense in the situation," and Turtle understood what he wasn't saying. She'd clipped out the next bone herself, and Martin had perhaps contrived the need for that.

Turtle carried the boards down the hillside, set them up in the clearing, and knelt in the wet leaf litter to predrill the holes. What once would've been a single night's work for her was now a grueling multiday project. Even walking down the hill had her grimacing from the pain in her guts. Dr.

Russell had said that the pain might wax and wane, but she would very likely have chronic pain for the rest of her life, and she could manage it with drugs or not. Turtle chose not. The ileostomy bag was a sweaty, plasticky presence fixed to her side. She braced the eight-foot board between her legs and, holding the four-footer against it, screwed them together, her hair falling into her face, grinning to herself, her whole body aching just from the effort of keeping the drill steady.

The next day, she carted each fifty-pound bag of topsoil down in the wheelbarrow, sweating and swearing and grinning, and she threw each in turn down onto the leaf litter beside her boards and stood wiping her face with the back of her hand and grinning, happier than she had been in months, and then she would lie down in the wheelbarrow and stare up at the sky and just breathe. Way up above her, the tips of the redwoods swung in the breeze and they were a delicate green and Turtle was alive. Preposterously alive, for how many mistakes she had made.

She cut the bags open and filled her beds with soil and then she dug out the holes with her bare hands, each seedling a handful of black earth and a coil of white roots. When she awoke the next day and cooked her oatmeal and came down holding the oatmeal in its warm pottery bowl with its dollop of Cinnamon Bear honey on top, the mist was rising off the forest floor, and it was so, so good.

Then the next day, she came out in the morning to find that the deer had cropped everything but the squash down to stubs. She'd stood there in her Smartwool tights and large pj T-shirt and the wool sweater, and she'd wondered how it would've been if she hadn't gone to Jacob's house, had just kept driving, knowing that Martin had Jacob's address, and that Martin was going there whether she went there or not, and she thinks, if he had gotten there, and Grandpa's truck wasn't there—what would he have done? Would he have kept driving? Or would he have parked and walked up the deck kicking aside red Solo cups? Sometimes she thinks that if she had just kept driving, it would've been okay. She can't get any clear picture of him, not of his face, just of his back, broad, shadowed. She had expected him to be there when she woke up in the hospital. It was just after the first surgery. Anna was there, looking ravaged, red with crying, and Jacob was there, reading. Martin wasn't there and she had thought, he is gonna be so fucking mad. Then she remembered.

After the deer got into the garden, she'd gone back to the hardware store and purchased two rolls of eight-foot chicken wire and fence posts and a fence-post driver, and because the posts and the rolls of wire did not fit in the Saturn, and because Turtle couldn't carry any of it, she'd paid to have it delivered and then she'd tried to do all the work herself, digging an eighteen-inch trench all the way around the garden, but she'd found that she couldn't lift the post hole driver, and so Jepson and Athena, Sarah's children from next door, came over to help her pound them in, and to stretch the wire from post to post. They were a year apart, both in high school, and careful of her. She repurchased her plants from Tim at North Star nursery and replanted them and she built a bamboo trellis for her snow peas and she had been so **proud**, knotting the trellis with twine, thinking how the peas would grow up over it, and then she'd come out to find that the raccoons had collapsed the trellising and laid their oily, stinking black shits all over the beds and that ravens had eaten the seedlings and the starlings were picking apart the twine for nesting material, and Turtle kept on, replanting and crossing her fingers, and slowly, the plants began to survive.

Then one morning Turtle came out to the garden and there was a fawn trapped inside the fence. The doe waited skittish at the edge of the clearing, dashing away and coming back, and the fawn leapt against the fence again and again without clearing it, leapt against it until the fence post leaned out and she tangled a leg in the wire and began kicking frantically, trapped. Turtle went to the toolshed and retrieved her wire cutters and a length of rope. She tied a lark's head around the two back legs, then wrapped the legs with four more coils and tied them off with another lark's head across the strands, a gentle knot, but one that kept the fawn from kicking. Then she took the struggling, panting creature in her embrace, the fawn surprisingly warm, small as a dog, heart hammering beneath heaving ribs, wrapped one arm around the fawn's gasping throat, and with the other hand worked the wire cutters, breathing onto the fawn's red-brown fur, smelling her wild, musty scent, and finally she lifted and carried the fawn out of the garden, set her down, and untied her legs. The fawn could not walk. She could only stand and collapse, stand and collapse. Turtle left her there that night, curled nose to tail, and when Turtle came out in the morning, the fawn was still there and the doe was gone. Turtle stood with the fawn curled at her feet. Quivers chased themselves down the small flanks. Turtle sat down beside her and thought, get up, goddamn it, but the fawn would not rise.

That night, Turtle took the head off the pick mattock and walked out with just the haft. The fawn was again curled head to tail, now shaking all over, blowing snot. She turned and looked at Turtle with one large eye, so dark it was almost black except for the bottom crescent of the brown iris, and Turtle killed her in a single downward stroke. Then she sat down on the duff, splay-legged, still holding the pick mattock haft, and she looked at the small corpse and did not know what to do, and if she knew, she didn't know if she could carry it through. She pitched a line over a madrone trunk, hauled the child-sized corpse into the tree, drew her belt knife, and stood shaking all over, dropped the knife and sat down and stood up, walked away and came back and picked up the knife and cut the fawn from asshole to throat, and it was as bad as she thought it would be, the feel of the flesh beneath the knife, and she walked away and stood leaning over and threw up into the huckleberries, and then she opened the leathery skin and pulled out the bloody entrails and didn't stop, and didn't think about it. She cut the fawn into steaks, and put them into the freezer and stood in the kitchen afterward, washing her hands in the sink. With Athena's help she tore out the fence and carried the rolled-up wire and posts to the shed.

Turtle walked the North Star aisles on shady, foggy spring days bundled up in wool with her hands tucked into her armpits, moving among the now familiar tables and picking up plants to put in her red wagon, something that had never lost its wonderfulness and which was slowly replacing the pleasures of novelty with the pleasures of the familiar, and she kept searching on the clear, warm days of summer, dressed in short sleeves and Carhartts, with Anna waiting in a deck chair reading **The Captive & The Fugitive**, part of her project of "Big Reads" that had eluded her through college, when she'd mostly been busy, she said, with white-water kayaking and with boys. She'd read

War and Peace, **Moby-Dick**, **Infinite Jest**, **The Brothers Karamazov**, and she'd started Marcel Proust's **In Search of Lost Time**. Anna had no patience for the writers she called the "dude boys," which meant Hemingway and Faulkner. Abutting the nursery, there was a kind of slough with a small green island and murky water covered in weeds and beyond that a tangle of trees, and sometimes Turtle would draw her red wagon of plants up to the edge of the nursery's gate and stand looking out at the wild, run-down plot of woods and her whole body would fill with a feeling that she could not name, her dread and her wonder mixed with the sunshine and the aisles of plants and the crunch of the gravel, with her new life here among these people, with Anna sitting in her deck chair reading Proust.

When Anna was too overworked, Turtle would walk through the redwoods to Sarah's house, which she and her husband had built in the late seventies, and knock on the door and Sarah would let her in and Turtle would sit at the counter in the dark kitchen—Sarah's house was also off the grid, and they used as little electricity as they could—and Turtle would crack walnuts from a large woven seaweed basket and Sarah would talk to her about the Mendocino school board or about the runoff election for the vacant position on the Mendocino water board, and Turtle would listen without talking, just watching the way the woman tromped around her home, energetic, unstoppable, with her shock of prematurely white hair and her replaced hip, and when Sarah was done cleaning, or baking, she would lean on the counter and say, "Well, honey, you probably want to go to the nursery," and Turtle would nod and they'd get into the car and Sarah would drive them into Fort Bragg and stand beside the gate talking to anyone she met about the Mendocino school board, or about global warming, or about how to run your house off solar, all with a kind of unstoppable vigor, and Turtle would pull her red wagon down the aisles of plants and look at them, and think, yes, yes.

Sometimes watching Sarah cross-armed and holding forth, or watching Anna turning a page, Turtle felt that she was looking up at these people through a tossing hoop of quicksilver water, and all she wanted in the world was to crawl up through it and she did not know how. She would wake in her little lofted bedroom in the middle of the night and feel her way along the window in disbelief, stunned, not understanding and thinking, this is not my bedroom, and then she would think, he is coming for Cayenne, I have to get to her, I have to find her, and Jacob, and Brett, and she'd feel her way along the wall, forgetting the flashlights Anna put by her bed, blind with panic and thinking, I have to get out of here, they need me, they need me, and trying to keep it together as she groped along the paneling for anything familiar, telling herself this, keep it together, Turtle, keep it together, and then she would find the light switch and sit crouched against the wall sobbing and she would be unable to get to sleep, panting and terrified and thinking, what is wrong with you, why are you afraid, you are in Comptche, you are at Anna's, and you are safe, and Cayenne is back in Yakima with her aunt, and Brett is not far from here, he is on Flynn Creek Road with Caroline, and Jacob is in Ten Mile, asleep in his mahogany sleigh bed with the sound of the estuary coming in through his windows, and you are here, trying to get better. Martin is dead and you are alive. During the day, she feels very far from these nighttime terrors, she feels very far away from it and from any belief that Martin might still be alive, and yet she isn't in Mendocino, either, isn't on Buckhorn Hill, isn't fully back home, not yet, and the closest she gets to it is with the plants in their plastic trays, and when she cuts them out of the plastic and the soil is loose about the tender coil of white roots.

Six months after she'd been released from the hospital, and two months since she'd started her garden, Turtle had the surgery to reverse the ileostomy. The doctors felt that they could try reconnecting Turtle's intestines, and because she was young, and because she was strong, they had high hopes that it would take, and it did. Dr. Russell reminded her to chew her food. "Chew and chew

and **chew**," he said, sitting by her bed and looking at her in that wondering way he had, impressed
and concerned and a little delighted, rubbing
thumb and forefinger together, and finally saying, "Well, Turtle, I'd love to see you again, but I'd
hate to see you back **here**," and she returned from
Stanford University's pediatric hospital to find
that everything was dead and the soil was choked
solid with redwood roots. It had been happening
for months, but it must have come on very fast
at the end. She dismantled the planters, and the
earth in the beds had been so knitted with roots
that it held its shape, even after the boards were
removed, and Turtle had to chop it up with a pick
mattock. The soil and compost, yards and yards of
it, had not been salvageable.

Her solution had been to rebuild the planters on
raised concrete slabs with augered drain holes. She'd
built the molds, mixed and poured the concrete,
put hardware cloth over the drains, and crocked
the bottoms of the beds. Then she'd had soil
trucked in at seventy dollars a yard plus sixty dollars delivery, which she then had to wheelbarrow
from its delivery heap into her new planters. She'd
been so sure that it would work this time. She was
building her little garden and this would be it, and
for a while, it was.

Tuesday was Turtle's day in town. She would
drive in with Anna at 4:30 in the morning, when

Anna liked to get out onto the beach, and Turtle would go in to Lipinski's Juice Joint while Anna surfed, and there she would drink green tea and sit at a funky, hand-painted wooden table, and then at 8:00 she would walk to the Independent Study office, a low redwood building on a rarely visited part of the school, across the field from the auditorium. There she met with Ted Holloway, a quiet guy who grew his own wheat and oats and ground them himself and baked his own bread. He was patient and soft-spoken. Turtle would sit with him in his office, which looked out at the always vacant, always gopher-warrened, always rain-sodden field and they would talk and go over her workbooks and he would assess her progress. He treated her like she was anybody else, and she liked that, wanted to be taken like she was. She and Ted met every Tuesday from 8:00 until 9:00, but their conversations often went on much longer. Turtle was careful to leave before 11:30, because Jacob often came over at lunch to work on his Independent Study Attic Greek, and she did not want to meet him and she didn't want him to see her. She didn't know what she was afraid of, couldn't articulate it and couldn't think about it, not closely, and still the thought of seeing him was unbearable, the thought of all she could lose, unbearable, because she felt she had lost him already, had lost so much and wouldn't know what it would look like for Jacob to keep his faith in her, and she thinks, to see Jacob would just make it sure, how much she had lost.

For Ted's birthday, she brought him a Country Living grain mill with stone burrs. It was in the basement of her house, and she was not using it, and she liked her talks with him. The mill was expensive, and at first he refused to accept it, but in the end, he took it. After her meeting with Ted, she had a four-hour private session of Shotokan karate at a dojo in town and from there, Turtle would walk up Little Lake and meet Anna at her car. All the while, her squash plants grew enormous and prehistoric-looking, thick green star-shaped stalks covered in bristly hairs.

Now, in the clearing, Turtle begins to shovel dirt out of the ruined planter onto the tarp. She works steadily without stopping and she is careful with the soil and careful not to scar the insides of the planter. The deeper she goes, the more roots she finds. Six inches down, she has to use the adze. The roots have spread artery-like across the bottom of the planter. After the first, unraised planters had succumbed, Turtle had been so sure, so certain that raising the planters off the ground would work. The concrete slabs had seemed like such a solid, permanent solution. Now she walks to the next planter, gets on her knees, and looks beneath it. She can see a forest of roots heaved up from the earth, long brown trunks snaking through the drain holes, chinking every gap. She sits down, leans against the side of the bed. Shit, she thinks. The beds are a loss. They all need to be emptied and replanted and she will need to check each planter for roots from now on. She just wants the garden to work. She just wants to build a garden and water it and have everything grow and everything stay alive and she does not want to feel besieged. She wants a solution that feels like a solution, a solution that will stick. This is all she wants. She wants garden beds in an unfenced sunny plot near the cottage and she would like to plant peas, squash, green beans, garlic, onions, potatoes, lettuce, and artichokes.

Thirty-one

ON THE FENCE POST, ZAKI TURNS HER head and Turtle looks up and hears it, the rusty screel of the Forest Service gate. Then the Saturn coming down the rutted road past the pump house. Turtle stands up and walks to the driveway to meet Anna, and Anna gets out, exhausted, and leans against the car and rubs her eyes with an unpleasant squelching noise. Strands of hair hang in front of her face and she purses her lips and blows the errant strands away. Turtle smiles for her, also tiredly, and opens the back door and takes out a bankers box of papers. Tonight is the homecoming dance, almost the one-year anniversary of the shooting, and Turtle knows Mendocino will be filled with high school students getting ready. Anna tilts her head toward the house, and they go on together. In the front yard, there is a deck with a small outdoor shower and an awning where surfboards and kayaks lean up against the wall. Turtle puts the bankers box on her hip and opens the front door for Anna, and then carries the box in through the living room with its big south-facing windows and into the office. The walls are painted blue with sponged-on clouds and there is a hobbit chair with a sheepskin throw and a big oak desk, a **SurfGirl** calendar on the wall. Turtle sets the box down and comes out into the living room. Anna is lying on the green velvet couch as if thrown there, and she gives Turtle a deeply humorous, exhausted look. Zaki bolts in with the flip-flap of the cat door and scurries across the room and takes her position on the corner of the couch. She looks from one to the other of them and then lids her eyes approvingly.

"Dinner?" Turtle says. She has a throaty voice.

"Dinner," Anna says.

Turtle goes into the kitchen and turns on the avocado-colored gas range, which clicks several times before sparking to life. She sets some quinoa to cooking before starting a skillet with butternut squash and olive oil. She stands watching the squash griddle. She breaks open a pomegranate and when she runs the water to fill a basin, she hears Zaki, who is for whatever reason fascinated by water, leap off the couch and come first clicking across the tile, then fishtailing around the corner, a sound like **gallop gallop gallop— Screeeeeeeeech!—gallop gallop gallop**.

Zaki vaults up onto the counter and wraps her tail around her feet and stares at the running water. Turtle submerges a colander in the basin and begins breaking the ruby-red pomegranate rind and the heavy white pith apart with her hands. Zaki yawns hugely and drops off the counter and parades away, tail upright, the very end flicking this way and that. From the other room, Anna sighs. Then sighs again and gets up and pads into the kitchen and pulls up a screw-top five-gallon bucket of brown rice and sits on it. They buy their food in bulk and use the three- and five-gallon buckets like furniture. Turtle gets Anna out an Atrea Old Soul Red, pours her a glass, and Anna takes it and smiles. She swirls her wine, and Turtle stirs the skillet, cuts up kale, and measures out handfuls of pumpkin seeds.

Anna says, "So how did your day go?"

Turtle looks down into the frying pan and then chews on her lip and says, "The roots are into one of the planters."

"But they're on risers," Anna says.

"Yeah."

"Oh, baby," Anna says.

"I don't know what to do," Turtle says. She is beginning to cry and flushes with annoyance. Anything can make her cry now. A week ago, she'd been in the living room doing her independent study reading when Anna screamed from the shower. The blood had drained out of Turtle, run out of her face and out of her guts and down to her feet and left her cold and, somehow, with no memory of crossing the intervening space, Turtle had been at the door and the door had been locked, and Anna had yelled from the other side, "Stop! Turtle, it's fine! It's fine!" and Turtle had stepped back and thought, you have to get through this door, and the doorjamb tore away and then she was in the steam-filled bathroom, Anna leaning around the shower curtain saying, "Turtle, it was just a spider. It was just a spider, it startled me," and Turtle had leaned back against the wall and cried then, too, her heart hammering and hammering, and Anna had come out of the shower, dripping everywhere, and she'd knelt down beside Turtle and put her head against Turtle's head and said over and over again, "It's okay, Turtle. It's okay. Nobody's going to hurt you," and Turtle had been unable to say anything, couldn't even say what she was worried about, had wanted to say, I know, I know nobody's going to hurt me, but she'd been unable to stop crying.

Now, in the kitchen, Anna takes Turtle in her arms and knocks her forehead against Turtle's and she says, "Turtle, we'll figure it out. We'll figure it out, okay? I'm sorry about the garden bed, but there's a solution, and this one, this one is easy." Turtle is already shaking her head, grinding against Anna's forehead, saying, "There's no solution. There's no solution. How can you say that?" It feels like Anna is lying to her, because how can Anna, who has seen Turtle's life, how can she say that things will work out? The truth is that things do not work out, that there are no solutions, and you can go a year, a whole year, and be no better, no more healed, maybe even worse, be so skittish that if you're walking down the street with Anna, and if someone opens a car door and gets out and slams the door you turn around, honest-to-god ready to kill them, turn around so fast that Anna, who knows what is happening, cannot even open her mouth in time and then you're standing there, crying, and there's some guy in a leather jacket and a fedora getting out of his Volkswagen Rabbit staring at you like, **is this girl all right?** and you want to be like, **this girl is not all right, this girl will never be all right.**

Turtle just wants the garden to work. She gave Jacob a year. They'd moved her from the ICU to a children's surgical unit, and when the swelling in her damaged vocal cords subsided, she told him in her harsh rasp of a voice that she didn't want to see him for a year. She didn't want him to see her broken and useless, gutted, lying in her hospital gown draining septic filth out through long, clear, bundled tubes into graduated plastic bags and collection chambers. She didn't want to yield to circumstance. She didn't want to talk to him or see him or think about him, and after a year he could come back, and if you picked the homecoming dance as your anniversary, today **was** a year, and if you picked the calendar date, he had two days, and if you picked the date she'd had the conversation with him—he had longer yet, and she wishes she'd been more specific, but it hadn't felt right, exactly, to hammer out the details. It doesn't matter, though, because she is sure that he will not come, and if you really wondered if people were for real when they said that you would be **all right**, the proof would be if Jacob came back, if Jacob thought you were going to be all right, and more than needing him to come back, she needs his faith in her.

Turtle slides down the fridge to the floor and the two of them sit together in the cramped little kitchen, the windowsills lined with mason jars full of sprouts and Turtle sobbing and snotting all over while Anna holds her and says, "Turtle, I'm sorry that the roots are into the bed. That's frustrating." Turtle cries harder because she just wants to have a plot of good earth where she can grow things, where she can dig out the weeds and let peas tangle up her lattices and let squash grow huge and sprawling, and it isn't working. Other people can do it, so why not her? The deer. The raccoons. The ravens, the starlings, the earwigs, the banana slugs, and the roots itching their way up through the planter bottoms. She doesn't want to be fighting a losing battle against everything here, against **everything**, and she hates herself, hates the whiny, ineffective person she has become, hates how wounded she is, deeply and terribly wounded, and how long that road home is going to be.

"Turtle," Anna says, "I'm sorry, but I'm going to have to go."

"What?" Turtle says, looking up. She can hear the kale in the skillet frying. "What?"

"We need another chaperone for the dance. A couple of the teachers have the flu and I've got to go down and chaperone the dance."

"What?" Turtle says, disbelieving. "No."

"I have to," Anna says. "You'll be all right here, tonight?"

"What?" Turtle says. "I don't want to be here."

Anna sits back and purses her lips. It is the look she gives Turtle when she has to make another concession she's willing to make but didn't expect, and Turtle can see that Anna is going to give in, going to call someone and say that she just can't do it, Turtle needs her here, Turtle just can't be alone tonight, and Turtle begins to shake her head because she **hates** that this is who she is to Anna.

"No, you should go. You should."

"I'll stay here, Turtle. If you need me to."

"No, it's fine," Turtle says.

"They **really do** need another chaperone for the dance," Anna says.

"But you're so tired," Turtle says. They sit together on the floor, knee to knee, head to head, and Turtle gets up. Much of the kale has burned and she picks out the worst bits. The pumpkin seeds, too, are more charred than she wants them. She takes down Anna's hand-thrown pottery bowls, dishes up the quinoa and kale and squash, the charred pumpkin seeds and red pomegranate, and they sit and eat on the kitchen floor, backs against the cabinets, and Turtle has to remind herself that he is not here, that bullets will not come through the walls, that the house will remain quiet moment after moment. She picks at her stir-fry with chopsticks. Beside her, legs akimbo, Anna says, "I really shouldn't leave, should I? That's a shitty thing to do, Turtle, I'm sorry. I just— I wasn't thinking."

"No," Turtle says. "You should go. I'm going to be okay."

Anna leans her head back against the cabinets. She turns and looks at Turtle and smiles at her and laughs and Turtle laughs and Anna says, "Look at us here. This is a little sad, Turtle."

Turtle says, "If I wanted to go to the dance, could I?"

Anna's face quirks as if trying out a number of expressions and she says, "Yeah, I guess you could if you wanted to. But, Turtle—"

Turtle says, "I know."

"The music—" Anna says.

"Yeah."

"It's gonna be **really** loud."

"You're right."

Anna knocks the back of her head against a cabinet in frustration. She sits looking up at the window above them with its rack of mason jar sprouts. The tops of the lids have been replaced with screens. The sprouts grow in a tangle. It is Turtle's job to wash and untangle them, twice a day.

"There will be a lot of people there," Anna says.

"Maybe another day," Turtle says.

Anna nods. "Maybe another day."

"We have some Netflix movies," Anna says.

"Oh. What?" Turtle says.

"I'm not sure."

"I'll look."

"No, I'll get it."

They both sit on the kitchen floor. Anna takes a drink of her wine and sets it aside and sets her bowl aside as if she is about to get up and go look at the Netflix movies, but she does not get up.

Turtle says, "If I went to the dance, though, and I couldn't do it, I could just get your keys and go wait in the car."

Anna hesitates. She says, "I think it was, like, **The Philadelphia Story** or something. Does that sound right?"

"I don't know what that is," Turtle says.

"I wish you'd been able to meet my grandmother. I wish she was here."

"I wish so, too."

"I bet she would've known how to garden out here."

"I could, though, right?" Turtle says. "I could go, and if it was too much, I could wait in the car."

"I don't think waiting in the car is a good idea, Turtle. I think if you go and it's bad—I don't think you're going to want to wait in a dark car outside a party. I don't know if that's a good idea. That might be triggering."

"I know," Turtle says.

"Another day," Anna says.

"Another day," Turtle says, and nods.

"Just tuck in and watch some movies."

"What if it never gets easier?"

"It will."

"What if it doesn't?"

Anna turns her head, still leaning it against the cupboards. She says, "Turtle. I'm so sorry. I'm so sorry for what happened. I wish I'd known. Or done something."

"No," Turtle says, because they've been over this before and it does no good. Anna's guilt for what happened is, to Turtle, exhausting and misplaced.

"God," Anna says, "I wish. I wish so bad."

"There was nothing you could do."

"That isn't true," Anna says.

"It is," Turtle says.

"I fucked up," Anna says. "I knew. I had no proof, but I knew and I fucked up. I dropped the ball. And I wish it hadn't happened. And I believe, Turtle, that you're going to be all right. And the problem is that you want to be all right **now**. We'll get there, but tonight . . ." She blows air out of her pursed lips. "It's just not the night."

"Yeah," Turtle says.

"Is that okay? Are you okay with that?"

Turtle looks around the kitchen.

Anna doesn't say anything, and Turtle knows that she is sorting through all the ways Turtle isn't ready, all the ways Turtle is not **all right**, and unable to voice them, and it is infuriating to Turtle that Anna's assessment is worse than her own, that even Anna, who believes in Turtle, who is the only person in the world whom Turtle knows believes **for sure** that Turtle will wind up all right, even Anna doesn't think Turtle is there yet, and Turtle sits beside her in the kitchen and she thinks, Turtle, you're even worse off than you knew and she doesn't want to break it to you.

"Why not fight for it?" Turtle says.

"I just—" Anna begins delicately.

"I want to go," Turtle says.

"Why?" Anna says. "You don't have to do this. Turtle, you **shouldn't** do this."

"I don't care. I want to try."

"Jacob will be there," Anna says warningly.

"I know."

"Turtle," Anna says, "you'll get there."

"Will I?"

"I think so," Anna says.

Turtle says nothing.

"And when you're ready, then we'll go. But this? This is rash."

They wait in silence. Turtle rises, runs the sink, refills her glass of water, and Zaki scrambles off the couch, gallops down the hall, runs in, tail high, and seats herself across from the two women and looks at them and yawns hugely and licks her lips, seemingly deeply contented, lidding and un-lidding her eyes in the slowest, most self-satisfied look of lazy approval, curling her tail around her paws and then flicking it up and resettling it.

"Zaki thinks I should go," Turtle tells Anna, and Anna laughs and then sets her bowl down exhaustedly and lies there as if unable to get up.

"I am so tired," Anna says. Then she looks at Turtle. "You **really** want to go?"

"I want to try," Turtle says.

"All right," Anna says.

Turtle waits beside her in the small redwood kitchen, the two of them sitting on the floor, Anna with her wine, Turtle still with her bowl, and neither of them rises. They just wait, taking each other in.

Acknowledgments

For her guidance, I would like to thank my agent, Joy Harris, the staunchest and best of allies. For her counsel and advice, Michelle Latiolais. For hard work, insight, and courage, my editor, Sarah McGrath. For her blazing intellect and her convictions, Jynne Martin. For all the help, Danya Kukafka. For being the first to believe, William Daniel Hough. For her brilliance, Shannon Pufahl. For thoughtfulness and support, Scott Hutchins. For their friendship, Charles and Philip Hicks. For sharing his love of the wilderness, Ray Tallent. I would also like to thank Teresa Sholars for patiently fielding questions about botany and phenology. For classroom questions, Meghan Chandra. For medical questions, Steve

Santora, Ross Greenlee, and Patricia Greenlee. I also need to thank Ross and Patricia Greenlee for all their love and support, in addition to the technical help. All of the numerous mistakes are mine alone. For stocking all the best books, Christie Olson Day and the Gallery Bookshop. I would like to thank a few teachers who meant the world to me: Jenny Otter, Derek Hutchinson, Jim Jennings, Ryan Olson Day, Tobias Menely, Mike Chasar, and Gretchen Moon. My parents, Gloria and Elizabeth, for more than words can say. And lastly, Harriet, for catching me when I fall.